W9-ARD-400

LULLABY AND GOODNIGHT

Books by Wendy Corsi Staub

DEARLY BELOVED

FADE TO BLACK

ALL THE WAY HOME

THE LAST TO KNOW

IN THE BLINK OF AN EYE

SHE LOVES ME NOT

KISS HER GOODBYE

LULLABY AND GOODNIGHT

WENDY
CORSI
STAUB

LULLABY AND GOODNIGHT

PINNACLE BOOKS
Kensington Publishing Corp.

PINNACLE BOOKS are published by

Kensington Publishing Corp.
850 Third Avenue
New York, NY 10022

This novel is a work of fiction. Names, characters, places, and incidents are either the product of the author's imagination, or are used fictitiously. Any resemblance to actual persons, living or dead, or events is entirely coincidental.

ISBN 0-7394-5456-0

Pinnacle and the P logo Reg. U.S. Pat. & TM Off.

Printed in the United States of America

For my new baby nephew,
Andrew Caleb Sypko,
who came a long, long way to get home at last.

And for Mark, Morgan, and Brody,
who are my home.

The author gratefully acknowledges the contributions of ever-supportive family and friends, particularly: Sonya Aydell, Kathy Barker, Beverly Barton, Janine Bauert, Anne Boehm, Anita Borgenecht, Tricia Caitlin, Kathy Carson, Toni Cramer, Gaile Davis, Patty and Rick Donovan, Cindy Gaston, Elizabeth Hannah, Meredith Haynes, Thjodie Hess, Denise Hodder, Lisa Jackson, Brooke Dunn-Johnson, Sheryl Madden, Gena Massarone, Michele Mazur, Joanne Masten, Doug Mendini, Patti Nota, Phil Pelletere, Elaine Pharrel, Katie Plotkin, Rhoda Rudnick, Helen Rush, Joan Siegel, Kelly Spagnola, Mark Staub, Natalie Syrba, Jan Wallace, and Wendy Zemanski.

And an especially warm hug to my agent, Laura Blake Peterson, and everyone at Curtis Brown, and my editor, John Scognamiglio, and everyone at Kensington Publishing.

PROLOGUE

"Please. Please don't hurt me. I just want to have my baby. . . ."

"Oh, you will." The stranger's lips curve upward to reveal chalk-white, even teeth. "You'll have your baby."

Far from reassuring Heather, the words—and the smile—strike her as sinister, sending a new wave of dread shuddering through her.

She struggles to keep full-blown panic at bay, her pregnancy-swollen body tethered to the four posts of the bed. She can't possibly escape. Even if she were left alone long enough to work the ropes free, even if she were in prime condition to run, she wouldn't get far. She has no idea what lies beyond the door of this room. She was brought here blindfolded, at gunpoint. The blindfold is off and the weapon now concealed, but she senses its deadly presence nearby. She can't take a chance.

And so, physically helpless, she can only search wildly for a mental way out, for some logical explanation to grasp.

The only rationale Heather's fear-muddled brain can conjure is that she isn't really here; this simply cannot be happening. She must be home in bed. This has to be another one of those crazy nightmares she's been having these last few weeks, between bouts of heartburn and frequent nocturnal trips to the bathroom.

Squeezing her eyes closed, she promises herself that when she counts to ten and opens them, she'll see familiar pink-and-white-striped wallpaper, her Beanie Baby collection, the bulletin board above her bed, still decorated with pictures from the prom with Ryan and from cheerleading camp last summer.

One . . . two . . . three . . .

Mom made her go to camp. The year before, Heather had begged to go and Mom said they couldn't afford it. This year, her mother somehow scraped the money together despite Heather's protests. She wanted to stay home to be near Ryan, who was lifeguarding at a borough pool.

Of course, Ryan was the very reason Mom wanted her to get away from Staten Island for the summer. She thought they were spending too much time together. She was worried that what had happened to her would happen to Heather. No amount of begging would change Mom's mind about camp.

"You're going, Heather. Period."

. . . four . . . five . . . six . . . seven . . .

Period. Ha. She didn't even realize she had missed hers until she got home from camp. Overnight, she had become a walking stereotype—the Roman Catholic schoolgirl who lost her virginity on prom night and found herself pregnant. She had become her mother's worst nightmare.

No, she had become her mother.

. . . eight . . . nine . . . ten!

There is no pink-and-white-striped wallpaper.

No Beanie Baby collection.

No bulletin board.

Renewed despair launches in Heather's gut as she gazes frantically around the nondescript box of a room. Painted white walls. Dresser, chair, four-poster wooden bed. One window with the blinds drawn and plain beige curtains hanging from a metal rod.

Where the hell am I?

A wave of longing sweeps through her; longing for the frilly white priscillas Mom bought on clearance at Kmart last year. At the time, Heather complained that they were too babyish for a fifteen-year-old. Now she'd give anything to see them again. To see Mom again.

"Please . . ." she whimpers, succumbing to the realization that this is no nightmare.

This is real.

As her captor looms over the bed, she's certain that her life—and her baby's life—is in danger.

"What's the matter? You're afraid, aren't you? Poor thing."

The eyes that gaze down at her are oddly vacant, betraying no hint of human empathy. Gone is the cheerful voice that asked if she needed a hand loading her packages into the car, having given way to an eerily detached monotone.

"It's almost over. Don't worry."

What's almost over? Oh, God. Please help me.

Heather has been transformed into yet another stereotype: the pretty teenaged girl who's disappeared from a shopping mall.

Once again, she has become her mother's worst nightmare.

"You should calm yourself down. All that shaking isn't good for the baby, you know."

Oh, please. Please.

I want my mommy.

I want to go home.

"Are you hungry? What am I thinking? Of course you're hungry. You're eating for two, and it's almost six. Time for dinner."

Only six o'clock?

Hours seem to have passed since she waddled out of the mall and across the icy parking lot through freezing rain. Heather automatically attempts to lift her left wrist to check her watch, but it's held fast by the twine that binds her hand to the bedpost.

She whimpers in frustration, closing her eyes. A series of images rush at her.

The shocked expression in Ryan's beautiful blue-green eyes when she told him the EPT was positive.

Bitter disappointment, etched with resignation, on her mother's face.

A shapeless blob on an ultrasound screen, one she wished would miraculously disappear so that Ryan would reappear in her life.

But that was eight months ago.

That was before she ever heard her baby's rapid heartbeat; before she felt the little flutters of life stirring beneath her swelling belly; before the flutters gave way to kicks and punches and sometimes, the staccato taps the doctor told her are the baby's hiccups. Somehow, the hiccups made the whole thing seem real.

The pregnancy she once cursed has transformed into a blessing; she now longs with anticipation for the date she once dreaded. And it's almost here.

Less than forty-eight hours until her due date.

She's been so exhausted, and the weather was so crummy. Why didn't she just stay home? Why did she feel compelled to make one last trip to Baby Gap and Gymboree?

Because she hated that her baby's layette was so skimpy. Because she convinced herself that the baby would need a few more Onesies, a few more little knit caps and tiny socks . . .

And maybe, because some part of her longed for one last trip to the mall; longed for that link to the carefree teenaged days she'd left behind as her stomach ballooned and Ryan and her girlfriends abandoned her.

"Hey!" A painful jab in her arm startles Heather back to the horrific present. Her eyes snap open to face her tormentor once again. "You didn't answer my question. Are you hungry?"

Oh, God. Please. Please don't let this sick lunatic hurt me. Please.

"I want to go home."

A surprisingly gentle hand strokes her head. "Hush. Everything will be all right."

Hush . . .

Hush, little baby, don't say a word . . .

The melody of the folk lullaby she's been humming for months, whenever she's alone, drifts into Heather's head.

"Please. Please let me go home."

Please. I want to rock my baby and sing lullabies. Please.

"Sorry, that's not possible." Her captor's smile has been replaced by an all-business demeanor that strikes Heather as even more chilling. It's as though there is a specific agenda, a purpose to her being here.

"What do you want to eat? Do you have any cravings? Pickles and ice cream, maybe?"

The laughter that follows is maniacal, subsiding just as rapidly as it began.

"Now, what can I make for you to eat?"

Maybe this is just a harmless crazy person, Heather tells herself. Maybe the best thing to do is go along until somebody shows up here to save her.

Wherever *here* is.

She has no idea which way they traveled after she was shoved into the back of a van that was parked close to her mother's car in the mall parking lot.

The van was so damned close. Why didn't she notice that? Why didn't she carry her own damned packages?

Why didn't she listen to Mom when she said never to talk to strangers?

"I'm waiting," the stranger says now, in almost a singsong voice. "Tell me what you want to eat."

"Anything." It's all Heather can do to push the lone word past the sodden lump of fear in her throat.

"Oh, come on. You must have a request. Even prisoners on death row get to place an order for their last meal."

Their last meal.

Heather knows then that she's never going home. She's never going home to her mommy, and she isn't going to *be* a mommy.

Erupting in tears, she begins to beg for her life, knowing it's futile.

"Please," she says, over and over. "Please let me go. I just want to have my baby."

"But you will. I promise. Trust me, I never break my promises."

"Please . . ."

"Relax. You're going to have your baby . . ."

It doesn't make sense, Heather thinks wildly, just before she hears the most ominous words of all.

"You're going to have your baby, right after you have your last meal. And believe me, you're going to need your strength for what's coming."

Ten Years Later

Month One

February

CHAPTER ONE

"I have some good news for you, Ms. Somerset," Dr. Lombardo announces, striding into the examining room, clipboard in hand and a broad grin on his handsome face.

"Oh my God!" Tears spring to Peyton's gray eyes. "When am I due?"

"Due? What are you talking about? The good news is that the Dow just jumped forty-one points."

He's teasing, Peyton assures herself—and nevertheless feels a slight twinge of too-good-to-be-true trepidation. "I *am* pregnant . . . right?"

"You *are* pregnant." The obstetrician reaches for her right hand and clasps it warmly in his own. "Congratulations."

She heaves a sigh of relief. Not that she had any doubt, really. Four home pregnancy tests can't be wrong. Still, the nurse instructed her to come in for blood work, just to be certain.

So. Now she's certain.

Nine months from now, give or take, she'll be a mother.

"I'm going to write you a prescription for prenatal vitamins," the doctor informs her, flipping briskly through his notes. "And we'll need to schedule some tests. Ultrasound, amniocentesis . . ."

"Amniocentesis?"

"I recommend one for all my patients who are over forty. The risk of certain birth defects rises in older mothers, so—"

"I won't be forty until September." According to her calculations, the baby is due the following month.

The doctor shrugs. "It's your call, really. I'll give you some information so that you can make an educated decision."

She nods, already knowing what her decision will be. Lord knows she's done enough reading in preparation for pregnancy, childbirth, and motherhood. As far as *this* informed patient is concerned, the tests would be useless. Even if, God forbid, she found out that the baby in her womb has some terrible birth defect, she would choose to have it. Period.

When Peyton Somerset makes up her mind to do something, she does it. *Her* way.

She interrupts the doctor, who has launched into an array of possible symptoms she might experience. "Do you mind if I run and get my purse so I can write some of this stuff down in my organizer?"

"You don't have to do that. I'll give you a pamphlet we have that explains everything."

"Great, thanks." Peyton is relieved that she doesn't have to parade, naked beneath an ill-fitting gown, into the adjoining room where her belongings are stashed on a hook.

Yes, technically, he's already seen it all, and then some. But she can't help it. He's handsome.

He goes on, reminding her that this is a combination practice with several doctors and a certified nurse midwife on staff, then moves on to what she should expect at the next few appointments. She barely listens, too caught up in visions of her immediate future. Morning sickness? Maybe. Maternity clothes, definitely.

She smiles to herself, wondering what could possibly be more fun than mandatory spring shopping. She'll need to buy a full maternity wardrobe, nothing frilly or pastel . . .

"I strongly recommend that you enroll in a childbirth preparation class," the doctor is saying. "We have one sponsored by our on-staff midwife, and there's also a good one at the hospital that covers not just breathing, but pain medication options."

Peyton back-burners visions of the many Manhattan boutiques that cater to upscale corporate mothers-to-be, and informs Dr. Lombardo, "I think I'll go for natural childbirth."

"You might think that sounds like a good idea now . . ."

Yes, she does, and he doesn't know her well enough to realize she can't be easily swayed by delivery room horror stories. Not much frightens Peyton Somerset these days. Or ever, for that matter.

In fact, the only truly scary thing she can think of is not being in utter control . . . of her body, her emotions, her future . . .

Yes. Control is key.

"But," Dr. Lombardo goes on, "if I had a dollar for every patient who said no drugs in the beginning and changed her mind by the time she was dilated a few centimeters, I'd be one young retiree."

Peyton offers the obligatory chuckle, wondering just how old he is. He looks about her age, maybe a little younger.

Basically, he's your garden-variety Tall, Dark, and Handsome M.D. who could easily be playing the part on an afternoon soap.

"You should also choose a labor coach, Ms. Somerset," Dr. Lombardo tells her.

"Call me Peyton."

He smiles. "Peyton. Get a labor coach. Somebody who's going to be by your side day or night from the time you feel the first cramp until you've delivered the baby."

Peyton forces herself to maintain eye contact and nod. "No problem."

"Good."

No problem?

If she had somebody like that—somebody willing to be by her side, day or night, to help her through the biggest challenge of her life—she wouldn't be here in the first place.

She'd be back in Talbot Corners, having a baby the old-fashioned way.

But here she is, in Manhattan, facing childbirth—and parenthood—entirely on her own.

It's your choice, she reminds herself, lifting her chin. *You're living your life on your terms. And now there's no going back. Not that you want to. . . .*

But for Peyton Somerset, to whom control is key, the future suddenly seems uncertain.

What if she loses her job now that—or *because*—she's pregnant?

How will she support herself and a child?

Assuming she keeps her job, what if she can't find decent child care?

What if something happens to her baby?

What if something happens to *her,* an only parent, after she has the baby?

Stop it, Peyton. Since when do you doubt yourself, or your plans?

Insecurity isn't allowed. Period.

"Well? Any questions, Mom?" asks Dr. Lombardo.

Mom. Wow. She's going to be somebody's mom.

"No," Peyton says firmly, her head spinning. "No questions at all."

"I'm sure you'll have some the minute you leave. Feel free to call the office any time, or you can e-mail us if that's more convenient. We're here for you, and we're accustomed to patients who are going it alone."

"That's good." Because she certainly fits that bill. In fact, she's never felt more alone in her life.

"Mr. and Mrs. Cordell?"

Derry looks up from an outdated issue of *Redbook* she's been pretending to read while chewing her fingernails down to nubs.

Dr. Lombardo's receptionist is beckoning.

Beside her, Linden promptly gets to his feet and tosses aside a copy of *Popular Mechanics* or *Popular Science* or whatever it is that's kept him utterly absorbed for the last twenty minutes. You'd think he'd be as agitated as she is. To Derry's complete irritation, her husband seems utterly relaxed. He's been relaxed ever since he found out that this visit is covered by their insurance plan.

Linden, who always likes a bargain, didn't even complain about coming up with the ten-dollar copay.

"Ready?" he asks, and she nods.

But of course she isn't ready.

Is any woman ever ready to find out why, after more than a year of trying to get pregnant, her period arrives as predictably as the Verizon bill every single month?

Don't worry, it'll happen.

Yeah, right. That's easy for Derry's mother to say; easy for her older sisters to say; for her friends to say. Things are different for all of them. Things are normal. They decided to have children, and they did.

That's how it's supposed to work, but—

"Derry?"

She looks up at Linden.

"Okay." She stands and replaces the issue of *Redbook* on the cluttered table beside her chair. She takes a moment to straighten the table's contents, to neatly align *Redbook* on top of the other magazines, telling herself that if she does it just right, everything will work out okay.

Yes, if she makes sure all the edges of all the pages are lined up, then Dr. Lombardo will have good news for her.

He'll tell her that there's no medical reason for her infertility. Or that there is, but he can give her a prescription and she'll be good as new by tomorrow.

Don't you think tomorrow is a little unrealistic, Derry? These things take time.

Yeah, no kidding. All right, then she'll be good as new by next week. Or next month. The next time she and Linden try, conception will be guaranteed. Problem solved.

"Mrs. Cordell?" The receptionist sounds concerned. "Are you all right?"

"I'm fine." She straightens and starts across the room.

Of course I'm fine. I'm not sterile, or barren, or whatever it is they call women who can't have babies.

I have to be fine.

Please, God, let me be fine.

If I can make it to the door behind the reception desk in less than ten steps, Dr. Lombardo will tell me everything's okay.

She counts silently as she follows her husband across the waiting room, conscious of the other couples glancing at them as they pass.

Some do so idly, then quickly go back to their magazines and newspapers and whispered conversations. Others seem more curious, or as anxious as Derry was, sitting there waiting. Especially the women.

They're the ones who are new to this, like we are, Derry tells herself. *They're thinking there's hope, or they've just found out that there isn't and they're here to discuss further options . . .*

Whatever those are.

Derry refuses to allow herself to think that far ahead.

For one thing, she and Linden are flat broke. Much too broke to even consider further options. They're already a month behind on their Co-op City mortgage. He's been urging her to ask her parents or sisters back in California to help them, but she can't do that. She isn't particularly close to any of her family these days. Anyway, her parents are barely surviving on Social Security; her sisters have mortgages and bills of their own.

Besides, potentially expensive medical options won't be necessary for Derry and Linden unless the doctor says one of them is sterile.

And that's not going to happen.

All those tests they took last week are going to show that there's nothing wrong.

After all, Derry made it to the doorway in only eight steps.

So the doctor is going to say that there's no reason she can't get pregnant. That in a year, maybe less, she could be holding a newborn with her auburn hair and green eyes, or Linden's blond hair and blue eyes, or perhaps a striking combination.

That's all she wants. A child all their own, a biological child with Cavanaugh and Cordell blood running through its veins. Is that too much to ask?

"Right this way," says a familiar, perpetually smiling nurse who greets them at the door with a clipboard and a manila folder in her hand. "How are you today, Mrs. Cordell?"

"Fine," Derry murmurs.

In the corridor, an attractive woman with shoulder-length light brown hair slips past them on her way out of the dressing room adjacent to the examining room.

She's wearing an expensive-looking suit the same chestnut shade as her hair, and has a camel dress coat draped over the crook of one arm and a chic leather shoulder bag over the other.

She's the kind of woman Derry has always envied: tall, sleek, slender. Her shiny hair is tucked behind her ears in an effortless yet elegant style. She probably has a perfect manicure, and pedicure, too. Derry, whose nails are ragged from incessant biting and whose wavy tresses are caught back in a plastic banana clip, is just over five feet tall and perpetually carrying an extra twenty-five pounds.

As the other woman passes, Derry does her best not to stare. Or glare.

"Thanks again, Nancy," the woman says over her shoulder to the nurse.

"Congratulations again, Peyton," the nurse replies, beaming.

Congratulations? In this office, that can only mean one thing. The woman is pregnant.

Derry is momentarily stilled by a fierce stab of jealousy as she stares after the retreating stranger in dismay.

You should feel hopeful, not resentful, she chides herself. *If she's pregnant, you can get pregnant, too.*

But what if the woman paid a fortune for infertility treatments? She looks as though she can afford it. Derry, in five-dollar Kmart clearance sneakers and too-snug ten-year-old jeans, cannot.

She shouldn't even be here, really. Her regular ob-gyn is up in the Bronx, where she lives. But one of her neighbors recommended this fancy Manhattan doctor, saying that if it weren't for him, her daughter couldn't have given her three grandchildren.

Derry would like nothing more than to give her aging mother three grandchildren. Then perhaps they could find the common ground that has eluded their relationship, particularly since Derry moved across the country against her parents' wishes.

"Right in here," the nurse says pleasantly, indicating an empty examination room.

"Thanks, Nancy." Derry nods, as though she and Dr. Lombardo's nurse have always been on a first-name basis when in reality, she never even paid attention to the woman's name tag in the past.

You should be more aware of things like that from now on, she tells herself.

Not that being casually friendly with the fertility specialist's staff has any bearing on whether or not she'll eventually find herself on the receiving end of pregnancy congratulations. But it can't hurt, right?

Linden steps back to allow Derry to step over the threshold ahead of him.

She's careful to do it with her right foot.

Yes, if she steps over the threshold with her right foot, everything will be all right.

Out on the street, Peyton is greeted by a burst of icy air. Overhead, the midtown skyscrapers are outlined against a pastel blue backdrop, milky February sunshine cascading down between them to cast her lanky shadow on the dry concrete sidewalk.

She smiles at the notion of how drastically that silhouette is going to change in the coming months. Glancing down at her stomach as she buttons her long cashmere coat over it, she imagines that it's the tiniest bit swollen. She knows it isn't, not yet. But soon enough, it will be.

A man in a trench coat brushes by her, jostling her slightly with his briefcase. Peyton's arms automatically cross in front of her, shielding her midsection and its precious cargo. In that momentary instinct, she grasps the scope of the tremendous responsibility that awaits.

Another human life is in her hands. Forever.

How can she do this alone?

Too late to turn back now, she reminds herself, reclaiming her staunch Somerset mentality. *And you can do it. Plenty of people do it, these days.*

Single motherhood may still bear a stigma back home in the Midwest, but it's become commonplace—almost trendy—here in the city, not to mention in the media.

Reassured for the time being, Peyton checks her watch, then looks around for a vacant taxi. The only yellow cab in the immediate vicinity is occupied and trying to back its way out of a turn down East Fifty-second Street, and no wonder. The block is clogged with traffic, funneled down to one lane at the corner because of construction. Jackhammers vibrate, car horns blare, pedestrians jaywalk, bike messengers weave in and out . . . typical midtown midday pandemonium.

There are times when she inexplicably longs for small-town Kansas, wondering why she ever traded serenity for chaos. But that always passes quickly.

Especially today, she thinks, absently watching the hapless yellow cab attempting to retreat to the avenue. Nothing is going to burst her bubble today.

Peyton is happy to be right where she is, just as she is, Kansas and her past a mere speck in a rearview mirror she rarely bothers to check.

And that, Peyton tells herself, again resisting a strange pang of foreboding, is just as it should be.

Startled by the sudden screeching of tires and the discordant clash of metal against metal, she looks up to see that the cab has backed into another car. Both drivers are already out in the street, shouting at each other in two different languages, neither of them intelligible.

So much for not checking the rearview mirror, Peyton tells herself with a wry shake of her head as she heads on down the block on foot.

Anne Marie Egerton would kill to have a nanny on days like this.

Or at least, to have a husband who isn't currently somewhere over the Atlantic Ocean, flying off to London—*again*—on business.

Since the second option is out of the question, she collapses into the nearest kitchen chair and briefly considers the first.

Again.

Jarrett has been telling her for months to hire somebody to help her with the boys. He doesn't understand why she won't. Money certainly isn't an issue. His latest promotion has pretty much guaranteed that money will never be an issue for them.

Not that it ever was.

It's just as easy to fall in love with a rich man as it is a poor one.

Grandma was right about that. As for the rich man falling in love with Anne Marie in return . . . well, she's always been certain that her Italian grandmother had a hand in that. There's no doubt in Anne Marie's mind that Grace DeMario is as controlling in death as she was in life, a celestial puppeteer. That would certainly be her idea of heaven.

This—being married to Jarrett Egerton III, the mother of his children, living in Bedford, wearing the finest designer clothes and Italian leather shoes—would have been Anne Marie's idea of heaven, at least in theory.

She ruefully remembers another of her grandmother's favorite sayings.

Be careful what you wish for.

She takes a deep breath to steady her nerves, gazing out the tall, arched window at the sunken brick terrace and the barren white trellises of her landscaped rose garden beyond. The New York winter has been harsher than usual. It's hard to remember the lush foliage and fragrant blossoms that have been replaced by clumps of brown, thorny stalks.

But the roses will come again. They always do, if you wait long enough.

Anne Marie forces her weary body up out of the chair.

"Mommy's coming, boys," she calls, picking up a tray that holds three individual portions of applesauce, three pieces of buttered toast, three sippy cups filled with whole milk, three napkins, three spoons.

Three.

Three of everything.

All for a trio of three-year-olds who almost didn't make it.

Stepping into the breakfast room, Anne Marie smiles cheerfully at her noisy sons, who are seated at a small table parked directly in front of the enormous, wall-mounted plasma television.

The Wiggles video she turned on before she left the room mere moments ago only adds to the cacophony.

"All right, guys, snack time," she chirps above the din, and begins handing out cups and spoons.

In a matter of minutes, the floor is littered with crumbs, a puddle of spilled milk is seeping dangerously close to the imported wool area rug, and the boys are wearing most of their applesauce, clamoring for more.

Anne Marie surveys the mess with a weary sigh.

This is heaven?

She smiles. It is. It really is.

This is heaven.

If anybody knows that, she does.

Because if anybody has ever truly been to hell, it's Anne Marie Egerton.

Falling into step in the throng of scurrying New Yorkers, Peyton shoulders her way to the corner of East Fifty-second and Lexington, then turns down the avenue toward Grand Central Station and the subway. If the 6 train is running without delays, she might be back at her desk thirty blocks away before Tara notices she's taken a two-hour lunch.

She suspects she might be doing that fairly often in the months to come. With any luck, her boss will understand and bear with her. In fact, maybe she should just march right in today and tell Tara she's pregnant. Get it out in the open from the start.

Then again, maybe she shouldn't. Maybe that would be a big mistake.

She's set her sights on a promotion to management rep, aware that a spot will be vacant after Alain transfers back to the Paris office in April or May. Tara might be reluctant to offer it to Peyton if she suspects a maternity leave is looming.

Having seen several of her childbearing female colleagues get passed over for promotions and perks, Peyton concludes that her best bet is to keep the pregnancy to herself for as long as she can. Nobody at work would ever suspect there's a Mommy Track in her future.

Just a few years ago, when she was still living in Talbot Corners, Peyton herself wouldn't have imagined it, either. She had long since put aside her dreams of New York, of a high-powered career on Madison Avenue, of motherhood.

She set them aside nearly two decades earlier, the moment her stepfather of five years, Douglas, died on the heels of her college graduation.

Realizing she couldn't abandon the widowed mother who had raised her single-handedly, Peyton watched her childhood sweetheart head to the East Coast without her. For a while, she convinced herself that she might somehow still marry Gil Blaney and have his children. But while she was writing him long letters and sending her resume to every corporation within a hundred-mile radius of Talbot Corners, he was embarking on a Wall Street career—and on a relationship with the woman he would soon marry.

Mercifully, the wedding was at a New York cathedral, rather than at the First Community Church of Talbot Corners, a stone's throw from Peyton's front porch swing.

By then, Peyton was over him, anyway. She had found a job commuting to Eaton Brothers, a Kansas City packaged goods company, where she eventually worked her way from an entry-level position in shipping to marketing and finally, to product manager.

All that time, she was oblivious of the silent ticking of her biological clock. But somehow, she turned into a time bomb on her thirty-seventh birthday—which happened to coincide with a broken engagement, her second since Gil left.

Three shattered relationships. Maybe she wasn't meant to be married.

Looking back, Scott, who followed Gil, was all wrong for her. He was older, somewhat arrogant, and far too controlling for her. She got cold feet, and it was a good thing. She would never have been happy as Scott's wife.

But with Jeff, who came later, she was head over heels in love. Who wouldn't be? He was a former NFL running back, the pride of Topeka. Everyone in Talbot Corners knew who he was; everyone was thrilled that a hometown girl had landed a Kansas hero like Jeff. He'd retired comfortably from football and now traveled as a sports commentator. With his fame, strapping good looks, and financial security, he was too good to be true.

At least, that was what Peyton's mother said.

Unfortunately, she was right.

Jeff didn't exactly leave his bride at the altar, but he came pretty damned close. Close enough that the First Community Church of Talbot Corners was already decked out in a thousand dollars' worth of white roses and organza pew bows, and Peyton found herself with a paid-for white silk gown in her closet and a truckload of crystal and china to send back.

He got cold feet, he said.

What goes around comes around, Peyton's mother said profoundly, as if she were the one who had coined the stale phrase.

But there is truth in cliché.

What goes around comes around.

Once again, Beth Somerset was right.

In the wake of the fairy-tale wedding that wasn't, the only way Peyton could escape the probing questions and sympathetic stares was to get the hell out of Talbot Corners.

She might just as easily have found herself in Los Angeles, Chicago, Boston, Phoenix. But an account management job fortuitously presented itself at Kaplan and Kline, the Manhattan ad agency that had long handled the Eaton Brothers account. With her client-side experience, she was a shoo-in for the position.

She's settled in the big city at last, twenty years after she first dreamed of doing so. Pregnant at last, twenty years after she all but dismissed motherhood as an option.

Scott had two teenagers from a first marriage and didn't want more children, period. Looking back, maybe that was part of the reason Peyton wouldn't let herself go through with marriage to him. Maybe somewhere deep down inside, the first fragile tendrils of midlife maternal instinct had already taken hold.

Now that it's crept into every part of her, irrevocably entwined around her heart and soul, there's no doubt about her destiny. She, Peyton Somerset, is going to have a baby.

A baby!

She can't wait to tell . . .

Somebody.

Anybody.

If only there were somebody to tell.

So.

This is it.

All the months of hoping and planning to conceive; the weeks of worrying and wondering why she hadn't yet; the days of waiting and praying for test results . . .

It's all come down to this.

No more planning, wondering, praying.

Now she *knows.*

Feeling numb, Derry struggles to maintain eye contact with Dr. Lombardo. She nods slightly, feigning interest in whatever it is that he's saying when in reality, her brain shut down a few minutes ago.

Right after he informed her and Linden that they are incapable of having children.

Rather, *Derry* is incapable of conceiving and carrying a child.

Impaired fecundity, he called it.

Impaired fecundity? What the hell does that mean?

"I know this is difficult for you, Mr. and Mrs. Cordell," Dr. Lombardo is saying gently, wearing a suitably somber expression.

Difficult? All her life, Derry assumed she would be a wife and mother.

It isn't the *only* thing she ever wanted to be, not like her oldest sister, Peggy, who never even wanted to go to college or have a career.

But Derry wanted motherhood, just as she wanted college and a career. She wanted to have it all.

Now . . . she'll have nothing.

"You'll need to investigate other options at this point," the doctor goes on.

Sure. Options. Options mean she'll have to settle, just as she settled once before, after graduating from high school back home in California. She was accepted to several private colleges on the East Coast, but couldn't swing it even with tuition aid. And her parents couldn't— or perhaps wouldn't—help her. They had her late in life; they had raised two other daughters; they were depleted.

So she went to community college in San Diego for a few semesters, thinking she might be able to at least transfer to a state university if she kept her grades up.

Her grades were fine; her finances were not.

She dropped out of school to waitress full time, telling herself it was only temporary.

Yeah. Right.

Some career. Her parents and sisters treated her as though she were an embarrassing disappointment; her old friends were busy with college life. She was consumed by loneliness and depression.

But that fell away when she found Linden. All she wanted then was to shed her pervasive loneliness and move across the country to be with him in New York, to become a wife and mother, to fill the gaping void in her life with a family of her own.

She made it to New York, although not Manhattan, as she pictured. She and Linden live in Co-op City, in a one-bedroom apartment they can barely afford on their salaries as a welder and a waitress.

Three years have passed since she fled the West Coast, her family, and all her old friends to wed the man she swore she would marry before she ever laid eyes on him.

Derry and Linden may have met over the Internet in a Classic Rock chat room, but everything else about their courtship, their lifestyle, their plans for the future, has been old-fashioned.

It never occurred to her that she—that *they*—would be denied something so basic.

Something so many people take for granted.

It isn't fair. Derry swallows hard over the monstrous lump in her throat. *So many women who don't plan it, who don't deserve it, are walking around pregnant. Some of them have abortions, some of them toss their babies into Dumpsters. It makes me sick.*

Clutching her middle as though she can somehow curb the hollow ache of loss, Derry knows she would do anything to have a baby.

Anything.

At eight o'clock that evening, Peyton emerges from her office building onto East Twenty-first Street to find that this afternoon's pleasant weather has given way to wind-driven sleet. Oh, ugh. Who knew this was coming?

Probably anyone who wasn't too distracted by baby thoughts to check the weather forecast, that's who.

With a sigh, Peyton reaches into her bag for the emergency umbrella she keeps there, hoping she didn't remove it in her recent scatterbrained pregnancy preoccupation. As she feels around inside the bag, she gazes out into the raw darkness. There are plenty of cabs sailing up Third Avenue—all of them occupied, just as one would expect on a foul-weathered night like this.

Her apartment is in Chelsea, a ten-to-fifteen-minute walk she covers round-trip most days. Taking the subway or a bus would mean transferring a few times, as there's no direct crosstown route from here. Anyway, in bad weather it's much too crowded and slow.

She ponders and dismisses the mass transit option after locating her compact spare umbrella. Since moving to the city, she's discovered that walking is not only the quickest means of transport, it's also conducive to clearheaded thinking.

Even better, there's a maternity clothing boutique in the next block, with a display of darling spring dresses in the window.

Nasty weather aside, on the heels of this afternoon's exciting news and a typically hectic day at the office, she'll welcome the chance to window-shop a little—and to be alone with her thoughts.

Having found her compact Burberry umbrella, Peyton raises it and splashes out onto the sidewalk, wishing she were equally prepared with boots, or at least sneakers, to wear home. Her stocking-encased lower legs and designer-pump-clad feet are soaked in seconds.

Terrific. What if she gets a cold?

Normally, the possibility wouldn't faze her, but she no longer has just her own health to consider.

If she gets sick, her baby might be harmed.

Isn't that a little dramatic? an inner voice scoffs. *A cold never killed anyone.*

Has it?

Riddled with uncertainty, she wonders if she's about to become the kind of woman who worries about everything—every sniffle, every hangnail, every bowel movement or lack thereof. A phobic-ridden woman like her own mother, who raised her only child alone, every maternal decision permeated by uncertainty. It's a wonder Peyton didn't turn out to be a fretful, frightened person as well.

No, she's just the opposite.

Her mother hated being alone, hated not having anyone to lean on. It's why she clung so desperately to Douglas when she met him—and why she clung to her daughter after he died. Even decades after she was widowed, Beth Somerset was profoundly distressed over Peyton's plans to move halfway across the country.

"What if you need me?" she kept asking, and Peyton knew that what she really meant was *What if I need you?*

"I'll be fine, Mom," Peyton said. *And you'll be fine, too.*

She is, now. Most of the time. But it's taken her a long time to get used to taking care of herself.

I will never become my mother, Peyton vows grimly, skirting around a deep puddle. *Not even when I* am *a mother.*

Which reminds her . . . she'll call Mom when she gets home,

to tell her about the baby. She wasn't thrilled when Peyton told her she was going through artificial insemination with plans to be a single mother, but she'll be excited to hear the news. Any child-loving, prospective grandmother would be.

Pausing to gaze longingly at the garland-bedecked display in the maternity shop's window, she pictures herself wearing that adorable blue empire-waist dress at Kaplan and Kline's annual spring outing.

If there weren't a CLOSED sign on the door, she'd be tempted to go in and try it on. Maybe tomorrow, during her lunch hour.

But then she might be tempted to buy it, and she probably shouldn't tote maternity boutique shopping bags back to the office until she's made an official announcement.

Despite her giddiness over the pregnancy confirmation today, she couldn't have spilled her news to Tara or her coworkers even if she were prepared to. They were simply too busy preparing a client presentation—and so, of course, was she. Too busy to chat, or answer the phones, or even grab coffee or a snack.

But that has to change, Peyton tells herself sternly, suddenly conscious of her empty stomach. She'll have to start eating regular meals, something she hasn't done in years. She'll have to take better care of herself.

Don't worry, little one, she silently croons to the child in her womb. *From here on in, it's all about you.*

As she turns away from the store window and heads west past Madison Square Park, deserted in this icy deluge, her thoughts are consumed by all the things she will do differently from her mother as she raises her own child.

She barely notices the raw, wet weather.

Nor does she notice the figure that slips out of the shadows and falls into step behind her, trailing her all the way home.

Compared to the last one, years ago, and the donor just selected last month, this new one is going to be a piece of cake.

She lives alone; doesn't even live in one of those fancy doorman buildings you'd expect.

No, she disappeared into a four-story brownstone, and if the lights that came on moments later are any indication, she resides on the ground floor.

The ground floor. In this neighborhood.

Doesn't she realize that a single woman with enough money

to afford a designer coat, shoes, and bag shouldn't leave herself so vulnerable?

There are bars on the street-level windows, of course—but they're an obstacle that can easily be skirted when the time comes. Far more easily than an uptown doorman.

Not that there isn't a way around any obstacle, if one is resourceful enough. Resourceful, and patient.

Patience will certainly be necessary in this case. Seven or eight months' worth of patience.

But that will allow enough time to set the wheels in motion so that the rest of the plan can fall into place. There's so much to do, with everything up and running again at last.

It's been a while, but not so long that one might forget the painstaking steps that must be taken.

Now that a second future donor has been designated, the next order of business is to select another worthy recipient.

Somebody who longs for what this woman is so undeservedly about to obtain.

Somebody with a loving heart, empty arms . . . and a husband.

Month Two
March

CHAPTER TWO

Brooklyn is the last place Peyton wants to be on this snowy evening. In fact, the only place she really wants to be is at home, preferably in bed.

But Dr. Lombardo's helpful nurse, Nancy, strongly recommended that she join the office's brand-new pregnant singles support group. She even e-mailed her at work to let her know about tonight's meeting, which caught Peyton off guard. She still hasn't told anybody at Kaplan and Kline that she's pregnant. But she probably should do it soon, before someone figures it out.

Anyway, here she is, straight from a grueling day at the office, standing in the vestibule of a rectangular brick apartment building in Carroll Gardens.

Stifling a yawn, she presses the buzzer for apartment 3F, beside a nameplate that reads *J. Cooke.* The door buzzes back within seconds, releasing the lock. She steps into the hall and glances in dismay at the steep flight of stairs before realizing there's an elevator. Good thing. The steps up from the subway and the three-block walk over here just about did her in.

Peyton presses the Up button and fights back another deep yawn, longing for her bed. She's never been so utterly exhausted in her life. These days, she sleeps for ten hours a night and still never feels well rested; it's all she can do not to shut her office door and nap on the floor in the afternoons.

Then there are the dreams—the most vivid and bizarre dreams she's ever had in her life. There was one in which she delivered a salamander instead of a baby. And a shockingly erotic one that involved Dr. Lombardo. . . .

The mere thought of that dream still makes her blush and wonder how her subconscious mind managed to conjure such titillating images about a married man, her ob-gyn at that.

Well, technically, he's the one who got her pregnant.

Apparently, her subconscious mind wishes he'd done it in the conventional way.

A year of involuntary chastity will do strange things to a person. Unfortunately, that state isn't about to change any time soon, given Peyton's physical condition. She isn't exactly a candidate for casual dating these days.

So. Indefinite celibacy, sheer exhaustion, aching breasts, increasingly tight waistbands, morning sickness that lasts around the clock . . . can any of this be worth it?

Peyton keeps telling herself that it will be. Yes, when she's holding her own baby in her arms, she'll look back and wonder how she ever had a doubt.

At least, she hopes she will.

Somewhere high in the shaft above, the elevator groans and begins its descent as the door buzzes once again in the vestibule. Peyton turns to see a woman stepping into the corridor.

An enormously pregnant woman, walking in a back-tilted, wide-legged waddle that's as pronounced as the watermelon-shaped bulge beneath the buttons of her red dress coat. She has a head full of inky black curls and horn-rimmed glasses, and she's loudly munching a chocolate bar.

A week ago, in the throes of craving anything chocolate, Peyton would have been inappropriately tempted to ask her for a bite. But overnight, she seems to have developed an aversion to the candy bars she devoured by the handful.

Chocolate, coffee, seafood, spaghetti . . .

Her list of aversions is as endless as her list of current cravings. There are sleepless nights when she willingly ventures out into the cold for butter pecan ice cream, canned peaches, bologna and Wonder Bread and yellow mustard.

Watermelon, Peyton decides now, stealing another glance at the stranger. *I could really go for some watermelon.*

"Hi," the newcomer says, coming to a breathless stop before the elevator.

"Hi."

The woman clenches the chocolate bar between her teeth as she removes her gloves. A glance at the bare fourth finger of her left hand is all the encouragement Peyton needs to inquire, "Are you going up to the pregnant singles meeting?"

"How'd you guess?" the woman asks with an easy laugh as the elevator reaches the ground floor at last. She finishes her chocolate bar in a single bite. "You're going, too?"

"Yes."

"First trimester?"

"Yes," Peyton says again, as they step into the elevator together.

"I'm Allison Garcia."

"Peyton Somerset."

"Nice to meet you. I'd shake your hand but I've got melted chocolate on my fingers." She pops them into her mouth and licks them.

Peyton turns queasily away. Even the smell is getting to her.

The elevator lurches and starts to climb.

"When are you due, Peyton?"

"October." She adds politely, though the answer is obvious, "How about you?"

"June."

"*June?*" Peyton echoes in disbelief, her jaw falling open. Realizing how rude that is, she forces it closed and averts her gaze from the woman's giant belly. Judging by that, she'd have guessed labor was imminent.

Allison laughs, saying in a Latina-tinged New York accent that's thicker than her waistline, "It's my third. I swear, I was showing before the sperm made contact."

Full of questions, Peyton is too polite to voice any of them. At least, not yet. Maybe when she gets to know Allison better . . .

If she gets to know her better. She isn't entirely convinced this support group thing is up her alley. Sharing the details of her private life with a bunch of strangers is about as appealing as . . .

Well, as going through pregnancy and childbirth all alone.

But Nancy was pretty adamant about her joining this group. The nurse has a no-nonsense attitude that's part maternal, part drill sergeant, as Dr. Lombardo laughingly likes to say. She takes a vested interest in all his patients, but especially the single ones.

Peyton is grateful for the support, but—

"So how'd you get pregnant?" Allison asks abruptly.

Aware that her eyebrows have collided with her bangs, Peyton fumbles for an answer that's less direct than the bold question itself. Realizing there isn't one, she shrugs and admits, "Artificial insemination."

"Donor sperm?"

"Yes."

"Same here. My mother thinks I'm crazy to get pregnant by a total stranger, but I told her that if I knew a decent guy well enough to ask him for his sperm, I'd be sleeping with him in the first place, know what I mean? Of course, she nearly had a heart attack when I said that, and she told me to go to confession."

Peyton can't help laughing. There's something appealing about Allison's direct approach.

Maybe if she knew her better, she'd tell her what Beth Somerset said when Peyton called to announce her pregnancy.

Now that you're ready to settle down and raise a family, you'll be able to find a nice man and get married.

Yeah. Sure. As if the streets of Manhattan are just teeming with nice men seeking pregnant single women.

On the third floor, Allison leads the way down the hall to the last door, which is ajar, held open by a white New Balance cross-trainer.

"Hello, hello," Allison calls, stepping into the apartment without knocking.

Peyton hesitates only a moment before following her.

A trio of women in various stages of pregnancy are seated in a tiny living room. Norah Jones is playing on the stereo, candles are flickering, and a large platter of nachos is on the coffee table.

"Guys, this is Peyton," Allison announces, her coat already draped over a chair and her hand reaching for a chip.

Introductions are made. It turns out this is only the group's second meeting, but Peyton can't help feeling like an outsider. The others seem so comfortable with each other already.

Julie Bernard is the hostess. Long, kinky blond hair, wire-rimmed John Lennon glasses, no makeup, seven months pregnant.

Wanda Jones is a stunning, statuesque African-American woman, well into her first trimester but still barely showing.

The slightly aloof, redheaded Kate Dunham is in the throes of Braxton Hix contractions but says the midwife claims she's still a week away from delivery.

All three women are single, although Kate has a live-in boyfriend and a diamond engagement ring. Only Allison has been through this before, with two teenagers at home, the products of a disastrous early marriage.

Despite her reservations, Peyton finds herself drawn into the conversation as it bounces from nursing pads to epidurals to home delivery.

"No way," Wanda declares, munching a tortilla. "I want to be in the hospital and as medicated as legally possible."

Julie's mouth tightens. "You should at least consider other options, Wanda."

"Uh-uh. I'm not good with pain."

"Oh, come on, who is?" Allison asks. "At this point, I say, bring it on."

"Where are you going to deliver?" Julie asks, turning to Peyton.

"The hospital, definitely."

"Which one?"

"I'm not sure. I guess whichever one Dr. Lombardo sends me to."

"You really need to be more proactive," Allison tells her. "Take charge of your pregnancy from the beginning."

Peyton protests defensively, "I am in charge. I just . . . I haven't had a chance to ask all of my questions yet. That's all."

"Too bad Rita couldn't make it to our meeting tonight. She was going to talk to us about cardinal movement and delivery empowerment."

"Rita?" *Cardinal movement? Delivery empowerment?* Peyton feels like she did as a high school freshman who boldly joined the Spanish club despite barely knowing what *hola* meant. That tiny detail couldn't hold her back. She had made up her mind to be in the Spanish Club the moment she found out about the biennial trip to Acapulco.

Mexico was wonderful, but it can't hold a candle to motherhood, she thinks now, smiling inwardly at the preposterous comparison.

Then again, maybe not so preposterous. For the second time in her life, she's learning to speak a whole new language, one that she'll carry to a foreign destination.

Cardinal movement. Delivery empowerment. And now . . . *doula?*

That's the term Allison just used to define the Rita she mentioned.

"Actually, Rita isn't a doula. She's technically a midwife," Julie contradicts. "We met her last month, at our first meeting."

"Doula, midwife . . . same thing," is Allison's laid-back response, but Julie begs to differ. According to her, a midwife is certified to do everything a doctor does, but in the comfort of the patient's own home.

"*Anyway,*" Allison says pointedly, making it abundantly clear that she isn't someone who enjoys nit-picking over technical details, "none of that really matters because what Rita *really* is, is a guardian angel. That's what I call her, anyway. She's been so sweet about taking all my calls and answering all my crazy questions that I just gave her a guardian angel pin with my baby's birthstone in it."

"How do you know what the birthstone will be?" asks Julie, who is quickly establishing herself as a nitpicker, in Peyton's opinion.

"I'm due in the beginning of June. It's a pearl."

"June is moonstone."

"It's actually pearl."

"I don't think so, but whatever. Anyway, the baby might be born in May. That's an emerald."

"It won't be. Both my other kids were two weeks late and induced."

Julie persists, "Yes, but that doesn't mean this one will be."

"Trust me. It does."

"So Rita's going to deliver your baby?" Peyton asks Allison, to steer the irksome conversation away from birthstones and back to the midwife.

"Yes, and Kate's and Julie's, too. And maybe Wanda's."

"Maybe not," Wanda pipes up.

"Oh, you'll be convinced the second you meet her. She's great. Hopefully she can make the next meeting." To Peyton, Allison says, "Rita had to cancel tonight because she has a patient in labor."

Peyton can't think of anything to say other than a lame "Oh."

As the conversation drifts on, she can't help wondering if she's out of her element, and not just amidst these know-it-all New Yorkers. Maybe she should have given single motherhood more thought before jumping headlong into artificial insemination.

But Dr. Lombardo encouraged her not to delay. Her fertility was diminishing with every month that brought her closer to her fortieth birthday . . . or so he said.

She got pregnant on the second attempt.

"Yes, but what happens if you do meet somebody now?" Kate is asking, wincing as another contraction subsides. "It's hard enough when you're on your own. But now you've got to find somebody who's going to love you *and* your baby."

"Or babies," Allison contributes wryly. "Believe me, he doesn't exist."

"Yeah, and what are you talking about, Kate? You have somebody. You and Gary are getting married in the fall, right?"

"Right. I'm just saying—"

"You just want the rest of us to live happily ever after, right?" Julie says. "But trust me, Kate, some people aren't meant to be married. I'm one of them."

"But don't you want your baby to have a father someday?" Wanda asks. "I know I do. Babies need two parents."

"Well, if that's how you feel, you should have married the guy who got you pregnant," Allison tells her.

"Not an option."

"Why not?"

"He's already married, remember?"

On that bleak note, Peyton tunes out of the conversation again. She's fallen in love three times, to no avail. That part of her life is history. Looks like she'll have to be content with sex dreams about her ob-gyn from here on in.

"If you hold out a few more hours, you can have a Saint Patrick's Day baby, Laura."

". . . Few . . . more . . . hours?" the woman sprawled in the bathtub grunts between gasps for breath. "Are you . . . out . . . of . . . your goddamned mind?" The last few words are hurriedly snarled before giving way to a high-pitched moan.

"Laura!"

"It's okay," Rita assures Laura's embarrassed husband with a smile. "Believe me, I've heard worse. And I was only kidding about holding out, Laura. Bad joke, huh?"

"You don't really think it's going to take a few more hours, then?" the man asks, face pale, mouth drawn. "I don't think she can take much more of this."

It's been a grueling twenty-hour labor already. Suspecting that Michael Chesterson is as worried about his own stamina as his wife's, Rita shakes her head and assures him, "It won't be long now."

Leaning over the tub, she dips another clean cloth into the

warm water and wrings it out swiftly with one hand as her patient's grip tightens painfully on the other. "You're doing great, sugar pie," she croons, expertly mopping the woman's sweaty brow.

". . . Hurts . . ." Laura says through clenched teeth as the contraction wracks her body.

"I know it does. Try not to fight it. If you're tense it's more painful."

"Need . . . music . . ."

"Quick . . . go change the CD," Rita orders Michael.

He rises to his feet, looking relieved to have a few moments' reprieve. "Which one do you want to hear next, Laura? The Rachmaninov or the Beethoven?"

"I . . . don't . . . give . . . a . . . flying—"

"I'll put on the Rachmaninov," Michael says quickly, and disappears into the next room.

"Men," Rita says conspiratorially, catching Laura's eye.

Her patient manages to smile, then says, amidst grunts and pants, "Yeah. They're . . . morons."

"Not always. Michael will be a good daddy. You'll see."

"He . . . better . . . Ow . . . here comes another one. . . ."

Waiting for the contraction—and Laura's anguished howling—to subside, Rita takes stock of the items she placed earlier on a clean towel draped over a small folding table wedged between the sink and the toilet. In addition to her blood pressure cuff, stethoscope, fetoscope, and Doppler, there are two sets of sterilized towels, a bottle of mineral oil and one of ammonia, sterile gauze, a small bowl in case Laura vomits during delivery, a plastic bag for the placenta. Her bag in the next room holds other equipment she rarely uses: an oxygen tank and mask, a laryngoscope, an IV line, and drugs including Pitocin and Methergine.

Everything is ready. Glancing at her patient, Rita notes that the torturous pain seems to have momentarily receded.

Swiftly trading the washcloth for a rubber glove, she says apologetically, "I'm going to have to check you again, Laura."

"Oh, no . . . no . . ."

"I'll be as gentle as I can. It might be time to push, but I won't know unless I see how far you're dilated."

Expertly inserting her latex-covered hand into the birth canal, she murmurs, "I'm so sorry," at Laura's primal scream of pain.

The cervix is at ten centimeters. Time to start pushing.

"Come on back in here, Dad," she calls to Michael, discarding the glove and smiling down at the writhing woman in the tub. "We're going to have ourselves a baby."

"Welcome," the familiar electronic mail voice announces as the sign-on screen gives way to a mailbox icon with the flag raised. "You've got mail."

Mouse in hand, Derry left-clicks on the icon, then takes a handful of cheese popcorn from the bag in her lap as the list of incoming messages pops up.

Singing along with the Journey CD on the stereo, she scans the subject lines, looking for something more interesting than spam, bargains, and endless dirty jokes forwarded by her teenaged nephew. She licks the salty cheese dust off her stinging index finger, its nail bitten painfully low thanks to a lifelong habit that's intensified in the stress of these last few weeks.

After drying her finger on her sweatpants, she repeatedly presses the Delete key, scrolling down the list of mail.

Boring, boring, boring . . .

Baby?

The single-word subject line is enough to set her heart pounding. She glances from it to the unfamiliar sender—dreamweaver777@cradletocradle.org—and back again.

Baby.

Probably spam.

She should just delete it.

Her finger twitches on the button, but somehow, she can't make herself do it.

Holding her breath, she double-clicks on the message.

Dear Mrs. Cordell:

If you and your husband are interested in adopting a healthy white infant, please respond to this e-mail as soon as possible. We specialize in discreet, affordable adoption for deserving couples.

Sincerely,

Rose Calabrone, Cradle to Cradle Adoption Agency.

Pulse racing, Derry rereads the e-mail several times before clicking on the underlined blue link at the bottom.

A web page begins to load.

This old computer is so damned slow. If only she could afford a new one, or even a high-speed connection. But the monthly Internet access fee has tapped out the household budget as it is. Linden keeps threatening to get rid of AOL altogether. Especially since Derry got laid off from her latest waitress job earlier this month.

She needs AOL more than ever, though, considering she's been spending more and more of her time in front of the computer.

She can't help it. She hasn't been in the mood for anything other than junk food and idle Web surfing these past few weeks. She doesn't feel like going out, or job hunting, or watching television, or making love.

Especially making love. Why bother? She isn't going to get pregnant, ever.

As an increasingly frustrated Linden pointed out, there are other reasons to sleep with your husband.

Whatever. Lately, Derry is too depressed to think about his needs, let alone any of her own, beyond the unattainable one: motherhood.

As she waits for the Cradle to Cradle Web site to load, she chews her ragged thumbnail and gazes absently out the window at the lights of Co-Op City and the east Bronx, reminding herself that adoption is out of the question. She and Linden can't afford it, even if she manages to land a better-paying waitress job.

Nor would they have been able to afford expensive infertility procedures even if Dr. Lombardo had presented that option. Linden ruled that out before they even got the crushing verdict. It wouldn't be covered by their health insurance, and they can't afford it. They can't expect her parents or his elderly mother in a Florida nursing home to provide financial assistance.

Maybe one day, he said to appease her, if *we win the lottery, we can look into adoption. . . .*

Derry shakes her head and shoves another handful of popcorn into her mouth. She's been over and over the "options," or lack thereof. The bottom line is that the Cordells are too poor for parenthood.

Unless . . .

All at once, a chubby Gerber baby materializes on her screen.

Derry gazes at the image for a moment, tears slowly filling her eyes. She wipes them with her sleeve, rubs her popcorn-dusted hand on her sweatpants. *You're a mess,* she tells herself miserably. *Pull yourself together, for God's sake.*

In the background, Steve Perry is singing "Don't stop . . . believing. . . . Hold on to your dreams."

It's a sign, Derry tells herself. Sniffling, she reaches for the mouse with a trembling hand and clicks again.

The baby gives way to a montage of images: pregnant birth mothers hugging ecstatic-looking couples, women cradling newborns, happy toddlers, a close-up of a baby's fist wrapped around an adult's sturdy finger. The soft strains of a Brahms lullaby play over the computer's speakers, all but drowned out by Journey until Derry reaches over impatiently and turns off the stereo.

This isn't the first time she's looked at an adoption Web site . . . but it's the first time an adoption Web site has directly solicited her. How did they get her e-mail address?

It's spam, she reminds herself. That e-mail probably went out to anyone who's ever looked at an adoption Web site.

But it was so personal. It was addressed to her. *Dear Mrs. Cordell . . .*

So? That doesn't mean it isn't spam.

And anyway, you can't afford to adopt, remember?

If she were wise, she'd sign off the computer and crawl into bed in the next room, where Linden is already snoring.

Instead, she takes another handful of popcorn and hits the Reply button, telling herself that it can't hurt.

Nothing can hurt any more than she already does.

The best thing about New York, as far as Peyton is concerned, is that you can get anything you want at any hour of the night.

Including fresh, ripe watermelon just after midnight on Saint Patrick's Day. The small market is surprisingly bustling at this hour on a weeknight.

God, it's late. She should have fallen into bed the second she walked in the door of her apartment, instead of checking the refrigerator for snacks—and then deciding to venture out in search of some.

The truth is, she would have been asleep hours ago if she hadn't lingered so long at the Pregnant and Single meeting. But once her initial reservations gave way to female comraderie, she found herself reluctant to leave.

Nurse Nancy was right. Those women understand what she's going through in a way nobody else in her life can. She's looking forward to seeing them again.

Now, heading purposefully toward the produce case, Peyton sidesteps a group of attractive, well-dressed men, all in varying shades of green, obviously fresh from a party or pub. She finds herself fighting the urge to check them out, the earlier conversation at the support group still fresh in her mind. She really has no business interacting with members of the opposite sex from here on in, unless it's on a professional—or medical—level. Or in her dreams.

"What else?" the smiling Korean grocer asks as she plunks down a clear plastic container filled with luscious pink cubes.

"That's it."

She watches him weighing the purchase, then punching the numbers into the register.

"That's seven sixty-three."

"Seven sixty-three?" she echoes in dismay. She has only the five-dollar bill she shoved into her pocket along with her keys on her way out of the apartment. Who would imagine that a small container of melon could be so pricey?

Then again, this *is* the middle of March. And this *is* New York. She should have brought her purse along.

Or, better yet, she should have gone right to bed. She shouldn't indulge every midnight craving that hits.

Still, when you want something as badly as she wants that melon . . .

She stares at the package, swallowing hard, her mouth watering. The thought of hurrying two blocks back home for her purse, and then back and forth again, is daunting. But she wants the melon, damn it. *That* melon. Now.

"Short?" asks a voice behind her.

She turns to see a man standing there. Lanky, handsome, exuding an easygoing charm. Exactly her type. Just like Jeff, and Scott, and Gil were exactly her type. And, yes, Dr. Lombardo.

"Short?" the man repeats, and she blinks.

"Excuse me?"

"Are you short?" he asks patiently, motioning at the money in her hand.

"What? Oh!" She grins and finds herself saying, "I've actually always thought I was on the tall side."

He laughs at the unexpected quip, and so does she, wondering why the heck she's bothering to flirt in her condition.

Then she turns sheepishly back to the grocer. "I'll have to come back."

"You come back," he agrees with a curt nod.

He shoves the box of melon aside and motions for the next customer to step forward.

The man behind Peyton sets a six-pack of beer and a container of mixed nuts on the counter. Out of the corner of her eye, as she turns to leave, she sees him pick up the melon and add it to his purchases.

Scowling, she makes her way to the door. Yes, there are other containers of melon in the store. Other containers of melon in the world. But she wanted *that* one.

Oh, God, she's actually whining. Only to herself, but still . . .

Chalking up her immature, irrational behavior to pregnancy hormones, she zips her jacket up to her neck and steps out into the windswept rain. Five minutes home, a minute to get her purse, five minutes back, and she'll have her melon.

No, the thieving stranger has *her* melon. But in ten minutes, she'll have *some* melon. Then another five minutes back home again before she can actually eat it. Unless she steals a bite or two along the way . . .

A few steps into the journey down the dark, deserted block, she's tempted to forget about the melon. She has to be up early, and she's too tired for all this walking.

Besides, it really isn't safe to be out on the street alone at night. You never know when somebody might—

Suddenly, above the wind and rain, the sound of pounding footsteps reaches her ears.

Somebody is upon her before she can react, a masculine hand closing over her forearm just as she turns her head.

"Hush, little baby, don't say a word. . . ." Rocking her sleepy child on her lap, trying to soothe away the nightmare, Anne Marie sings softly.

Sings and rocks, back and forth, back and forth; an age-old rhythm in time to age-old lyrics that have lulled many a child to slumber.

The nursery is illuminated only by the moon-shaped night-light plugged into an outlet between the beds where her other children lie soundly sleeping. Hopefully, it won't be long before their brother joins them again. It's all Anne Marie can do to stay awake herself as she croons the lullaby, the one her mother sang to her, the one she sang to her own—

No. Don't go there.

But it's too late.

Anne Marie stops singing, stops rocking, braces herself for the chilling memories.

They pelt into her, fast and furious and startling as unwelcome summer hail, culminating in the shocking moment last summer that triggered the final descent.

At first she was certain that she was imagining things. She had grown accustomed to seeking that face everywhere she went for a decade. Sometimes she actually found it—but only for a moment, superimposed over a stranger's features in an ultimately cruel mirage.

But that morning, it was different.

That morning, it was real.

It wasn't the first time she had taken the boys to the Bronx Zoo. She and Jarrett are patrons; she takes them every week when the weather is good, and often when it isn't. They never tire of the silly orangutans, the reptile house, the butterfly exhibit . . .

It was there, among sweetly scented blossoms and thousands of fragile, fluttering wings, that Anne Marie happened to look in the right direction and spot the face.

In that breathtaking instant, she was given a fleeting, astonishing glimpse through a magical window into the past, and it profoundly changed everything.

Then the face was gone, swallowed up in a throng of children, all of them wearing identical orange T-shirts emblazoned with the name of a school on the back.

Edgewood Elementary.

Maternal instinct swept her and she wanted to run after the group; stronger maternal instinct held her in place. There were hordes of strangers packed into the garden; little boys clung to her hand on either side, their bolder brother going after a flitting monarch in the opposite direction. She had three children to watch over; she couldn't go chasing an illusion the way Avery was chasing a pretty orange butterfly.

But it wasn't an illusion.

Edgewood Elementary.

She's harbored the lone tangible clue for months, turning it over and over in her brain the way she used to mull seemingly impossible scenarios.

"Mommy . . ."

Only the realization that her son has stirred in her arms and is beginning to whimper jars Anne Marie back to the present.

"It's all right, Caleb," she whispers, pressing a kiss on his feverish temple. "Go back to sleep. Mommy is here."

"Mommy's sad." A small hand reaches up to touch the tears trickling down her cheeks.

She brushes them away with the sleeve of her nightgown, clasps her son's fingers in her own trembling hand. How long can she go on like this? How long can she continue to live one life by day, another beneath the shroud of night?

"You're crying, Mommy. What's wrong?"

"Mommy is fine, sweetheart. Everything is fine. Hush."

Hush.

Slowly, Anne Marie sets the chair in motion again, rocking and singing once more, cradling her precious child against her breast.

"Hush, little baby, don't say a word. . . ."

"Hey, miss, you forgot this," says the man from the store. The one who stole her melon.

Relief courses through Peyton. When somebody came up behind her, she was certain she was about to be mugged, or worse.

He smiles and thrusts a white plastic bag into her hands. "Here. I bought it for you."

Speechless, her heart still racing, she accepts it mutely, too shaken to offer her thanks.

"You okay?" the stranger asks, peering at her, and she nods.

She reaches into her pocket and pulls out the five-dollar bill, holding it out to him.

"Nah, keep it. My treat. You know, it's not a great night to be out buying fruit," he points out conversationally.

Finding her voice, Peyton says only, "No."

"Do you have far to walk?"

She shakes her head, still holding the fruit in one hand and the money in the other.

"Going that way?" He gestures straight ahead.

She can hardly about-face. There's nothing to do but nod.

"So am I. I'll walk with you."

Peyton hesitates. He doesn't look like a crazed killer. But then, Ted Bundy didn't, either.

She should tell him to get lost. New Yorkers don't trust strangers.

But the latent naive, mannerly midwesterner in her stirs to

protest that this nice man just spent seven dollars and sixty-three cents on her. The least she can do is allow him to fall into step beside her as she heads home.

She glances around, hoping to see that a crowd has materialized on the sidewalk and traffic in the streets.

In the distance, she can see cars flying along up Eighth Avenue on one end of the block and down Ninth on the other end, but the cross street is quiet.

Still, there are well-lit apartment buildings and brownstones all around them. If this guy tried anything, all she'd have to do is scream and someone would help her.

Then again, maybe not. This is Manhattan, not Talbot Corners.

Peyton glances again at the man by her side.

He *seems* safe. And he's incredibly handsome. Even more handsome than Dr. Lombardo, with the same brand of dark good looks. She can see that he's wearing a suit and tie beneath the collar of his black overcoat.

She decides that he's an exceptionally gallant man, and nothing more.

Besides, what is she supposed to do? Tell him he can't walk down this public street in the same direction?

Reluctantly, she starts walking again. So does he, saying, "I'm Tom."

Peyton says nothing, her thoughts racing.

"I know what you're thinking," he says after a moment, and she glances up at him in surprise. "You're thinking that I'm some kind of lunatic prowling the streets for innocent women. Right?"

She can't help but laugh at his expression. "Actually, I . . . Right."

"I don't blame you. But I'm really a nice, normal guy."

"I'm sure you are," she says, though she's anything but.

"No, you aren't." He reaches into his pocket for . . .

A gun? A knife? A . . .

Business card.

According to it, Thomas M. Reilly is a biomedical science research technologist at a major pharmaceutical company.

His safety level rises a notch.

But what if this card isn't really his? Short of asking him for photo ID, there's no way Peyton can be sure.

She hands the card back to him without comment.

"You're probably wondering why I'm out talking to strange women at this hour."

She shrugs. That's exactly what she's wondering.

"I had the day from hell at the lab—I just left now, in fact. I'm on my way home to an empty apartment and an empty fridge. I desperately need a beer and I desperately need sleep, but I guess I'm even more desperate for somebody to talk to. Lucky you, right?"

She can't help smiling at his expression . . . or glancing down at the fourth finger of his left hand.

He catches her, and laughs, holding it up and waving it in her face. "No ring. I'm divorced. You?"

Pregnant and single.

"I'm not divorced."

"Married, then?"

"No. Just . . ."

Pregnant and single.

But she isn't about to tell him that. Why would she? He's a stranger. She'll never see him again. It's none of his business.

"Not interested?" He shakes his head, laughs again. "It's okay. I get it. I guess I won't bother asking if you want me to walk you the rest of the way down the block. Here's where I turn off."

They've reached Ninth Avenue. The crosstown light is red.

"Thanks for the melon," Peyton tells him as she waits for the DON'T WALK sign to change.

"You're welcome. Thanks for the ear."

Feeling a twinge of guilt that she wasn't more receptive, she sees that the light is green.

"Good night." She waves and steps off the curb.

She forces herself not to turn back as she crosses the street, but she can feel his gaze on her. Or so she believes.

When she reaches the opposite side, she allows herself to turn her head briefly.

The spot where she left him is empty.

Maybe he wasn't watching her walk away after all.

Maybe you shouldn't flatter yourself that way.

She can't help smirking. She's been in the city long enough to know about the notorious dearth of handsome, professionally successful eligible bachelors her age. She's had only a few dates since she moved here—in part because her job consumes all her free time, but also because interesting men don't pop up and fall in love with her on a regular basis.

It isn't until Peyton reaches her brownstone in the middle of the next block that something Tom said comes back to her.

I guess I won't bother asking if you want me to walk you the rest of the way down the block.

It almost sounded as though . . .

No.

She's never seen the man before in her life.

Why would she think he might know where she lives?

It's just that the way he phrased it—*the rest of the way down the block*—seems telling. How does he know she doesn't live in one of the blocks beyond the intersection? Or around a corner?

She's probably just paranoid. More pregnancy hormones at work.

Still, she checks the locks on her door several times once she's inside, and, feeling foolish, looks under the bed before climbing back into it.

The watermelon sits untouched, still in its plastic bag, her craving having vanished just as unexpectedly as the stranger who paid for it.

Month Three
April

CHAPTER THREE

"I'm Rose Calabrone," the woman across the threshold announces in a friendly tone that almost puts Derry at ease.

Almost.

Standing there beside her husband, facing the stranger who holds their parental fate in her hands, Derry can't help but fret. She clenches her fists in the pockets of the new corduroy pants she found on final markdown at Strawberry's during yesterday's emergency shopping trip.

Less than twenty-four hours ago, as she scurried around the city on her fashion mission, it was sleeting, reducing the remnants of a late snowfall into ugly gray slush in the gutters.

Today, the April breeze is so unseasonably balmy that Derry could conceivably be wearing shorts instead of corduroy and this polyester-blend sweater she bought to go with the pants. She bought a couple of new blouses that would have been better. A ruffled blue one, and a peach one with a broad collar.

But she chose the sweater because she was going for an upscale, suburban housewife look. Very classic, very together. Hopefully, Rose Calabrone won't notice that her hair-spray-tamed bangs are dampened with sweat.

"Come on in," Linden says cordially, stepping back and holding the door open. He looks awkward in the suit and tie Derry insisted he wear. Maybe his regular clothes would have been better, she thinks, noting that the suit doesn't fit right and the tie's shape is outdated. The powder blue dress shirt beneath the jacket has short sleeves. Like the suit, it's the only one he owns. Linden is under strict orders not to remove the coat, no matter how hot it is.

"Why not?" he asked sourly just before the buzzer rang.

"Because nobody wears short sleeves with a suit. And because sweaty armpits will show up on that light blue."

As the visitor steps into their home at last, Derry sweeps the freshly scrubbed living room with the same critical eye that found grievous fault in her husband.

Is it obvious that the "coffee table" is really a piano bench long ago scavenged from the curb? Or that the peach-colored drapes in the room's lone window are homemade? Or that the throw pillows are as frayed as her nerves?

At least the throw rug is new, and you can't see the worn spots on the couch slipcover. Thank God for Odd Lot, and for the dimmer switch on the overhead light.

"Can I get you some coffee, Ms. Calabrone?" Derry asks, wishing she had thought of making a pot in advance. The scent of brewing coffee would make any house more homey.

"It's *Mrs.* Calabrone, actually, but you can call me Rose."

Derry can't help thinking that bodes well for a long-term relationship. You don't encourage a first-name basis with people you don't expect to see again.

Or maybe Derry's just grasping at straws, looking for signs that this, at last, is the answer to their prayers for a child.

"Coffee, Rose?" she asks again, and the woman hesitates, then politely declines.

Perhaps she would have accepted a cup if she thought it were no trouble. If she had stepped in and the apartment smelled like fresh coffee.

Yes, and Derry should have baked cookies, too, rather than buying those Easter-themed Oreos with the pastel-tinted cream. Now they're sitting on a plastic-wrapped plate in front of the couch, ready to serve. What was she thinking?

You were thinking that fancy-colored Oreos were a step up from the generic-brand sandwich cookies you and Linden usually buy. You were thinking that a child should grow up in a home with plenty of Oreos on hand.

Meanwhile, Mrs. Calabrone—Rose— probably thinks that a child should grow up some place where homemade treats are the norm.

Well, it's too late for cookie-baking and coffee-brewing now. It's sink or swim time for the Cordells.

At least I'm not working anymore, Derry tells herself optimistically. *They probably don't like working mothers.*

Linden has led Rose to the couch, having completely forgotten—or ignored—Derry's adamant previsit instructions.

She hastily sidesteps the makeshift coffee table and says, with a pointed glare at her husband, "I think you'll be more comfortable in this chair, Rose."

Yes, because the chair, though threadbare, doesn't squeak or sag or smell like cat pee.

Hopefully the lilac-scented candle flickering beside the plate of cookies masks the odor, because the woman has already seated herself on the couch, saying, "This is fine, thanks."

There's nothing for Derry to do but sit in the chair herself, with Linden perched on the arm. He rests a loving hand on her shoulder, as though the two of them haven't been at each other's throats all day in the frenzy to prepare for the adoption agency representative's arrival.

"Tell me a little about yourselves," Rose suggests, her pink-lipsticked mouth curving into a pleasant smile.

Derry would much rather she told them about the unwed Iowa teenager who, miracle of miracles, selected their profile from the dozens the agency sent her.

Who would ever have expected that to happen so quickly after Derry responded to the initial e-mail? She's heard nightmarish stories about all the red tape, high costs, delays, and false starts that go along with the adoption process, but this was easy.

Almost too easy.

And, remarkably, affordable. The fee is much lower than the tens of thousands she anticipated. Even better, it can be paid in small monthly installments that will commence only when the adoption is complete.

At this rate, Derry could be a mother in just a few months.

". . . and then we realized we can't afford infertility treatments," Linden is saying, having conveniently forgotten that Derry's case was so futile Dr. Lombardo didn't even present that option, "so we sort of knew that we probably aren't going to be parents."

Sort of knew?

There was a time when Derry was charmed by his poor grammar. She used to be drawn to that rough-around-the-edges quality of his.

Not anymore. She has to get him to shut up, or he's going to ruin this. No adoption agency wants to give a child to a father who says *ain't*. Of that, she's certain.

"But then, just when we figured it wasn't gonna happen, Derry got that e-mail," Linden goes on, oblivious of her disgust, "and she was so happy when she heard back from you. You should have seen her face. I don't think she's stopped smiling since that day."

Derry melts a little, touched by the glance her husband sends in her direction. His grammar stinks, but anyone can see that he loves her. Surely two happily married parents meet the most important adoption criteria.

"I'm happy to hear that, because your future as parents looks very bright." Rose includes them both in her pleasant smile, revealing a row of perfect, ultrawhite teeth. Still, there's a slight air of detachment about her expression. The smile doesn't quite reach her brown eyes.

That's because she's the epitome of professional decorum, Derry tells herself, relaxing a bit despite her anxiety. This isn't as scary as she expected. Everything is more casual than she expected, almost as though the slim blonde on the couch is a new neighbor from down the hall, dropping by to introduce herself.

Not that she can quite picture Rose living here in Co-op City. There's a vaguely upscale air about her. Her hair is styled in a country club pageboy, and she's wearing a trim black suit and a pair of leather pumps that look as expensive as her perfume smells. And if that square-cut diamond ring on the fourth finger of her left hand is real, it's worth almost as much as this apartment.

Derry always pictured adoption agency employees as nuns, or social worker types. In a way, that might be easier. She wouldn't feel as self-consciously inferior.

Shifting her gaze away from the woman's huge ring, she notices that at least her nails aren't long and perfectly polished, as one might expect in a city where weekly manicures are requisite. Derry unclenches her own ravaged fingertips a little, no longer quite as desperate to hide them in the folds of her sweater.

There's nothing critical in Rose's mascara-fringed eyes as she says, "I'm sure you have a lot of questions. Why don't you go ahead and ask them?"

Linden, who has been skeptical about this process from the start, promptly opens his mouth.

Before he can throw a wrench—or a dangling participle—into the precarious proceedings, Derry blurts, "Tell us about the mother in Iowa."

A shadow crosses Rose's attractive face.

Uh-oh. Clearly, Derry said the wrong thing. She should have let Linden do the talking after all.

Rose seems to be choosing her words with care.

Finally, she says, "At Cradle to Cradle, we prefer to call expectant clients 'donors.' If everything works out the way we expect it to, Mrs. Cordell, *you* will be the mother. Not her."

Derry grins, the last of her reservations melting away like ugly late-winter slush.

Rita's cell phone rings just as it's her turn to be waited on.

"Can I help you?" the deli counterman is asking impatiently.

She holds up a finger, motioning him to stand by while she answers her phone. "Hello?"

"Rita. I've been trying to reach you all morning. Where have you been?"

"Delivering twins," she tells Nancy wearily. "And I worked up one hell of an appetite, so hang on a second."

To the impatient counterman, she says, "I'll have a turkey sandwich on whole grain bread with lettuce and mustard."

"Cheese?"

"No."

"Tomatoes?"

"No. Just lettuce and mustard," she repeats with forced politeness, wondering why New York deli men always seem bent on making things more complicated. She orders the same exact sandwich every time she comes in here. Which is at least once or twice a week.

Rita isn't crazy about complications these days. Or ever. No, sirree.

Into the phone, she says, "The second twin was breech. What a nightmare for the mother."

"And for you."

"She did all the work."

"Not all the work. Don't sell yourself short."

Rita smiles, shaking her head.

Leave it to Nancy to turn her into the hero. The woman's specialty, aside from gossip and perpetually feeling sorry for herself, is definitely stroking egos. No wonder Bill Lombardo hired her years ago. Nancy always knows just what to say to flatter him.

It's a God-given gift, as far as Rita's concerned.

"You know how I feel about my work, Nancy. It isn't brain surgery. I just make sure I'm there, and I let nature take its course."

"Most midwives would beg to differ."

"Listen, sugar pie, you and I both know that women have been giving birth for quite some time and anyone is capable of doing what I do," says Rita, who frequently points out that it wasn't so long ago that most women acted as midwives for their daughters and sisters and friends.

"You'd better not say that in front of your patients, or they won't be willing to pay you," Nancy warns her. "Anyway, listen, I was wondering if we could set up another home-birth seminar here in the office for sometime next month."

"You don't think I'm busy enough?" Rita asks with a laugh, plucking a bottle of sweetened iced tea from the refrigerated case adjacent to the counter. "I've already got my hands full with patients and support groups—which reminds me, I've got to reschedule that Pregnant and Single meeting. I've had to cancel on them twice at the last minute."

"Nature of the business," Nancy says lightly. "And they've been meeting anyway. I think they just like bonding with other women who are in the same boat. So can we set something up for the office?"

"I'll call you later, from home," Rita promises. "I don't have my appointment book with me."

"Turkey on whole grain with lettuce, onion, and mustard," the counterman bellows, thrusting a wrapped sandwich in her direction.

Rita sighs. "I've got to go, Nancy. I've got to take care of a problem here."

"Patient complications?"

"No," Rita says with a smile, shaking her head. "Sandwich complications. Talk to you later."

"You were right. This is a great restaurant, Peyton," Allison announces around a mouthful of Tequila Moon's famous refried beans. "Do you come here a lot?"

"Pretty much every day lately, the way I've been craving cilantro." Peyton dips another tortilla chip into the restaurant's addictive salsa. "Good thing it's only a block from my apartment.

Then again, I'd be more than willing to take two subways and a bus to get here if I had to."

"That's pretty much what I have to do to get my Indian food fix. Only it's one subway and two buses."

As they share a laugh, Peyton marvels at how quickly she and Allison have bonded over cravings and nausea, layettes and maternity catalogs, even a mutual hobby of collecting classic children's books.

It's only been a few weeks since that first Pregnant and Single meeting, but Allison feels like an old friend, more so than the other members of the support group.

Kate has already delivered a baby boy and advanced to the foreign land of breast pumps and colic. Julie is a bit too militant in her views on home birth and neonatal care, and Wanda is caught up in the ongoing drama of her affair with the married father of her child.

Still, Peyton has more in common with all of them than she does lately with coworkers she's known for a few years. Those at the office who have children are married; those who don't seem to be determined nonbreeders. In fact, Peyton wonders how she never noticed until now how often her boss, Tara, seems to make disparaging remarks about children and motherhood. It's almost as though she might suspect Peyton's pregnancy and is hinting that she's about to derail her career.

"Do you think I should talk to Tara on Monday?" she asks Allison, who is a longtime secretary at a midtown law firm and a self-proclaimed expert on corporate politics.

"I thought you were going to wait until you're really showing."

"I was going to, but . . . I mean, why wait? What's she going to do, fire me?"

"Maybe."

Peyton sticks out her tongue. "Let her try. I want that promotion when Alain leaves in a few weeks, and I've worked hard for it. Nobody deserves it more than I do."

"Then don't tell your boss you're pregnant until after she's promoted you. Tell her now and she'll have you flying down the mommy track so fast you'll need Dramamine. Trust me. I see it happen all the time at the firm."

"So why doesn't anybody sue? They're lawyers."

"Who knows? Maybe because once they become mothers, they aren't as passionate about their jobs. You'll see."

"I doubt it. I know I'll love the baby, but I also love my career." Less at the moment than ever before, but she's worked hard to build it, and she's certain she'll regain the passion. "And anyway," she goes on, heaping her fork with spicy yellow rice, "I've got to support the two of us somehow."

"Maybe you'll find a nice rich husband. Like Dr. Lombardo."

I never should have told her about those dreams.

Peyton knows her cheeks must be redder than the habanera chiles on her plate.

"I don't want a nice rich husband," she assures Allison. "And anyway, Dr. Lombardo is already somebody else's nice rich husband."

"Okay, then how about a great-looking husband with a good sense of humor? Because I was thinking that one of the lawyers at the firm would be perfect for—"

"I don't want *any* husband, Allison. Trust me. I don't want to answer to anyone."

"Hmm, let me guess: your fiancé was a total son of a bitch. Am I right?"

Peyton shrugs, not in the mood to ask *which fiancé?* She must have mentioned one of her broken engagements to Allison in the flurry of confidences they've exchanged these past few weeks—not that she recalls doing so. She's pretty forgetful these days, though. And she must have brought up Scott or Jeff at one point, because Allison is now regarding her with a knowing look, obviously convinced that one of them turned her into a man-hater.

Again, Peyton regrets blabbing her personal business. It isn't like her. There's just something about candid, easygoing Allison that tempts Peyton to open up more than she usually would. And something about being pregnant that has her reaching out to other women in a way she never has.

Oh well. No harm done, she assures herself.

She just isn't eager to discuss Scott or Jeff or the reasons neither of them became her husband.

She says simply, "I'm going to do this on my own."

Allison's expression isn't exactly disapproving, yet she shrugs and asks with a touch less warmth than usual, "What are you going to do with the baby once your maternity leave is over?"

"Hire a nanny," she says, hating that it comes out sounding like a confession and wondering what the heck Allison *thinks* she's going to do. "Or maybe I'll use day care. I don't know."

"Have you started looking?"

"Not yet. There's plenty of—"

"You'd better start looking now," Allison cuts in. "This is New York. People put fetuses on waiting lists for private high schools."

Peyton laughs.

Allison shakes her head soberly. "I'm not kidding."

Her smile fading, Peyton wants to tell her friend to stop trying to spook her. It's not as though she's assuming this will be a cake-walk. But neither is she willing to focus on the challenges ahead without mustering every shred of optimism she possesses.

Don't let her scare you off. You'll make it. You'll be a terrific mother, and you'll raise a terrific kid.

"Look," Allison says earnestly, "I'm not trying to be the prophet of doom. But I feel like you think you know what to expect and you're positive you can handle it on your own, when in reality, parenthood is full of surprises. I don't want to see you with your hands full, wishing you had waited until you were married."

"*You're* not married."

"Not this time, no. But I have a support system under my roof. You're all alone."

"Which is my choice," Peyton insists. "And it's a good one, for me. This didn't happen by accident, remember? I chose this. I want this. More than anything." Her voice breaks, and she looks down, needing to steel her wayward emotions.

"Just don't rule anything out, okay? You might change your mind."

"About getting married?"

"That, and working so many hours in such a demanding field."

Peyton laughs. "You don't know me very well, Allison. I rarely change my mind about anything."

"All right, Ms. *Obstinado*. We'll just see about that."

"Hey, don't call me that!" Peyton protests, though it isn't the first time somebody has done so.

"What?"

"Bullheaded."

"I didn't realize you spoke Spanish."

"Only what I learned in high school."

"Well, if the *zapato* fits . . ." Allison smiles. "Listen, all I mean is that becoming a mother is going to change everything. You can't know in advance how much, so keep your options open. You might wake up a year from now and decide you want a husband or a three-day workweek or a nice cushy job share like I have."

A job share. Even if that kind of thing weren't frowned upon at the agency, it's out of the realm of possibility for Peyton. She couldn't afford the salary cut now, let alone with another mouth to feed.

Allison has the luxury of living with her parents.

Luxury, or misfortune, depending on how you look at it.

Peyton would never want her mother judging her every move the way Allison's reportedly does.

Then again, she can't help secretly thinking it might be nice to have a built-in babysitter. Or a few of them. Allison's parents helped to care for her children when her husband left her. Now her teenagers are old enough to take care of themselves, and to pitch in with their new sibling.

Allison will have plenty of willing hands standing by when the baby comes along. Peyton will have none. Nobody to help . . .

But nobody to interfere, either, she reminds herself, and decides to change the sore subject.

"I keep wondering what the baby looks like," she tells Allison. "It's hard, you know? Never having seen the father."

"I know, but just think. Maybe his genes won't matter anyway. Maybe it'll look just like you did as a baby."

"God, I hope not. I was totally bald until I was about a year old."

Allison laughs. "Well, I had so much hair when I was born that my uncle Norberto nicknamed me *Peludo.*"

"*Peludo?*"

"You don't know that word? It means shaggy. He still calls me that. I hate nicknames. When my kids came out looking just like me, with piles of shiny black hair, Uncle Norberto tried to pull it again. But as soon as I told him I'd teach them to call him *Pelado* in return, he cut it out."

"What does *Pelado* mean?"

"Baldy," Allison says with an evil grin, and turns her attention to the menu in her hand. "So what should I order for dessert? What's good? The margarita ice cream?"

"No liquor, young lady," Peyton says with mock disapproval. "Not for another two months."

"Yeah, well, the second I deliver, I'm breaking out the tequila."

"Want me to bring you a bottle of Cuervo in the hospital?"

"Make it Patron and you've got a deal." Allison grins, her old sunny self once again.

Watching her friend scanning the dessert list, Peyton decides that she'll definitely ask Allison to be her labor coach. It's something she's been mulling over all week.

For one thing, she can't think of anybody else to ask. For another, Allison's irreverent sense of humor will be welcome in the delivery room. Yes, and she'll certainly be well acquainted with the rigors of childbirth by that time.

Before Peyton can pop the question, though, Allison poses one of her own. "How's the flan here?"

"As good as you'd expect."

"Does it have a lot of caramel sauce?"

"Yup."

"Is it good caramel sauce?"

"Delicious."

"Then that's what I'm having." Allison snaps the menu closed. "Oh, and speaking of delicious, that hottie over by the bar has been watching you for the last ten minutes. If you weren't so opposed to husband hunting, I'd tell you to turn around and wink."

"Wink?" Peyton laughs, shaking her head, trying to imagine herself winking at a strange man. "Who am I, Betty Boop?"

"Oops, too late, Betty. It looks like he's leaving. Anyway, men are off-limits to you, unless you've changed your mind already?"

Peyton assures Allison that men are as off-limits in her immediate future as margarita ice cream is.

Still, curiosity gets the best of her, and she turns around.

Just in time to glimpse a vaguely familiar face in the split second before the figure disappears out into the street.

For a few minutes, she can't seem to place him.

It isn't until she and Allison have given the waiter their dessert orders that she realizes, with a twinge of excitement oddly tainted by a vague sense of uneasiness, who he was.

Tom.

The complete stranger who bought her the watermelon that night a few weeks ago.

Tom . . .

The complete stranger who seemed to know where she lived.

The thing about New York is that you can be utterly anonymous, utterly unnoticed. It takes a lot more than a river of mascara running down a person's cheeks to capture attention on a crowded sidewalk.

Anne Marie wipes her face and eyes with a futile swipe of a tissue, but the tears refuse to subside.

What now? she wonders, looking down at the envelope clutched tightly in her hand. She's afraid to let go even to tuck it into her bag.

If only you never let go in the first place, she tells herself, thinking not of the envelope but of the loss it signifies. *Why did you let go?*

Somebody slams into her from behind and she realizes she has stopped walking altogether. "Sorry," the pedestrian flings brusquely over his shoulder, striding on.

Anne Marie forces her legs to start moving again, forces her thoughts into action as well.

What now?

I should probably call him, tell him. But I don't even know where he is.

His whereabouts can be discovered easily enough, she supposes.

But that would mean letting him in, to share not just the burden but the decisions that will have to be made.

Is that really what she wants?

She clasps the envelope possessively to her chest, to her heart, knowing that isn't what she wants.

This is hers, for now. All hers.

For now, and perhaps, forever.

"Peyton, wait—"

She turns back toward Allison and finds her still poised on the top of the subway steps.

"What's wrong?" Peyton asks, retracing the few steps she had taken down the busy street. "Did you forget something?"

"Yeah. I forgot to ask if you'll be my labor coach."

"I was going to ask you the same exact thing!" Peyton exclaims, touched and surprised by Allison's invitation.

"You were? I'll do it. It'll be an honor."

"Same here. Only . . . are you sure you want me? What about your mother? Or . . . someone else from the group?"

"My mother?" Allison's gaze darkens. "She's the last one I want in the room. No, I just want you. You're calmer and stronger than anybody else."

Honored by the praise, and determinedly ignoring the jostling crowd edging by her as she hovers beside the green globe lamp at the subway's entrance, Peyton asks, "So what do I have to do to prepare for this?"

"Rita will tell you. If I have you and Rita, I'll get through it just fine. And I'll get you through it, too, when it's your turn. You'll see. All you need when you're in labor is to be surrounded by people you totally trust."

After making plans to meet Allison for coffee after work on Monday, Peyton waits until the subterranean staircase has swallowed her friend's glossy black curls.

Then she turns back to the bustling avenue—and realizes that she isn't quite ready to go home just yet.

Maybe it's spring fever, thanks to the unseasonably warm weather that has driven New Yorkers outdoors this balmy Saturday afternoon: on foot, on Rollerblades, on bicycles.

Or maybe, Peyton tells herself as she walks slowly down Seventh Avenue toward home, *you're looking for* him.

She certainly shouldn't be.

Nor should she assume that Tom Reilly's appearance in Tequila Moon had anything to do with her.

When you come right down to it, that's hardly a remarkable coincidence. After all, Tequila Moon is a popular Mexican restaurant, and he lives right here in the neighborhood.

So it isn't as though he's following her.

Nor, on the other hand, is it as though he's avoiding her.

But if he was staring, as Allison claimed, then he probably recognized her. Why didn't he come over and say hello? Why did he just disappear?

Because you're virtual strangers, Peyton reminds herself, feeling foolish for caring. *A container of watermelon hardly creates a lasting social obligation.*

Particularly when one is hardly in prime condition for a romantic relationship.

So he happened to be there, and he apparently remembered meeting her that night, and he didn't say hi. So what?

So, it's bothering me. I can't help it.

And she just isn't sure whether she wishes he'd greeted her, or is glad that he didn't.

Nor does she know why, when she reaches her cross street a few minutes later, she keeps walking rather than turning the corner.

Where the heck are you going? she asks herself, frowning even as she strides on down the sidewalk.

Who knows? is the hardly satisfying answer to her silent question.

Unaccustomed to harboring wishy-washiness, Peyton decides to chalk it up to pregnancy. Maybe aimless wandering is just another incongruous symptom, right up there with the leg cramps and facial pigmentation Allison warned her about earlier.

Allison also mentioned a great maternity boutique called Baby Blue that happens to be located down on Fourteenth Street, not far from here.

Okay, that's a desirable destination. She's far more comfortable heading some place specific rather than simply strolling the streets.

Strolling is for people who don't know—or don't care—where they're going.

That's so not me.

No, Peyton's always known exactly where she's going. She prefers to have every detail of her life mapped out with the same precision that landed her in New York, and in Dr. Lombardo's office.

Dr. Lombardo.

The thought triggers an image of dark good looks, and a forbidden stirring.

Stop it, Peyton.

She forces herself to think in strictly professional terms about her upcoming visit with the doctor on Tuesday afternoon. His nurse, Nancy, sent Peyton an e-mail last week suggesting that she arrive with a list of questions she wants to ask the ob-gyn. So far, Peyton has come up with only one that's not entirely inappropriate: how does Dr. Lombardo feel about home deliveries?

The more she's read—and the more time she spends with her support group—the more interested she is in that particular topic. There's something reassuring about going through a traumatic experience like childbirth right in your own home, surrounded by familiar things and familiar faces.

Familiar faces . . .

As she walks downtown, Peyton finds herself scanning the crowded sidewalks for another glimpse of one familiar face in particular.

Every so often she looks over her shoulder, feeling as though somebody is watching her. Which is ridiculous. Odds are, she'll never see Tom again.

Not necessarily, she can almost hear Allison saying.

As her friend pointed out in the restaurant when Peyton told her about her initial meeting with Tom, sometimes New York is a smaller town than legitimate small towns.

"You'll probably run into him again in your neighborhood. Or maybe where you least expect it," Allison informed her, and went on to tell Peyton about how she once found herself sharing a subway car with her ex-mother-in-law.

"The thing about this city is that its boundaries are relatively small, and people are absolutely everywhere," Allison said. "You're bound to cross paths with everyone in town, sooner or later."

Peyton doesn't know about that theory. She's never run into, say, the mayor. Or any of her favorite local movie stars. Or her ex-boyfriend Gil Blaney.

She's heard through the Talbot Corners grapevine that he's living and working in midtown Manhattan. In fact, both her mother and Peyton's old friend Caroline, with whom she exchanges e-mails, have mentioned recently that Gil would love to hear from her. Peyton's mother even mentioned that he had called there last Christmas, hoping she was home for the holiday. He asked for her phone number, but Mom didn't feel comfortable giving it to him.

"I know how much he hurt you," she told Peyton. "I wasn't sure you'd want to speak to him ever again, but I took his number for you anyway, just in case."

Peyton still has it, scribbled on the back of a bill envelope and stuffed into her desk drawer. Just in case.

It wouldn't be so horrible to talk to Gil. Or even see him. Presumably, he spends most of his time a stone's throw from her own apartment and office, but their paths have yet to cross by chance.

Sometimes, out of sheer nostalgia, Peyton is tempted to pick up the phone and give him a call. Yes, she thinks, as she spots the Baby Blue down the block near the subway station, she really should call him. Someday. Just for old times' sake. Just in case—

"Oh, I'm sorry!" blurts a slow-moving passerby, who stopped directly in Peyton's path to gaze into a store window.

"It's okay." Peyton sidesteps the stranger, who is licking an ice cream cone and who, like the majority of New Yorkers on the sidewalk today, obviously has nowhere in particular to be.

Striding on toward the store, Peyton resumes thinking about Gil.

You should look him up . . . in case what? In case he's available again? Come on. You don't want Gil back. You just finished telling Allison that you don't want anyone.

She meant it. Yet, lost in memories of her first love, she continues to weave her way amidst the drifting herd, oblivious of the fact that not everyone walking behind her is strolling aimlessly on this mild April Saturday.

One pedestrian, careful to keep a safe distance, has a distinct purpose: to go wherever Peyton Somerset does.

Mouse in hand, Derry left-clicks on the icon that whisks her to yet another baby clothing Web site, glad Linden isn't here to look over her shoulder.

He would undoubtedly tell her she's being premature, ordering all these tiny socks and hats and Onesies with money they don't necessarily have. He'd say she shouldn't get her hopes up, that it's too soon. That she should at least wait until they get the call from Rose's agency, telling them that they are the Iowa teenager's final choice—or, even better, that the girl has gone into labor and the Cordells' parenthood is imminent.

Those are precisely the comments Linden made when Derry made a beeline for her stash of *Right Start* catalogs the moment Rose left their apartment.

Naturally, Derry snapped, her temper having already been stretched dangerously thin in all the previsit stress. She found herself engaged in yet another screaming battle with the husband who claims to want a child as badly as she does, yet is somehow maddeningly detached from the emotional trauma of obtaining that goal.

Finally, Linden grabbed his coat and left the apartment, headed God knows where. He didn't say; Derry didn't ask. Nor did she point out that he doesn't need a coat in this weather. Let him sweat it out somewhere. She couldn't care less about his comfort at this point.

Derry peruses a tantalizing array of old-fashioned pink floral dresses with tiny tucks along the bodices, the kinds of dresses she wore in her baby pictures and always imagined putting on a daughter of her own someday.

It would be nice to know if that girl in Iowa is expecting a girl. Has she had a sonogram?

"Please feel free to call my office with any questions you have," Rose said when she left, handing Derry a business card emblazoned with the now familiar Cradle to Cradle logo: two tiny cradles and a winged cherub midflight between them. "Or you can always e-mail me. And of course I'll be sure to call or e-mail you and Linden with any updates."

Derry finds the card and dials the number—a local one with a Manhattan exchange—not really expecting to get a human answer. After all, it's a weekend, and late afternoon. Then again, maybe adoption agency offices don't keep regular business hours. Maybe staff is on hand around the clock to field calls from potential mothers-to-be.

Rather, *donors.*

She smiles, Rose's words echoing in her head.

If everything works out the way we expect it to, Mrs. Cordell, you will be the mother. Not her.

Was it Derry's imagination, or was the final word uttered with a hint of distaste? As the number she dialed rings on, unanswered, Derry contemplates the fact that Rose didn't exactly seem to hold the unwed pregnant teenager in high regard.

Well, who can blame her? In her line of work, she's probably seen a lot of neglect. She must weary of working with women who are carrying babies they can't raise for one reason or another. She probably feels as though they're recklessly irresponsible, or—

There's a sudden click in Derry's ear.

"Your call is very important. Please leave a message."

Derry hangs up abruptly, confused. Was that a private residence?

She presses Redial and checks the number that comes up in the caller ID window, comparing it to the one on the business card.

The numbers are the same.

After three rings, the call is answered, and she hears an identical message, succinctly delivered in a female voice that may or may not be Rose's.

"Hi, this is Derry Cordell," she says tentatively, after the beep. "I just . . . I had a quick question for Rose, if she could call me back."

She recites her phone number, utters her thanks, and hangs up, still feeling a bit uncertain.

You'd think the agency's recorded greeting would be a little more . . . businesslike. And specific. At least the message could have mentioned the name of the agency, Cradle to Cradle. Or even have some kind of answering service or hotline for expectant mothers who call when they're in labor.

No, Derry corrects herself again.

At Cradle to Cradle, we prefer to call expectant clients "donors."

Well, that's just fine with Derry. She prefers to think of herself as a mother-to-be from here on in.

Smiling once again, she redirects her attention to the onscreen cursor blinking alongside that display of tiny pink floral dresses.

If Jarrett ever finds out she lied to him about where she was going today . . .

With a squeal, the subway train lurches into motion again.

No, he won't find out, Anne Marie tells herself, holding the manila envelope with its precious, shocking contents close against her side with one hand and reaching overhead for the metal bar with the other. *And anyway, you didn't lie. You're in the city, just like you said.*

Yes, but she hasn't been at a matinee for the new Andrew Lloyd Weber show on Broadway. She was taking care of business. Business that Jarrett knows nothing about.

What if he asks her specific questions about the musical?

She'll have to stop at Hudson News to pick up a copy of *New York* magazine before she gets on the commuter train at Grand Central. Hopefully, there will be a review in the Theater section.

Then again, what does it matter? It's not as though Jarrett is apt to ask her about the plot or lyrics or acting. He's about as interested in Broadway shows as he is in art galleries, fine dining, the Yankees, window-shopping on Fifth Avenue . . .

Anne Marie frequently tells him that he might as well live on a desolate prairie for all the time he spends enjoying the city during nonworking hours. Jarrett's interests are confined to the stock market, his antique sword collection, and his children.

Yes, and sometimes, it seems, in precisely that order.

To be fair, she knows he loves the boys, just as she knows, deep down, that he loves her.

She loves him in return. Jarrett Egerton saved her when she was at her lowest, a drab shell of the vibrant woman she once was.

Seven years ago, she was working in a Revolutionary War

museum on the Hudson River, spending her days, fittingly, in isolation, cataloging dusty relics as she attempted to come to terms with her own past.

There was a time when she longed to be an archaeologist, but of course, college was out of the question for her. She had to earn a living, and until ten years ago, she earned it working as a salesclerk by day, a waitress by night.

But there she was, finally employed by a museum—not as an archaeologist, of course; by then she had long since given up the childish dream. She was content simply to support herself, to exist in relative anonymity.

Then Jarrett came along, a longtime patron interested in donating historic weaponry from his private collection.

He took her to dinner; he took her to Paris; he proposed. It was an unexpected fairy-tale ending to a bleak existence . . . or so she foolishly believed.

She should have known her newfound happiness could be little more than a temporary bandage on a festering wound.

She doesn't expect it to heal, even now. But she must find a way to cope with the chronic suffering, if only for her children's sake.

So stop feeling guilty about today.

On Jarrett's account, anyway.

She only regrets that she had to leave her cherished boys at home all afternoon with a father who isn't accustomed to being solely in charge. But she had no choice.

She has to see this through.

She owes it to herself . . .

And I owe it to you.

She closes her eyes in brief, painful remembrance, only to open them abruptly as the careening train screeches around a curve in the dark tunnel.

Anne Marie instinctively adjusts the position of her black leather pumps to keep her balance with the ingrained expertise of someone who hasn't ridden a two-wheeler in decades, yet finds that her body instantly remembers how.

These days, she's far less accustomed to the subway than she is to the upholstered seats on MetroNorth's commuter trains. She certainly wouldn't be riding the downtown local now if cabs weren't so sparse in the neighborhood she just left. Within the circles she travels as an Egerton of Bedford, nobody rides the subway. Few ever did.

The moment she passed through the turnstiles that now demand to be fed fare cards instead of metal tokens, Anne Marie's senses were seized by familiarity. Tokens may have fallen by the wayside but the rest is intact: dingy mosaic signs and bare-bulb lighting; the passing roar of express trains one track away from the platform dragging newspaper and food wrappers into the dark tunnels; the pungent, distinctively dank odor of the universe far beneath the city streets.

This almost feels like home.

But of course, it isn't.

Home is a three-story brick colonial fortress forty miles and a world away from here. It won't be long before Anne Marie finds herself on another train—a regular, commuter train—back to Westchester.

Home.

Home to a life that has nothing to do with any of this, a life where nobody—including her husband—knows about her past, or about the secrets contained in the unmarked manila envelope.

"Can I help you, ma'am?"

Peyton looks up from the clothing rack to see a svelte salesgirl whose plastic name tag reads *Sue.*

Cripes. You'd think a maternity boutique would make a conscious effort *not* to hire model-thin help.

Trying to ignore the blatant contrast to her own burgeoning waistline, Peyton lifts a hanger-draped arm and says, "I'd like to try on a few things."

"Sure. Do you want me to take those and start a room for you while you keep browsing?"

"No, thanks, I'm through browsing." And highly disappointed in the pickings, she might add.

It isn't that the clothes aren't well made, because they are. They'd better be, given the price tags.

But Peyton can't help noticing that everything in this place, from work suits to jeans, seems to be vaguely frumpy. Allison must have very different taste in clothing. The way she raved about Baby Blue, Peyton was expecting Dolce and Gabbana meets A Pea in the Pod.

"When are you due?" Skinny Sue asks conversationally, leading the way into a large, carpeted dressing room.

"October. I guess it's a little early to be trying on maternity sundresses and bathing suits, right? Maybe I should just come back when I've got more of a belly so I'll know how things will fit."

"Oh, that's not a problem. Hang on a second." The girl disappears around the corner.

Peyton slips out of her loafers, noticing that the room is furnished with two guest chairs and a little table stacked with magazines. *Sports Illustrated* is on top of the pile, a not-so-subtle reminder that most occupants of this cubicle are apparently accompanied by a male companion.

"Here we go." Sue reappears in the doorway with an armload of what looks like cushions. "These are prosthetic tummies. You strap one on underneath whatever you're trying on to see what you'll look like in a few months. Here's a six-month one to start."

With that, she leaves Peyton alone in the dressing room with a fake belly and floor-to-ceiling mirrors, saying to call out if she needs any help.

"I will," Peyton promises, eager to get down to business.

She hurriedly strips down to her bra and panties, then pauses to inspect the faint swelling across her stomach. Yes, she's definitely starting to show—but only when she's naked. It'll be quite some time before anyone can tell, just by looking at her, that she's expecting.

She straps on the prosthetic device with surprisingly little effort, then reaches for the nearest stretch-panel pants and T-shirt, putting them on over the belly.

Wow.

So this is how she's going to look in just a few months.

Unexpected tears spring to her eyes.

Pregnancy hormones. Lately she finds herself misty at the slightest provocation. Anything can set off a wave of sentimentality. Romping puppies at a pet shop. Children's choirs on PBS.

And now fake bellies.

It's just . . .

Here's the proof that it's really happening. After all these years, motherhood is happening.

Peyton turns from side to side, admiring her reflection. She looks like Allison. All right, not as big as Allison is; Allison seems inordinately tremendous, anyway. But Peyton is wearing the six-month tummy, and boy, is it convincing! Nobody looking at her would have a clue that she isn't really pregnant.

After examining herself from all angles, she exchanges the

six-month tummy for the nine-month tummy. It looks just as real, filling Peyton with giddy anticipation.

This will be me, next fall. This is how I'll look, and how I'll feel.

She leans back a little, resting a hand in the small of her back, emulating Allison's frequent stance.

"How's it going in here?" Skinny Sue knocks and pokes her head in. "Oh, you look adorable!"

"Thanks." Peyton smiles, wholeheartedly agreeing. "I don't suppose you sell these things?"

Sue looks mystified. "The clothes? Of course we—"

"No, I meant the belly. I want to wear it from here on in."

"Are you serious?"

Kind of.

"Not really," Peyton says reluctantly. "But it's so cute."

"It is, isn't it? Sorry to say we don't sell them. But we have had people smuggle them out of here, if you can believe that."

"You're kidding."

"No, it happens every couple of months or so. Really. And we did officially loan one to a customer's husband last Halloween. He was a big hit at the masquerade party."

"I'll bet." Peyton turns to the side again, marveling at her rounded profile that looks for all the world as though a baby really is growing there. The couch pillow she tried on once or twice at home doesn't hold a candle to this prosthetic, that's for sure.

"Can I help you with any sizes?" Sue asks, still hovering.

"Sizes?" Oh. Right. She looks down at the pants and top, not about to admit she's been so busy with her fake tummies that she hasn't bothered to try on anything else. "No, I, um . . . I'll just take this outfit."

"Do you want to wear it home?"

No way. The stretch pants and T-shirt are decidedly dowdy once she's reluctantly removed the belly and handed it back to Sue. These pieces will be relegated to the back of her closet for a few months, until she can fill them out with an authentic tummy of her own.

She pays for her purchases and a baby name book she plucks from a rack beside the register.

"So you don't have any picked out yet?" Sue asks, handing Peyton the shopping bag.

"Names? No, not yet. Not officially, anyway. I like Whitney for a girl."

"As in Houston?"

"As in the museum, actually." Peyton immediately crosses the name off her mental list. She can't have people thinking her daughter is named after an erstwhile pop diva.

"Well, good luck with the names. I have two boys, and my husband and I had the hardest time coming up with names for them. We agreed on girl names, but boy names . . ." She shakes her head.

For some reason, Peyton feels compelled to say, "Well, I don't have a husband, so it's my call."

There she goes again, confiding her private business in a perfect stranger. What is *with* her lately?

"Lucky you." Sue seems unfazed. "Well, come back and see us again when you're ready."

"Oh, I definitely will, thanks."

Swinging her paper shopping bag along, she steps out into the April dusk, too absorbed in thoughts of baby names to notice the chill creeping into the air, or the person who waits only a few moments before falling into step behind her once again.

CHAPTER FOUR

Sloshing along down Fifth Avenue past the vast International Toy Center at the western edge of Madison Square Park, Peyton finds herself noticing every child she passes.

Babies pushed along in tarped strollers; toddlers clinging to mothers' hands; school-aged kids in groups, too young, in her opinion, to be unsupervised on city streets.

Maybe that will change by the time the little one inside her is that age.

She smiles, picturing a demure little girl in pigtails and knee-socks, or a spirited, freckle-nosed boy romping in dungarees.

Right now, she can't imagine ever wanting to let her child out of her sight. Right now, all she wants is to cradle her baby safely in her arms.

But she'll have to wait. Five months at least, perhaps almost six, according to the measurements at her last physical examination.

With every day that passes, she finds herself more enchanted by the miracle inside her.

Dr. Lombardo's office did an ultrasound on her yesterday. Not one of those fancy new 3-D ultrasounds that look like a picture, but the old-fashioned black-and-white variety.

The technician couldn't tell the baby's gender, but he did identify the snowy streaks on screen as a head, a spine, limbs, as Peyton lay with tears rolling down her face. This is real. The sonogram, its grainy prints tucked into her shoulder bag, provides tangible proof that she's carrying a child, that she's going to be a mother.

For the rest of her life, no matter what happens, she will be joined with this precious, precious person. Already, she's enveloped in a swell of emotion never before experienced in such profound permanence.

Love. Earth's oldest love.

Maternal love, powerful enough to brighten even this gloomy Sunday morning with its abiding warmth.

She smiles at a little boy splashing toward her in bright yellow rain boots; at another stomping in a pond-sized puddle to his mother's vocal dismay.

If April showers really do bring May flowers, Manhattan will be one big blooming garden in just a few more days. The last three weeks have been nonstop soggy grayness, to the point where she could hardly get out of bed this morning.

But of course she did, despite the fact that it's a Sunday, because she spontaneously and stupidly made this brunch date with Gil.

Why on earth did she have to go and call her first love?

Because you've been feeling nostalgic lately, she reminds herself, holding her umbrella closer to her head as a wet gust tries to slip beneath it.

It's as though certain details, innocuous relics, of her past have been locked away in a dusty attic that she suddenly has the urge to explore.

Is inexplicable nostalgia another bizarre pregnancy symptom, like the enhanced sense of smell Allison warned her to watch for?

It must be. Otherwise, she wouldn't be eating canned Spaghetti-os every day for lunch, just the way she used to back in elementary school. Nor would she have spent last Saturday night sorting through old photos while watching a *Green Acres* marathon on cable.

And she certainly wouldn't be reuniting with Gil Blaney on this gloomy Sunday—or ever.

He sounded so surprised when she called the other night. Pleasantly surprised—but only after initially telling her to hold on a moment, then apparently closing the door to whatever room he was in. She heard the click, and realized that he wanted privacy to take her phone call.

That bothered her. Was he afraid his wife would be upset? Maybe she shouldn't have called him at home. In fact, she hadn't even been sure she *was* calling him at home. She merely dialed the number he'd left with her mother.

If he didn't want her to call him at home because it might upset his wife, why would he have left that number? Why would he have left *any* number?

"I just wanted to say hi," she said with forced breeziness, trying to think of a reason to hang up quickly.

But as those first awkward moments turned into what felt for all the world like a casual conversation between two old friends, she found herself relaxing. Relaxing to the point where she agreed to have brunch with him.

She reaches the historic Flatiron Building and makes a left along Twenty-third Street, glad she picked this particular dining spot amidst the row of trendy bistros and bars across from the park's southern entrance. He had mentioned a restaurant on the Upper West Side, but she stepped in and insisted on a place she's frequented on business lunches, a place that isn't the least bit intimate or romantic. That would be awkward, should the conversation lag. Better to be on familiar turf; noisy, bustling, familiar turf.

"That sounds fine," Gil said, more accommodating than she expected—or remembered. "Is eleven okay?"

"Noon would be better."

He laughed. "So you're still calling all the shots. It's nice to know some things never change. I'll see you at noon."

She doesn't expect to spot him the moment she steps in out of the dismal drizzle. She thought she'd have a moment to make herself presentable, to gather her thoughts.

But he's right here, sprawled on a seat by the door, his lanky legs stretched in front of him and one arm hooked casually over the back of the chair. Peyton pauses to take in the familiar posture, the upturned Kevin Bacon nose, the shock of sandy brown hair that betrays not a strand of gray.

He looks up, sees her, smiles. "You look exactly the same, Runt," he says, standing and crossing over to her.

Runt. The word, his tone, the way he looks at her when he says it . . .

Memories burst unbidden from the dim recesses of her mind. Fond memories.

"So do you, Gil. You look great."

He squeezes her upper arms, and she sees that up close, there's a network of fine lines around his blue eyes and his smile. He's gotten older. Not *old,* just older.

Well, so has she.

Time is running out.

The ominous thought strikes out of nowhere. Why?

Time might be rushing by, but it certainly isn't running out. She's getting older, yes, but that doesn't mean her life is drawing to a close. In so many ways, it's just beginning.

"Are you okay?" Gil asks, putting a hand beneath her elbow as the hostess beckons.

"Sure. I'm fine," Peyton assures him, trying to shake the strange, sudden sense of foreboding.

The phone rings, and it has to be him. He must have got the latest message by now.

Yes, this time, it *has* to be him.

But it isn't. It's a telemarketer.

A rude, pushy telemarketer who deserves to be cursed at and disconnected with an abrupt click.

When the line is tied up, nobody else can call. *He* can't call.

Then again, how can he, when he's busy with *her?*

It isn't that he wants to be with her. It's all part of the little game, remember? He doesn't really feel anything for her. You're the one he cares about.

Sometimes, it just doesn't feel that way. Sometimes, it feels as though he's really gone.

Abandonment.

Lately, this life feels as empty as a hollow womb.

Yet the work goes on, as it must. Donors and parents have been selected; babies are coming into the world. The donors must be punished and eliminated, the parents established and blessed.

Now that it's resumed, this important work, this vocation, can go on forever, if necessary.

But it all depends on him.

The restaurant is typical Chelsea: high-beamed ceilings, exposed brick, wide-planked floors. What it isn't, at least not today, is crowded. Perhaps it's the weather, or maybe this place just isn't as busy on weekends. In any case, the candlelit far reaches of the cavernous space could almost conceivably be romantic and intimate.

"Is this okay?" the hostess asks, leading them to a large booth in the corner.

It isn't as far as Peyton is concerned, but Gil assures the hostess that it is.

He motions for her to slide into the curved seat and she does, careful not to bump her stomach against anything.

A regular table would have been better. At least at a table they'd be sitting on opposite sides, a safe distance from each other. Here, they're forced to sit ridiculously close, the only way to have a conversation without speaking across an unreasonable expanse of table.

"So," Gil says, once they have menus in hand, "it's about time you called me."

"What do you mean?" She knows exactly what he means. But it's something to say.

"It took you long enough to get in touch. When I found out you've been living here for years—"

"Only a few," she amends, glancing wistfully at the wine list, the laminated page trembling in her hands. What she wouldn't give for a nerve-calming glass of that California Pinot Grigio. She's still feeling vaguely uneasy, and it isn't just about having brunch with an old flame.

Or is it?

There are times lately when Peyton feels almost like a squatter in somebody else's body. This pregnancy has changed her profoundly, in ways she never expected. She's more emotional, less secure. More . . . paranoid. She finds herself scanning the restaurant again, looking for the nameless, faceless *something* she senses lurking nearby.

"But you should have called when you knew you were coming to New York," Gil is saying, and she forces her attention back to the conversation. "I would have helped you get settled, shown you the ropes . . ."

"Thanks, but I managed to negotiate the ropes and get settled all by my little self," she assures him, wondering how she could have forgotten about the faint scar beside his eyebrow, courtesy of a childhood playground accident. For all the time he's crossed her mind these past two decades, she never remembered the scar. Never remembered how she used to touch it gently with her fingertip before kissing it.

"You always were big on figuring things out on your own. You never liked me to do anything for you. Or anybody else, for that matter."

"I never cared what you did for anybody else, Gil. And it's a good thing, because you were quite the good-deed doer back then."

He laughs. "I meant that you never wanted anybody else doing anything for you, either. You had it stuck in your head that accepting help—or God forbid, asking for it—was weak. I guess nothing has changed with you."

If you only knew, she thinks, resisting the urge to rest her hand on her stomach.

"Not in that respect," she says aloud. "Tell me about your life. Wife, kids, job . . . ?"

"Job is great. I'm an analyst now. Kids are great. Josie's twelve, Randy's eight. I'd show you pictures, but I didn't bring them."

"You mean you don't carry them around in your wallet?" She thinks of the sonogram stills in her purse.

He shakes his head. "I guess I'm a bad daddy."

"Well, I would have loved to see them."

"Next time."

Next time? As far as Peyton is concerned, this is a onetime event.

"Do they look like you?" she asks.

A shadow crosses his eyes. "Not really. They—"

The waiter appears to recite a list of specials and ask if he can get them started with Bloody Marys or mimosas.

"I'll stick with coffee," Peyton says. "Decaf."

"Oh, come on, live a little." Gil looks at the waiter. "We'll have the mimosas. And I'd like to select the champagne."

"Wait, Gil, no. Seriously, I just want decaf," she tells the waiter, who, to her absolute irritation, looks at Gil as if for confirmation.

"She'll have decaf. And I'll have regular. With a splash of Bailey's."

"In both?"

Unlike the waiter, Gil looks expectantly at Peyton.

"Just plain decaf, thanks."

The waiter leaves.

"You're no fun, Runt."

Hearing the old familiar nickname, Peyton is transported instantly to the day they first met, back in grade school. He was throwing a tennis ball against the brick wall behind the gym and it bounced away, over his head, just as she was walking by.

"Hey, Runt," he called, "can you get that for me?"

They laughed about it later—about her indignation that he assumed she was younger than him just because he was a whole head taller. In truth, he was a whole head taller than everybody their age, having inherited the notorious Blaney height genes.

Not to mention the notorious Blaney fondness for Irish cream, and Irish whiskey, she thinks, shaking her head with a smile.

"What?" he asks.

"It's not that I'm no fun, Stretch." The last word rolls off her tongue as effortlessly as *Runt* rolled off his.

Runt and Stretch. The pet names lasted as long as their romance did. How could she have forgotten?

She says lightly, "It's just that you're such the party boy that next to you, normal fun-loving people seem dull."

"You weren't opposed to a little cocktail back in the day, as I recall."

"We were underage back in the day, remember? It was forbidden contraband. Now that I'm all grown up . . ."

"The formerly forbidden stuff isn't half as much fun, right?" he asks with a spark in his eye that tells her he isn't just talking about liquor.

Gil always was a flirt. So was she. But things are different now. Vastly different.

"Your wife," Peyton says abruptly.

"My wife? What about her?"

"How is she?"

"I wouldn't know."

She looks down at his left hand, where a gold band encircles his fourth finger. "Is she traveling or something?"

"We're separated."

"Oh, Gil . . . I'm sorry."

"Yeah, me too."

"Is it . . . permanent?"

"Who knows? I've been trying for optimism, but she's made it pretty clear that she can't stand the sight of me."

"What about the kids?"

"Oh, she likes *them.*"

"No, I meant—"

"I know what you meant. I was just being funny. Or trying to, anyway. Not that there's anything funny about any of this," he adds soberly. "She's talking about moving out to Oregon."

"Oregon! Why?"

"She said she wants to live on the coast. I told her that the last time I checked, this *was* the coast. Apparently, it's the wrong one. But I swear I'll fight her on it. I can't let her take my kids from me."

"Of course not. I'm sure it won't happen." This time, Peyton can't keep her hand from coming to a sheltering rest on her belly.

Her child isn't even born yet, and she can't stand the thought of somebody wrenching it from her life. She can only imagine how intensely emotional this is for Gil—and wonder how his wife can even contemplate such a thing. What on earth could he have done to deserve losing his children?

He gives a bitter laugh. "Don't be so sure it won't happen. You've never met Karla, have you?"

"No." But she glimpsed the statuesque blonde once or twice from afar in the first few years after Gil left. Back then, he came back to Talbot Corners more often, much to Peyton's chagrin. It wasn't easy, seeing her former love and his new bride, making certain that he didn't spot her.

Their coffees arrive. Stirring his, Gil says of his estranged wife, "What I loved about her when I met her was that she was strong and independent. A lot like you, actually."

But she didn't have a needy mother in Talbot Corners. Peyton can't help thinking of the road not taken, of what might have happened if her stepfather hadn't died just as freedom was within her grasp.

"But you're different," Gil goes on, looking at Peyton with a wistful expression that makes her squirm in her seat. "You have a heart."

"Yeah, well . . ."

"I heard it got broken a while back."

She sighs. "How'd you hear that?"

"You don't get engaged to a guy like Jeff Rieger without feeding the local gossip mill for a good long time. I'm sorry it didn't work out."

"I'm not sorry. Not anymore, anyway," she admits, unwilling to revisit the pain of being left at the altar.

"I'm not, either," Gil confides, leaning closer. "I'm so glad you walked back into my life now, just when I needed you. It's like all of a sudden, there is a God."

"Gil . . ." She has to tell him that she isn't back in his life. Not in that way, anyway. Not romantically.

"Let's have dinner Wednesday night. I have meetings tomorrow night and Tuesday, but Wednesday is—"

"I can't, Gil. I have a meeting, too."

"Right. We haven't even talked about your job, or your life—I swear I'm not always this self-absorbed. It's just been a tough couple of months."

"I'm sure. And it's fine. You need somebody to talk to." She instinctively reaches out and touches his hand, knowing she shouldn't give him the wrong idea, wondering if the instinct is purely platonic on her part. She can't ignore how deeply she loved him once.

First love.

She's long since dismissed their romance as infatuation, easy to do after Gil vanished from her daily life. But now, remembering the intensity of emotion she felt for him all those years ago, she can't help wondering if first love really was true love. Perhaps the feelings she thought she was burying forever weren't dead after all.

Just don't rule anything out, okay? You might change your mind.

She promised Allison she wouldn't . . .

And she won't. She has to nip this thing in the bud now, before it blossoms into a complication she doesn't need. And she knows exactly how to do it.

"So what time will your meeting be over on Wednesday?" Gil is asking. "Is it in your office? Because I can meet—"

"It's in Brooklyn, Gil," she cuts in. "And it isn't a meeting, exactly. It's a support group. For pregnant, single women."

"What's this? More baby clothes?"

Derry looks up from the cross stitch she's working on to see Linden standing over her with a cardboard carton. "Those are the pink receiving blankets I ordered last week. Remember? I showed you."

"I don't think you did."

She knows she didn't, but she shrugs and says, "You were probably busy thinking about something else."

He shakes his head and puts the box back in the corner behind the door, where it rests on top of a stack that's been accumulating for almost a month now.

Derry frowns and makes another pastel x in a configuration that will soon, she hopes, begin to look like the lamb it's supposed to be. The duckie bib she made turned out so well she thought she should tackle the lamb. Being new to needlework, she probably should have stuck with easy little yellow ducks.

Linden turns down the volume on the Foreigner CD she was playing and returns to the couch to sit beside her.

"Derry, we need to talk."

"About what?"

"All this crap you're buying for the baby."

"Crap?" She winces, not just at the offensive word but because a strand of embroidery floss just snagged on a bit of fingernail she earlier chewed to ragged splinters. She tosses the wooden hoop aside and bites at the ragged edge.

"Whatever it is. Little shoes and blankets and dresses—the baby isn't even born yet. You don't even know for sure it's a girl."

She removes her fingertip from her mouth to remind him, "Rose said the test showed it is, and we already said that we're going to name her—"

"Tests can be wrong," he cuts in. "I know what we said, but we don't know it's going to happen. And anyway, it's not just the dresses that bug me. Where are we going to put all this cr— stuff? You're going way overboard, don't you think?"

"You're being a little pessimistic, don't you think?" she returns, glaring at him. "We were approved, Linden. The donor chose us. In a few months, we're going to be bringing a newborn into this home, and I want to be ready."

"Yeah, me too . . . when the time comes. But don't you think you should hold off a little? Things can happen."

Yes. Things can happen. Donors can change their mind. About the chosen parents, about adoption. There can be complications in late pregnancy, complications in labor.

"Rose said everything will work out," Derry reminds Linden, refusing to allow her dreams of motherhood to be tainted by his negativity. "Why can't you just be optimistic?"

"I am optimistic."

Derry snorts, thinking he probably doesn't even know what the word means.

"Weren't you supposed to be going over to see Richie this afternoon?" she asks, anxious to get him and his bad vibes out of here.

"Yeah, in a little while. You trying to get rid of me?"

"Not at all," she says, wishing he'd leave her alone with her lamb bib and pink blankies and dreams of sugar and spice and everything nice.

Pulling into the puddle-dotted circular driveway in front of her three-story brick home, Anne Marie realizes that Jarrett's black Mercedes is parked just where it was when she left two hours ago.

Terrific. He'd promised to take the boys out to get some lunch, since the weekly groceries aren't delivered until Monday morning and the cupboards and fridge are in their usual Sunday barren state.

Now Anne Marie's going to walk in and find hungry children, and Jarrett absorbed in something else. Something selfish. It never fails.

She parks her own silver Mercedes in the garage, with no intention of venturing out again on this rain-soaked afternoon. Sunday is supposed to be a day of rest. With triplets in the house and a hands-off husband, there's no such thing. But if Jarrett refuses to take them out to eat, she'll scrape together something from the pantry.

Turning off the windshield wipers and then the engine, she leans against the leather headrest a moment to inhale the welcome silence. Then she reaches over to the seat to grab her cell phone and slip it into her Hermes satchel beside the small red-leather-bound Bible that accompanies her everywhere she goes.

Her heels tap on the concrete as she makes her way through the darkened three-car garage to the door that leads into the butler's pantry. She can hear little voices squealing and the din of a *Thomas the Tank Engine* cartoon in the background.

The moment she opens the door, she's met by the sound of pounding sock-feet and a gleeful chorus of one word sung in identical pitch and perfect unison. "Mommy!"

"Hi, everybody!" She bends to welcome her sons into her embrace, searching over their heads for Jarrett.

"How was mass?" he asks, coming around the corner from the kitchen.

Is it her imagination, or does he seem suspicious? Is he wondering if she really was at church? Did he snoop around the house while she was gone and find the envelope she slipped into the top drawer of her dresser last night, beneath the layers of bras and panties?

You're just being paranoid, Anne Marie scolds herself.

Jarrett asks the same question every Sunday. It's a polite non-question, in a league with "How's your meal?" and "How was your day?" He doesn't really want to know. It's just something to say, just another of his maddeningly impersonal interaction skills.

Early in their relationship, it bothered her that he didn't use endearments. She long since gave up longing for *honey* or *sweetheart.* Now she just wishes he would occasionally address her directly by name. She can count on one hand the number of times she's heard *Anne Marie* pass his lips.

She can almost hear her grandmother saying, *So what? There are worse marital offenses. He's faithful and a good provider, so why are you complaining?*

"Mass was fine," Anne Marie tells Jarrett. "Long sermon," she adds, in case he really was wondering where she's been all this time. She motions at the triplets, who are scampering out of the room, and can't help saying, "I thought you were taking them out for lunch."

"They didn't want to go out in the rain so we ordered a pizza."

Instantly, Anne Marie regrets her accusing tone. "Oh. Good idea."

"You thought I would let them starve?"

"No. I thought you didn't feed them . . . yet."

He shakes his head. "I'm not such a horrible father, am I?"

"No," she says, looking down at her Ferragamo pumps. "You're not a horrible father at all."

I'm just a horrible mother.

No. That isn't fair. It isn't true . . . not now, anyway.

Anne Marie Egerton loves her babies fiercely. *All* of them.

CHAPTER FIVE

"Don't I know you?"

Glancing up from the keys in her hand, Peyton spots Tom Reilly standing on the sidewalk beneath her stoop. He's not even wearing a jacket, just navy sweatpants and a maroon sweatshirt that's spattered with raindrops.

She should be startled to see him, but for some reason, she isn't. If anything, it's almost as though she's been expecting him. Like Allison said, this city can be an awfully small town.

"You *sort of* know me," she tells him, wondering if her mascara has run and if her hair is as plastered to her head as it feels. "I'm the one who—"

"I remember. Watermelon, right?"

"That's me. Watermelon." She smiles briefly before turning back to the door, where she almost puts the wrong key into the lock. Her heart is pounding. Not out of fear, really. Not this time. She can't help noticing that he's one attractive man.

"So there I was, walking down the block, and there you were, coming in the opposite direction. We're the only two idiots out in this weather without umbrellas, so I looked at you, and . . . I recognized you." He rests an arm on the dripping wrought-iron railing beside the steps.

You'd think he would mention having seen her in Tequilla Moon that day a few weeks ago.

Why doesn't he?

Maybe he didn't really see you that day, she tells herself. Maybe Allison just said that because . . .

Well, because Allison seems to want to see her hook up with

somebody, almost as though she doesn't think Peyton has what it takes to raise a baby on her own.

Then again, maybe Tom saw her, and is . . .

What? Following you around the city? Stalking you?

It's all Peyton can do not to roll her eyes at the thought. She must have left the better part of her earlier paranoia behind at the restaurant along with her umbrella. Her spirits buoyed by two hours of laughter and reminiscing with Gil, she can't seem to muster much concern about this chance meeting with Tom Reilly.

In the broad, if gloomy, light of day, his being a sinister character seems about as likely as bright sunshine suddenly bursting through the oppressive storm clouds overhead.

He glances up as if he's read her mind, barely seeming to notice the droplets sprinkling him from the heavens. "This is a great building."

"Yes, it's . . . great."

"Is it full of fireplaces and French doors and crown moldings? Is there a beautiful garden out back?"

"No French doors, and the fireplace doesn't work, but there are crown moldings. And there's a garden, but it backs up to an alley and it's usually more overgrown than beautiful."

"Yeah, that's what I always picture in a place like this. Like the apartments in those Nora Ephron movies. New York apartments always look so charming in them. It's like nobody ever lives in a rectangular box in a high-rise building, you know?"

She laughs and nods, knowing exactly what he means—and pleased that he's no stranger to chick flicks. Macho Jeff used to scoff at romantic comedies, when she could get him to accompany her to one.

Still looking at the brownstone, Tom asks, "Which floor are you on?"

"I can't tell you that," she manages to say lightly. "You might be a lunatic prowling the streets for innocent women, remember?"

The moment the words are out of her mouth, she regrets them. Why did she have to refer to their former conversation? Now he'll realize that she remembers it in that much detail—if, indeed, he happens to remember it in that much detail.

He probably doesn't, she assures herself. *Of course he doesn't.*

"Nice day, isn't it?" He takes a step up from the sidewalk, ducking his head a bit as though he's trying to escape the rain.

She looks around dubiously. "A little wet, isn't it?"

"The weather? I don't mind. It's good for staying indoors and lounging around with the Sunday *Times*."

"That it is," she agrees, wondering why he isn't doing just that.

He lifts a white plastic shopping bag in answer to her unspoken question. "This is my *Times*. It didn't come this morning. I just bought it. I'm sorry to say I didn't grab some watermelon while I was at it."

"Yeah, well . . . you can't be expected to think of everything."

He laughs. Then he takes another step up and says, "I'm Tom Reilly. In case you forgot."

No. She didn't forget.

"Um, this is the part where you tell me your name. Unless you just want me to call you Melanie?"

"Melanie?" she echoes, puzzled.

"You know. Watermelon. Melanie."

She laughs, shaking her head.

"That was lame." He furrows his brow. "Now you think I'm a loser, and you'll never tell me your name. Or if you do, it won't be your real one."

He's wearing such a comically earnest expression that she can't help saying, "It's Peyton. My name. Peyton."

He looks dubious. "Real?"

"Real."

"First or last?"

"First."

"That's unique. Let me guess. You were named after Peyton Manning?"

At that, she can't help thinking of Jeff. Back when he was her fiancé, he introduced her to the famed young NFL quarterback, who was amused that they shared the same first name. She remembers how jealous Jeff was that night, accusing her of flirting. She wasn't then . . .

But she is now.

So sue me. I can't help it. Tom's cute.

"I'm just a tiny bit older than Peyton Manning," she deadpans, fighting the urge to tell Tom she's actually met him. He might be the kind of man who enjoys chick flicks *and* football. But she isn't eager to open the door on a discussion of her romantic history.

"How much older? I'm forty-two. In case you were wondering."

She was. "Well, I'm old enough for *Peyton Place* to be more my era. Only I wasn't named after that, either."

People—always adults—used to tease her about that. It was annoying when she was too young to know that *Peyton Place* was a steamy soap opera, and even more annoying after she found out.

"Where did the name come from, then?" Tom asks. "There must be some kind of story behind it."

"Sorry, there isn't one."

"Come on. Humor me. My name is Tom. *Thomas*. No stories there. Tell me yours."

She shrugs. "My mother just told me that my dad just happened to like the name Peyton."

"So your dad wasn't around to tell you that himself."

She's said too much. Warning bells go off inside her. She pictures iron gates slamming down to keep all her dark secrets safely locked away.

It's none of Tom's business that her father left her mother before she was even born, or that Mom gave her his favorite name in hope that when he found that out, he would come back to her. As if a name alone would be reason to return. As if it were possible he'd return for any reason at all.

He never came back.

For all Peyton knows, Arnold Somerset never bothered to find out whether she made it into the world at all. Mom stopped talking about him years ago, after Douglas came along. She married Peyton's stepfather and never looked back.

By then, Peyton was long over the days of wishing she had a daddy like everybody else. If anything, having seen her friends go through high school complaining about their strict fathers and ridiculous household rules, she figured she was better off with just a mom.

Sometimes it wasn't easy to grow up in a single-parent home, but she turned out just fine.

And so will her own child.

Derry is alone when she gets the shocking news. Linden left a while ago, saying he was going to his friend Richie's.

So when the door buzzes from downstairs, she's caught off guard.

She sets aside the cross-stitch bib and takes her time going over to the security panel on the wall, figuring Linden must have forgotten his keys. She isn't in any hurry to have him back in the apartment. Not with the way he seems to disapprove of every move she makes. She figured he'd be at Richie's for at least a few hours, the way he usually is.

She has no idea what he does when he's hanging out over there, and doesn't really care. The one time she bothered to ask, he shrugged and said, "Guy stuff," as though that explained everything.

Actually, it does. Guy stuff is undoubtedly watching sports and drinking beer and talking about the people they once knew as schoolkids together at Samuel Gompers High. Derry has no interest in that.

It will be nice to have a little girl in the house, she thinks as she presses the intercom button. A little girl who will be happy to do girly things with her mom.

"Who is it?" Derry calls into the receiver.

"Rose," is the unexpected reply.

"You're getting soaked," Peyton tells Tom, pushing her troubled past into the far rafters of her mind.

He shrugs. "I don't mind."

"Well, I'm getting soaked and I sort of mind, so . . ."

"I'm sorry. Go ahead."

She jabs the right key into the lock at last, wondering why he's lingering behind her.

"One more thing, Peyton . . ."

"Yes?"

"Do you want to have dinner sometime? Or maybe just coffee?"

Good Lord. What a day. First Gil, now Tom.

Mom would say, *it never rains, but it pours.*

Then again, Peyton thinks, looking up at the gray-shrouded sky, it always rains lately. And pours.

"I know it seems lame, asking you out on the street like this, but . . ." He shrugs. "I thought of it, and I tend to blurt out things as they occur to me. Odd habit, I know. So . . . ?"

"Coffee would be nice," she hears herself saying.

Which is almost the same thing she told Gil when he persisted in asking her out even after she dropped her pregnancy bombshell on him. He said he was happy for her. He told her she was in for the adventure of a lifetime. He congratulated her on taking charge of her maternal future, and said he wasn't the least bit surprised.

Long story made short, she and Gil are having dinner on Thursday night.

And now, she and Tom are having coffee on Saturday.

He, of course, doesn't know about the baby-to-be. She isn't about to tell him. She would if she thought she were embarking on a relationship with him, but coffee is just coffee. Just as dinner is just dinner.

"We can have lunch instead, if you'd rather," Tom suggests.

"No," she says quickly. "Coffee is fine." Coffee is just coffee.

"Okay, then . . . do you know the Starbucks on Union Square?"

"Yes." It's not far from Baby Blue.

Which reminds her, once again, that she's not supposed to be dating. Who is she trying to kid? Coffee isn't just coffee when you're feeling a mutual attraction with somebody who happens to be eligible. It's a date.

Before she can open her mouth to cancel, Tom says, "Great. I'll meet you there Saturday morning."

Meeting him there is more platonic than going over together. She relaxes a little.

He asks, "Is nine too early?"

The rain seems to fall harder all at once, pattering onto the concrete all around them. He takes a backward step down toward the street.

"Nine is definitely too early."

"So you're a late sleeper."

"Not usually, but . . ."

But I'm pregnant. Say it. I'm pregnant.

"How about ten-thirty, then? Later than that might border on lunch. And I know lunch is out. So ten-thirty is fine with me." Taking another step in his casual backward retreat, Tom is clearly oblivious of the fact that suddenly, none of this is fine with her.

Tell him.

"Actually, Tom—"

"See you on Saturday." He waves and jogs off into the rain, leaving her to wonder if he even heard her. Or maybe he did, and, sensing that she was about to back out, beat a hasty retreat.

Oh well. She can always just not show up.

It's a lousy thing to do, but it's an out. Just in case she wakes up Saturday morning and needs one.

Peyton returns her attention to the door to her apartment and unlocks it, this time finding the right key on the first try.

Amazing what nerves can do to you, she thinks wryly, remembering how she dumped the contents of her purse when she got up from the booth back in the restaurant earlier. Gil helped her put everything back, crawling around underneath their table and others to retrieve her loose change, her lipstick, her roll of Tums.

He smiled when he saw those, and mentioned that Karla always had heartburn when she was pregnant.

He said it almost fondly, and Peyton realized he wasn't over his wife, regardless of his bitterness or his dinner invitation to an old girlfriend. That was a relief.

He smiled again when he picked up the sonogram image, and he knew, without Peyton having to point them out, where the baby's skull, spinal column, and knees were. He knew better than she did, having been through this twice before.

"If you need anything, going through this alone," he offered before they parted, "I'm here for you. Really. Anything you need. I'm great at putting cribs together, shopping for diapers and formula, whatever."

"Thanks, Gil." She was warmed by the offer, warmed by his familiar friendship. She might even take him up on the offer.

Stepping over the threshold into her apartment, she tells herself that there's no reason she shouldn't simply enjoy time spent with an old friend.

And with a new one, she adds mentally, thinking again of Tom as she reaches out to blindly deposit her purse into its usual resting spot on the desk chair just inside the door.

She nearly drops her bag onto the floor before realizing that it's gone.

No, not gone. Just . . . moved.

Frowning, she stares at the chair.

It's over too far; just a foot or so, but it's too far. It's always been closer to the desk. It seems almost as if somebody moved it out of the way to get into the desk drawers, then hastily pushed it back.

Which, of course, is impossible.

Peyton is the only one who could have done that, and she didn't touch the chair or the desk before she left the apartment this morning. She was too focused on meeting Gil.

Okay, maybe she's imagining things. She backs up a few yards, out the door, and throws the strap of her purse over her shoulder again. She'll just retrace her steps without thinking about it. Just do what comes naturally; do what she does every single time she returns home.

You're just paranoid again, she tells herself, shaking her head in disgust.

She walks quickly into the apartment and reaches out to drop the bag using reflexive motion.

But she can't reach the chair unless she takes another step or two.

The chair should be closer to the door.

So if she didn't move it . . .

And it's not her imagination that it's been moved . . .

Somebody was in her apartment while she was gone.

Derry stares at Rose in stunned disbelief.

She must have heard her wrong. She *must* have.

Or maybe Linden put her up to this as some kind of cruel prank. Maybe he's trying to teach her a lesson about . . .

About what?

About preparing for motherhood? About being optimistic?

It doesn't make sense. None of this makes sense.

"Derry, I'm so sorry. Maybe you should sit down."

Derry, who refused that gentle yet ominous advice before Rose broke the news, sinks into the nearest chair.

"I know this is devastating for you. I know how much you wanted this little girl."

"You promised," she says, too numb to muster sufficient accusation. "You promised everything would work out."

"I know I did, and I'm so, so sorry, Derry. Sometimes donors change their minds. Unfortunately, that's the reality of this business."

Derry shakes her head, staring dully at Rose's enormous square-cut diamond. What does she know about reality? Sitting there in her prim black suit, with that big ring and fancy purse. What does she know about anything?

"We already had a name for her, Rose," she chokes out. "Rhiannon."

"That's beautiful."

"It's from the Fleetwood Mac song. It's how Linden and I met. We were both in this Seventies Rock chat room on the Internet, and somebody asked a trivia question, and we both knew the answer was Rhiannon. Ever since then, I knew that someday, we'd have a daughter with that name. It's like our own special code word. Rhiannon. We use it for everything. At least, I still do. Linden used to use it as his ATM code, but he said he changed it. Now I have no idea what he uses."

There's silence.

Then Rose says, "Derry, you're going to get through this. It's going to be okay."

"Do you have children?" she asks abruptly. Harshly. She can't help it.

Rose's head jerks up a little, as though something bumped beneath her chin. There's a sharp intake of air in her nostrils.

"No," she says after a moment, exhaling heavily as though she's been holding her breath. "I don't have children."

It's because she can't, Derry realizes. *She can't have children.*

She doesn't know how she knows that, but she does. Maybe because she recognizes a kindred spirit. Maybe because that would explain why a woman like her is doing a job like this.

It doesn't matter how she knows. She's as certain of Rose's *impaired fecundity* as she is that this isn't some cruel prank staged by Linden.

No, this is really happening.

The donor in Iowa really did change her mind. Not about adoption. About Derry and Linden.

"What did we do wrong?" Derry asks dully. "Why doesn't she want us?"

"It's not like that. Please don't—"

"It's Linden, isn't it? It's because he's blue collar. Or because he isn't well read, or well spoken." She hates her husband. She really does. This is his fault.

"Linden is wonderful. He'll make a wonderful father."

"Then why didn't that girl want him? Why didn't she want us?"

"It's nothing specific. Don't torture yourself. This just wasn't the right match."

"But it was!"

"Derry . . ." Rose kneels on the floor in front of her chair, taking both her hands.

"That was our little girl. I felt her. I knew her." She collapses, sobbing bitterly, into Rose's arms.

For a long time, she just cries, as Rose croons comforting words.

Finally, the initial wave of anguish subsides, leaving Derry as bruised and raw as if she's suffered a beating.

"I'm never going to be a mother," she says quietly, wiping her hot, wet eyes with the base of her palm.

"Yes, you are."

"No. I can't do this again. I'm finished. I can't handle any more pain. I'm not cut out for this kind of disappointment, and I'm not cut out for motherhood."

"I think you are, Derry. It just depends on how badly you want it."

"I want a child more than I've ever wanted anything in my life."

"But you say you aren't willing to go any further to make that happen."

She buries her head in her hands. "I just can't take it. To be so close, and then . . ."

"What if there was a guarantee?"

With those words, something has shifted. It happens so subtly that for a moment Derry isn't sure. Then she lifts her head, sees the expression on Rose's face, and realizes that one door might have been slammed shut, but another seems to have opened. Just a crack. Whether she forces her way through it is up to her.

She looks Rose in the eye. "How can there be a guarantee?"

Rose seems hesitant. "I don't know, Derry. I shouldn't—"

"How can there be a guarantee?" It's all Derry can do not to grab her by the shoulders and shake her. "You've got to tell me!"

"This is highly sensitive. Highly confidential. If it ever got out . . ."

"It won't."

Still, the woman hesitates.

"Please, Rose. You've got to help me. I'll do anything if you can help me get a baby. Anything."

For the first time since they met, Rose's smile seems to reach her eyes. "That," she says, "is exactly what I was hoping to hear."

She's just lucky the intruder didn't steal her valuables. At least, that's what the police officer tells Peyton when she returns from one last trip to her closet to confirm that nothing is missing.

"Why do you think they didn't take anything?"

The police officer, who barely looks old enough to shave, shrugs. "Who knows? Maybe you came home before they could get the television or computer out the door."

She shudders, remembering how she was delayed coming inside, talking to Tom out on the stoop. Was somebody lurking in her apartment even then? Did the sound of her voice carry a warning to beat a hasty retreat?

What if Tom hadn't stopped her before she came in? Would she have interrupted a robbery in progress? Was the intruder armed? Would he have hurt her?

She wraps her arms around her waist with protective maternal instinct, unable to bear the thought of what might have happened. To both of them.

The apartment that has always felt like a haven in a ruthless city now feels as unfamiliar as it did the week she moved in. She gazes from the hardwood floors she sanded and refinished herself to the walls she transformed with warm-hued paint to the yards and yards of trim she restored to its original finish. She just finished paying off the shabby chic furnishings she bought brand-new at Domain, and the custom window treatments designed with filmy sheers to make the window bars less obtrusive.

Accustomed to looking around her home and admiring anew the hours upon hours of handiwork that turned this small apartment into a pleasant refuge, Peyton now sees only the shadows, the potential hiding places, the blocked escape routes.

"Those are things they usually go for. Electronics," the officer is saying. "That, or jewelry. You're sure it's all here?"

She nods. What little she has is all here in its case in her top bureau drawer, left ajar by whoever rifled among her belongings. The thought of foreign hands touching her clothes, her lingerie, makes her sick.

"If I interrupted a burglary," she asks the policeman, "don't you think the place would look like it had been ransacked?"

"Possibly."

And wouldn't you think a cop might be a more compassionate type of person? His job, after all, is to help people. She can see where somebody in his position might become detached after years on the job, but if he isn't a rookie, then she isn't just past her first trimester of pregnancy.

Resenting his jaded expression, she points out, "Everything was pretty much in its place when I walked in here. Except the desk. And there's only one door in and out of here. I'd have seen somebody coming up the stairs." Unless the person had slipped hastily into the shadows before she passed.

She clenches her midsection more tightly, shielding her precious cargo from the mere thought of potential harm.

You're okay, she tells the baby—and herself. *We're okay. Nothing happened. Nothing violent, anyway.*

She sinks onto the couch and watches while the officer takes another cursory look around the apartment and jots more notes on his report.

Then he tells her to have her locks changed immediately.

"You think whoever it was got in here with a key?" she asks in disbelief.

He looks over at the bars on the street-level windows. "I'd say it's likely."

"But . . . how?"

"Have you lost a set of keys recently, had your purse snatched, anything like that?"

"No," she says, indignant that he'd assume she wouldn't have changed the locks already if that had happened, or at least have given him that kind of information right from the start.

"Who has your spare keys?"

"Nobody." This is New York, not Talbot Corners. She's not foolish enough to trust a neighbor with her key, let alone hide it under the doormat as her mother does. "I keep one in my desk at work."

"Is it locked?"

"The desk? No, but my office door is."

"All the time?"

"Well, not during business hours."

"And during business hours, you never, ever leave your desk unattended?"

"Of course I do. But people are always around," she says defensively. "It's a busy ad agency."

"Exactly. People are always around. Maintenance guys. Messengers. Coworkers."

"Believe me, nobody could go through my desk drawers in broad daylight without getting caught," she informs him. "And after hours, my office is always locked."

"Who has the spare key to that?"

Her heart sinks. Suddenly feeling foolish, she admits, "I don't know. Probably the janitor. The secretary, maybe."

He nods. "You need to change the locks here. Today."

"But . . . it's Sunday."

"This is New York, Mrs. Somerset," he says, as though she's a naive bumpkin fresh off the Midwest Express. "We have round-the-clock locksmiths."

"Of course we do." She emphasizes the *we*. "And it's actually *Ms.* Somerset."

He doesn't hear her. His radio is blasting with static and an unintelligible, apparently urgent announcement.

He speaks into it, saying something equally unintelligible and urgent.

Already intent on some other, more pressing crime, he thrusts the clipboard and a pen at Peyton and asks her to sign the report.

"You're going to leave?" she asks frantically, making an effort to sound more peeved than plaintive. "Isn't there something else you can do?"

"Like . . ."

"Like . . . I don't know, solve the case?"

He looks at her as though she's asked him to pretty please stay and hold her hand.

Clearly, the NYPD isn't going to dispatch their best detectives on a break-in, or provide twenty-four-hour protection to a woman terrorized by a mere prowler.

Left alone in her apartment, Peyton barricades the door with her desk. The same desk somebody found reason to search.

Did she really interrupt a burglary?

Maybe not. She was out for hours. Whoever it was could have come and gone this morning, right after she left.

But if that's the case, then the question remains: why didn't the prowler steal anything?

Again, Peyton opens the top desk drawer, half expecting to realize that something, indeed, is missing.

No. It's all there.

Her checkbook. Her Palm Pilot. The credit cards she doesn't carry around with her unless she's traveling.

Yes, everything that should be in the drawer is accounted for, she concludes, about to close it and move on to the next.

Then, tucked in beside the rubber-banded stack of unpaid bills, she spots something that shouldn't be there at all.

Something that sends a chill slithering down her spine.

No, the intruder didn't steal anything.

The intruder left something behind.

Month Four
May

CHAPTER SIX

Peyton awakens abruptly from a restless sleep and lifts her head to look at the bedside clock.

Dawn is still at least another hour away.

She rolls onto her side, trembling.

Which is worse? Returning to the nightmare she just escaped? Or lying awake in utter darkness, thinking frightening thoughts?

Neither option is appealing.

After a few minutes of the latter, she realizes slumber has evaded her more effectively than she was able to evade the demons in her dreams.

Turning on a lamp and the television do little to banish the wee-hour Sunday morning gloom. On-screen, the heroine of a black-and-white movie is clutching her jaws and screaming.

Terrific.

Peyton hurriedly points the remote and clicks until she reaches the Weather Channel, hoping the innocuous meteorological banter will help calm her nerves.

It doesn't. Not even the local forecast—a hot, sunny day to begin another week of unseasonably mild weather—lifts the pall.

Propped on pillows, Peyton huddles in bed beneath her quilt, knees clasped against her chest. She can't help but dart wary glances from one shadowy corner of the room to another, her heart pounding as she searches for a lurking figure amidst familiar possessions.

It's been two weeks. This has to stop, she tells herself, unsuccessfully battling a tremendous yawn. *You can't wake up paralyzed in fear every night for the rest of your life. Somebody broke into your apartment. So what? It probably happens to everybody in New York sooner or later.*

But not everybody in New York is left a bizarre calling card.

Tossing the remote aside, Peyton gets out of bed and pads barefooted over to the desk drawer to retrieve it. She's kept it there ever since she came across it, taking it out every so often to puzzle over its significance and who could possibly have broken into her apartment with the sole purpose of leaving it.

The only thing that's entirely clear is that somebody knows her secret.

Somebody who doesn't approve.

Somebody who chose to convey that message with a small, annotated red-leather-bound Bible.

"Happy Mother's Day, Mommy!"

Jarred out of a deep sleep, Anne Marie rolls over to see a row of cherubic faces beside the bed. Her babies.

"Happy Mother's Day!" Caleb says again.

Realizing that sunlight is streaming into the room through the cracks in the shutters, Anne Marie glances automatically at the bedside clock. Nine-fifteen? How can that be? She's usually up with the kids at the crack of dawn.

Wonder of wonders, Jarrett must have risen with them today so that she could sleep.

"We have really special surprises for you," Justin tells her, struggling over the r's as always. Really is "weely"; surprise is "sue-pwize." There are times when Anne Marie patiently corrects him; times when she revels in the sweet baby talk.

He'll grow up soon enough. They all will.

"We made breakfast in bed so you can eat it before you get ready for church!" Avery jumps up and down with excitement.

"We made the breakfast all by ourselves," Caleb says proudly.

"All by ourselves, except Daddy helped," amends the ever-ethical Justin.

"Daddy helped a little," Avery explains, "but we mostly made it all by ourselves."

Justin says, "Except Daddy helped a lot."

Anne Marie laughs, gathering the chattering trio into her arms, embracing them against her heart.

"Good morning." Jarrett appears in the doorway bearing a tray, looking uncommonly tousled for a man who tends to shave, shower, and dress before leaving the master suite every morning. "Happy Mother's Day."

She opens her mouth to thank him, touched by his efforts.

"The boys wanted to make you breakfast in bed," he announces before she can speak, and sets the tray on a table.

"Just like the bear cubs did for Mama Bear in that video you got us from the library," Avery pipes up.

"Daddy only helped a little," Caleb puts in, as Anne Marie surveys the whole grain toast, bowl of strawberries, and mug of coffee.

"He helped a lot," Justin says again.

There's something perfunctory about the kiss Jarrett plants on top of her head before saying, "It was a team effort."

"Well, thank you, team Egerton." Anne Marie can't help feeling a little wistful. If only Jarrett were the type of husband who came up with things like this on his own. If only he were a little more attentive, a little less preoccupied . . .

But there are worse marital offenses, intones Grace DeMario, who certainly knew that firsthand. Anne Marie's grandmother was abandoned by her own husband early in her marriage, left destitute to single-handedly raise five children . . . and, years later, Anne Marie herself, after Lisa, her teenaged mother, ran away.

Not that Lisa was ever a true mother to Anne Marie. She later discovered from one of her aunts that her grandmother had taken over that role from the time she was born . . . before she was born, actually. It was Grace who decided that she was to be named Anne, after the patron saint of expectant women. She had prayed to Saint Anne daily throughout Lisa's pregnancy, worried that her wayward daughter might do something drastic to end it.

But Grace never admitted that. She was fiercely protective of both her daughter and her granddaughter.

She loved you enough to give you to me, Grace would tell Anne Marie, when she grew old enough to ask about her mother.

"Are you okay, Mommy?" Caleb asks. "You're not eating."

"Yes, sweetie, I'm fine." *Just listening to voices in my head again.* Yawning loudly, she says, "I guess I'm still not fully awake."

"The boys thought you might like to sleep in," Jarrett says.

"The boys were right. Thank you, boys. And Daddy."

If only they let her sleep in every weekend morning, she thinks, stretching and sitting up. But if one day a year is all she gets, she'll make the most of the indulgence.

One day. Mother's Day.

A day to be endured before the triplets came along. Dreaded, and endured.

Now it's cause for celebration.

Reaching for the creamer, she dumps some into the coffee.

If only she could be as lighthearted as Mama Bear on that cartoon video she watched with the boys.

But Mama Bear doesn't carry the burden Anne Marie has borne all these years. Mama Bear didn't wait, day in and day out, in growing desperation for news she both longed for and dreaded. Mama Bear and her cubs live in an insulated utopia, very much like—

"Mommy?"

She looks up to see the children and Jarrett watching her.

"How come you're still stirring your coffee so much?" Caleb asks. "Aren't you going to drink it?"

"And you have to eat the strawberries, too," Justin says.

"But can I have a strawberry?" Avery asks. "Or four strawberries?" Since the triplets' birthday last week, four has replaced three as their favorite number.

"Of course you can have four strawberries, honey."

"Avery! No! Those are for Mommy."

"It's okay, Caleb. I'll share. Come on up here," she says, scooting over to make room on the bed for the children, who clamber right in to nestle beside her.

"They're going to spill the coffee," Jarrett warns her, as if spilled coffee is the worst thing in the world.

"Then I'll clean it up," she informs him, darkly thinking that there are far more horrible things in the world. Things her husband, in his own insulated utopia, can't possibly begin to imagine.

Rita checks her watch as she and Nancy step out of the cab in front of the Amsterdam Avenue high-rise apartment building. "We're late."

"Just five minutes. No big deal. Hey, what are you doing?"

"Paying the driver." Rita hands him a ten, says yes to a receipt, tells him to keep the change.

"But I was going to pay," Nancy protests as he drives away. "I'm the big whiner who insisted on a cab instead of the subway. I'm sorry. I guess I just didn't feel like taking two different trains, changing at Times Square to come uptown. . . ."

"That's okay." Rita pockets the receipt. "I'll write it off as a business expense."

"Which it is. You should write off that coffee, too," she adds as Rita deposits her empty hot cup, along with her mostly unread newspaper, into a nearby trash can.

"That isn't a business expense."

"You drank it on the way to a business presentation." Nancy tosses her own newspaper and coffee cup in after Rita's. "Come on. What are the chances you'll get audited, anyway?"

"That's my Nancy. Always trying to bend the rules."

"Who, me?"

Rita grins. "Yes, *you.* The same *you* who tried to get me to take an extra paper out of that machine by the taxi stand."

"Well, I had already paid and the door was open, so—"

"You paid for one, Nancy, not two."

"Who would know? They don't keep track of that sort of thing."

"I'm sure they do. And I already had my quarters in my hand."

"That's my Rita. Always a fine upstanding citizen, trying to set a good example. No wonder your kids turned out so well."

"Oh, I don't know about that."

"Come on, Rita. John's a surgeon, Paul's a pediatrician. They definitely turned out well."

"I'm not arguing about how they turned out. I'm just not sure how much of that is to my credit."

"Oh, stop being modest. It's all to your credit. Admit it, you're an incredible mother."

"So I suppose it would be all my fault if they were both jailbirds?"

"Absolutely," Nancy says with a laugh.

The May sun is warm on Rita's bare shoulders as they cross the sidewalk to the building. She initially had put on a light sweater this morning when she went to early mass back home in Queens, but changed into a sleeveless cotton T-shirt afterward.

According to the weather report she did manage to get from the newspaper amidst Nancy's incessant backseat chatter, this is apparently going to be one of those years when winter seems to give way directly to summer. After weeks of steady, chilly rain, it's been sunny and humid with temperatures in the eighties for the past few days.

"Oh, did you remember to bring that pamphlet on cephalopelvic disproportion?" Rita asks as they step into the dim lobby of the prewar building.

Nancy lifts her canvas bag. "Got it. Also that new one on postdatism."

"Good thinking."

"I figured I should make myself useful so you wouldn't regret agreeing to let me come along."

Hearing the familiar poor-little-me note creeping into her friend's tone, Rita thinks, *Uh-oh, here we go again.*

"It's not that I didn't want you here, Nancy. It's just that I could have handled this fine on my own."

"Yeah, well, it's Mother's Day. I needed something to do to get my mind off that."

Oh. That's right. Rita touches Nancy's arm gently. "Are you okay?"

"I'm fine. Really," she insists, seeing Rita's concerned expression.

"I'm just making sure. I know this is hard for you."

"Thanks. I'm fine," Nancy says tightly, and looks away.

In the marble-tiled lobby, they're greeted by a uniformed doorman, whose name tag reads *Jamil.* "What can I do for you today, ladies?"

"We're here to see Wanda Jones in 28J," Rita says, and he grins.

"What is this, a Tupperware party? Ms. Jones is getting one lady visitor after another this afternoon."

"Not a Tupperware party, exactly," Nancy says with a friendly smile, looking like her old self again.

Until Jamil says, "Oh, I get it. It's Mother's Day. Must be some kind of special luncheon or something."

Neither Rita nor Nancy bothers to correct him. Moments later, they're in the mirrored, carpeted elevator on their way up to the twenty-eighth floor.

"What are you doing after this?" Nancy asks, checking her reflection and patting her ash-colored hair, which is meticulously styled and sprayed, even on a sweltering day like this.

"I'm meeting my sons for dinner on the East Side," Rita tells her. "Why?"

"Never mind. I just thought maybe we could see a movie or something."

"I'm sorry. I'd invite you to come along, but it's supposed to be just the three of us—J.D. isn't even coming along, and the boys are treating me, so . . ."

"I totally understand. It's Mother's Day," Nancy says with a disheartened shake of her head, obviously feeling sorry for herself. "Don't worry about me. I'll be fine."

She wants me to insist that she come along anyway, Rita realizes. *She's thinking that if I were a good friend, I'd tell her that my sons won't mind and she should join us, rather than let her be alone on a day that's so painful for her.*

Suddenly, the silence in the elevator seems strained.

Don't start making excuses for yourself, Rita tells herself sternly. *Don't let her make you feel guilty.*

The elevator has reached its destination. Stepping out into the carpeted twenty-eighth-floor corridor, Rita says, for lack of anything else, "Here we are."

"Yes, here we are." Nancy's voice is chipper, but Rita can't seem to ignore the shadow in her dark eyes.

"Oh, Mrs. Cordell! I didn't even recognize you!"

"Hello, Abe. Hi, Jerry." Derry stops pushing her grocery-filled metal cart to speak to the two elderly men playing checkers in the sunshine in front of the building. The Yankees game blasts from a battery-operated radio at their feet.

"Gorgeous day, isn't it?" Jerry says.

Derry looks up at the blue sky and bright yellow sun perched above their building. "Definitely a gorgeous day," she agrees wholeheartedly. "And it's about time. I thought spring was never going to come."

"Feels like we skipped spring, if you ask me. This feels like summer." Jerry lifts his Yankees cap to wipe a trickle of sweat from his silver temple. "If this keeps up, we'll all be complaining about the heat before summer really does come in June."

"Especially you, Mrs. Cordell," Abe says with a meaningful glance at her stomach. "I see that congratulations are in order."

"Thank you." She knows she must be beaming brighter than the May sun. This is the first weekend she's been able to shed her jacket and parade around for all the world to see.

"When are you due?" Jerry wants to know.

With her fingertips curled to conceal their savagely chewed nails, Derry pats the rounded belly protruding beneath her sleeveless maternity blouse.

"Late September or early October," she says, just as Rose told her to.

* * *

"Shouldn't we wait another few minutes?" Peyton protests when Nancy announces that it's time to get the presentation started. "I talked to Allison last night. She said she was coming."

"Maybe she changed her mind," Rita suggests, seated on a folding chair facing the women gathered on the velvet couch and love seat.

The new furniture was recently bestowed by Eric, Wanda's wealthy married suburban lover. He also paid a contractor to convert the alcove off Wanda's bedroom into a nursery, and furnished it with an Ethan Allen crib and changing table.

Wanda proudly led the group on a tour of the apartment, including the lovely terrace with a dazzling view, before settling them in the living room.

It amazes Peyton how candid she is about being a so-called kept woman. She likes Wanda, but can't help wondering how she can live like this, let alone bring into the world a child whose father is openly married to another woman.

But then, it isn't up to her to judge.

With a shiver, she pushes aside an image of that red leather Bible sitting in her drawer back home.

She's told nobody about it, not Gil last week at dinner, not Allison, not even the police.

Oddly, the only person she's been remotely tempted to confide in is Tom.

Tom Reilly, the man with whom she's shared two coffees, lunch, and some soul-searing kisses. To her relief, her first impression of him was dead-on; he's turned out to be charismatic and easy to talk to.

Peyton could easily allow herself to fall in love with him, if she let her guard down.

So she won't let her guard down.

And she certainly won't go confiding in him about the Bible she found in her desk drawer. He knows she had a prowler; she prefers to leave it at that. He's so concerned that every time they part company, he insists on walking her to her door and making sure her apartment is empty.

At first, she thought he might be an opportunistic cad hoping she'd invite him in, but now she believes he's really just a gentleman, and a concerned friend.

A concerned friend who has no idea that she's carrying a

child, or that she's apparently being stalked by a shadowy religious fanatic who disapproves of her choice.

The pertinent passages were from the Book of Wisdom. They were painstakingly highlighted in yellow marker, pages paper-clipped and marked with yellow Post-it notes so she'd be sure to find them. She felt ill from the moment she read the first line, from chapter 3, verse 16: *the progeny of an unlawful bed will disappear . . .*

Unlawful bed? There *was* no bed, Peyton wanted to scream at the faceless intruder. There was a steel table, and a test tube and a syringe.

How dare somebody judge her?

How dare somebody invade her private space?

How dare somebody scare the hell out of her?

Yes. She's *scared.* When she isn't angry at the violation, she's downright terrified. Terrified that whoever it was might find a way past the changed locks and window bars, this time with a more ominous purpose.

But who? Who would want to hurt her? Only a handful of people know about her condition. Could this possibly be somebody in her trusted circle of confidantes? Somebody who keeps up a normal facade yet harbors a secret religious extremism?

Or is it a neighbor, or somebody at the office, a passing acquaintance who guessed that she's pregnant, knows she's single . . . and saw fit to pass judgment?

None of it makes sense. She resents having to endure her days looking over her shoulder, and her nights lying awake listening for intruders.

Maybe she should tell somebody. The police, or even just Tom, or Allison.

Allison.

Peyton looks at her watch. Allison is now almost an hour late for the meeting.

This isn't like her, she thinks, as worry for her friend begins to edge out anxiety over her own situation. She knows Allison well enough to realize that she's responsible about appointments.

Or does she know Allison at all? How well does she know anybody, really?

Linden is still parked in front of the television set watching the Yankees game when Derry emerges from putting the groceries away in the kitchen. She crosses the room and ceremoniously sets a bowl of ice cream in front of her husband.

"What's this?" He looks up in surprise.

"Chunky Monkey. I bought it at the store just now. It was on sale," she adds, before he can tell her they can't afford premium-brand ice cream.

"What's the occasion?"

"No occasion. I just thought you deserved a treat, and I know it's your favorite."

"Yeah," he says, grabbing the bowl and digging in. "Thanks."

"You're welcome." Deciding to sit with him for a while, she arches her back, bends her knees, and gingerly lowers herself until she makes contact with the chair.

"What the hell are you doing, Derry?"

"I'm practicing. This is how I'll have to remember to sit as I get bigger. It's going to be pretty uncomfortable."

Linden says nothing, just lifts another spoonful of ice cream to his mouth and stares at the television set.

Derry fights the urge to ask him, once again, when they can call his mother in Florida and tell her their news. He keeps putting her off, saying his mother is half deaf and too old to be thrilled about a first grandchild at this stage, anyway.

Having met her mother-in-law a few times and realizing she was never the most maternal person in the world, she knows he's probably right. He's probably trying to shield Derry from a disappointing response, knowing that her own family's reaction was less enthusiastic than she had hoped.

In the fiercely Catholic Cavanaugh circle, babies are a dime a dozen. Derry's oldest niece in Sacramento is expecting her second. Everybody offered congratulations, but nobody seemed particularly sympathetic to the long, hard infertility road Derry and Linden have traveled. And she couldn't elaborate on the details of her nonpregnancy, so she kept the calls short and sweet.

"I saw Abe and Jerry on the street just now," she comments, leaning back against the cushions. "They both congratulated me."

"Yeah? That's good."

She struggles to keep from blurting that he's not being very supportive.

Because the truth is, he's being far more supportive than she ever expected. The mere fact that he's agreed to this at all . . .

Well, she'll be grateful to him for the rest of her life. To him, and to Rose.

"Did you tell Richie yet?"

"No. I haven't had a chance," he elaborates when she raises a questioning eyebrow.

"I can't wait to tell more people. I tried calling Emily and Cara yesterday, but neither of them was home."

"Who are—" he starts to ask, before recognition dawns. "Oh. Your friends from the restaurant."

"Right. They'll both be so happy for us. They know how hard it's been."

Not that she's kept in touch with either of them since she lost her job. Strange how isolated you can become when you stay at home day in and out, rarely even bothering to get dressed in the morning, utterly wrapped up in nesting. Not in a bad way, necessarily. Most of the time, she doesn't need anybody other than Linden.

But he isn't exactly fulfilling all her emotional needs these days—and vice versa, to be fair.

Wishing things could be different, but not sure how to make that happen, Derry sits stiffly beside her husband. Her back is beginning to ache from the awkward posture.

It's more difficult than one might expect to keep both feet on the floor. Normally, she's prone to curling up with her feet tucked under her, or sprawling with her legs draped over the arm of the sofa.

But she has to get used to carrying herself differently, even when she and Linden are home alone. That way, she won't slip up in public.

"Aren't you going to take that thing off?" he asks, glancing over a few minutes later, when the game goes into a car commercial. "It's so freaking hot in here."

"The A.C. is on."

"It's still hot. You must be dying."

Derry scowls. "No, I'm not going to take it off. If I were pregnant, I wouldn't be able to take it off the second I felt uncomfortable."

"Yeah, well, in case you forgot, you're not pregnant."

Ignoring the cruel phrasing, Derry points out, "I have to wear this all the time. What if somebody pops in unexpectedly and sees me without it?"

Linden casts a skeptical glance at the triple row of locks on the door. "Nobody can pop in unexpectedly without buzzing first."

"You never know."

"Sure you do. *I* know. Nobody's popping in here unless we let them in. I think you're safe," he says with a trace of sarcasm.

Derry props an elbow on her belly and chews a fingernail in frustration.

Linden couldn't possibly understand. No man can.

This is her chance to experience, on some level, the miracle that can never be a reality for her. No, she can't carry a baby in her womb, but she can wear maternity clothes and notice strangers' glowing smiles as she waddles about her daily business. And in September, or perhaps October, she'll have a baby in her arms, just like a real mother.

Rose promised. And this time, nothing can go wrong. This time, Derry isn't just counting on the donor—the donor is counting on her.

According to Rose, the thirteen-year-old girl from a strict, ultrareligious family was date-raped after she snuck out to go to a party. She's hiding the pregnancy from her parents, knowing they'll disown her if they ever find out.

"How can she hide a pregnancy for nine months?" Derry asked Rose.

"It happens all the time," was the woman's disconcerting response. "Especially with kids her age and size. They just wear baggy clothes and nobody has a clue."

"But . . . isn't that wrong? How can you go along with something like this?" *And how can I?*

How can she go through with faking a pregnancy and a home delivery so that the girl's baby can be passed off as hers? Rose told her and Linden that nobody would ever find out. There would be no adoption, no financial paperwork whatsoever, and the birth certificate would be legitimate.

"But . . . how can that be?" Derry asked incredulously, unable to accept that the plan could be as simple as it seemed.

"It happens every day, all over this country," Rose told her. "Women give birth at home all the time. Do you think none of those babies have birth certificates?"

But . . . it's wrong.

"Of course it's wrong, Derry, technically. But it would be more wrong to let this distraught young girl give birth in an alley somewhere and put the baby into a garbage can. I've seen it happen over and over again in cases just like this one. That's why whenever a girl in her predicament comes to me for help, I help. I do what I have to do. We all do what we have to do. This isn't a game. There are no rules. We're saving babies' lives."

Rose's passionate discourse made it sound like Derry would be heroic to take on this challenge.

She must have said more or less the same thing to Linden when Derry asked her to explain the situation to him. She knew that if Linden heard it from her, there was a good chance he'd tell her she was out of her mind and would have nothing to do with this bizarre charade, despite the appeal of not having to pay a dime for a baby.

Derry wasn't in the apartment when Rose spoke to her husband. She couldn't bear to be. She knew that their marriage would be over if her husband dashed her fragile hopes just when they were on the verge of making their dreams come true.

So she left Linden and Rose alone with her parental fate in their hands. She went to the playground down the block and she sat on a swing in the rain, praying the whole time that her husband would somehow come through for her.

After all, it wouldn't cost him anything. And it wasn't as if he had never done anything morally ambiguous in his life. Hadn't he wired the apartment for illegal cable? Hadn't he rolled back the odometer on his old car so that he could sell it for more money?

But this is different, Derry told herself. *This is huge.*

Still, it helped to know that Linden wasn't above cheating, under the right circumstances. Especially when he had financial motivation.

To this day, Derry has no idea what Rose said in the apartment that afternoon, only that Linden later commented that the woman could talk a cow into volunteering for the slaughterhouse.

That, Derry told him with a shudder, was not a welcome comparison.

"I don't think Allison would change her mind about coming without calling to let us know," Julie comments, as Peyton's apprehension escalates by the minute.

Where on earth is Allison?

"It's Mother's Day," Nancy points out. "Maybe she's busy with her kids. She has two older ones, doesn't she?"

"Yeah, but she said they didn't have any special plans this afternoon," Wanda says. "They spend Sundays with their father."

"But it's Mother's Day."

Wanda snorts. "Have you ever met Allison's ex-husband?"

"I take it *you* have," Rita says.

"No, but he's a bastard. She's told me enough about him. Whatever, she said she really wanted to be here today because her due date is so close, and she needs to hear all about cardinal movement and delivery empowerment. There's a full moon this weekend and she's afraid she'll deliver early."

"A full moon?" Peyton can't help echoing. "What does that have to do with anything?"

"Rita says full moons can trigger labor."

Peyton shoots a skeptical glance at the midwife.

To her surprise, Rita shrugs. "There's actually some documentation of that."

"Well, then, she probably went into labor." Emanating impatience, Tisha checks her watch. "Can't we just start without her?"

The lone newcomer at today's meeting, Tisha is an outspoken nineteen-year-old who reeks of cigarettes and looks closer to thirty—apparently thanks to hard-living high school years. Her pregnancy, unlike the others', is unplanned.

Given the fact that she's fully made up in this heat and exhibiting her swollen belly between a snug cropped top and low-slung shorts, Peyton can't help comparing her to one of those self-absorbed Hollywood starlet types you see flaunting their bellies in magazines.

Especially after listening to her complain about one symptom after another in the first fifteen minutes after they met. Just when Peyton was on the verge of informing Tisha she really didn't want to hear any more, and that she'd be doing herself and the baby a favor if she quit smoking, the woman apologetically said, "I'm really sorry I'm unloading on you, Parker."

Parker? Peyton opened her mouth to correct her, but Tisha went on, her voice quavering a little, "It's just that when you're pregnant and single, there's nobody to talk to, really. Nobody who understands. I feel so alone."

A wave of empathy washed away Peyton's irritation. "*I* understand. We all understand. That's why you're here."

Now, feeling a vague uneasiness over Allison's unexpected absence, she finds herself annoyed with Tisha all over again.

Before she can speak up, Wanda utters the words that are on the tip of her tongue. "Tisha, if Allison went into labor, Rita would know about it. She's going to deliver Allison's baby."

"Well, maybe she missed the call," Tisha persists.

The midwife reaches into the pocket of her slacks and pulls out a cell phone. "I carry this with me wherever I go. I'm on call twenty-four-seven, just like room service at the Waldorf Astoria."

"*You've* stayed at the Waldorf Astoria?" Tisha asks dubiously, looking the midwife over from her unfashionably thick, overgrown gray-streaked bangs to her plain white Keds.

"Hell no. Who do I look like, Trump?"

As they all laugh at Rita's sassy response to what could have been perceived as an insult, Peyton finds herself liking Tisha even less than she did upon meeting her, and liking Rita even more.

The midwife's easygoing smile and quick sense of humor are a welcome addition to today's gathering. As Nancy has pointed out more than once, and as Kate affirmed after her son's birth, Rita has borne two children of her own. She's been through the rigors of labor twice, and her bedside manner is proof.

Peyton isn't entirely sold on home delivery and childbirth, but she's definitely anxious to hear what Rita has to say.

Not until Allison arrives, though.

She shifts her position, wondering if it would be rude to get up and stretch for a moment. Beside her, Julie is tapping her foot rhythmically against the leg of the coffee table, and Wanda has sighed more than once.

"Just think," Nancy says brightly, gazing around the room. "Next year at this time, you'll all be mommies celebrating your first Mother's Day!"

"Yeah, and just think, last year at this time I was going to my prom," is Tisha's glum response.

"Cripes, who invited Debbie Downer?" Wanda mutters to Peyton.

"She's one of Dr. Lombardo's patients. Nancy said she needs us."

"Yeah, well, the last thing we need is to listen to that for the next few months. Somebody needs to set her straight and if she keeps up that 'tude of hers, it's going to be me," Wanda retorts under her breath, before going to answer the abrupt ring of the telephone.

She returns a few minutes later. The group falls silent at her grim expression.

"That was Allison's mother. She went through Allison's organizer and found out about today's meeting. She wanted to know if she might have shown up here."

Wanda pauses, taking a deep breath and steadying her bulk against the doorjamb.

Peyton's nagging worry for her friend escalates into full-blown fear even before Wanda goes on, "Her mother was in a panic. She kept talking to me in Spanish, but what I think she was saying is that nobody has seen Allison since she went to bed last night. They've already called the police."

Across the river in Bayonne, Mary Nueves sits beside a cradle in the moonlight, rocking it gently with her foot, humming the Spanish lullaby her mother hummed to her forty-one years ago. She knows, because her mother told her when she gave Mary a music box that played the melody as a gift for her first pregnancy.

Mama's lovely voice was silenced forever almost three years ago, but the music box sits now on top of the little white chest of drawers nearby, beside a neatly folded stack of receiving blankets and Onesies that have to be put away.

Laundry to be put away, another load to be folded, dishes to be washed . . .

So much to do.

But Mary can't seem to bring herself to do anything other than rock the baby.

She's waited so long for her to be here. So very long. That she arrived on Mother's Day is a meaningful gift from heaven—one last perfect gift from Mama, as far as Mary is concerned.

A footstep creaks in the hallway.

Mary stops humming.

The door slips open a few inches, and her husband is silhouetted in the shaft of light that spills into the cozy little room.

"Are you still awake?" he asks in a hushed tone. "You should get some sleep. She'll be up for another feeding soon."

"I know, I can't help it. It's her first night in the world. I don't want to leave her alone."

He laughs softly, peering over her shoulder into the cradle. "She doesn't even know you're here. She's sound asleep."

"I know. But I just want to sit here and watch her. We've waited so long for this, Javier. So many months . . ."

"So many *years*. I know."

Mary sighs with contentment and stops rocking the cradle, careful not to jar it as she stands at last. She reaches over to the dresser and lifts the music box. The brass key beneath it gleams in the moonlight as she winds it.

The tinkling strains of a lullaby fill the room. Mary gently sets the music box back on the dresser, remembering the day she hurtled it against the wall in despair. Miraculously, it didn't break.

Was that after she lost that first pregnancy? Or her second? Or third?

It's all a terrible blur.

And it no longer matters.

It's all behind them now: the countless miscarriages, the many futile attempts at conception, the dashed hopes when they accepted Mary's infertility—and again when they realized they simply couldn't afford to adopt . . .

It's all behind them, like a nightmare that vanishes the very moment you open your eyes.

Less than eighteen hours ago, as the morning sun cast its first pink rays over New Jersey, this tiny, precious daughter was delivered to Javier and Mary Nueves.

They named her Dawn.

It was a fitting name, Rose said with a smile, having exchanged the delicate bundle in Mary's arms for the prosthetic stomach she would no longer need.

"I can't believe she's really here," Javier says now, gazing down at the baby, bathed in the silver glow of the full moon.

"Neither can I. It's been so hard, Javier. So incredibly hard . . ."

Years' worth of pent-up emotion escape Mary, and she finds herself sobbing. Her husband pulls her close, crooning to her in their native tongue until the tears subside.

"Did we do the right thing?" Mary asks, searching his eyes for the guilt she can't quite seem to suppress.

There is none. His conscience is clear. Perhaps hers should be, as well.

"We saved her life, Mary. You heard what Rose said. If it wasn't for us, she might be wrapped in a garbage bag and thrown in a Dumpster somewhere."

Mary shudders, gazing down at little Dawn, watching the reassuring rise and fall of her tiny chest with every feather-soft breath.

"We all do what we have to do, Mary. There are no rules."

"Right," she says quietly, recalling Rose's words as clearly as her husband does.

If there are no rules, then no rules can be broken.

"Come on. It'll be okay. Let's go get some sleep."

Javier kisses the top of his wife's head, then bends to do the same on their new daughter's shockingly full head of glossy black hair.

CHAPTER SEVEN

On Monday morning, Peyton arrives at the office more than an hour late, bleary-eyed beneath the obligatory layer of eye shadow and mascara.

She slept perhaps an hour in total last night, so frantic about Allison that her own worries of the past two weeks have almost faded in comparison.

She called Allison's home number just before bed, praying that she'd turned up in a hospital somewhere, perhaps because she fainted on a subway in the oppressive heat. That was the most plausible and optimistic explanation she could conjure.

A man, presumably Allison's father, answered the phone on the first ring, as though he had been waiting beside it. He told her in broken English that there had been no news.

When Peyton asked if there was anything she could do, he said simply, "*Rezar.*"

Pray.

Reaching her office door, Peyton spots a yellow Post-it note at eye level.

Two words are scrawled on it in bold scarlet ink, her boss's signature tool for written communication.

See me.

Peyton stifles a groan and unlocks the door, leaving the note stuck to it. Tara will have to wait until she can pull herself together. She might be here, but she's not ready to face the day . . . and she hasn't had a chance to prepare for the bombshell she needs to drop as soon as possible.

She can't wait any longer to tell her boss she's pregnant.

She has to leave early this evening to meet Rita, who graciously offered a private consultation when yesterday's presentation was cut short. She was thinking she'd have to make up something to tell Tara about her early exit, but she can't rely on the dental appointment excuse again. It's been overused as it is, every time she comes back from an extended lunch hour at Dr. Lombardo's office.

Anyway, she can't hide this from her colleagues much longer even if she wanted to. It's as if her stomach popped out overnight. Today, for the first time, she's wearing a maternity skirt whose spandex panel is concealed beneath an old spring jacket whose buttons are gaping slightly around her breasts.

Until now, she's gotten away with rubber-banding the buttons at her waist and looping them through the buttonholes, a trick Allison taught her.

Allison. Where are you? What happened to you?

A lump rises in Peyton's throat even as her desk phone lights up and rings. Too choked up to answer, she lets it bounce into voice mail, doodling absently on a pad and thinking about her friend.

Maybe, she tells herself, not for the first time in the past twelve hours, Allison couldn't deal with the pressure of being pregnant and alone, and took off for a few days to pull herself together.

She's seemed a little tense lately, now that Peyton thinks about it. More introspective; preoccupied, almost.

When Peyton asked if she was okay, she said she was just exhausted, fed up with her mother's blatant disapproval, and worried about the upcoming delivery.

"I'm so huge that I don't know how Rita's going to get this baby out of me," she told Peyton morosely. "I keep hearing horror stories from people at work about big babies whose shoulders get stuck, or women who need emergency C-sections. I guess I'm just afraid that I can't do this."

"You can do it," Peyton said, squeezing her friend's hand, riddled with unaccustomed uncertainties of her own.

The nature of the beast, she remembers thinking.

Now, looking back on that conversation, she wonders if she could have done something more for Allison; if she could have said something more effective, more comforting.

"Peyton?"

She looks up to see Tara's secretary, Candace, standing in the doorway.

An ambitious college graduate with a business degree and

hopes of working her way into agency management someday, Candace is dressed, as always, in a Tara-style tailored business suit and pumps. Behind horn-rimmed glasses—which she confided to Peyton she wears strictly to enhance her professional appearance—her expression is serious.

"How's it going, Candace?"

"Okay." She doesn't seem to be her usual upbeat self. Uh-oh.

"Tara just told me to find you and tell you to come in to see her. Right now," Candace adds somewhat apologetically, as if sensing Peyton is about to stall.

"Okay, thanks. Tell her I'll be right there."

With a reluctant sigh, she hoists herself wearily from her chair, checks to make sure her jacket has stayed buttoned, and marches off to her corporate duty.

Thank goodness for supermarkets that deliver, Anne Marie thinks, stacking another can of the boys' beloved beef ravioli in the rapidly filling pantry cupboard.

Once upon a time, she actually enjoyed the grocery shopping ritual, even relished the challenge of clipping coupons and perusing the circulars for bargains. But that was in her old life. The life where every precious dollar counted.

These days, she feels a mixture of relief and guilt whenever she tosses into the garbage the circulars that come in the weekend papers.

It isn't that she squanders money now that she's moved up in the world. Not at all.

But when the triplets came along, she realized there was no way she could negotiate supermarket aisles with three small boys in tow. So she joined the ranks of her Bedford neighbors who receive weekly grocery deliveries without batting an eye. And she hired a housekeeper.

Not full-time, not live-in. Having somebody here day in and out would be out of the question.

"Mommy?" Avery calls from the next room. "Is it time for lunch?"

"In a few minutes," she promises, thinking it's far too early for that. She hasn't even eaten breakfast yet. The bowl of cereal she poured an hour ago for herself is still sitting soggily on the table, abandoned when Caleb fell off the back of the couch while trying to fly like a superhero.

Anne Marie removes the can of ravioli she just put into the cupboard, along with the one beneath it. There. Lunch.

She knows what her Italian grandmother would say about that. Pasta from a can? *Veleno!*

Poison.

Grace DeMario made only homemade ravioli, a daylong job for which Anne Marie was frequently pressed into service.

She actually enjoyed the chore: mixing the meat or cheese filling, rolling out sheets of pasta, pressing the dough into the antique molds Grandma had brought with her from Sicily. They were made of metal, and resembled shallow ice cube trays hinged together.

How well Anne Marie remembers the painstaking process: put a scoop of filling into each small pasta-lined cup, lay another sheet of dough across the top, and fold the empty half of the tray over to press, crimp, and cut the ravioli all at once.

Filled with the bittersweet nostalgia that consumes her whenever she thinks of her grandmother, Anne Marie wonders if she still has those old molds somewhere. They're probably packed in the attic with the rest of the relics from her blue-collar Italian past. Jarrett has no interest in any of it, of course.

She sighs, about to reach for the can opener, when the phone rings.

Not the home phone.

Her cell phone, tucked into the pocket of her jeans, always close at hand. The phone she programmed with different musical ring tones so that she'll know who's calling before she answers.

It's a handy feature, one that allows her to weigh the likely importance of the call in advance. She can decide whether a call is worth scrambling to answer while she's driving. Or whether a call should be taken in privacy, where there's absolutely no risk of being overheard.

Yes, it's important to know what to expect when the phone rings.

The standard tone belongs to Jarrett, who rarely calls this number.

The "Happy Days Are Here Again" riff is assigned to Lena, Anne Marie's perpetually cheerful next-door neighbor.

Karen, a southern-born friend from her mothers-of-multiples support group, laid claim to "Dixie."

Now the opening notes of a Brahms lullaby reach Anne Marie's ears for the first time since she programmed in that particular ring.

Anticipation darts through her as she scurries toward the nearby powder room to answer it in seclusion.

Anticipation . . . and sheer, bone-chilling dread.

"I'm sorry I was late," Peyton immediately tells her boss, who is seated behind her desk in a corner office with a sprawling view of the East River. "I had some personal business I had to deal with, so . . ."

She trails off, wondering if she should mention her missing friend, or just leap right into the pregnancy issue.

Before she can decide, Tara speaks up.

"Close the door," she says, adding a cursory "please."

Peyton obliges, and takes the chair that's silently indicated.

"Your being late isn't what this is about." Tara steeples her fingers on her blotter. "But I would definitely appreciate a phone call in the future if you're going to be late. If nothing else, so that I won't worry that something horrible happened to you."

She offers a taut smile. The words are kind in the abstract, but in reality, they're hardly genuine.

Peyton has always recognized her boss for what she is: a shrewd, driven businesswoman who can turn the warmth on—and off—the way other people flip light switches.

"I'll make sure I call in from now on," Peyton nods, swallowing the urge to vocalize her fears that something horrible might actually have happened to a good friend.

Tara doesn't want to hear about that, and she isn't interested in excuses. She's the kind of woman who would probably stop in at the office on her way to her own mother's funeral.

"Alain is leaving to go back to the Paris office, Peyton, as I'm sure you know."

Her breath catches in her throat. "Yes, I know. Soon, isn't it?"

"We just finalized it. Next week."

She's going to tell me that she's promoting somebody else, Peyton realizes, trying to analyze Tara's unyielding expression.

Which, she realizes unexpectedly, is absolutely fine with her. She's got enough on her plate now. More responsibility at work is the last thing she needs.

"How do you feel about taking on more responsibility?" Tara asks, as though she's read Peyton's thoughts.

In utter disbelief, she asks, "You're promoting me?"

"Not yet. It would be a trial run, for, say, six months. If you take the challenge and prove you have what it takes, you'll get the title and pay increase retroactively when you come up for review in October."

October.

October is precisely when she'll be getting something far more valuable than a title and pay increase.

"You can move into Alain's office as soon as he leaves," Tara goes on briskly, as though it's a done deal. "It's much bigger, and he has a window."

Peyton's madly whirling thoughts alight on the most insipid: "Actually, my office has a window."

"His has a view," is the dismissive response. "I'll have Candace come in and help you box up your files next weekend."

"Tara . . ."

"Yes?" She pauses with a hand on the telephone receiver, clearly about to set the wheels in motion without Peyton's go-ahead.

"Wait. Just . . . wait."

"What's the matter?"

She knows, Peyton realizes, spotting the provocative gleam in Tara's tawny gaze. *She knows that I'm pregnant and she's baiting me.*

For a moment, she just holds her breath, aware that her professional future is teetering in the balance.

Part of her longs to tell Tara what to do with the no-imminent-title, no-imminent-raise, more-immediate-responsibility offer. Or order, as the case may be.

But, with the mettle she's always been proud to possess, she lifts her chin. "I just wanted to say thank you for the challenge, Tara. I'm definitely up for it."

Derry doesn't bother to get off the couch when she hears Linden's key in the lock late Monday afternoon. The air-conditioning has been on the blink all day and it's too damned hot to move. Even lying directly in front of the spinning box fan has done little to ease her discomfort in the humidity.

She hasn't stirred in an hour, except to change the CD on the stereo from REO Speedwagon to Journey. If she weren't so wiped out, she would get up to play "Don't Stop Believin'" yet again. The song has become her own personal anthem.

"Derry?" Linden asks, tossing his key and lunch pail on a chair. "Are you sleeping?"

She closes her eyes belatedly, wishing she had thought of that before he walked in. Then she wouldn't have to speak to him until she's good and ready.

But she can't fake it now, so she opens her eyes and says only, "No, I'm not sleeping."

"What are you doing?"

Does she have to be doing something?

Apparently, she does. Linden resents the fact that she hasn't tried harder to find a new job—especially since she took the MasterCard and went shopping for maternity clothes.

A dozen new outfits now hang in a neat row in her half of the closet. They hang on newly purchased plastic, not wire, hangers, as do the two new blouses she bought in April and never even had a chance to wear yet. Linden claims not to understand how she can buy clothes she supposedly doesn't need with money they supposedly don't have.

That, in fact, was what started the huge fight they had last night—a lovely way to top off the first Mother's Day she's ever been entitled to celebrate.

Which was another sore spot with Linden. When she suggested that he take her out to dinner to mark the occasion, he had the nerve to tell her she'd have to wait until next year. He also pointed out, sarcastically, that she isn't really pregnant, in case she forgot.

"Derry? What are you doing?" he persists. She expects him to ask her if she's okay, but he doesn't.

"I'm resting. The air is still out and it's too hot to move."

She doesn't look at him. She doesn't feel like seeing his expression, knowing what he thinks of somebody who lies around all day without a legitimate reason.

If she were really pregnant, would he be this callous?

Probably not. He'd probably be waiting on her hand and foot, telling her to lie back and put her feet up every chance she gets, and forget about working.

Then again, maybe he wouldn't. Maybe his true nature has finally emerged. Maybe he doesn't care about her or the baby. He only cares about himself.

"Thought about dinner?" he asks, after a moment.

Himself, and food. Jerk.

This time, she glares right at him.

"We'll have to get takeout. I can't cook in this heat."

"If you'd take off that damned rubber belly around the house, you'd be cooler."

"You know I can't do that." He opens his mouth to protest and she cuts him off with, "If we had air-conditioning, I'd be cooler."

"We can't afford air-conditioning. And we can't afford takeout. We're broke, in case you haven't noticed."

"If that's another dig about my not working—"

"Maybe it is."

At that, she screams an obscenity at him, an obscenity she's never spoken to another human being in her life and never could have imagined hurtling at her husband.

He stares at her for a long moment. Coldly.

Oh God. What has she done? What has she become?

Tears well in her eyes; a lump clogs her throat.

But before she can voice her heartfelt contrition, her husband silently turns on his heel and walks out of the apartment, slamming the door hard behind him.

Seated at a table in Tequila Moon, the Mexican restaurant Peyton suggested, Rita surveys the boisterous after-work crowd at the bar. Nearly everybody is attractive and fashion-fad young, sipping lime green cocktails, munching chips, having a grand old time.

She can't help wondering what that must feel like. Her own youth was fleeting, certainly never as unencumbered as the lives of these happy hour inhabitants.

Oh, please. You don't know that. You don't know what kind of lives they really have.

No, but chances are, they aren't facing the weighty issues and responsibilities Rita did at their ages, and far younger. They might technically be adults, but the burden of adult problems still lies on the distant horizon.

You don't know that, she scolds herself again and sips her lemon-garnished seltzer, irritated by her own broad assumptions and the bittersweet memories they trigger.

Memories of being positively saturated in blessedly requited love, married at twenty-one, and then—

"I'm sorry I'm late!" Peyton Somerset breezes up to the table and deposits a briefcase on one of the empty chairs. She looks much more sophisticated than she did in yesterday's shorts and

T-shirt. More noticeably pregnant as well, in a snug-fitting jacket she probably won't be able to wear again for quite some time.

"Have you been waiting long?"

"Not long at all," Rita assures her. "I figured you might have gotten hung up at the office."

"You figured right." Peyton collapses into a seat, her face flushed from the heat and, most likely, the flurry of crosstown rush-hour travel. "I was about to walk out the door when my boss dumped a huge project into my lap. She has a way of doing that."

Rita, who has never had a boss, murmurs something appropriately sympathetic.

Then, after weighing the question's impact on their meeting, she realizes she can't ignore it and asks if anybody has heard from Allison Garcia yet.

Peyton's eyes promptly mist over. "No," is the only word she seems capable of uttering for a moment.

Then she dabs the corners of her eyes with the cocktail napkin Rita offers and takes a deep, nerve-steadying breath. "I called Wanda right before I left the office. She just talked to Allison's mother. Nobody's heard from her."

"My God. I can't believe this." Rita reaches for Peyton's hand, squeezing it hard.

At the physical contact, a choking sound escapes Peyton, as if she's been holding in her emotions all day and the floodgates are about to open.

Rita rubs her wrist and uses the soothing voice she normally reserves to comfort laboring patients. "We just have to pray that she's okay. We have to think positive thoughts. Maybe she just needed to take off and go somewhere."

Peyton seizes that—and Rita's hand—like a lifeline. "That's what I keep hoping," she says fervently.

Hope.

Hope, Rita wants to warn her, can be as fragile as a newborn. It's meant to be gently cradled, not held in a potentially crushing grip.

But Peyton needs desperately to believe that Allison's disappearance had nothing to do with foul play. And Rita needs to reassure her, at least for now.

She says cautiously, "I don't honestly think her running away is out of the realm of possibility."

Peyton's head snaps up. "You don't?"

"Well, I've seen her a few times these last few weeks, as a patient, and I thought she seemed a little bit . . . removed."

"I thought the same thing!"

"You did?" Rita raises her eyebrows in surprise. "Have you told her family that?"

"No, I only talked to her father for a few minutes last night, and he was too upset. But if you think she was subdued lately, too . . . maybe we should tell her parents. Or the police. Maybe she ran away."

"I hope that's the case. And I hope that wherever she is, she'll have help if she needs it when she goes into labor."

"So do I." Peyton sighs heavily and slips her hand from Rita's. She rubs her red-rimmed eyes, seemingly unaware of the makeup she's wearing.

Smudged mascara is the least of her problems now, Rita thinks, and decides not to mention it. The restaurant is dark, and anyway, Peyton Somerset is beautiful regardless of makeup. She's the kind of woman, Rita senses, who will be beautiful even when she's sweating and straining to bring a child into the world. Beautiful, and in control.

"I can't stand to think of Allison afraid and alone out there somewhere . . . and in labor, no less. Maybe she'll call you if that happens, Rita. She trusts you."

Rita pulls her cell phone from her pocket and taps it. "Twenty-four-seven. Remember?"

"Just like the Waldorf Astoria." Peyton gives a nod of recognition. "If she calls you, will you get in touch with me right away? I'll give you all of my numbers."

"You'll be the first to know if I hear anything . . . after her parents, of course. They must be going crazy. I just can't imagine." She shudders.

"What are they like? Have you met them?"

"Only once. They're overbearing, like Allison says. But loving, and they mean well. They're kind of like I am with my kids."

"And like my mother was with me. You have two children, right?"

"How did you know?"

"Nancy told me."

"Oh, Nancy. She loves to talk, doesn't she?" Rita shakes her head, marveling at her friend's willingness to discuss with patients—and, no doubt, Dr. Lombardo—the intimate details of everybody's life but her own. "Yes, I've got two kids, a dog, and a husband. But John and Paul are grown, the dog is old and tired . . . and so, frankly, are J.D. and I," she adds as an afterthought.

"John and Paul are your sons?" At Rita's nod, Peyton asks, unnecessarily but politely, "And J.D. is your husband?"

"Yes. We've been together forever." She sees a fleeting, wistful expression cross Peyton's face, and is compelled to ask, "Is there anybody in your life right now? Or is that a sore subject?"

"Not a sore subject, just . . ."

"I guess it's just a useless question. I don't know why I asked it. If there were somebody, you probably wouldn't be coming to Pregnant and Single meetings, would you?"

"Actually," Peyton says, wearing a secret little smile, as though she's momentarily forgotten her burdens, "there wasn't somebody when I started in the group, but there is now."

"Really? Who is he?" she asks, intrigued, yet trying to sound casual, sensing Peyton isn't a woman who freely dishes about her personal life.

"His name is Tom."

Rita waits for more, realizes nothing more is coming, and is hardly surprised by the reticence. She noticed a quiet reserve about Peyton yesterday at the meeting; saw that she seemed to hold herself apart from the others, even after the frightening news about Allison.

Especially after the frightening news about Allison.

While Wanda and Julie cried openly and dramatically discussed worst-case scenarios, Peyton seemed to retreat emotionally. She was obviously accustomed to finding her strength inside, rather than reaching out, leaning on others.

Well, that quality will serve her well when she finds herself faced with the childbirth challenge ahead. Some of Rita's laboring patients have collapsed into screaming, begging, panicking, tortured souls. That isn't good for anyone—not the mother, not Rita, and certainly not the baby fighting its way into the world.

But Peyton isn't going to fall apart when the time comes. She gives off an aura of absolute fortitude. Working with her, Rita concludes, will be a rare pleasure.

If you wind up working with her at all.

She can ask more about Tom later.

For now, it's time to get down to business.

"I know you must have a zillion questions, sugar pie," Rita

says, beginning the heartfelt speech she's given so many times before. "I may have been pregnant a lifetime ago, but I remember it like it was yesterday. I especially remember wanting to know absolutely everything about what I was going to go through, because knowledge is comfort."

Peyton's eyes light in recognition. "That's exactly how I feel!"

Rita smiles. "I figured. I've been there, remember? Twice. So why don't you go ahead and start asking me about what a midwife does, and anything else you want to know?"

Peyton shifts her weight. "I'd really rather you went ahead and started telling. If that's okay with you."

"A take-charge attitude is always okay with me," Rita says with a smile.

With that, she launches into the information she meant to provide at yesterday's meeting, before Allison Garcia fell off the face of the earth.

Alone in the house with her sleeping children, Anne Marie knows better than to steal into Jarrett's study, where rows of gleaming battle swords line the walls, and pour herself a glass of Jarrett's scotch.

She knows better, yet she does it anyway, filling the glass to the brim with amber liquid that might somehow numb the assault on her heart and soul from the moment she answered her cell phone twelve hours earlier.

This isn't the way it's supposed to be.

Mothers are supposed to protect their babies, shelter them from harm.

Well. You'll just learn to live with this, won't you?

This isn't the first time you've had to face harsh reality. You've done it already and survived, haven't you? Survived every time. Haven't you?

Seated in Jarrett's leather recliner, surrounded by lethal blades that glint in the lamplight, Anne Marie lifts the glass to her lips and sips. She feels the potent heat sliding past her shattered heart, feels it swallowed into the depths of an injured soul where it stokes the flames of fury.

Fury is all that remains now.

Jarrett and the boys are all but forgotten in this moment; there isn't a glimmering shard of love to light the smothering cloak of darkness that surrounds her. Not a flicker of warmth, nor a speck of hope.

Just a familiar, burning fury that she thought she'd tamped out long, long ago.

CHAPTER EIGHT

Three days have passed.

Three days in which Anne Marie has gone through the motions of living while thinking every waking moment of dying. Of what it must be like.

Death, decay, extinction.

The stench of it seems to permeate her every breath; the repulsive reality of it seeps into her sleep, transforming dreams into bloodcurdling nightmares. She's consumed by visions of rotting flesh buried in rain-dampened earth, haunted by clinical terms like *dental records* and *DNA*.

"Mommy, can I have more milk, please?" Caleb asks, and she pours rich, creamy milk into a glass, seeing only crimson blood flowing from gaping wounds.

"Mommy, tickle me, please," Avery begs and she wriggles her fingers in his squirming midsection, imagining knives splitting flesh, wounds so deep they leave slashes in bone.

It didn't have to be this way.

You did it yourself. You have nobody else to blame.

Yes. She can blame fate, blame the perceived immortality of reckless youth. Blame the dearly departed, or blame the devil that saw fit to punish, to extinguish life.

Or, Anne Marie can try to forget, try to move on.

Try . . .

And fail, time and time again.

You opened the door in the first place, she reminds herself as she washes supper dishes heedless of the dishwasher, needing hot water running over her hands in a futile effort to cleanse them, to cleanse her soul.

You opened the door.

It's become a warped refrain, one she can't escape. Yes, she opened the door. And now it's too late to close it, too late to shut out the demons.

She turns off the water, dries her hands, dries the tears rolling down her cheeks. She remembers to be glad Jarrett is late coming home from the office again, too far away to ask questions that might mean something for once.

The irony, she thinks as she mindlessly bends to pick up a stray sock, a small car, a crust of bread, is that ten years ago, nobody would have known her if they found her.

Now, thanks to the miracle of science, anything is possible. These days, remains of one who lived centuries ago can be identified by a single strand of hair. A human who would otherwise have gone on in infinite anonymity can be given a name, a face, grieving loved ones who crave answers.

It just takes time, and patience, but the answers will come to misguided souls who seek them.

"Mommy, I'm tired," Justin says, tugging the hem of the shirt she hasn't changed in three days.

"I'm tired, too," Anne Marie says wearily, bending to gather him into her arms.

Goddamned miracles.

In the three days that have passed since Allison's disappearance, Peyton has thought of little else—other than work, of course, when she's there.

Alain hasn't even left for Paris yet, but already, Tara is piling on the assignments, to the point where Peyton was too bogged down yesterday to even attend the annual Kaplan and Kline spring outing. Not that she minded. She was hardly in the mood to socialize.

But her boss didn't know that. And it seems as though Tara secretly gloats every time she allocates a new task to Peyton.

Or maybe that's just my paranoid imagination, Peyton reminds herself as she wearily covers the last block heading home Wednesday night.

Half the time she's able to convince herself that Tara doesn't suspect that she's pregnant. After all, Peyton's made an effort to conceal her bulge beneath looser-fitting suits these last few days.

Then again, Tara did make that catty comment when she found Peyton carrying a bag of microwaved popcorn out of the kitchenette late this afternoon.

"Eating again?" was what she said, or something along those lines. Almost as if she expected Peyton to defend herself with an explanation.

Well, let her think I'm just getting fat, Peyton thinks, digging into her pocketbook for her keys as she mounts the steps of her brownstone building. *Fat can't get you fired.*

Neither can pregnant, officially. But it can keep a woman from getting promoted, no matter what anybody claims. It isn't fair, but it's true.

Damn that Tara, anyway.

Peyton has repeatedly told herself that she can take whatever her boss wants to dish out. She wants this promotion. Or maybe she doesn't *want* it as much as know that she *deserves* it.

In the end, she's too preoccupied to truly *want* anything these days, other than Allison back where she belongs.

After descending the steps to her apartment, Peyton locks the door, checks it twice, then goes straight to her blinking answering machine.

Please let it be Allison, she prays as she presses the button and listens to the tape rewind. *Or news about Allison. Good news.*

It isn't. But it's the next best thing, and she finds herself smiling faintly despite her anxious state.

"Hey, Peyton, it's Tom. I just got back from D.C. . . ."

D.C.?

Oh, that's right. That last-minute business trip he mentioned on Saturday. She forgot all about it in the drama since.

No wonder he hasn't called her these last few days . . . not that she really even acknowledged that fact until now.

"Listen," Tom's recorded voice goes on, "I've got two tickets to see the Yankees annihilate the Red Sox next Saturday afternoon. Are you game? Pun intended, ha, ha. Call me when you get home."

Well, she's home, but she can't call him. Maybe later. Or tomorrow. Or whenever something as inane as a baseball game seems to matter again.

She busies herself filling a cup with tap water and setting it in the microwave. A nice hot cup of tea is what she needs right now.

Herbal tea.

That should steady her frayed nerves.

Herbal tea, and—

She reaches for the phone again.

She can't help it. Baseball aside, she suddenly, desperately, needs to hear Tom's familiar voice.

Her own breaks unexpectedly at the sound of it when he answers on the first ring.

"Peyton?"

"Yes," is all she can manage.

"Are you okay? What's wrong?"

"It's my friend. Allison. She's missing and she's . . . pregnant."

There's so much more she wants to tell him, things she couldn't say even if words were flowing easily past the anguish welled up in her throat.

"Allison. I think you mentioned her," he says, although Peyton is certain that she hasn't.

She was careful not to, knowing that there was an off chance he might ask too many questions.

Like how she met Allison.

She tearfully spills the details, careful to stick with only the most cursory of them.

Eventually, she'll tell him more. But if he finds out that Peyton is pregnant now, he might very well walk away. And she isn't ready to handle that. Not yet. Not tonight.

"Do you want me to come over?" Tom is asking.

"No. I'll be okay. I just . . . I got your message and I thought I should call you back tonight. You know. To tell you what's going on."

"I don't think you should be alone, Peyton. Especially after that break-in you had. It's been hard enough for you to deal with that."

The break-in. This is the first time she's arrived home since it happened and entirely forgotten to search the closets and under the bed.

She begins to do so now, carrying the phone and turning on lights as she goes.

"Let me come over," Tom says again. "I can be there in two minutes."

There's a certain comfort in knowing that. Knowing that if the phone rings in the middle of the night with bad news, she doesn't have to be alone.

"You don't have to come over, Tom. I know you just got back from your trip, and—"

"But I—"

"Look, I promise I'll call you if I need you, okay?"

He hesitates. Then says, reluctantly, "Okay. I'll be here. And I can be there, too. Two minutes. Remember?"

"I remember." She smiles, but only briefly.

A sudden twitch in her stomach has caught her off guard.

She goes still, wondering if it could possibly be—

A startled gasp escapes her as she feels another sharp twitch, down and to the left of her navel.

This time, there's no mistaking it.

The child within her has just kicked for the very first time.

"Are you all right?" Tom is asking. "What happened?"

"Nothing. I—I stubbed my toe."

"Are you okay?"

She says nothing, standing motionless, hoping to feel the miraculous stirring of life once again.

"Peyton?"

"Hang on a second," she says abruptly, and sets the phone down.

She wraps her arms around her abdomen, pressing gently in the spot where the baby's tiny limb was moving.

Where are you, little one? What are you doing in there?

No response.

For a long time, she waits.

Are you sleeping now, baby? she asks silently, feeling less alone, less *lonely,* than she did just minutes ago.

Then the sound of Tom calling her name emerges from the receiver.

She reaches for it slowly, realizing that she can't go on fooling him, or herself. She can't sustain this relationship—if it can even be labeled a relationship. They've seen each other only a handful of times.

Yes, there's an undeniable connection. An attraction. Yes, this could go somewhere, if she let it.

But she won't. She has to tell him she can't see him again. Now.

Or at least, tell him that she's pregnant—and let him be the one who curtails the relationship because of it.

Why prolong the inevitable? That isn't fair, and it isn't healthy.

Steeling herself for the turmoil to come, she lifts the receiver to her ear. "I'm here. Sorry."

"I think I should come over. I'm really worried about you."

"No, you shouldn't come over."

"But—"

"Tom, just wait. Just . . . stop. I need to talk to you."

A beat of silence. Then he asks quietly, "What's going on? Is there more? More than just your friend?"

She's poised to tell him about the baby.

Just say it. You have to.

She does. And she will.

But not tonight.

Because before she can utter another word, her confession is curtailed by the urgent beep of call-waiting.

Lowering the receiver to check the ID window, she recognizes Wanda's number.

"I've got to get that, Tom," she says hurriedly. "It could be something about Allison."

"Want me to hang on?"

"No, hang up. I'll call you if I need you."

But I won't, she tells herself firmly, ending the call with a trembling finger. *No matter what happens, I won't let myself need you.*

"Here." Derry walks across the living room, lit only by the flickering blue light of the television. "You forgot this."

She's tempted to fling the alarm clock at Linden, newly settled on the couch with his blanket and pillow.

If I do that, he might haul me into jail for spousal battery, she thinks wryly, though the premise isn't entirely without validity.

"Yeah, I'll take it since you don't need it anyway. *Ever*." He sits up, snatches the clock from her outstretched hand, and plugs it in.

Yet another nasty crack about her unemployment.

The fight that erupted earlier in the bedroom didn't even revolve around her idle lifestyle, nor around the prosthetic that strains the bodice of her lone summer nightgown.

No, this time, they were at each other's throats over Linden's failure to say good night. It started out as yet another a minor tiff in a week filled with them, but quickly escalated.

All because he just plopped himself down in bed beside her

with a grunt, and ignored her when she said good night. He pretended he was asleep, which irked her because she's not gullible enough to believe that a person can possibly be that deep in slumber two seconds after hitting the pillow.

Linden claimed that it's possible for him, because he works so hard, of course. What he didn't say—at least, not aloud—is that he wouldn't have to work that hard if she would get a job.

Things plummeted from there, snowballing to encompass other topics, stupid topics, things Derry was once able to live with.

His grammatical skills. His ever-present monosyllabic pal Richie. His snoring.

"What are we going to do when the baby comes?" she demanded. "How is the baby going to sleep through all that noise?"

"What the hell can I do about it?"

"You can see a doctor, like I've been telling you for years."

He dismissed that idea with a curt "What the hell for?"

"So you can have an operation to fix your nose so you won't snore!"

"An operation? Where are we going to get the money for that?"

"Oh, stop it, will you please? Stop harping on me about money. It's always about money with you."

That was when he grabbed his bedding and stormed out of the room, leaving her to flip over and mutter a heartfelt "good riddance" into her pillow.

But she couldn't sleep. She was too worked up. She couldn't just leave it alone.

"I told you I'd look for a job this week, remember?" she spits at him now.

"Yeah, well, I've got news for you. This week is already happening."

"Well, *I've* got news for *you.* It isn't over yet," she shoots back at him. "Or as you would say, it *ain't* over yet."

A week ago, that would have been a lower blow than she'd have been capable of dealing to the man she promised to love, honor, and cherish. The man with whom she once had everything in common. Everything that mattered, anyway, from a unique shared affinity for retro rock music to a mutual vision of their ideal future.

Not anymore. Things have changed.

These days, they seem to have very little in common. Derry is no longer sympathetic to Linden's underprivileged upbringing, his typical excuse for not being as polished as she would like. Her usual gentle hints and good-natured teasing about his grammatical lapses have given way to white-hot anger.

He used to make an attempt to speak properly. Now he seems to deliberately choose the wrong words, just to get on her nerves.

It's working.

Linden glares at her from the couch.

She glares back. Then, seething, she marches back to the bedroom, so blinded by fury that she accidentally bumps her fake stomach into the doorjamb.

"Ouch!" she blurts, though it more or less bounces off like the rubber ball it technically is.

Linden snorts.

How dare he?

"You wouldn't think it was so funny if our baby had been injured," she snaps at him over her shoulder.

"I hate to break it to you, Derry, but our baby isn't in there."

"It could be!"

"But it isn't!"

"No kidding!" Those last two words, screeched, are met by a loud pounding on the wall.

Old Mrs. Steiner next door again. She banged earlier, during the bedroom argument. She bangs whenever there's the slightest noise from the Cordells' apartment, which would be forgivable if she didn't pretend to be deaf whenever they pass her in the hall.

"Will you please just shut up?" Derry hisses at Linden. "What if she hears what we're saying about the baby?"

"You're the one who's screaming," he says with a maddeningly docile shrug before pointing the remote at the television.

He turns up the volume to spite Mrs. Steiner, and Derry.

She spins on her heel and storms into the bedroom, somehow resisting the urge to slam the door.

"Wanda?"

"Yeah. Were you on the other line?"

Ignoring the question, Peyton clutches the phone against her ear and poses one of her own. "Any news?"

"No. I just couldn't sleep, and I knew you'd be up, too. Were you on the other line?"

"It's okay. I hung up." Deflated, Peyton sinks into a chair. "I was hoping you were calling to say they found her. I can't believe this."

"I know. I keep thinking she might be out there somewhere . . ."

"Or she might be . . ." Peyton can't say it.

She doesn't have to.

"I know," Wanda says again, her tone hollow. "I talked to her uncle Norberto just now. He answered the phone there. He started crying so pitifully when I told him I was a good friend of Allison's."

Uncle Norberto. The bald uncle who teasingly called Allison and her lookalike newborns *Peludo.*

Peyton swallows hard over a painful lump in her throat, remembering her friend's tale that afternoon in Tequila Moon barely a month ago. Will she ever see that mischievous grin again?

Wanda is still talking; Peyton forces herself to listen when all she wants to do is break down and sob.

"He said her parents weren't there. They're keeping a vigil in church."

"I can't imagine what they're going through," Peyton says, although in truth, she can. She rests a trembling hand on her stomach. "What about Allison's kids?"

"I guess they're home with the uncle. You'd think the parents would stay with them at a time like this."

"But they're not tiny children," she points out. Remembering her herbal tea, she stands and returns to the galley kitchen. "Allison's kids are teenagers, right? They don't need a babysitter."

"No, but still . . ." Wanda sighs. "You know what I mean. Allison always said that with her mother, God comes first and foremost."

"That's not such a bad thing, Wanda," Peyton says cautiously, knowing Wanda is a self-proclaimed atheist.

"Well, I think her priorities are messed up and so did Allison. God has always come before Allison's father, before Allison, before the grandkids."

Knowing it's best to get off the hot-button topic, Peyton says simply, "I think Allison can use all the prayers she can get right now, wherever she is."

"I know. It's just that she just always resented her mother's holier-than-thou thing. She'd probably be pissed about this vigil. She never even went to church."

"I know, but I don't think she resented her mother for going,"

Peyton murmurs, finding Wanda's words harsh no matter what her beliefs.

She dangles a tea bag into her cup and swishes it around at the end of its string, absently watching the tinted swirls permeate the clear water.

"Maybe she doesn't resent her for going to church," Wanda concedes, "but trust me, Allison's mother's been in her face preaching at her from the second she found out she was pregnant."

That, Peyton doesn't doubt. She heard the same thing from Allison, time and again. But she says nothing, allowing Wanda to continue her tirade, sensing that she needs to vent.

"I mean, give me a break. She even left a Bible under Allison's pillow, for God's sake, all marked up with references to illegitimate children."

Peyton cries out as hot water sloshes off the side of the teacup, burning her hand. She flings the cup into the sink, where it shatters against the porcelain.

"Peyton? What was that?"

On the verge of hysteria, she asks shrilly, "Are you sure her mother left it there? The Bible?"

"That's what she said. Why? What's wrong?"

"Nothing, I just . . . I burned myself. I have to go. I'll call you tomorrow."

Peyton hangs up on Wanda's protest.

She clutches throbbing fingers to quaking lips.

A Bible.

References to illegitimate children.

Peyton's brain whirls with thoughts so terrifying, so utterly impossible, that she fears not just for Allison's life . . .

But for her own.

"You're doing great, Jessica." Rita wipes the panting woman's head with a cool washcloth.

". . . can't . . ."

"Yes, you can, sugar pie. You're almost there."

Taking Rita's cue, Jessica's husband leans over and says, "You did it before, honey. You can do it again."

". . . hospital . . . please . . ."

The husband, Kevin, looks up at Rita. "Is it too late to take her in?"

"Yes, and it isn't what she wanted."

"She just said it. Maybe she needs drugs. She's been at it for hours. How much more can she take?"

"She doesn't need drugs or the hospital," Rita informs him, checking the birth canal again, shuddering inwardly at the sight of the deep scars from Jessica's episiotomy.

She doesn't want one this time, and she doesn't want drugs like they gave her with her son two years earlier. That's what she told Rita when they met last winter, and Rita assured her that neither would be necessary.

"Promise me," Jessica said with absolute conviction.

And Rita promised.

"Beautiful," she says now, lifting her head and smiling at her patient, whose face is contorted in agony. "We're almost there."

"No . . ."

"Come on, Jessica. This push can be the one. Kevin and I are going to hold your legs and we're going to count to ten."

"No," Jessica wails pitifully. "Please . . . stop . . ."

Kevin looks at Rita with tears in his eyes. "Oh my God, can't you see she can't take this? Please help her."

"I'm helping her. We both are."

"But you've got to do something."

"No, she's going to do it," Rita assures him with the serenity of somebody who has been here before, hundreds of times. "Now."

"No! Not now!" Jessica protests, yet her body is straining forward, bearing down on its own accord.

"You take her other leg, Kevin," Rita commands, gently but firmly lifting Jessica's ankle. "Come on, let's go. One . . . two . . . three . . ."

A piercing scream fills the room.

And then, moments later, the warbling cries of an infant who just took her first breath.

The proud daddy cuts the cord, freeing his child at last.

"It's a little girl," Rita gently tells the exhausted mother as she places the blood-slicked newborn against her mother's warm, bare breasts.

"Oh my God. Look at that. Look at her." Kevin peers into his daughter's solemnly alert gaze. "She sees me. She's turning her head. She knows I'm her daddy."

"Of course she does. She's heard your voice for the last nine months," Rita tells him with a smile, as she gently dabs a smear of blood from Jessica's inner thigh.

"She's beautiful," Jessica whispers in awe. "Thank you, Rita. Thank you for being here. I needed you. You're . . . you're like a guardian angel."

A guardian angel.

Rita nods and looks away, unable to find her voice, haunted once again by memories of Allison.

"And you say you didn't see the Bible that was left under your friend's pillow?"

Peyton shakes her head, wishing the police officer were a little less . . . dubious.

Well, at least he's older and kinder than the last one who was here.

Aloud, she says, "I don't even know if there's a connection between mine and hers. But it seems like an odd coincidence, doesn't it?"

He doesn't answer, merely leans over the counter to scribble more notes on his report. If he's noticed the broken china in the adjacent sink, he hasn't mentioned it.

"So what you're saying, ma'am, is that your friend's mother might have broken into your apartment and left a Bible for you, same as she did for her daughter?"

"No! I mean . . . maybe. I don't know." Peyton rakes a hand through her hair, exhausted. "What do you think?"

"Frankly, I don't know what to think. It's definitely an odd coincidence."

Terrific. That's precisely what she just said. Isn't the policeman the one who's supposed to put the clues together?

"You say you've never even met this woman?"

"Allison's mother?" Peyton shakes her head. "No."

"But she's some kind of lunatic Holy Roller who—"

"I don't think she's a lunatic," she interrupts.

"So she's some kind of Holy Roller," he amends, though it's clear from his expression that he thinks Holy Rollers qualify as lunatics, "and she goes around quoting the Bible, and you think she might have—"

"I don't think anything," Peyton cuts in again, frustrated. "I just know that I found this Bible after the break-in, and Wanda told me Allison found one, too. I haven't seen hers, and I don't know which quotes were highlighted, but if they're at all similar, I think it would be obvious that there would be a connection."

"So you think your friend's mother disapproves of both of you for being unmarried and . . ." He pauses, as though trying to figure out how to put it delicately.

"Knocked up," she supplies impatiently. "And yes, I know her mother disapproves, at least of Allison. But—"

"So you think that's why your friend took off? Because of her mother?"

"I don't know if she took off," Peyton tells him wearily, folding her arms and leaning against the fridge for support. It's been a hell of a long day. Maybe she should have waited to call the police.

But you have to do this. For Allison.

Aware that her throat is beginning to constrict with emotion, she says quietly, "I'm worried that she didn't take off. I'm worried that whoever left that Bible for her might have . . ."

She trails off, unable to say it aloud.

"Abducted her?"

The officer's words are more benign than the scenario in Peyton's worst nightmares. His scenario is difficult, but one she can handle.

"Yes," she agrees, "abducted her."

He scribbles more notes on his report, then returns his pen to his pocket, looks up, and promises, "We'll look into it."

"Now? Tonight?"

He hesitates. "Ms. Somerset, you have to understand that another precinct is involved and—"

"What does that have to do with anything? This isn't some little petty break-in. It's a missing-person's case, for God's sake."

"I'm aware of that, and I'm also aware that ninety-nine percent of the time in cases like this, where the kid and the mother were at odds, it turns out to involve a runaway."

"Allison wasn't a kid! She isn't some teenaged runaway! She's a grown woman!"

"I understand that. But she lived under her parents' roof, with a mother who was driving her crazy. Chances are, she just snapped and took off for a while. Adults are allowed to do that, you know."

Peyton nods. Yes, she knows. She knows, at least, intellectually, that he could very well be right.

But she can't ignore the nagging feeling in her heart, in her *gut*, that there's more to this.

That whoever left her the Bible is behind Allison's disappearance.

That it wasn't Allison's mother.

And that something catastrophic has happened to a woman who had everything—well, the most seemingly relevant thing, anyway—in common with Peyton herself.

A twig snaps amid a chorus of crickets, and she freezes, her foot frozen in place, waiting to be exposed in the sudden glare of floodlights.

A moment passes, and then another, and, reassuringly, another.

She dares to breathe again. The house remains dark, at least on the outside. Lamplight spills from the bay windows on the first floor and a gabled corner one on the second, above the porch. The glow illuminates peeling paint, a gap in the spindles, a broken shutter.

Is that *her* room? Is she up there somewhere beyond the twin swoops of parted curtains, preparing for sleep?

There's a trellis alongside the porch. It looks rickety, but it wouldn't be difficult to climb it if it holds her weight. Not at all difficult to creep across the porch roof and peek inside. Just to get a glimpse.

She'll never suspect. Even if she did happen to hear something, or even see something, she might chalk it up to a suburban Peeping Tom.

For a few more minutes, she waits, standing absolutely still, her black-clad figure blending with the inky night.

Then, satisfied that nobody heard the twig snap beneath the heel of her Ferragamo loafer, she begins to move forward again.

She assures herself that she won't be discovered even if she slips through the darkness to the porch. That she can scale the trellis, take a quick look, and then be on her way.

That's all I need. Just one look. At least, for tonight.

She's taken precisely six painstakingly counted steps toward the trellis when she hears the rumble of a distant motor. Growing rapidly closer, the rumble is swiftly followed by the arc of headlights as a car turns onto the end of the street.

Panic swells within.

Heart pounding, adrenaline surging, driven by primal instinct like one of the deer that roam the woods beyond her Bedford rose garden, Anne Marie Egerton flees toward the shelter of shadowy undergrowth.

But you'll be back, she promises herself, and the unwitting stranger in the room above the porch.

Because once the door has been opened, there's nothing to do but go through it.

Month Five

June

CHAPTER NINE

"How about Saturday, then?" Gil asks Peyton as they stroll down Seventh Avenue on a humid Wednesday evening in June. "We can have dinner and then go downtown and listen to some music or something."

"I can't, Gil. I already promised Rita I'd have dinner with her that night."

"Again?"

Peyton shrugs, unwilling to explain to him the fast friendship she's formed with Rita, and with Julie, and Wanda, and Nancy . . .

Irrevocably united in tragic loss, the women have formed a solid bond, spending as much free time in each other's company as possible.

Almost a month has passed since Allison disappeared, with no sign of her.

Hope has all but died. Even if she did run away, she'd surely have come back eventually for the sake of her other children. And she'd have had the baby by now.

All you need when you're in labor is to be surrounded by people you totally trust.

Remembering her friend's heartfelt assertion, Peyton is certain she wouldn't choose to be alone somewhere to deliver her child. She'd have at least called Rita from wherever she was, for emotional support if nothing else.

"I sound like a jealous boyfriend, don't I?" Gil asks ruefully, intruding on her grim thoughts. "Whining because you actually have friends and a life, Runt, and I don't."

"You still have friends and a life, Stretch."

"Not really. You're my only friend these days. Karla's poisoned all our mutual ones. And my life consists of work and sleep."

"Yeah, well, I can relate to that. How about Sunday?" Peyton asks to placate the poor guy, whose loneliness is palpable.

One minute he was married with children; the next, he's being forced to move into a rented apartment, alone.

He just showed her around his new place. Never having seen the town house where he lived with his family, Peyton found it exceedingly livable. But Gil kept pointing out all its shortcomings, to the point where she had to remind him that there are worse things in life than living without a dishwasher or linen closet.

Far worse things.

"Sunday is Father's Day," he informs her now. "I get the kids all day. I'm taking them to a baseball game."

A baseball game.

Peyton can't help but think of Tom, whose two tickets to the Yankees she was forced to turn down last month, along with all the other invitations he's extended since. At first he seemed undaunted by her avoidance, much to her frustration. He just kept popping back into her life, and she kept insisting she was too busy at work, too upset about Allison, to see him.

In truth, to let him see *her,* and the pregnancy that's challenging to hide under even the baggiest of clothing.

Mercifully, he finally left for the Orient on business for ten days.

A few days ago, knowing he was back, she stopped wondering when he would call, stopped answering her phone at all, stopped caring.

Well, no. She hasn't stopped caring about him.

But Lord knows she has tried.

"Okay, so at least you get to see the kids on Father's Day," she tells Gil absently, her thoughts still on the man who might have been perfect for her, if things had been different.

"Yeah, terrific. I get to see them after Karla has spent the week filling their ears with lies about me."

"I'm sorry, Gil. I know how hard this is for you."

"Thanks, Runt. I keep telling myself that I'm lucky. You know, that it would be much harder if she took them to the West Coast."

He goes on, talking about his ex-wife and devious plans and

her evil lawyer, and his own barely competent lawyer and the unjust separation agreement he was refusing to sign.

Peyton fulfills her role as sympathetic listener with an occasional comment, but her thoughts are wandering again.

To Tom. To Allison. To the baby, now making its presence known on a regular basis with bold kicks and unexpected flutters.

The prospect of motherhood is her unwavering anchor in these tumultuous times. Sustained by the realization that there can be moments of pure bliss in the midst of such discouragement, she continually manages to get out of bed in the mornings and face whatever lies ahead.

Aside from the all-too-fleeting, magical interludes when her child stirs within, her long days consist of a montage of meetings and pink message slips, client presentations and stacks of paperwork.

Now that she's showing, a number of coworkers have at least politely acknowledged her pregnancy, if not grilled her about the father, the due date, her plans.

But not Tara.

It's become a bizarre, ridiculous waiting game, as far as Peyton is concerned. Tara refuses to comment, clearly expecting Peyton to state the obvious.

She has no intention of doing that.

Call her stubborn—Allison did—but she isn't in the mood to hear Tara's take on single motherhood or what it will do to her career. Sooner or later, it will have to be addressed, but not until Tara brings it up—or Peyton herself is forced to when, say, maternity leave is imminent.

If her days are difficult now, her lonely, restless nights are excruciating.

Her apartment, her bright little sanctuary, no longer feels safe.

She had yet another dead bolt installed, along with an alarm system, but she might as well be sleeping out on the sidewalk for all the protection they seem to offer. All she can think is that somebody slipped in before, and they might somehow do it again.

The police don't seem to think so. To her frustration, they aren't even taking seriously the possibility of a link between her break-in and Allison's disappearance.

She's called the precinct nearly every day since the officer took away as evidence the annotated Bible she found in her drawer.

According to them, Allison's parents couldn't find any such Bible among her possessions. Her grieving mother was so incensed at the mere suggestion that she could have had anything to do with her daughter's disappearance that the detectives presumably dropped that line of questioning.

Peyton has only Wanda's word that Allison found the Bible under her pillow, and Wanda claims she never saw it. Allison didn't mention it to anyone else in the group, or to Nancy, or Rita.

None of them knows what to make of that, or of the Bible that was left by Peyton's prowler. Nobody is certain that Peyton is even in danger, although everyone agrees that she should watch her step.

Big help that is.

How can she watch her step when she has no idea whether there's even a legitimate threat? And if there is one, where on earth does it lie?

There are times when the marked Bible seems ominous, times when she feels ridiculous dwelling on that in light of everything else she has to deal with.

For all she knows, the culprit could be somebody she knows—somebody who disapproves of her choice, but isn't brazen enough to confront her directly. Somebody who has access to her everyday life, to her home, the way a total stranger would not.

"Who's that? One of your neighbors?"

At Gil's question, Peyton glances up to see him pointing at the stoop of her brownstone down the block.

Somebody is sitting on the steps, legs sprawled onto the sidewalk, as though they've been there for a while. Waiting.

Peyton's heart quickens as she recognizes the figure.

"No," she murmurs to Gil, her feet instinctively picking up their pace. "Not one of my neighbors. It's a friend."

A friend whose abrupt reappearance has caught her utterly off guard.

"You can't just leave! What about the baby?" Derry screams at Linden as he slings his hastily packed bag over his shoulder.

"For God's sake, will you listen to yourself? There is no baby!" he roars.

"Yes, there is!"

She hates him. She honestly hates him, with every ounce of energy she possesses.

"You *know* there's a baby. In October, the donor is going to—"

"I don't care about October," he cuts in, fury gleaming in his eyes. "I care about now. And right now, you're out of your freakin' mind! You're obsessed with this!"

Obsessed? Because she turned down a lousy waitressing job this afternoon? A job that would have kept her on her feet for ten-hour shifts nights and weekends?

When Linden came home just now and asked—no, demanded to know—why she turned it down, she initially considered making something up. Something he would agree was understandable.

But in the end, she didn't. In the end, she told him the truth: that she turned down the job offer, her first in a month, because the manager was clearly unsympathetic to her condition.

"You don't have no condition!" Linden bellowed.

Don't have any *condition,* Derry thought silently, clenching her jaw.

"You are not even pregnant!"

"Shut up!" she hissed, casting a wary glance at the open window. "The manager thinks that I'm pregnant, and he couldn't care less. That means he won't care, either, when it comes time for me to take time off to give birth, or be with the baby."

That made perfect sense to her.

It merely convinced Linden that his wife has plunged off the deep end.

"I'm not obsessed," she says now, lowering her voice slightly in response to Mrs. Steiner's renewed pounding on the wall. "I'm just not willing to work in a place that isn't conducive to family life."

"We don't *have* a family."

"We're about to."

"You don't need time off to give birth because you're not giving birth."

"Why do you keep saying that? You're trying to hurt me."

"No, I'm saying it because it's true. And I'm starting to think that you really think you're having a baby." He leans in, eyes glittering with accusation. "I'm starting to think you're really crazy."

"Shut up!" She reaches out to shove him away, but he stands his ground like a steel pole rooted in cement.

"No, you are. You're crazy." His voice is tight with conviction. "Every day, I see you getting more and more into this thing. Every day, I tell myself that it's not right."

"What are you talking about?"

"I'm talking about *this.*" He reaches out and snatches the prosthesis from beneath her blouse, wrenching it from the belt fastenings and heaving it into her face.

That's when she really does go crazy.

She pummels Linden with her fists, calling him every heinous name she's ever heard.

He holds her off, infuriatingly, with just one strong arm, telling her that he's through. Through with her, and through with the crazy adoption plan, as he calls it. He has no interest in pretending for even a moment longer that they're expecting a child.

"You mean you're going to tell Richie, and all the guys at work, that I'm just no longer pregnant?" she asks in disbelief, tears streaming down her cheeks.

How can he betray her this way?

"Are you kidding me? I never told anyone that you were pregnant in the first place."

"Why not?"

"Because you're not. And I can't do this."

"Can't do what?" she asks, already knowing.

"I can't pretend."

"But you told Rose—"

"I know what I told Rose. But it ain't gonna happen. I changed my mind."

"But if we don't take this baby, it could die! You heard what Rose said. People like this donor, they don't care about the baby. They don't care about anything except making sure nobody knows they were ever pregnant."

"Yeah, well, I don't care about any of this right now. I just want my life back. I'm not a superman, who's gonna fly around this city saving babies from garbage cans, and neither are you."

"Oh, yes, I am," she hurtles at him. "I'm doing this whether you are or not."

"I'm not."

"Fine. Leave. I don't need you."

For a long time, he just stares at her.

Then, with sudden, chilling composure, he says, "No, you don't. You're right. You don't need me at all."

He reaches again for the doorknob.

She hurriedly straps on the prosthesis again, smoothing her shirt over it in case anybody happens to be lingering in the hallway.

She looks up to see him watching her.

To her surprise, he looks sad.

"Good-bye," he says, shaking his head.

"Where are you going? Running away to Richie's again?"

"I don't know where I'm going. All I know is that I'm not coming back. I mean it, Derry. If I walk out the door, I'm gone for good."

She glares at him.

He shrugs.

And then he walks out the door.

Seeing Peyton approaching with Gil, Tom Reilly scrambles to his feet, a bouquet of flowers in one hand and a white plastic shopping bag in the other.

The first thing that goes through his head, Peyton discerns when she's close enough to see the look on his face, is that she's been avoiding him because she's obviously involved with somebody else.

She's opening her mouth to spew the first cliché that comes to her tongue—*this isn't what it looks like*—when she sees his gaze—and then his jaw—drop.

She glances down at the blatant bulge of her midsection and then, reluctantly, back up at him. "Tom . . ."

She falters. What is there to say?

This isn't what it looks like is no longer valid.

It *is* what it looks like. From his standpoint, it's even worse.

"You're pregnant." His tone is accusatory; his expression is not. There's an oddly pensive note in his gaze, as though he's experiencing some emotion she can't quite identify.

She doesn't know what to make of it. She only knows that it isn't the anger she might expect—and that along with her own dismay and humiliation, she's experiencing an unexpected measure of relief. At least her secret is out there at last, after weeks of wondering how to tell him, trying to dodge him at every turn.

She wipes a trickle of sweat from her temple and wishes the saturated night air would give way to the predicted thunderstorms.

Anything to curtail the awkward silence.

Finally, knowing she has to say something, Peyton echoes the obvious: "I'm pregnant." Then she adds, "This is Gil. He's an old friend."

Always the gentleman, Gil sticks out his hand.

Preposterously, Tom juggles his flowers and shopping bag to shake it. "Tom Reilly."

Aren't we all just so civilized?

Peyton wearily wishes she were anywhere else.

"I didn't know," Tom says, first looking at Gil, and then at her. "About . . . this"—he motions at her stomach—"or . . . you. Two. You two."

Peyton wishes Gil would speak up and inform Tom that they aren't a couple, but he says nothing. Why would he? Of course, he's left it up to her. This, after all, is her scene. He has his own messy relationships to handle.

How tempting it is to support Tom's misconception. It would be less complicated, perhaps more merciful, to let him think there's somebody else.

But she's never been one to take the easy way out and she's not going to start now. *Especially* not now, on the verge of becoming somebody's mother.

A mother sets a good example. A mother doesn't lie.

"Gil isn't the father," she says bluntly. "He's just an old friend, like I said. From Kansas."

"So you're visiting New York?" asks Tom, who can't possibly give a damn who Gil is or where he comes from. He probably wants to get out of here as fast as he can.

He can't—won't—because he's a nice guy. A great guy. A guy who has too much class to beat a hasty retreat, let alone say whatever is on his mind. Peyton can only imagine.

"No, I live here. Are you . . . ?" Gil lets the question dangle.

"Tom and I went on a couple of dates, Gil," Peyton explains, unwilling to partake in awkward niceties. "He lives in the neighborhood. And he didn't know, obviously, about the baby." She turns to Tom and repeats, "Which isn't Gil's. He's married with kids of his own."

She can feel Gil stiffen beside her; knows that it's all he can do not to elaborate on his disrupted marital status. But this isn't the place. This has nothing to do with him, and he knows it.

Tom asks Peyton, "So you and the father are . . . ?"

Together? Apart?

He doesn't say whatever it is he means to imply, forcing Peyton to explain further. But she won't give him the whole story. The whole story is none of his business.

"The father isn't in the picture," she tells him, wishing Gil weren't standing beside her. This is a conversation she and Tom should have been having in private.

"So you're on your own?"

She nods, struggling to keep things as straightforward as possible.

Yet she's aching inside, aching for Tom to grab her and tell her it doesn't matter. That he still wants to be a part of her life.

"Why didn't you tell me?" he asks.

"Because . . ."

Because I knew you'd take off as soon as I did. And I wasn't ready to let go.

"I'm sorry," is all she can muster. "I should have."

As if spurred by the tension gripping her body, the baby abruptly shifts position within, sending a ripple of sensation across her navel.

That's right, she tells the tiny being who so depends on her, *I should have told him about you all along. I should have let him know that nothing else matters to me.*

Nothing but you.

CHAPTER TEN

"Where are you going?"

Startled, Anne Marie looks over her shoulder to see Jarrett. He's standing above her, poised halfway down the back stairs, clad in the silk boxer shorts and T-shirt he wears in lieu of pajamas on warm nights.

She removes her hand from the doorknob that leads to the garage and wishes she weren't wearing potentially incriminating black from head to toe.

"I'm running to Shoprite for milk. We need it for the boys' cereal in the morning."

Not that he'd ever know that. Not unless he's broken with his long-standing tradition of letting her handle the care and feeding of the children.

"Now? It's late." He yawns loudly.

What is he doing out of bed, anyway? He turned in a good hour ago and was asleep when she peeked into the master bedroom earlier.

"It won't take me long, Jarrett. We need milk. What am I supposed to do?"

"Why don't you wait until morning?"

"And drag the boys out with me? No, thanks," she says, knowing he'll be unwilling to offer to take a later commuter train.

No, but he is willing to offer something far more unexpected.

"I'll go get the milk."

Her jaw drops. "You will?"

He nods.

For a moment, they just stare at each other, Anne Marie in disbelief, and Jarrett with a knowing look that tells her he suspects she's up to something.

What is there to do but toss her keys aside and thank him?

Together, they retreat to the master bedroom where only his side of the California king has been disturbed.

As he dons street clothes, she takes hers off, putting on a summer nightie and stretching with an exaggerated yawn.

"Tired?" he asks.

"Exhausted." It's the truth. These last few days, these last few *weeks*, have been positively draining.

"Get some sleep. The boys will be up early in the morning. See you."

With that, he's gone.

Peering through a crack in the blinds, she waits until his car has left the driveway, and then the block.

Then she scurries downstairs to the kitchen, to pour a nearly full gallon of milk down the drain, wash out the sink, and bury the container in the garbage.

"Rita? Are you asleep?"

"Me? Sleep?" Rita says into the phone with a laugh. "I'm just sitting here watching TV. J.D. snores louder than a jackhammer. Who can get any sleep around here?"

"I figured you might be up." Peyton sounds troubled. "I wasn't going to call, but . . ."

"What's up, sugar pie? Please don't tell me you're having labor pains, because I'll have to tell you it's just gas again."

Peyton laughs. "No early labor pains this time. I swear I won't do that to you again."

"Oh, you will. And don't worry, I'm used to it. So what's going on?"

"It's just . . . I ran into Tom a little while ago, on the street. I had to tell him."

"About the baby."

"Yes."

"What did he—" Rita interrupts herself to say, "Wait a minute. You just 'ran into' him?"

"Sort of. He was actually waiting on the steps of my building when I got there."

Rita mulls that over. "That seems a little presumptuous, don't you think?"

"No, it was okay. Gil was with me. He's been asking me to go over and see his new place, so I finally went tonight."

"He's another one."

"Gil? Another what?"

"He's way too attached to you for a married man."

"He's separated."

"But not divorced."

"Tom is," Peyton says.

"Good for him." Realizing that sounds harsh, Rita checks herself, adding, "Trust me, you don't need men with baggage at a time like this. I'm saying that as your friend, not as a health practitioner."

"Well, I'm calling you as a friend, and not as a health practitioner, so I'm glad we've got that straight. But, Rita, I can't help being there for Gil. He just needs somebody to talk to right now. He's going through hell."

"A lot of people go through hell."

Peyton doesn't say anything to that. Rita knows she's thinking of Allison, clinging to the hope she's carried so valiantly since Mother's Day.

Rita should probably state the obvious here: that chances for Allison coming back to them are slim at this point. Wanda said as much earlier, when they met for lunch. She was full of information on missing-persons' cases, a wealth of discouraging statistics and percentages.

According to Wanda, with her flair for bleak irony, Allison is as likely to turn up alive and well as Wanda's married suburban boyfriend is to get a divorce, move to Manhattan, and marry her.

"Meaning," Wanda told Rita decisively, "it ain't gonna happen in this lifetime."

But then, Peyton probably knows that in her heart as well as anyone does. What harm is there in letting her cling outwardly, at least, to her optimism?

"Don't worry, Rita," she says finally. "I'm not letting any guy get too close."

Rita adapts her efficient, no-nonsense, doctor-patient demeanor. "Listen, if you could find a nice, sincere guy who would be daddy material, I'd be the first one to say go for it."

"I'm not looking for daddy material," Peyton tells her. "And if I thought Tom might be it . . . well, I didn't think that so it doesn't matter."

"What did he say when you told him?"

"I didn't tell him, exactly. He saw my stomach before I could.

He was just sitting there on the stoop, waiting for me, with flowers, and it was like he just . . . crumpled."

Rita shakes her head. "I'll bet."

"I feel so guilty. . . ."

"That's understandable, but remember that you haven't done anything wrong. You went on a few dates with the guy, and you chose not to tell him something very personal."

"Something *huge,*" Peyton amends.

"Yes, huge, but personal. Nobody can blame you for that."

"You're right. I know you're right. But I get the feeling he doesn't see it that way. The way he looked at me when he saw me with Gil . . . well, I have to admit that I was scared for a minute there."

Rita clenches the phone more tightly. "Don't make me worry about you, sugar pie."

"Maybe scared isn't the right word . . ."

"You're not thinking he's actually dangerous, are you?"

Silence.

Then an unconvincing "Of course not."

Rita asks the logical question. "Do you think there's any way he could have been the one who broke in last month?"

"I don't think so. I mean, I know deep down that it wasn't him."

"Are you sure?"

"Yes. I'm positive," she says, and Rita wonders whom she's trying to convince. "What's scaring me is that he seems more attached to me than he should be, and I . . . I was kind of starting to feel the same way about him. Seeing him again reminded me."

"Well, I think you'd better keep your distance from him, sugar pie. It's just a gut feeling, but I don't like him."

"You would if you met him. He's not a bad guy. In fact, he's a great guy."

"Sure, go and defend him now, after you get me all worked up."

Peyton laughs. "Sorry. It's just— You know how you get a feeling about somebody, even somebody you've just met? Like they're just a good person who wouldn't be capable of hurting you? That's Tom. I'm a good judge of character. I trust him."

"Don't lose your backbone, is all I'm saying."

"I won't. I promise." Peyton sighs. "Oh God, look at the time. I'm so sorry I called you so late. I guess I just had to talk it out with someone."

"That's what I'm here for. You want me to come over there?"

"No, I'll be fine. Is J.D. still snoring?"

"Are we still breathing?"

Peyton chuckles. "Go back to bed."

"Not without earplugs," Rita says on a rueful laugh before hanging up.

Stealing gingerly across the nursery in the soft glow of the night-light, a heaping basket of still-warm, freshly folded laundry in her arms, Mary Nueves is careful not to step on one of the many creaky floorboards in this old two-family house. She knows precisely which spots of the threadbare rug to avoid, having learned the hard way these last few weeks that her newborn daughter is a light sleeper.

Pacing the floor with a crying baby night after night is a small price to pay for the blessing of parenthood, she reminds herself.

It's a shame that isn't the only price she must pay.

If only she were capable of setting aside that crushing burden as easily as she rests the laundry basket on the floor beside the dresser.

But the debt she thought she'd paid in full a month ago is carried with her still, like a weight that grows heavier with every day that passes.

She should go to confession. That would help. But sometimes, she thinks her sin is so great that she can't reveal it even to Father Roberto, the trusted parish priest who smilingly blessed her growing stomach every week when she took communion.

Other times, she tells herself that it wasn't a sin at all.

Gazing at the cherished, sleeping infant in the secondhand cradle Javier so lovingly refinished, Mary tells herself that she only did what any human being with a conscience would do.

How could she leave this child's fate in the hands of the thirteen-year-old rape victim who never wanted her in the first place?

Surely Rose could have found somebody else to take her, to save her.

But you're the one she chose, Mary reminds herself, echoing the words Javier spoke earlier, when she voiced her belated contrition. *And you wanted a child so much.*

Only now, when both the fierce longing and the heady elation have subsided, is she able to question her actions.

"Dawn is ours," Javier reminded her just an hour ago, as he has with increasing frequency as his wife's remorse grows with every passing day. "We have the birth certificate to prove it. It's legal. You heard what Rose said. Nobody can possibly question it. And why would they, anyway? The whole neighborhood, the whole world, saw you pregnant."

Yes. The whole neighborhood, the whole world, saw the lie she lived for almost nine months. The lie she agreed to only after that first Cradle to Cradle adoption fell through, when the birth mother—or rather, the *donor*—unexpectedly changed her mind.

Not about giving up the baby. Merely, as Rose put it so delicately on that awful day, about Mary and Javier's suitability.

They had been through so many miscarriages by then, so many false starts and lost opportunities.

She couldn't bear to give up on the dream now that Cradle to Cradle had rescued them. It all fell into place so easily, from the moment Mary impulsively answered the letter that came in the mail. Junk mail—that was her first impression. Thank goodness she got past it. Thank goodness she called, and met Rose.

Miraculously, within weeks of submitting their paperwork, Mary and Javier found themselves chosen as adoptive parents by that teenager in Idaho. It was too good to be true. Even the fee was an amount they could afford, an amount that could be paid over time without hardship.

It was as though it was meant to be.

So when Rose broke the news a month later, about the donor changing her mind, they found themselves facing a more shattering blow than ever before. It seemed as if their lives were over . . . until Rose told them about this opportunity.

It was their last chance for parenthood.

They knew it, and Rose acknowledged as much, when pressed.

Otherwise, Mary would never have agreed to the charade.

Now, she tells herself, staring down at her precious child, *you have no choice but to live with what you did.*

You'll have to suffer the consequences . . . and be grateful that this terrible guilt is the worst of it.

"Derry? I just got your message. What is it? What's wrong?"

The sound of Rose's familiar voice is as reassuring as the obvious concern that emanates over the telephone line.

I'm not as alone as I feel. Not really.

Rose cares about me. And she'll see to it that I get this baby, no matter what. Then I'll never be alone again.

Clutching the phone tightly against her ear, Derry allows herself to exhale, telling herself, for perhaps the hundredth time in the past hour since Linden left, that everything is going to be okay.

Yet even as she thinks it, a tide of heartbreak rushes through her to sweep away her voice, her composure, every bit of hard-won confidence in her soul.

She loved him. He was her entire world.

What is she going to do? How will she survive?

Thankfully Rose is silent, waiting patiently, as if sensing Derry's crisis.

"It's Linden," she says in a small voice when at last she can speak. "He's . . ."

"What?" Rose persists gently when she trails off. "Did something happen to him?"

Yes. He turned into an absolute bastard. That's what happened to him.

"He moved out," she tells Rose reluctantly, wishing that with the revelation she could put behind her the anguish of their final fight.

The one that sent him out the door.

Not for the night.

Forever.

That's what he said and she knows in her heart, in her gut, that it's true.

Their marriage is over. All she has now is the baby.

He told her that was the only thing she really wanted anyway, but he was wrong.

She wanted to be a family. She just lost sight of her husband's role in the struggle toward that goal.

"He moved out?" Rose is echoing in disbelief as Derry wipes away the fresh tears that sting her swollen eyes. "What happened?"

"Things have been bad for a long time. We're splitting up. It's better this way, though," she says, sniffling. "He didn't really want the baby. Not like I did."

Rose is silent. Ominously so, Derry realizes.

"This won't change anything, will it?" she beseeches the woman in near desperation. "I mean, this girl—the donor—she has to know that one parent is better than none."

"I would think so," Rose agrees after a pause. "But—"

"No, Rose, don't say it. Please just say she'll still let me have the baby. Please. That's all I have left and we've come so far. Everybody knows that I'm pregnant. They're all expecting me to have a baby. I can't suddenly undo everything, take it all back, say that I wasn't really pregnant after all."

"No," Rose agrees again, after another brief hesitation. "You can't."

"Please talk to the donor for me. Can you? Can you convince her that we have to go through with this?"

Derry holds her breath, sensing that everything is hanging in the balance now, waiting for the verdict. She thrusts a fingertip into her mouth, and then another, and another, searching for a ragged edge to chew, finding nothing but raw nubs.

"I think it's time that you met her yourself," Rose tells her at last.

"When?"

"As soon as possible. I'm sure that if she hears your story firsthand she'll be more apt to agree that you can handle this as a single mother."

"Just name the time and place and I'll be there," Derry says in sheer relief, hugging the rubber mold close.

"All right. But, Derry . . . ?"

"Yes?"

"Please don't say a word about this to anybody. Not even Linden."

"Linden and I aren't speaking," Derry reminds her, wondering why Rose sounds so adamant. Of course Linden is already aware of the pregnancy charade in the first place. Did Rose forget somehow that she was the one who convinced him to go through with it?

"I realize that, but if you by any chance see him again before we meet the donor, don't say a word about it. I mean it, Derry, this has to be absolutely confidential from here on in—between you, and me, and the donor. Do you understand?"

"Of course," Derry promises. "I won't tell anyone."

". . . and the progeny of an unlawful bed will disappear . . ."

Suddenly hearing Jarrett coming up the stairs, Anne Marie shoves the red leather Bible and envelope back into her bureau drawer and slips swiftly and silently into bed.

Heart pounding, pulse racing, she pulls up the duvet on her side, hoping to duplicate her usual even-breathing huddled sleep posture before he arrives in the room.

To her relief—and surprise—she hears him pause on his way down the hall to look in on the slumbering triplets, just as she did mere minutes ago. Jarrett stays in the nursery just briefly, presumably tucking them in more securely, but the unexpected paternal gesture fills Anne Marie with unaccustomed remorse.

He's not all bad. In fact, he's *not* bad, at all. He loves their children. Perhaps not as fiercely as she does, but then, her motivation is unique.

If he ever knew . . .

She quells the thought that's flitted through her mind countless times lately.

He doesn't know. He'll never know, unless she tells him.

And why would she do that?

Because you can't keep this up much longer, she acknowledges wearily, closing her eyes, pretending to be sound asleep as he comes into the room.

Because sooner or later, you might just crack . . . and confess.

If Jarrett hadn't come down earlier and found her before she left, she'd have stolen off into the night without thinking of the consequences, just as she did before. She'd have driven two hours on a useless, impulsive mission borne of this obsession that's taken over her life.

What if she hadn't been so lucky this time? What if she'd been caught, prowling around a stranger's home? What if she'd had an accident, speeding along the highway to get back home before dawn?

What was she thinking?

She *wasn't* thinking.

She was *feeling.*

Maybe it's about damned time she traded an anesthetized existence for a confrontational one. It's about damned time she found him, called him. It's about damned time she decided to seek closure.

But for now, closure will have to wait.

She hears Jarrett tiptoeing across the floor, pausing at the upholstered bench by the bureau, where he tossed his discarded boxers and T-shirt earlier.

Only when she realizes that he hasn't yet put them on does she surreptitiously open her eyes.

She finds her husband standing absolutely still, looking into the top drawer of the bureau, left inadvertently ajar in her haste to cast aside the incriminating evidence: the Bible and the manila envelope.

* * *

Well. Talk about an unexpected turnoff in a well-mapped road.

Not that this is entirely unwelcome.

She wasn't the right choice from the start. Though she technically fit all the requirements, there was always something vaguely impetuous about her.

Now she's gone too far. There is simply no room in the meticulous plan for a loose cannon.

Something must be done.

And it can't wait until tomorrow, or next week, or next month.

No, she'll have to be dealt with tonight.

"I'm coming over," Tom Reilly informs Peyton the instant she picks up the telephone. "In two minutes. I'll be right there."

"But—"

Her protest is met by a dial tone.

He's coming over?

There's nothing to do but cast aside her summer pajamas, hurriedly throw on a T-shirt and shorts, comb her bed-rumpled hair, brush her teeth, and wonder why he can't just leave it alone.

She honestly assumed whatever it was that they had ended when she bade him a firm and final good night outside, after Gil tactfully hopped into a passing cab, leaving the two of them alone on the stoop.

"I need to talk to you," Tom said even then, before and after her goodnight, but Peyton brushed him off, escaping into her building to call Rita.

Now he's coming over.

She can always just not let him into the building when he buzzes from the door outside.

But that isn't her style. She isn't a person who ducks confrontation.

Oh yeah? What about avoiding all his phone calls until now?

And, aside from Tom, what about not telling Tara you're pregnant?

The truth is, she's becoming a wimp, and she doesn't like it. She's let Allison's disappearance and her own break-in unnerve her to the point where she's no longer capable of handling her own problems.

The old Peyton Somerset would face Tom head-on, listen to what he has to say, and stand up for herself.

"Wimp," she accuses, glaring into the bathroom mirror. "What's happened to you?"

He probably wants to tell you off because you led him on, she informs her infuriatingly anxious-looking reflection. *Or maybe he's just curious and wants to know who the baby's father is.*

She can handle that. She can at least listen. She can at least talk to him.

Feeling reassuringly decisive, infinitely more like her usual self, she splashes cold water on her face. If only she could somehow wash away the purplish trenches beneath her sleep-deprived eyes.

Yes, she can talk to him . . . but what can she say?

Maybe she should actually come right out and explain the circumstances of her pregnancy. Maybe she owes him the truth because . . . because . . .

Because she cares about him. There. She'll admit it, if only to herself.

Certainly not to Rita. Peyton felt her friend's disapproval for Tom, and she knows Rita has her best interests in mind. That's why she called her. Because she needed a sounding board, a voice of reason.

All her life, though, she has relied on her own instincts. She's never needed anybody else's input. Why now?

Because this pregnancy has wreaked havoc on her chemistry, her emotions. How can she trust herself when she frequently feels like an outsider in her own body?

It's been five months now. She should be used to it. She should make an effort to go back to listening to what *she* wants, what *she* needs.

Beginning tonight. Right now.

All right, then, Peyton. What do you *want?*

I want to see Tom again.

Yes. She's glad he's coming over . . . even if it's only to have the final word.

The playground, jam-packed with romping children every single day, is virtually deserted at this late hour on a weeknight, just as Derry expected. The only person she passed on the way to this part of the park was a homeless man collecting discarded cans from a trash bin.

She figures that's why Rose selected this remote corner as a meeting spot, knowing the pregnant teen would be skittish.

But couldn't they have waited at least until daylight?

Derry looks over her shoulder as she takes a seat on the designated bench right on the edge of the pond, where little boys sail remote-operated boats on beautiful summer afternoons.

She can't help feeling a little spooked. It's easy to imagine danger lurking in the underbrush a few feet away from the bench; easy to imagine that she hears something rustling the branches.

She slaps at a mosquito that rises from the murky water to buzz around her sweat-sticky neck, manages to find a sliver of fingernail to gnaw, and wishes Rose would hurry.

The evening's oppressive humidity threatens to give way to a thundershower any second now. There's an ominous rumble in the distance, and heat lightning flashes are coming more frequently above the skyline in the western sky.

Derry would hate to be caught out here alone in a storm.

If Rose and the girl would show up, the three of them could go some place to talk. Even back to Derry's apartment, which is what she should have insisted upon in the first place.

But when Rose called to hastily present this last-minute plan, she agreed.

What else could she do?

Rose is calling all the shots, clearly, from here on in.

And with Linden gone now, Derry reminds herself grimly, *this is definitely my last chance for—*

Her final thought is forever incomplete as, with a single, shattering blow from behind, her world goes blacker than the night sky.

"Here." Still in the gray shorts and navy T-shirt he had on earlier, Tom thrusts the familiar white plastic shopping bag and flowers into Peyton's arms. "These are for you."

"But—"

"Please take them," he urges. "I want you to have them."

What is there to do but accept? She peers into the bag, sees a clear plastic deli container filled with watermelon chunks, and looks up at him, not sure how to react.

She's afraid that if she tries to speak, she might cry. And she never allows herself to cry in front of anybody. Not even over Allison.

"It's almost in season," he says with a shrug. "I thought you might like it."

"Thanks," she murmurs, setting both the bag and the flowers on the counter of the kitchenette. Riddled with unaccustomed uncertainty, she wonders if she should put the melon into the refrigerator and the flowers in a vase. The gestures seem somehow inappropriate, in light of the grave undercurrent in the room.

"This is just how I pictured it," he comments, and she turns to see him looking around, walking around, seemingly inspecting the place. "Crown moldings and all."

She nods again, wishing she could find her voice, and something worthwhile to say.

"Are you going to stay here when the baby comes?" he asks unexpectedly. "I mean . . . do you have room?"

"Yes."

He looks as though he's waiting for her to elaborate.

What else can she possibly tell him? That she'll buy a cradle, then a crib, then a toddler bed, and keep them beside her in the apartment's lone bedroom? That someday, with luck, she'll be able to afford a bigger place, and private school, and all that lies ahead?

"There's something you should know." Tom sits, uninvited, on her couch. He pats the cushion beside him. "Come sit with me. Okay?"

She does. Her pregnancy-enhanced senses drink in the familiar smell of him. Not cologne, exactly, but the clean, woodsy scent of soap or shampoo, a scent that is uniquely his . . . a scent she realizes she's been subconsciously craving for weeks.

"You should know why my marriage ended," he tells her.

She throws up her hands, instinctively fending off an unwelcome onslaught of information.

He captures her hands gently in his, squeezing them. "Look, I wouldn't be telling you this if it wasn't relevant."

"None of this is relevant," she tells him, but she doesn't sound convincing, even to her own ears.

"My wife didn't want kids, Peyton. I love them. It's that simple."

Peyton merely gapes at him, pretending to wonder what that has to do with anything.

"I should have known from the start. But I was crazy about her. Or maybe just crazy." He gives a humorless laugh.

She should slip her hands out of his, but she can't seem to bring herself to pull away. It's been so long since she's had human contact like this.

But it isn't just that. It's *him.* She's drawn to him. She can't help it.

"Amy was never good with my nieces and nephews—I have eleven of them—but I thought she'd change," Tom goes on. "All my friends kept telling me her biological clock would start ticking eventually, and she'd want a baby after all. Of course that didn't happen. People don't change."

"No, they don't." Peyton thinks of Jeff, and Scott, even Gil. Of the reasons none of them is right for her.

But Tom isn't, either, she reminds herself. He could have been, if things were different. . . .

"Why are you telling me this?" she asks abruptly, pulling her hands from his grasp at last.

He takes a deep breath. "I know this sounds corny. I can't even believe I'm telling you this. But I felt something for you from the first time I saw you that day in the park, even before we ever met. I took one look at you and it was like I knew there was going to be something—"

"In the park?" she cuts in, her mind reeling. "We didn't meet in the park. We met in the Korean grocery. Remember? On Saint Patrick's Day."

"But that wasn't the first time I saw you," he says without flinching. "I noticed you around the neighborhood before. I even knew where you lived. I saw you coming out of this building a couple of times. Once you must have been Christmas shopping . . . you had all these bags and it was snowing and I kept thinking I should run up and help you open the door . . . but I didn't."

Oh God. She remembers that day. Remembers her weighted arms, and blowing snow, and being in a festive, carefree mood anyway. Carefree . . . and blissfully unaware that she was being watched.

Unsettling as that realization may be, Peyton can't deny that she still feels something for Tom.

Nor can she help asking, "Why didn't you? Help me, I mean."

"I just never got up the courage to go up and start talking to you out of the blue. Don't get me wrong—I'm not the kind of guy who has a problem talking to women. But there was something . . . I don't know . . . different about you. You just struck me as sophisticated, and independent, and I guess I didn't think you'd be interested. Until that night I saw you in the Korean grocery."

The night she fell apart because she didn't have enough money to indulge her watermelon craving.

So what he's saying is that he glimpsed her vulnerability, and he took advantage of it?

"I figured it was fate that we were both there at that hour. Like fate throwing you right in my path, saying, 'go ahead and do it already! Talk to her!' So I did. But you thought I was a lunatic preying on innocent women," he goes on with a grin.

"No, I didn't. Wait . . . were you in Tequila Moon one afternoon, watching me?" she demands suddenly, remembering. "After that night?"

He averts his gaze. "Probably."

A chill slips down her spine.

"Oh, hell," he says abruptly, looking up at her. "Yes, I was there. It's one of my favorite restaurants. I saw you, and I was going to come over. I kept trying to catch your eye, but you were busy with your friend, so—"

"Allison," she tells him. "She's the one who—"

"Disappeared? I've been wondering about her." He's holding her hands again, without her even realizing it until his fingers are wrapped comfortingly around hers. "I've been trying to reach you, to see how you are, and if you'd heard anything. I kept leaving messages, but . . . you never called me back."

"No," she agrees, looking him in the eye. "I never called you back."

"You're probably wondering why I can't take a hint, huh?"

She smiles faintly. "Probably."

"I figured you'd lost interest, but there was this part of me that thought I should give it one more shot. That's why I hung out tonight, waiting, hoping I'd see you. And I did."

"You sure did." She slides a glance down at her protruding stomach, knowing what a shock that must have been.

"Well, at least now I know why you were avoiding me," he says, following her gaze. "But when I got home and thought it through . . . about what you said about the baby's father . . . well,

I couldn't go to sleep tonight without letting you know that I'm game to go forward. If you are."

"Go . . . forward?"

"I love kids," he says simply.

Maybe it's only because she feels so damned defenseless now, after everything that's happened . . .

But it doesn't matter why. She only knows that he's reaching out, and she doesn't want to push him away.

You don't want to . . . but you have to. You have to be strong.

She shakes her head, pulling her hands away from his and clenching them in her lap. "I can't do this now, Tom. There's just too much that I have to—I can't be in a relationship."

She doesn't dare look at him.

Just leave me alone, she beseeches silently, waiting for his response. *Can't you see that I'm overwhelmed? Can't you see that this isn't the right timing?*

"I understand why you can't be in a relationship," he says at last. "But can you have a friend? Because that's fine with me, too. I just want to be in your life. I care about you. I want to help you. I can be your friend. Like Gil."

Startled that he somehow remembered the name, she looks up to see if he's being sarcastic.

But all she finds is a smile so warmly genuine that she can't say no.

"Sure," Peyton tells him, knowing Rita is absolutely going to kill her when she hears about this, "you can be my friend."

The storm has passed. For now.

Thunder rumbles as the clouds roll to the east, carrying the violent weather away.

A night bird calls in the distance and is answered by its mate. Crickets have begun to chirp once again; mosquitos rise once more from the swampy edge of the pond to buzz annoyingly in their thirst for human blood, oblivious of the feast they might have had minutes ago.

Stupid creatures.

Stupid, stupid girl.

Did she truly think she was deserved a precious, innocent baby *now?*

Did she honestly believe she was capable of raising a child

single-handedly while picking up the pieces of her shattered marriage?

It no longer matters what Derry Cordell believed.

The height of the storm lasted no more than five minutes—just long enough to provide protective noise and screening for the completion of the macabre task, should anyone have happened along.

Nobody did. Of course not. The playground is deserted at midnight, especially in weather like this.

It's time to go home, with a quick stop in Co-op City along the way, just to make sure there are no traces. Derry's keys were retrieved as a brilliant afterthought, along with her identification. Even if she's eventually found, nobody will realize who she is for a long, long time . . . if ever.

Rhiannon.

It's like our own special code word. . . . We use it for everything. At least, I still do.

With luck, Derry used it as the password to her computer screen name.

Time to go find out.

A gentle rain is falling now, washing away any traces of blood and brain matter that exploded from the axe-inflicted gaping skull wound.

Dewy droplets patter softly onto the cedar chips beneath the playground equipment and plop into the pond, radiating small rings across the black surface wherever they land.

In time, the expanding circles will meet the deeper ripples that still emanate from the depths of the pond, where the concrete-weighted tarp carried its human remains to rest in a turbid grave.

Month Six

July

CHAPTER ELEVEN

The building on a narrow side street east of Little Italy is as dilapidated as they come: crumbling concrete steps, broken security buzzer, cracked windowpanes. The smell of old boiled vegetables, cooking grease, and body fluids permeates the vestibule.

It was ostensibly built as a tenement before the turn of the century, and hasn't changed drastically since. This isn't a place anybody in their right mind would want to live, but of course, the people who live here have little choice. They're grateful to have a roof over their heads, the chance to work for a living, the opportunity for their children to get an education and make something of themselves someday.

If they have children.

Those who don't—because they can't—have no hope of changing their childless state. Fancy fertility specialists are out of the question for the uninsured; adoption is well out of their reach.

Somebody has to help people like Hamal Khatir and his wife Khadijah realize their dream.

Somebody has to give these otherwise worthy people the precious gift too many take for granted, and don't deserve.

Somebody will.

Even if this is the last thing I feel capable of doing after what happened last night.

But there was no choice about that. It had to be done.

In some ways, it was far easier than snuffing out the lives of women who realize exactly what's happening to them; women who are still in their prime; women who fight back. Women who don't even have the promise of eternal salvation to carry them through the final bitter struggle to live on after having given life.

In many ways, though, this was far, far more difficult. There was no struggle. It was over swiftly, silently. A noble human life, snuffed out in an instant.

But it must be seen, quite simply, as yet another unexpected obstacle, another unexpected person who had to be eliminated. Any other viewpoint only perpetuates a frightening sense that this is uncharted territory, that things are careening out of control.

Did you get carried away, so caught up in doing good that you forgot to tread carefully?

Are too many people now involved? Would it have been better to see through one complete cycle at a time, rather than simultaneously dealing with two donors?

Perhaps.

Perhaps the mistake was in playing the game too close to home, as well as trying to juggle so many lives all at once.

And now you've gone and ended one that was purely devoted to goodness and God.

Surely one who lived such a long and exemplary life welcomed a fast, painless death and the prospect of a glorious afterlife. In some ways, maybe it was a blessing bestowed upon the most worthy person of all.

Yes, and in other ways, it was cold-blooded murder.

But dwelling on that won't help, nor will it change anything.

It's over. Nobody will ever know.

And the first donor has also been eliminated, the baby safely placed in her new mother's arms.

Mary and Javier Nueves will be good parents.

It's time now to attend to the urgent business at hand, to designate another deserving pair of recipients.

The apartment is on the third floor, at the end of an unlit hallway. Here, there is no hint of the warm morning sun that shines just beyond these walls. It might as well be the dead of night, but for the cacophony of domestic life that emanates from every door along the way: children playing, adults arguing, televisions blasting, babies crying.

The Khatirs' door opens on the first knock. The couple stand together to greet their anticipated guest. The man's gaze is blatantly hopeful; the woman's is averted, yet her wringing hands betray her fervent aspirations.

"Come in, Mrs. Calabrone." Hamal Khatir graciously opens

the door wide for the stranger who holds his future in her hands, the stranger who miraculously promised a newborn infant by early October.

"You're measuring exactly right for thirty weeks," Dr. Lombardo tells Peyton, removing his latex gloves with two snaps. "How are you feeling?"

"Hungry."

"Well, that's a good sign." Still seated, he rolls his stool up to the head of the examining table. "Most women do have a hearty appetite at this stage of the game."

"I'm kind of hungry myself. Do you want me to order Chinese food?" Nancy asks dryly, accepting the clipboard the doctor hands her.

"Chinese food? At this hour of the morning? God, no." Peyton cringes. "I guess Rita didn't tell you that's my latest aversion."

"No, she must have forgotten to mention that. Sorry. She did say that you're having leg cramps, though. Perfectly normal. Right, Doctor?" Nancy asks belatedly.

"Glad to know I'm still in charge," he says, clearing his throat. "Yes, leg cramps at this stage are perfectly normal, *Doctor.* I mean, *Nurse.*"

He isn't entirely teasing.

And this isn't the first time Peyton has noticed that he isn't always thrilled with Nancy's chummy, take-charge attitude. Clearly, the obstetrician is the boss, and he wants that to be abundantly clear not just to his patients, but to his longtime nurse.

"Trust me, Peyton, if anybody knows his stuff, it's Dr. Lombardo," Nancy says in obvious response. "He's the best in the business, hands-down."

Good save, Peyton thinks, amused by the nurse's quick effort to stroke her boss's ego.

"Any questions?" he asks Peyton, who turns her attention back to him and finds herself making an immediate effort not to find his dark eyes positively mesmerizing.

"Just one that I can think of. Do you think I'm having a boy or a girl?"

"I *know* you are."

It takes her a moment to get the joke. "Oh!" She laughs. Good looks, tender bedside manner, and a sense of humor to boot. Maybe she should have him deliver the baby after all.

But then, Rita is just as proficient. More so, perhaps, as a woman and mother. And she's become a friend.

I'll stick with her, Peyton concludes.

"Let's see . . ." Dr. Lombardo has taken her chart back from Nancy and is flipping through it. "We did an ultrasound back in April."

"Right. It was too early to tell."

He nods. "I'll try to find a reason to schedule another one at your next appointment, but I should tell you insurance companies frown on our ordering unnecessary testing."

"So I guess they think gender-determination is unnecessary."

"Pretty much," he agrees. "But with luck, we'll come up with some not too serious reason to do the test and be able to tell you if you've got a little Joey or Josephine in there."

Peyton wants to tell him not to bother. There's something vaguely—all right, boldly—unethical about creating a mythical symptom to justify a test. Her level of respect for Dr. Lombardo has just gone down a few notches.

But before she can speak up, Nancy is saying, "Just think of all the pink or blue you'll be able to go out and buy after the ultrasound!"

"As long as you know that even if we give you the likely gender, the test isn't definitive like an amnio would have been," Dr. Lombardo injects.

"I know." Peyton still has no regrets about not having the invasive amniocentesis he suggested way back in her first trimester. If she ever lost the baby, she . . . well, she just couldn't go on. An icy fist of dread constricts her heart at the mere thought of miscarriage.

"I can understand your wanting to know what you're having." Dr. Lombardo smiles that empathetic smile of his, the one that makes Peyton feel as though he's somehow been in her shoes. "The majority of my patients choose to try and find out. But you'll be pleased with a healthy baby, no matter what it is. Right?"

"Of course!"

"Just making sure. Some women I see have their hearts set on one or the other."

Peyton thinks of Wanda, who desperately wants a girl. But of course that can be attributed to the baby's father, who already has sons of his own.

"Have you signed up for a childbirth education class yet?" Dr. Lombardo is asking. "And did you designate a labor coach?"

A labor coach.

Allison.

Even now, it stings.

"I'm going to have Rita do the delivery at home," she reminds him. "As long as there are still no potential complications by that time."

"We hope there won't be, but I'll be standing by. And you should still have a labor coach in attendance."

Peyton nods. She knew this was coming eventually, but she can't bring herself to replace Allison yet. Anyway, whom would she choose? Whom would she want at her side during the most intimate, meaningful moments of her life?

Mary hands over her gurgling baby girl to Javier, who manages to smile down at Dawn even as he tells his wife, "I can't believe you're doing this."

"I have to." Mary picks up her good black purse, the one she carries to church on Sundays and to her weekly confession. "I've been telling you for days now that I have to do this, and that I'm doing this today."

Javier looks away in stone-faced silence.

"You know Father Roberto is the only person I would ever dare to tell, Javier."

"I know that, but . . . why do you have to tell anyone at all?"

"This isn't telling. It's confessing. He's the only person I would trust with something like this. You know that."

"He might go to the police."

"He can't," Mary reminds him with a certainty she doesn't feel. "Priests aren't allowed to—"

"He might convince you to go to the police, then."

"He'll guide me, Javier. He can guide us both. Why can't you see that?"

"Why can't you see what you're doing to us? We have everything we ever wanted, Mary. And now you're going to throw it all away. Please don't do this."

For a long moment, they stare at each other.

Then she tucks her black purse under her arm and walks unsteadily toward the door.

Well aware that Dr. Lombardo is still waiting for an answer to his question about a labor coach, Peyton finds her thoughts careening down a too-familiar path, one that meanders maddeningly to no clear destination.

Beth Somerset would be the logical choice, if she weren't terrified of flying. Peyton's mother has never been on a plane in her life. She did halfheartedly offer to take a train up to New York when the baby comes.

She was relieved when Peyton told her there were no direct rail routes to the city from Kansas, that such a trip would probably take days and cost a small fortune.

"I'll bring the baby down to visit as soon as it's safe to travel, Mom," she promised.

So her mother is out as a labor coach, as are her friends at work. Though everyone but Tara has been vocally supportive, Peyton has no desire to blur the line between her personal and professional lives.

That leaves her friends from the support group—of whom petulant Tisha is out of the question, and Wanda is the closest. But her due date is in a few weeks. By the time Peyton reaches hers in October, Wanda will be far too busy with her own baby to drop everything and rush to assist in childbirth.

"I'll find somebody to ask," she assures Dr. Lombardo.

But there's nobody to ask.

Nobody except perhaps Gil.

Or Tom.

Gil would do it in a heartbeat. And he's been through the delivery room experience twice before.

Tom never has, but he's offered, more than once, to be with her when the time comes.

"I'd be happy to do it if you need me," Nancy reminds her now. She, too, has offered before.

"Thanks, that's sweet of you," she murmurs. "I'll keep that in mind."

Peyton can't help but feel as though the person she chooses should be somebody very close. Somebody she trusts implicitly to be there for her, no matter what.

Somebody like . . .

Tom.

But asking him to be her labor coach might lead him on to think that they have some kind of future together.

The telephone extension on the wall behind the doctor rings suddenly.

"Excuse me," he says to Peyton, and reaches up to answer it.

"I'm meeting Rita for an early lunch in an hour," Nancy says, leaning chummily against the examining table. "Do you want to stick around and come with us? We're just going over to the diner on Forty-second. It's fast and cheap."

"I'd love to, but I really can't. I've got to get back to the office. Tell Rita I said hi, though."

"I'm sure she'd love to see you in person."

"I'm actually meeting her for a movie later, so . . ."

"You are? She didn't mention it. Maybe I'll tag along."

Peyton merely nods awkwardly, wishing she hadn't said anything. She gets the impression from Rita that Nancy can be a bit pushy.

"I mean, I love her to death," Rita has said, "but she's got a way of working her way in wherever you least expect it."

Hanging up the phone, Dr. Lombardo informs Nancy, "There's a patient's husband in the waiting room. He wants to talk to both of us after we're through here."

"No appointment?"

"No. He just walked in. He said it's important. I'm sorry, where were we?" he asks Peyton distractedly, rolling back over on the stool. "Did you have any more questions?"

Relieved to have the labor coach topic dropped for today, she shakes her head. "No, I think I'm all set for now."

"Great." He flashes a brief, but genuine, smile. "Go ahead and get dressed then, and we'll see you in a month. After that, it'll be every two weeks, and then every week of the final month. Sound good?"

"Sounds good." Peyton sits up and swings her bare legs over the table in the direction of the adjacent dressing room where her clothes and bag are stashed.

"See you later," Nancy whispers, and gives a little wave.

She follows Dr. Lombardo, who is striding out of the room, and asks, "What's the name of the patient whose husband is here to see us?"

In the last moment before the door closes behind them, Peyton hears the inconsequential answer.

"It's Cordell. Derry Cordell."

The biggest—perhaps only—drawback to living in Bedford, Anne Marie decides as she climbs back into her Mercedes in the post office parking lot, is that there are no working pay phones.

It isn't something she noticed until this sun-splashed July morning. But she's just spent the last half hour driving around the local business districts in search of one, to no avail.

That's because everybody in town, even the kids, presumably has a cell phone of their own.

One might also assume that everybody in the metropolitan area also has access to caller ID.

Which is why a pay telephone—and anonymity—is crucial for the calls Anne Marie is about to make. Even now, she isn't sure which call she'll place first, or what she's going to say—or if she'll manage to say anything at all. If she can't bring herself to speak, it's good to know she'll be able to hang up and go back to her life once and for all, without leaving a trail.

But if she makes this connection, opens this next door, and the one after that . . . well, who knows what she'll discover?

The calls, both of them, are a long time coming. And she's finally ready; as ready as she'll ever be.

The boys are safely ensconced in her friend Karen's vast basement recreation room, thrilled at this unexpected play date with her twin daughters.

"Take your time," Karen told Anne Marie when she dropped them off. "I hope it's not too painful."

She of course was referring to the emergency dental work Anne Marie claimed to be having this morning.

"Oh, it'll be painful," Anne Marie responded somberly, not talking about the mythical dental work at all.

But she has to do this. It's the next logical step. She can't go on indefinitely the way she has been. Now that Jarrett knows . . .

Not, of course, the whole story. He only knows the details she was forced to confess the night he found the Bible in her drawer.

She initially tried to pass it off as insignificant, but he's no fool. He somehow sensed something was going on.

He even had the audacity to accuse her of having an affair.

That was when she told him the truth.

The partial truth, anyway. He found the Bible, but not the envelope.

His reaction wasn't what she expected. He was shocked, of course—but also showed a compassionate side she's never really seen before.

Maybe because she wasn't looking. Maybe because it's just far less complicated for her to see in him only what she wants to see.

Steering down Railroad Avenue, she tells herself that if she doesn't find what she's looking for here, she'll return to Karen's to get the boys, and call it a day.

Already thinking ahead, she reminds herself to feign tremendous pain in her mouth when she gets there. That will be a good excuse not to stick around and chat over coffee or lunch.

"We haven't had a chance to sit down and catch up lately," Karen said in her sweet southern drawl when Anne Marie called this morning to beg the favor.

"I know, and we'll have to do that soon," Anne Marie promised her friend.

Just as soon as I take care of business.

Business that a sheltered former debutante like Karen could never comprehend.

Pulling into the train parking lot, Anne Marie widens her eyes.

Mission accomplished.

She parks, locks the car, and walks slowly toward the pay telephone, steeling herself for whatever lies ahead.

Never before has such a thing happened.

Well, you should have known. You took on too much at once, and the result was carelessness.

Never before has an infertile, impoverished couple turned down the opportunity to receive the precious gift of parenthood.

What did you expect? You skipped the most important step in the process.

Ah yes. It is perhaps the most clever element in a flawless plan, the phase that allowed it to unfold in the past without a hitch.

A pregnant midwestern teen suddenly changes her mind about the clients' suitability, instantly transforming their newfound, elated certainty into crushing disillusionment. A deliberate deception, yes, but psychologically brilliant, and of course it's for the couples' own good.

But this time, there was no midwestern teen who selected the couple's profile from among dozens of others. This time, there was only a bizarre proposition that would challenge any upstanding recipient's moral fiber, coming directly on the heels of a seemingly miraculous offer out of the blue.

Is it any wonder Hamal and Khadijah Khatir said no?

If they had been painstakingly baited and hooked as all the others have been, this wouldn't have happened. They'd have been reeled in slowly, then, with exquisite timing, abruptly released—

only to have another tantalizing lure immediately dangled before them. They'd have seized that with the same fervent hunger as the others, willing to do anything to avoid being cast back.

But there simply wasn't time, and there was all the distraction, the unexpected necessity of removing three additional obstacles. . . .

Of course, with the first—with Derry Cordell's unexpected demise—the key element was eliminated. Suddenly, there was no visibly pregnant mother waiting in the wings.

It was a mistake to attempt to replace her when there was simply no time to properly execute the plan.

Well, you live and learn.

You take things one step at a time.

And it's better to operate the plan with donors chosen randomly, from a distance, women with whom one is not required to interact on a regular basis. While the proximity to their lives is tantalizing and at times beneficial, it's too difficult to keep up this exhausting facade for months on end.

So what now?

Peyton Somerset will be preparing to give birth in a matter of weeks. That doesn't leave much time to find a suitable set of loving parents.

But the spark of an idea—a provocative, daring idea—has already begun to take shape. . . .

See Me.

With a scowl, Peyton rips the yellow Post-it with its bloodred lettering off her computer screen.

Leave it to Tara to show up in her office looking for her the moment she left her desk to make one of her increasingly frequent runs to the ladies' room.

Oh well. At least Tara doesn't realize she came in an hour and fifteen minutes late this morning because of her appointment with Dr. Lombardo. Thanks to Candace's access to Tara's daily calendar, Peyton knew her boss had a breakfast meeting downtown today. That's why she scheduled the appointment when she did.

At least Tara's secretary is sympathetic to Peyton's situation. Candace is even making a quilt for the baby. She works on it at her desk whenever Tara is away on business trips.

Today, of course, as Peyton approaches the secretaries' bay on her way to Tara's office, the quilt squares are nowhere in sight. Candace is busily typing, but looks up when she sees Peyton.

"How'd the doctor's appointment go?" she whispers. "Did you find out what you're having?"

Peyton smiles, touched by the girl's interest. "Not yet. Maybe next month."

"Well, the background is yellow, like I told you, but I'm putting both pink and blue diamonds into the pattern," she says. "That way, it'll work for either a boy or a girl. I want it to be done soon in case you have the baby early."

"Don't say that!" Peyton exclaims, clasping her stomach as if to keep the baby from going anywhere any time soon.

"Don't say what?" a voice asks.

She turns to see Tara standing in the doorway of her office, eavesdropping.

Might as well put an end to this ridiculous game, Peyton thinks wearily, lifting her chin.

"Candace just mentioned something about my having the baby early, and I told her not to say that. I'm not due until October," she adds, figuring Tara has probably been wondering.

Or maybe not.

Maybe she truly doesn't give a damn.

"October? That could be a problem. Come in and sit down, Peyton."

Here we go, she thinks, following her boss into the corner office.

Tara closes the door behind them, never a good sign.

They take their seats facing each other, the broad mahogany desk lying between them like a battlefield.

"I had asked you to come in here and see me because I need you to do some traveling in the near future for the new product launch," Tara crisply informs her.

Peyton's heart sinks. "When, exactly?"

"I don't know exactly. Over the next month or two."

Surely Dr. Lombardo wouldn't object to a short plane trip or two in her third trimester, even though the pamphlet he gave her back in the beginning said to stay close to home by that stage.

"Where would I need to go?" Peyton asks reluctantly.

"On location for the commercial shoot," is the somewhat reassuring reply.

Until, gloating a bit, Tara drops the bombshell. "In Prague."

* * *

"Bless me, Father, for I have sinned."

"*Si, mi nina,*" the priest murmurs, concealed behind the mesh window of the old-fashioned confessional.

With a pang, Mary realizes the voice isn't Father Roberto's familiar rumble, but that of a stranger.

"And when was your last confession?"

"One week ago." Her response is barely audible. She nervously fingers the rosary beads in her hand, wondering what to do now.

"Pardon?"

"One week ago," she says more forcefully. "I made my last confession one week ago, Father."

She makes her confession every week, without fail.

And every week since May, without fail, she has neglected to tell Father Roberto her most terrible sin.

It took every ounce of strength she possessed just to get here today, to tell the trusted priest what she did. A dozen times, she turned and started to retrace her steps toward home, unwilling to go through with it.

But in the end, she prayed for strength, and she found the fortitude to walk into the familiar sanctuary.

Father Roberto, she concluded, will guide her toward redemption. Perhaps, she even dared to think, he'll say that this enormous secret is better kept buried, the innocent child better left with the only parents she knows.

Mary was prepared to rest her future, her family's future, in his sturdy hands.

How is it that now, when she can no longer bear the burden; now, when she needs the kindly, trusted priest most of all, he isn't here?

What a cruel joke fate is playing on her.

"*Donde esta Padre Roberto?*" she blurts.

A minute later, she's running away from the church, away from the shocking news that the elderly priest died in his sleep last night.

CHAPTER TWELVE

Prague?

Prague?

It's been a good half hour since her boss sprang that on her, yet Peyton still can't seem to get past the sheer audacity.

Tara knows she can't go to Czechoslovakia any time in the near future.

Naturally, she had no choice but to come right out and admit it. Tara shook her head and informed Peyton that she'll keep that in mind when her evaluation comes up.

When she ran into a coworker in the ladies' room, Peyton spilled the whole story to her. She was silent at first, and Peyton assumed she was thinking, *Well, what did you expect?* But she ultimately urged her to march straight in to Human Resources and report Tara.

That might be satisfying in the short run, but it doesn't solve the problem at hand. If Peyton doesn't go to Prague—which she simply cannot do—she'll be proving she can't handle the new position. She won't be allowed to keep the promotion, with the lofty title, larger office, and pay raise that go with it.

Maybe I had no business agreeing to take over Alain's position in the first place, she tells herself now.

Either that, or she has no business having a child at this stage in her career.

The phone rings, jerking her thoughts back to the immediate present—and the memo she should have been typing these last five minutes she spent stewing about Tara.

"Peyton Somerset."

"Oh, hi, it's Claretta," the floor receptionist says. "There's a man out here who says he needs to see you."

"Is he a messenger?" Peyton asks, balancing the receiver between her shoulder and her ear so she can go back to her keyboard. "Because I'm waiting for storyboards to arrive, but you can sign for them."

"No, he's not a messenger. Sir, what was your name?"

There's a brief pause, during which Peyton continues to type. According to Tara, this memo needs to be e-mailed over to the client immediately. Or, as she so exasperatingly put it, "I need it done yesterday."

"His name is Gil Blaney," Claretta informs Peyton. "He said he's an old friend."

Gil. An old friend she hasn't seen in weeks. After a long silence, he's left a couple of messages on her answering machine over the last few days, but she hasn't had a chance to respond. Apparently, he's decided an in-person confrontation is in order. Terrific.

Shaking her head in frustration, Peyton tells Claretta, "I'm tied up now. I'll be out in ten minutes or so if he wants to wait."

She types furiously as Claretta relays her message to Gil.

"He says that he does want to wait, Peyton."

"Fine. Tell him to make himself comfortable." Peyton plunks the phone back into its cradle and goes back to her memo, her thoughts only half on the topic, which is, of course, the impending new product launch.

Gil has sounded increasingly needy with every message he's left her. She can't help feeling sorry for him, but she isn't capable of being his sole sounding board at a time like this. There's just too much going on in her own life to worry about somebody else's problems.

Memo finished and e-mailed, she returns two calls to the media department before going out to meet Gil. The calls could have waited a few more minutes, but she can't help wanting him to realize that she's truly busy, far too busy to drop everything just because he's dropped by the office.

Finally, she walks out to the reception area, where she sees him pacing. Obviously, he wasn't in the mood to make himself comfortable.

"Gil," she calls, and he stops walking and turns around.

Instant guilt. His face is drawn, his reddish hair needs a trim, and he hasn't shaved this morning. Maybe in a few mornings. He should be wearing a suit at this hour on a weekday, but he's dressed in rumpled cargo pants and a more rumpled T-shirt.

"What's wrong?" She goes over to him but stops short of reaching out to give him the hug he obviously needs, aware of Claretta's curious gaze. She's a notorious office gossip.

"What isn't wrong?" is Gil's sardonic reply.

"Come on, let's go into my office and talk."

Peyton leads the way down the corridor, conscious of several occupants of the secretaries' bay glancing up with interest. She can just hear them whispering, "Do you think he's the father?"

Let them speculate.

She closes the door and bends to move a stack of heavy binders from her lone guest chair. Rather than gallantly offer to help her, as he normally would, Gil walks to the window and gazes unseeingly into the air shaft.

"What happened?" Peyton asks, edging by him to sit down, looking nervously at her watch, then at the stacks of papers and folders on her desk.

"Karla's got the kids out in Oregon for the summer. And I lost my job."

"You were laid off?"

"I was fired, Runt."

"For what?" she asks reluctantly, settling back in her chair.

"For taking two and a half weeks' vacation."

"You don't have vacation time?"

"I get three weeks. I used one in February when I took Karla and the kids skiing. I wasn't supposed to take the other two until August. We go to the Outer Banks every August. I reserve the same house every year," he says desolately. "But now . . ."

"Why did you take your vacation early, Gil?"

"I went out West to be near her and the kids. But she didn't want me there, and the kids . . . I don't even know if they wanted me there. So I finally came back . . ."

"And lost your job?"

He nods. "I didn't clear the time off in advance. I left my boss a message, but apparently, he doesn't understand. He's been married thirty years and his kids are grown. What the hell am I going to do now, Peyton?"

"Listen, Gil, you'll get past this. I know you will. Everything is going to fall into place and . . ." She trails off, spotting Tara standing in the doorway.

"Peyton? Do you have the storyboards yet?"

"Not yet. They should be here any second."

"They should have been here an hour ago. Can you follow up, please? And if you can't get this resolved quickly please send me an e-mail recapping this situation. Thanks."

She nods, glancing uncomfortably from her boss to Gil, who steps forward, hand out, as if he's suddenly remembered to be civilized.

"I'm Peyton's friend Gil Blaney."

"Nice to meet you," Tara says curtly, not bothering to introduce herself. "Peyton, if you can check on those storyboards . . . ?"

"I'm on it, Tara," she promises as the boss strides off down the corridor. To Gil, she says, "I've got to do that right away or you won't be the only one without a job."

"Can you go to lunch with me?"

"Gil, I'm swamped."

"You've got to eat."

"I'll order something in."

"How about dinner?"

She starts to agree, then remembers Rita. "I've already got plans."

"With who? For what?"

The fact that he obviously considers his personal crisis more pressing than her social life shouldn't be surprising, considering his condition. Nor should it irk her the way it does.

After all, a friend in need . . .

But I'm in need, too, Peyton reminds herself stoically. *I can't deal with a divorced-and-unemployed sob session on the heels of a day like this. I just can't.*

"Sorry, Gil. Maybe tomorrow? Call me and—"

"Come on, Runt. I don't have anybody else to turn to. I'm falling apart, here."

Her phone rings before she can reply.

She seizes it gratefully. "Peyton Somerset."

"Peyton, the messenger just left your package."

"Thanks, Claretta." She hangs up. "Gil, I've got to go. Come on, I'll walk you out."

"Forget it, you don't have time." He heads for the corridor.

"I'm going that way anyway," she says, but he's already disappeared around the corner.

She stares after him, raking a hand through her hair.

He'll be fine, she assures herself halfheartedly, wistfully recalling the happy-go-lucky Gil she once knew.

* * *

"Peyton Somerset was in today for her monthly," Nancy mentions to Rita around a mouthful of tuna sandwich. "She looks great."

"She does, doesn't she?"

"She wants another ultrasound so she can tell what she's having. I bet it's a girl. What do you think?"

"I really don't have anything to go by."

"Neither do I. I'm going by instinct. What's your guess? Boy or girl?"

Rita takes a bite of her sandwich: her usual turkey on whole grain bread with lettuce and mustard. "I don't really like to guess."

"Why not? I love to guess. My mother always said that if you conceive on an even day of the month during a full moon, you're having a girl." Nancy's smile betrays the predictable note of sadness.

Searching for a cheerier subject, Rita asks, "How's your tuna?"

Nancy looks down at her half-eaten sandwich. "Not great. It's kind of runny. I hate when it's like that."

So much for cheer.

For a moment, they sit in silence.

Then Nancy says brightly, "You know, I forgot to mention to Peyton that I was window-shopping down in Soho over the weekend and I saw a painted yellow crib like she wanted."

"She already ordered a white one."

"Well, maybe it's not too late to cancel if she likes this yellow one. It would match the nursery walls."

"Actually, she doesn't have a nursery," Rita gently corrects Nancy. "It's a one-bedroom apartment. The baby will sleep in Peyton's room. We painted the walls in there yellow."

A flicker of envy in her eyes, Nancy asks, "You helped her?"

"I had to. She's got those high ceilings, and she can't go around climbing ladders. Listen, I'll tell her about the yellow crib when I see her later," Rita promises, to appease her, though she knows she probably won't mention it.

Peyton has enough to think about these days between her stressful job and her busy personal life. For somebody who claims to be mere friends with two men, she's been seeing an awful lot of both Tom and Gil, against Rita's advice.

"You're seeing Peyton later?" Nancy asks, a bit too casually. "Business or pleasure?"

"Business," Rita lies, knowing Nancy is prone to inviting herself along. "Hey, want to split a piece of blueberry pie for dessert?"

Nancy shakes her head. "I'm not really in the mood for pie."

She's hurt, Rita thinks. *She's hurt, and lonely, and she's thinking she has no life outside of work.*

The sad thing is, she doesn't.

Rita should come up with some way to lift her spirits. Something other than inviting her to the movies later.

"So tell me what's going on at the office today," Rita suggests, and is promptly rewarded when her friend's eyes become animated once again.

"Let's see," she says, "Elsa Lang was in with contractions—just Braxton Hix, though. And remember Helen Cantero? She's having twins."

Rita pops the last bite of her turkey sandwich into her mouth, thinking what a shame it is that poor Nancy must live vicariously through her patients.

Karen looks up from her magazine as Anne Marie follows the housekeeper into the spacious family room, and blurts, "Oh, my gosh. You look like you've been through hell."

Hell doesn't begin to cover it, but Anne Marie forces a smile, remembering to act as though it hurts to move her facial muscles.

"How are the kids?" she asks, needing to hold her boys close.

"They're downstairs eating sandwiches with Barbara," Karen tells her, uncrossing her barefooted legs and patting the love seat beside her. "I know you said not to give them lunch but you were gone longer than I expected and they were hungry."

"Thanks," Anne Marie murmurs, annoyed despite her preoccupation with her two brief telephone conversations, one more disturbing than the next.

Karen, with her full household staff including Barbara and a second nanny, considers herself Supermom and has a way of making veiled disparaging remarks about other people's perceived negligence.

Anne Marie isn't going to feel guilty, though. Not today.

"Sit down. Are you hungry?" Karen offers, flashing her southern hospitality smile. "Because I can have Louise make you some—"

"No, I can't eat for a few hours," Anne Marie cuts in, adding an explanatory "Novocaine," to offset her curt tone.

"Oh, right, I forgot. Did they prescribe anything to numb the pain? Because maybe you should leave the boys here for the afternoon. You probably shouldn't be alone with them if you're out of it from the medication."

Wishing there were pills to numb her pain, Anne Marie tells Karen, "No, actually, they said I'll be fine in a few hours. So I'll just get the boys . . ."

She's already walking toward the stairs, needing them.

Needing them in her arms.

Now.

"Want the rest of these?" Rita asks Peyton, offering an open box of Snowcaps as they head across Union Square.

"No, thanks. I've still got Jujubes stuck in my teeth." She pokes unsuccessfully at an embedded, sticky gel with her tongue, then asks, "So what did you think?"

"Of the movie? It was good, but I didn't think they should have ended up together," Rita says of the star-crossed hero and heroine.

"Why not? I thought they were perfect for each other."

"It just wasn't realistic." Rita tucks the Snowcaps into the pocket of her khakis.

"You know, for somebody who's been happily married forever, you're pretty jaded," Peyton informs her. "You of all people should believe in true love."

"Oh, I believe in true love. I just don't think it happens as easily as it did in the movie. Or for me and J.D."

"You're probably right," she says, thinking of Gil. "You know, I'd love to meet him someday. What's he like?"

"J.D.?" The midwife's face lights up. "He's sweet. He's caring. He'd do absolutely anything for anyone. Especially for me."

Peyton can't help smiling to herself, thinking that sounds an awful lot like Tom.

For a few minutes they walk on in companionable silence, surrounded by the square's typical nocturnal inhabitants: teenagers on skateboards, street merchants, strolling couples, briefcase toters, subway-bound students, hawkers thrusting sales fliers into the hands of passersby.

As immune to the chaos as any seasoned city dweller, Peyton finds her thoughts drifting back to the chaotic workday, to Gil's crisis, to Tom's welcome phone call just before she left the office.

"Bad day?" he asked sympathetically.

She told him that would be the understatement of the year.

"What can I do to make it better?" he asked, unaware that he just had.

She can't help it. Whenever she hears his voice, she finds her heart beating a little faster.

"What's the matter? You're so quiet."

Her thoughts interrupted by Rita's question, she looks around and realizes they've already reached Eighteenth Street.

"Just thinking about work." Peyton hasn't bothered to mention what's going on at the office, knowing the midwife is probably too far removed from the corporate world to offer much more than a sympathetic ear.

Allison would have understood completely, would probably have offered sound advice.

To stave off the melancholy mood that invariably settles over her whenever she thinks of her lost friend, Peyton muses, "I wonder how close Wanda is to going into labor."

"She's still a few weeks away from her due date, but you never know. Nancy said she had an appointment late this afternoon to be checked for dilation. I'm sure I'd have heard something if anything was under way."

"So what do you think will happen if she starts having contractions in the middle of the night? How will her boyfriend explain that to his wife?"

Rita shakes his head. "Who knows? Maybe he told her he's a volunteer fireman."

Peyton can't help laughing at that, adding, "Yeah, or a superhero."

"Don't laugh. I have a feeling she'd believe anything Eric told her."

They arrive at the intersection of Broadway and Twenty-first Street, and Rita says, "Here's where I turn off."

"Hey, how about coming back to my apartment for coffee? Tom is going to stop over to put up a bookshelf I bought. You can meet him."

"Meet the famous Tom at last?" Rita smiles. "That sounds good. But don't expect me to give you two my blessing or anything like that."

"Trust me, he's just a friend."

But in her heart, Peyton knows he might have been something more, if things had been different.

"How was your day?" Jarrett asks as always, standing in the front hall in his suit and tie, flipping through the day's mail.

"It was . . . fine." Anne Marie hovers in the archway, hugging herself against the chill that has nothing to do with the superefficient central air-conditioning.

He glances up at her as if he actually heard her for a change.

She reaches up to touch her cheek. "I had to have emergency dental work."

Jarrett stares at her. Then he sets the stack of mail on the Stickley table by the door and walks toward her.

Anne Marie forces herself to stand her ground when all she wants is to flee.

But you can't run away, she reminds herself as she has ever since she got home earlier. *You can't run away from Jarrett, from this life, from the past, from . . . the truth.*

"You didn't have emergency dental work, did you?"

It isn't a question.

"No."

She braces herself for the suspicious interrogation, the bitter accusations.

They don't come.

Jarrett merely searches her face, then takes another step closer.

She holds her breath, waiting for him to reach out and touch her, to grab her upper arms and demand an explanation, the way he did that night in the bedroom when he found the Bible. She knows that if he does touch her, this time, she'll fall apart.

But he doesn't.

He merely looks at her and says, barely audibly, "Anne Marie."

Her name. The name she hasn't heard him utter in so long, too long, and it affects her more profoundly than physical contact ever could.

With it, Anne Marie Egerton's shield of stoic resolve evaporates. At long last, she allows herself to fall apart . . . and into her husband's arms.

At long last, she tells him the whole truth.

* * *

"Is she asleep?" Mary asks, looking up when Javier walks into the kitchen.

"Finally. I think she might be cutting a tooth."

There is no joy in his voice as he speaks of the milestone, only a quick flash of resentment when Mary tells him, "She's too young for that."

"How do you know?"

"I just know."

And I've spent years reading everything there is to read about motherhood; every parenting manual, every month-by-month chart, every magazine article under the sun.

Time and time again, she prepared herself to care for the infant that was growing inside her, only to face loss after devastating loss.

Now, at last, she's a mother. A mother who will have the chance to witness every priceless milestone: first tooth, first word, first steps . . .

They stretch before her, beckoning landmarks on a golden path she can choose to follow . . . or not.

"We should call the rectory," Javier says quietly. "Find out if there are any arrangements yet."

She nods, a lump forming in her throat as she remembers the old priest's kind eyes and gentle spirit.

She'll never know now what might have happened if she had unburdened her soul to him. It's too late for that, too late for *what-ifs.*

Conscious of Javier's eyes on her, she finishes drying the last droplet of water on the last supper dish and places it carefully on top of the meager, chipped stack in the cupboard. Then she drapes the towel on the oven door handle and turns back to her husband.

"I keep trying to listen to God, trying to figure out what he wants me to do," she tells Javier. "And whenever I look at our daughter, I think I know. But I'm not sure whether it's God talking to me, or my own heart. I want her so much, Javier . . ."

"And now she's ours," he says, taking her in his arms when her voice breaks. "God wouldn't take her away. It's what Father Roberto would have told you. I know it is."

"Maybe you're right."

"I am right. Trust me. Even Mrs. Calabrone said so."

Mary frowns and pulls back to look up at him. "What do you mean?"

"I spoke to her a few weeks ago," he says, avoiding her gaze. "I called her."

"Why?"

"Because I needed to speak to her."

"About what?" Mary asks uneasily.

"About you, and your doubts. I told her you were going to go to confession because you felt like you had sinned. I said that besides me, the only two people in the world you could possibly talk to about it were Father Roberto and her. I thought, why involve him?"

"Because I trust him."

"But I figured maybe Rose could come talk to you instead, and make you see that it wasn't a sin in the first place."

"But that isn't her place to—"

"Listen, it doesn't matter. She said to let you work this out for yourself. She said you would come to realize that what we did wasn't wrong. She said even Father Roberto would know it was necessary to save an innocent child."

Mary takes a deep breath, praying she's doing the right thing.

Then she tells her husband, "I'm going to do my best to believe that. I'm going to pray for guidance, that I might eventually learn to live with this guilt."

"You're saying you won't tell anybody after all?" Javier holds her close again. "You're saying you'll forget all that and just move on, the three of us, as a family?"

"I'm saying I'll try."

Leaving Tom to hang the bookshelf in one corner of the newly painted bedroom, Peyton turns on the kitchen tap to camouflage her voice, then whispers to Rita, "What do you think?"

"Of the bookshelf? I love it. It's the same shade of yellow as—"

"Not the bookshelf. I mean *him.*"

"Oh. He's nice," Rita says noncommittally. "You're making decaf, right?"

"That's it?"

"Caffeine will keep me up all night."

Peyton narrows her eyes, certain Rita is deliberately misunderstanding her. "I'm pregnant, remember? I only keep decaf in the house now. I wasn't talking about the coffee."

"You mean Tom? What else do you want me to say?"

"I don't know . . . nice is so . . . I mean, everyone's nice."

"Not everyone."

"Rita, come on."

"Okay, then . . . he seems to know his way around a toolbox. Better?"

Peyton nods, filling the glass carafe and pouring the contents into the coffeemaker.

"And he's good-looking, too," Rita adds.

"He is, isn't he?" She begins scooping coffee grounds into the filter basket.

"It's just . . ."

At Rita's hesitation, she promptly loses count. "It's just . . . what?"

"He seems really intense."

"Intense? Tom?" Peyton frowns, her hand poised on the silver scoop. No wonder Rita has seemed so quiet and thoughtful ever since Tom walked in the door. Peyton never expected her to be utterly immune to his charisma. "How can you say that, Rita? He's one of the most laid-back people I know."

"It's just something about the way he looks at you. Like there's a lot more going on in his head than . . ."

"Than what?" she has to prod, when Rita trails off again.

"Friendship," Rita says reluctantly.

Fair enough. For if the whole truth be told, Peyton feels more than mere friendship for Tom Reilly in return.

She dumps the grounds back into the can and begins to count again. One . . . two . . .

"I just don't feel like you're getting the whole story where he's concerned."

Peyton looks up. "What do you mean?"

"I don't know . . . there just seems to be something off about him." Rita shakes her head and shrugs. "But, hey, maybe it's just me."

"I know you're trying to be a concerned friend. But I can take care of myself."

"So you don't want me to say anything negative about him, is that it?"

"No," Peyton says levelly, "I don't."

"Are you sure?"

"Yes. At least, not until you know him better. You just met him ten minutes ago, Rita. I don't think first impressions are that reliable."

"Really?"

"Not at all. I mean, the first time I met Tom, I thought he was a lunatic roaming the streets preying on innocent women." She laughs at the ridiculousness of it now.

Rita remains silent for a moment. Then she says darkly, "I'm a strong believer in first impressions. That's all I'm going to say, okay? I promise. Just promise me in return that you'll be careful around him, okay?"

Peyton hesitates, her heart pounding as she pretends to be absorbed in counting out six more scoops of coffee grounds and setting the appliance to brew.

She doesn't dare admit aloud that Rita's struck a nervous chord.

Her hand is shaking as she takes out the sugar bowl and an empty cut-glass creamer.

It's not that she thinks there might be any truth in her friend's warnings. It's just that she still can't help but feel wary. Not just around Tom, or around strangers, but around everyone she knows.

"I promise," she says at last, realizing her friend is still waiting for a response. "Listen, can you go ask Tom if he wants milk or half-and-half in his coffee? I have both."

"Sure."

Her back turned, Peyton nearly bolts out of her skin when she feels a hand on her arm.

She spins around and is relieved to see that it's just Rita.

"I thought you left the room!" she exclaims, resting a hand on her racing heart.

"I was about to. I didn't mean to scare you."

"Sorry, I'm jumpy."

"I just wanted to apologize. I didn't mean to be so critical. I'm sure he's a great guy."

"He is," Peyton tells Rita, wishing she believed that as wholeheartedly as she wants to.

On the glowing green dial of the digital clock, midnight gives way to the first minute of a new day, relegating the last twelve hours' worth of trauma officially to the past.

Another minute passes, and then another, and still they lie awake in the dark, waiting for sleep that refuses to come.

"What now?" Jarrett asks finally.

"I don't know." Anne Marie rolls over to face him, reaching

out to touch his shoulder with newfound ease. "What are you thinking?"

"You mean, about what you should do with what you've found out?"

"Yes. And with what I still haven't found out."

He's silent, presumably mulling it over.

How long has it been since they've lain awake in the dark, sharing confidences in hushed whispers? Have they ever done this? Will they ever do it again?

The walls between them were washed away by the earlier tide of tears, the long-buried foundation of marital trust laid bare in its wake.

"You don't have to do anything about any of this, you know. Maybe you can just sit with this awhile."

"Maybe. But I don't know."

She leans her head against him and he reaches out to hold her close. She didn't realize how much she's been craving a renewed physical connection with her husband; never comprehended just how much they somehow lost along the way.

Some things about him, about *them,* can never change. But in these dark moments, the darkest she's had in a decade, they've somehow managed to make contact again. For now, that's enough.

Perhaps it's enough to sustain her from here on in, without ever needing the answers she sought so desperately.

"Do you want to go out there again?" Jarrett asks, just when she thinks he might have drifted off to sleep.

"Maybe I'll just wait awhile." She sighs. "You know, like you said. Maybe I'll give it a few weeks . . ."

And pray, just pray, that this raw, all-consuming need somehow goes away.

For a long time, they lie there in the dark, in silence.

Only when Jarrett's breathing has taken on a telltale even rhythm does Anne Marie sit up and swing her legs over the edge of the mattress.

"Where are you going?" he asks, stirring.

"Shhh. I just can't sleep." She bends to kiss his brow, her thoughts already soaring away from this bed, this room, this life. "Get some rest. I'll be back."

There's no response from the man in the bed, whose concern for his wife's nightmare has once more given way to sweet dreams of his own.

* * *

"Well, that's a damn shame," Detective Jody Langella mutters, peering over the subway platform at the barely recognizable human remains on the tracks.

"So what the hell happened to him? Or was it a her?" she asks, turning to the two transit authority officers standing guard on this side of the yellow tape cordoning off the still unshrouded carnage.

"It was a *him,*" the older of the men informs her. "What happened?"

"What do you think? The usual."

A police photographer leans precariously over the platform to get a better angle, takes a couple of overhead snaps, then climbs down into the tracks.

The younger officer, an obvious rookie, watches the process, appearing too shaken to speak.

This is the first of many mangled corpses you're gonna see in your life, Jody wants to tell him. *Better get used to it.*

But why put a damper on the poor kid's day—let alone his freaking career—before it's even under way?

Addressing the older cop, Langella asks, "Did he jump or get pushed?"

"Pushed. By some homeless person."

Yeah. Same old, same old.

The transit officer unwraps a piece of Big Red and folds it into his mouth, then offers the pack to the rookie, who turns even paler and pushes it away.

Smirking inwardly, Langella gives the kid about a year before he'll be eating oil-slicked hero sandwiches within minutes of taping up a gory crime scene. All in a day's work.

"So you got witnesses?" she asks the gum-snapping spokesperson for the two.

"Platform was pretty much empty at that hour of the morning."

Sure it was. The Baychester Avenue station is the second stop on the number 5 line, in the northernmost reaches of the city. The accident occurred a few hours before throngs of neighborhood commuters would have begun heading south to Manhattan.

Maybe you'd have a coupl'a construction workers here at that hour, or some young punks heading home from an after-hours bar.

"We got three people who saw what happened." The cop indicates an ashen-faced trio seated on a bench nearby.

Bingo! Feeling smug, Langella gives herself an invisible pat on the back.

One construction worker, one club kid, and one wild card witness: an impatient scrubs-clad hospital worker who keeps looking at her watch.

Preferring to get the already-obvious scenario from the cop, she'll wait for her partner, Detective Sam Basir, before interrogating the witnesses. He's upstairs now with the distressed subway motorman.

Langella asks the cops, "So what happened?"

"Homeless person came up behind this poor schmo, gave him a shove just as the train was pulling in, and took off running."

"The perp a man or woman?"

"Nobody could tell. It happened too fast."

Jody nods, all too familiar with the scenario. Stalk, shove, and split.

Beautiful. Just one more demented soul left to wander the city streets.

"So anybody ID the schmo?" she asks, hearing a commotion on the stairs as the cleanup crew and medical examiner simultaneously arrive on the scene.

"Yeah, I did when I checked his pulse. I put his wallet back into his pocket. Name is Cordell. Linden Cordell."

Month Seven
August

CHAPTER THIRTEEN

"Special delivery for Peyton Somerset."

She gasps and opens the door wider, allowing Tom and the oversized stuffed elephant he's carrying to fit through the opening. He sets it in the middle of the living room floor and brushes his hands against each other in a satisfied gesture.

Peyton laughs, shaking her head. "Where on earth did you get that?"

"Oh, I have my sources."

"Your giant stuffed animal sources?"

He nods and pulls her as close as he can with her unwieldy midsection between them. "If you don't think the baby will like it, I can always exchange it for a giraffe or something."

"I only have eight-foot ceilings. I'll stick with Dumbo," she murmurs against his lips, before he kisses her.

"Stop," she protests after a few seconds, halfheartedly resting her hands on his chest.

"Why?"

"Because we've got dinner reservations and I'm starved."

"Oh, right. Almost forgot about that three-meal-a-day, eating-for-two thing you've got going on. Just let me go wash up. I've lugged that thing twenty blocks in ninety-five-degree heat."

He disappears into the bathroom, and Peyton hears the water running. She gingerly lowers herself onto the couch to wait, propping her swollen ankles on the coffee table and leaning against the cushions to rest her perpetually aching back.

Just weeks ago, she never could have imagined that she'd find herself caught up in a romance at this cumbersome stage of her pregnancy—or her life.

Then came the unexpected blackout that struck the city on a steamy July evening, just as the sun was sinking over the Jersey skyline.

She only panicked in the few seconds it took her to look out the window and realize all of Manhattan was dark. But in those harrowing seconds, her thoughts spun wildly from the prowler's possible return, to her own mortality, to what might have happened to Allison just before she vanished.

She was grateful when Tom turned up on her doorstep in remarkably short order, armed with flashlights, candles, and ice. Though she felt obligated to claim she was perfectly capable of taking care of herself in the dark, she was secretly relieved he insisted on staying with her until the lights came on.

That didn't happen until dawn—and when it did, he didn't leave.

Somewhere in the wee hours of that long, hot night, he had kissed her for the first time, transforming their friendship into something far more intimate, and far more welcome, than Peyton ever anticipated.

Neither of them has since discussed their future or what will happen when the baby arrives, let alone Tom's prospective role in that event. She hasn't yet asked him to be her labor coach, though she's pretty sure she's going to, with Wanda's blessing.

Her friend has met Tom and really liked him.

Not that she didn't put him through the third degree, grilling him about where he lives, where he works, what he does in his spare time, whether he has any pets . . .

"Who are you, Barbara Walters?" Peyton grumbled to her afterward.

"I was just making sure he's good enough for you."

"And . . . ?"

"He is," Wanda concluded. "I think your baby's going to have a future daddy."

"I think you're getting way ahead of us there, Ms. Jones," Peyton responded with a laugh.

The last thing she wants to do is speculate about what might happen next year, next month, even next week. For once, she's content to take things day by day.

It's hard enough to deal with the lingering sorrow over Allison, the brutal dog days of August in the city, and her physical metamorphosis as her due date looms.

Not to mention the fact that Gil, apparently stung by her inability to help him when he stopped by the office, hasn't been in touch since that day. She left a few messages on his home voice mail in the days that followed, but he never called back. For all she knows he's taken off for Oregon again. Feeling guilty for neglecting her old friend in his time of need, she keeps telling herself she should try harder to track him down. Yet, short of breaking into his apartment, she can't imagine how she can possibly reach him if he doesn't want to be reached.

For the most part, though, there's been too much going on at the office to dwell on Gil or anything else.

Tara hasn't officially demoted her yet—not necessarily surprising, considering that Peyton was never officially promoted in the first place. But her boss never misses a chance to give her tedious assignments typically reserved for underlings, or to make supposedly teasing digs about her pregnancy.

No, Peyton doesn't have the time or energy to analyze her love life. Where that's concerned, *que sera, sera.*

"Miss me?" Tom reappears in the living room, fresh-scrubbed and handsome. He's wearing a chambray shirt tucked into khakis and loafers without socks.

The man looks as though he stepped out of a J. Crew catalog.

Beside him, Peyton should probably feel positively ungainly, but he has a way of making her feel somehow beautiful despite her bulky figure.

She allows him to take her hand and hoist her out of the couch. Smoothing the wrinkles in her linen maternity jumper, she asks, "Do you think I'm underdressed?"

"I think you're gorgeous in anything you wear. Or don't wear," he adds salaciously. "Come on, let's get going so we can come back."

As they step out into the warm summer Friday night hand in hand, Peyton Somerset is blissfully unaware that the last tranquil moments of her life are rapidly falling away.

Anne Marie slips the red Bible and manila envelope, its flap now worn and tattered from use, into her bag.

She closes the bureau drawer, then looks up at Jarrett standing beside her.

"Finished packing?" he asks, and she nods.

"Do you have everything you need?"

"Even things I don't need." She pats the Bible, thinking that if he asks her why she's taking it, she'll have to explain. And that if she's forced to come up with an explanation, she might be able to understand her own motives for a change.

Because right now, nothing makes sense. For weeks, she's been operating on pure instinct, and nothing more.

Anyway, Jarrett says nothing.

Jarrett rarely says anything.

Anne Marie often wishes he were the type of man who has just the right words of support; the type of man who would offer to go with her tonight, and who, if he went with her, would know how to handle the challenge that lies ahead.

But in the end, she supposes she's grateful to him for doing the very least he could do—which is the most he is capable of—and who would expect anything more?

Jarrett is staying with the boys tonight, and tomorrow, and tomorrow night, if necessary . . . staying with them for as long as it takes her to put things to rest.

This has been eating away at her for weeks, ever since she made the pay phone call that morning a month ago, the call that raised more questions than it answered.

No, longer than that. She's been traumatized ever since she got the call back in June, the one that confirmed what she now realizes she already knew.

There are things a mother just knows, if she listens to her heart, Grace DeMario used to tell her children and grandchildren.

Usually she said it teasingly; say, when Anne Marie was up to something she shouldn't have been.

But what she has always remembered most vividly is the time her grandmother told her that her mother—Grace's daughter, Lisa—wouldn't be coming back to them.

Ever.

Anne Marie must have been about twelve then, a Catholic schoolgirl filled with wonderful fantasies about the mother she barely knew, the free-spirited wanderer who popped in and out of her life when she least expected it. A flower child, Grace used to call her wayward daughter, and Anne Marie would picture her smiling, beautiful mother with a wreath of roses on her long, straight blond hair.

She told the girls at school about her, inventing adventures that her mother wrote to her about in letters that never existed. But the girls didn't know. Most of them envied Anne Marie. They wished their own mothers—churchgoing types who cooked and cleaned and nagged them—were more exciting, like Anne Marie's.

Then Margarita Taylor, a girl with close-set eyes and a perpetually sour expression, told everybody that Anne Marie's mother wasn't a flower child at all. She said her parents called her a crazy hippie and said she was never coming back.

Anne Marie punched Margarita Taylor in her pinched little face on the playground and Father Joe, the principal, called her grandmother to the school. Anne Marie remembered thinking Grace didn't seem as angry as she expected. She didn't say much on the walk home. When they got there, Anne Marie asked her, once again, when her mother would be coming back.

Instead of offering her usual shrug or vague "soon, I suppose," Grace gave her the dreaded answer.

Never.

Never? But . . . how do you know?

There are things a mother just knows if she listens to her heart, Anne Marie, without having to be told.

Of course she cried then. They both did. But Anne Marie cried so hard and for so long that she still remembers the way her eyes ached, the terrible headache that lasted all day. Grace offered cold cucumber compresses, one of her old Sicilian remedies. Anne Marie finally accepted them, but refused to speak to her.

She so wanted her grandmother to be wrong. For years, she hoped she was.

In the end, of course, she wasn't. Lisa never did come home to her daughter—or her mother— again. Anne Marie still doesn't know what happened to her. Grandma assumed she was dead, but for all she knows, her mother might still be out there somewhere, an aging flower child with a wreath of roses in long gray hair.

Probably not.

But . . . maybe.

That's the thing about the not knowing.

Hope.

You get to keep hope in your heart, carry it with you, resurrect it when days seem darkest.

"Are you going to say goodnight to the boys?" Jarrett's question startles her back to the present.

"Oh . . . No."

He looks at her, raising his eyebrows.

She opens her mouth to rationalize her choice, to point out that they're probably asleep, that if they aren't, they'll cry if they realizes she's leaving. They might ask when she's coming back. And then what will she tell them? That she isn't sure?

Of course, she's coming back eventually. Sooner or later, she'll reclaim this charmed life that never quite seemed to belong to her in the first place. Of course she will.

A mother—a *good* mother, like Anne Marie Egerton—doesn't abandon her own children. A mother stays with them, protects them, until they no longer need her care. And even then, she's perpetually on watch.

A painful lump rises in her throat.

"You're ready, then?" Jarrett asks, lifting her heavy bag.

Somehow, she manages to reply. "I'm ready."

She kisses her fingertips and presses them to the doorknob of the boys' room as they pass.

Downstairs, in the hall, she regains her composure to ask Jarrett, "What if I'm wrong about this?"

"You could be right."

"What if I'm right?" she asks with a bleak, staccato laugh, before she walks out the door.

Rita is standing on the corner waiting for the light to change when she feels the sudden vibration of her cell phone in her back pocket.

She curses under her breath. There are times when she wholeheartedly welcomes the interruption.

This isn't one of them.

She pulls out the phone and flips it open. Seeing the unfamiliar number in the caller ID window, she's tempted not to answer it.

But of course, she has to. *Twenty-four-seven.*

"Rita?"

Hearing the familiar voice that greets her, she promptly bids farewell to her plans for the next twenty-four hours, and perhaps beyond.

"Wanda! Tell me what's going on." She steps briskly away from the pedestrians clogging the curb, heading for the relatively secluded storefront of a Duane Reade drugstore.

Rather than rushing headlong into a series of physical symptoms, Wanda asks only, "Did I get you at a bad time?"

She doesn't sound like a woman in labor, or even like a woman going on two weeks overdue with her first baby. She sounds oddly . . . calm.

Well, that proves you never know. Rita would have pegged her as a screamer.

"Not a bad time at all, sugar pie," she says soothingly. "I was just on my way to pick up J.D.'s dry cleaning. What's happening? Contractions?"

"No, no contractions."

"Well, any day now," Rita says automatically, just as she has for the past week. She mentally reclaims her evening plans, even as she takes mindless inventory of the back-to-school window display before her.

Black-and-white marble notebooks, packets of yellow pencils, pink erasers . . .

"Actually, Rita . . . I had the baby."

The plans instantly evaporate, taking the array of school supplies with them.

"*What?*"

"Eric came over early this morning and said his wife and sons were going out to their beach house in the Hamptons for the weekend, so it would be a good time for me to have the baby."

Barely able to keep the rage from her voice, Rita says, "Let me get this straight. He *told* you when to have the baby? Because it would be convenient for him?"

"It wasn't like that." Wanda gives a nervous laugh that tells Rita it was *exactly* like that. "He said he wanted to be there for me, no matter what. For me and the baby. And this way, he wouldn't have to figure out how he could get away, or leave to go back home as soon as she was born. Oh, I had a girl, Rita. Just like I thought."

"Congratulations," she says tightly. "Just how did you manage to accomplish that on command?"

"You mean, having a girl?"

"I mean, having a baby."

"Well, Eric made me a cup of this special tea he brought with him, and the next thing I knew, I was having contractions."

"Special tea?" she echoes in disbelief. "What the hell was in it? How do you know it was safe?"

"Don't worry, it was just herbs, Rita. He got it up in Harlem from some—"

"Voodoo shop?" Rita cuts in, familiar with the thriving uptown culture of island "medicine."

"Not a voodoo shop," she protests, her voice laced with uncertainty.

"Wanda, I have legitimate medication that will induce labor, if that's what you wanted."

The uncertainty gives way to a sassy retort. "It *is* what I wanted, two weeks ago, when I begged you to get this baby out of me. Remember?"

True. But . . . "You hadn't even reached your official due date then. And you know that I don't believe in induction unless the baby is either very large or very late. I told you we'd think about it on Monday if you still hadn't delivered."

"Well, I couldn't wait until Monday."

"Wanda, why didn't you at least call me?"

"I wanted to, really, but Eric . . . he didn't want me to deliver at home, and he didn't want me to go through it without drugs for the pain. He said he watched his wife suffer through labor and he didn't want that for me."

She says it with pride, as though it's proof that he loves her more, somehow, than the woman who wears his wedding ring and lives in his suburban mansion—oh yes, and Hamptons beach house.

Rita bites back the harsh words Wanda deserves, the even harsher expletives her lover deserves. She manages to sound positively civilized when she asks, "Where did you deliver?"

"At Saint Luke's Roosevelt. He brought me to the ER here once the contractions were regular and they admitted me. They gave me drugs, and an epidural, and . . . here we are. Only it wasn't that easy." She gives a bitter laugh that sounds almost like a sob. "They had to do a C-section in the end."

"Why?"

"I don't know, it wasn't progressing, and the baby was in distress. . . ."

Due, no doubt, to the "tea" provided by that wretched excuse for a father.

"But she's fine now." Wanda clears her throat, then proudly elaborates, "Her name is Erica."

Of course it is, Rita thinks grimly.

"Where are you now, Wanda? In the hospital?"

"Yeah. They're keeping me for a few days because of the surgery. Dr. Lombardo's office was already notified. I wanted to tell you myself, though. I'm sorry, Rita. I didn't want to upset you, but . . . I didn't want to upset Eric, either."

Rita shakes her head. What is there to say to this pathetic woman?

At last, she manages a heartfelt "Good luck."

Wanda and poor, innocent, undeserving little Erica are certainly going to need it, for the rest of their lives.

"Because you absolutely cannot pay every single time we go out to eat, that's why!" Peyton informs Tom, holding the check out of his reach with one hand as she reaches for her purse on the back of her chair with the other.

"Why not? I like treating you."

"Well, I might like treating you, too, if I ever had the chance."

He makes another grab for the check, reaching past the crumb-laden plate upon which they just shared a sinfully rich wedge of chocolate cake.

Laughing, she pulls it farther from his reach, digging blindly in her bag for her wallet as she says, "You just can't take no for an answer, can you?"

"You should talk!"

"Come on, Tom." Aware of other diners starting to glance over, she hisses, "Stop making a scene and let me pay in peace, will you?"

"Sorry," he says calmly, "I was brought up to believe that a gentleman should always pay the check."

"Well, I was brought up to believe that a lady should be allowed to pay the check at least once in a while," she returns, which is, of course, a complete lie.

Her mother spent years in a desperate quest to find a man who would take care of them both. Even back when Peyton was in high school, she often asked if Gil was treating her well—meaning not just, *Is he protecting you from the big bad world?* but also, *Is he keeping you in burgers and Cokes?*

If not for Beth's many weaknesses, Peyton probably wouldn't feel so compelled to reinforce her own strengths. One of which is being capable of—and entitled to—picking up dinner for two in an upscale Manhattan restaurant like this one.

"Aha!" she exclaims, locating her wallet at last by touch in the zippered pocket where she keeps it, well away from muggers' prying hands.

She pulls it out and opens it, whipping her American Express

Gold card from its protective slot with a flourish. She thrusts both the card and the bill at a fortuitously passing waiter and turns to shoot a smug but good-natured look at Tom.

But Tom isn't looking at her. He's gaping at something over her shoulder.

She spins around and realizes that what he's looking at is the waiter; that the waiter is standing there, still holding her credit card and the bill, both of which are smeared with what looks for all the world like blood.

Glancing over the autopsy report that just came across her desk, Detective Jody Langella mutters, "'Death occurred due to massive trauma.' Yeah, no kidding."

Her partner, Sam, looks up from the report he's filling out. "What's up?"

"That subway push case from a few weeks ago."

"The one at Pelham Bay?"

"The one at Bayview Avenue."

"No perp on that one yet."

"Nope." And she doubts they'll nail a suspect if it really was a dangerously deranged street person. At least, not this time. Not until he—or she—pulls another stalk, shove, and split. There's no question that'll happen sooner or later with the lunatic left on the street.

What is still in question, as far as Jody's concerned, is the perp's motive.

Random madness? Or is there something more?

"Only thing that's certain," Jody tells Sam, "is that there was, indeed, a perp."

"Yeah? What do you mean?"

"I mean he wouldn't be the first married guy I've ever known to off himself on the heels of getting a Dear John letter."

Yes, if it weren't for the witnesses who indisputably saw Linden Cordell being pushed in front of a southbound number 5 train in the early hours of that July morning, Langella might very well have concluded it was a suicide.

"You mean a Dear John e-mail," Sam corrects with a roll of his eyes.

"Right, e-mail."

That little nugget of information came from Cordell's old pal

Richie, whose name was listed after the wife's on the emergency contact card the welder dutifully carried in his wallet.

Poor guy was pretty shaken up by the news of his friend's untimely and gory demise at the Baychester Avenue Station, a stone's throw from the block where the two of them played stickball as kids.

"Does Derry know?" Richie asked when he finally pulled himself together. "Did you find her and tell her?"

"*Find* her?" Jody echoed, sensing a tantalizing new angle the way a seasoned bomb-sniffing German shepherd smells nitrates.

And so the sad marital tale came pouring out of Richie. Amidst shuddering sobs of genuine grief for his lost friend, he managed to inform Detectives Langella and Basir that Richie's wife Derry had left him "out of the blue, for no reason whatsoever."

She simply took off from their apartment one night, sending her husband a brief e-mail that said she was leaving, and that he shouldn't bother trying to find her.

"An e-mail?" Sam asked in disbelief.

"Yeah, I read it myself. He got it when he was staying at my place. He and Derry e-mailed each other all the time. That's how they met in the first place."

Ah, love in the Information Age, Jody thought at the time, shaking her head, laying a comforting hand on Richie's trembling shoulders.

Now, she can't help wondering . . .

It's been a month.

Linden Cordell's remains have been cremated and interred, based on instructions from his distraught elderly mother in a Florida nursing home. The case was virtually open-and-shut: a random homicide in a terrorism-ravaged city that rarely bats an eye these days at a lone, albeit tragic, death. Even the tabloids relegated the item to relative obscurity, caught up in a feeding frenzy that day over another missing fuel tanker from a local airport.

The tanker turned up the following day in Jersey.

Linden Cordell's wife never did.

And yes, now, even after a month, Jody Langella can't help wondering . . .

The witnesses weren't sure whether the homeless perp was a man or woman.

What if it was a woman?

What if the crime wasn't random after all?

What if Derry Cordell is simply lying low, waiting to cash in on her husband's life insurance?

No, it wouldn't be the first time Jody Langella has seen such a crime.

"We need to get a search warrant executed for tomorrow," she briskly tells Basir, who's packing away his papers for the night.

"Search warrant? For what?"

"For the Cordells' apartment."

"Are you kidding me?" Sam's bushy black eyebrows meet in a crease above his aquiline nose. "Haven't we got enough to do tomorrow?"

"We'll add this to the list," Jody says with a shrug, and he groans.

"Come on, Sam, something tells me there might be more to this thing than meets the eye."

"Yeah? Something tells me you're looking for complications where there are none."

She can certainly understand his reaction. There are enough cases to keep them going around the clock, and they probably would if they didn't have spouses and kids at home.

However, busy as they are, Jody figures the least they can do—if only out of respect for poor, dead, jilted Linden Cordell—is dig a little deeper.

Not tonight, though. It's getting late, and there's no reason to execute a night search warrant.

Time to head downtown to her own family, where she'll throw Tater-Tots and frozen chicken nuggets into the oven, open a can of corn, and call it dinner.

But tomorrow, they'll pay another visit to the Co-op City apartment building the Cordells called home.

Last time, the building manager let the detectives into the deserted apartment, where they sniffed around for any evidence that might show the crime was anything but random. Just as they expected, there wasn't a shred.

This time, however, they'll be more meticulous.

Maybe they'll even find the e-mailing Widow Cordell—or, perhaps, the e-mailing *Black Widow* Cordell—in residence.

Peyton's first thought is that she might have cut herself when she reached into her bag.

The fingers that dug for her wallet are sticky with what looks like blood. She turns her hand over and back again, looking for the source. But there's not an open wound to be found, not even a bleeding hangnail.

"My God, Peyton," Tom is saying, having come around the table to kneel beside her. "What did you do to yourself?"

"I don't know."

"Is it lipstick?"

"I don't think so." She doesn't own a bright scarlet shade. And this doesn't feel waxy, like lipstick. It feels . . . tacky.

Like blood.

The waiter has set the card and bill gingerly on the table and is quickly retreating, undoubtedly eager to wash his hands.

Peyton finds herself wondering vaguely if she should at least go after him and assure him that he has nothing to worry about where her blood is concerned.

But she can't be sure it's even her blood.

Tom has taken her purse from the back of her chair and is peering into it.

"Let me see." She snatches it from him and looks inside. In the flickering candlelight, it's difficult to see anything. "I'll be right back."

"Where are you going?" Tom calls after her as, bag in hand, she scurries toward the ladies' room, a familiar route she's already taken twice since they arrived here.

She finds it empty, thank goodness, and deposits the bag on the counter by the sink. She briefly considers washing her contaminated hand, but tells herself that can wait.

In the bright overhead light, she looks into her purse . . . and gasps.

There, tucked in among her belongings—her wallet, her hairbrush, her date book, her roll of Tums—is a coiled length of something gelatinous and bloody.

CHAPTER FOURTEEN

"Placenta," Rita pronounces, the moment Peyton opens her purse to reveal the heinous object.

"*Placenta?*" Her hands still trembling even now, hours later, Peyton drops the purse back on the coffee table and backs away with a shudder. "Are you sure?"

"Positive. I've seen enough of it in my time, that's for sure."

"Oh my God. Oh my God! Rita . . ."

Help me.

Peyton doesn't say it, but the plea is clear.

Sidestepping the garish stuffed elephant in the middle of the living room, Rita goes to her, placing a steadying arm around her shoulders. "Sit down."

"But—"

"Sit."

Peyton sits.

"You need to take some deep breaths. Try to relax." Rita sinks onto the couch beside her, keeping an arm on her shoulders as she shakily inhales, then exhales.

"Thanks for coming over, Rita. I probably shouldn't have called you, but I just . . . I guess I freaked out when I saw it."

"Who wouldn't? My God, Peyton, what on earth is that thing doing in your purse?"

"I have no idea!" Her voice is shrill, almost accusatory. "I didn't put it there, if that's what you're wondering."

"Of course I wasn't wondering that. I just meant . . ." She shrugs. "It doesn't make sense."

"I know. I keep thinking somebody must have done it as . . . I don't know, as a joke?"

"A joke? Well, it sucks. The one about the chicken crossing the road is a lot funnier."

Peyton fails to crack a smile at the halfhearted attempt at levity.

"Pssst . . . ever hear that story about the elephant in the room that nobody would mention?" Rita nudges her and points at the oversized stuffed animal. "Please tell me you see that."

"Tom brought it over tonight," is the dull reply. "For the baby."

No longer in the mood to make light of things, Rita asks, "So where is Mr. Wonderful now?"

"He went to buy milk."

"He went to buy *milk?*" Rita shakes her head, about to ask what kind of man leaves a woman in need to go on a silly errand at this hour of the night.

"My stomach has been upset ever since . . ." She indicates the purse with a cringe. "Tom thought some milk might settle it down, but I'm all out of it, so he went to get it."

"He left you alone when you're so upset you can barely speak?" Rita asks dubiously.

"It was my idea, actually. And I knew you'd be here any second. I told him it was fine, go ahead."

"Yeah? And what aren't you telling me?"

"What do you mean?"

"Something's up. With Tom. Tell me."

Peyton no longer even bothers to feign confusion. "I guess I just wanted to get him out of here for a few minutes so I could talk to you in private."

"About . . . ?"

"About . . . what if he's the one who put that . . . *placenta,*" she says with difficulty, "in my bag?"

"Why would he—and where would he get—"

"He works in a bio lab."

Rita clamps her jaw shut. "I knew that. I forgot. Oh, Christ."

"I'm afraid. I don't know why he would do it, but . . . what if he did?"

"Maybe he didn't. Think about it. Who else would have had access to your bag?"

"Anybody would have, I guess. I don't think I even opened it all day. I had my keys in my jacket pocket at work—I remember, because they kept jangling and I kept thinking I needed to put them into my bag, but I never did." She's thinking aloud, her brown eyes gazing off into the distance, her brow furrowed as she backtracks through her day. "And I didn't need my wallet to buy lunch because we had a meeting and they brought sandwiches in."

"So the last time you opened your purse was . . . ?"

"I guess yesterday."

"Has Tom been around?"

"He spent the night."

"Last night?"

"And the night before."

Rita takes a moment to absorb the news. Then, shaking her head, she murmurs, "I told myself I was never going to tell you about this."

"About what?"

This is going to kill her, Rita tells herself. She squirms, looks up at Peyton. "I shouldn't even say it. Because it probably has nothing to do with—"

"Rita, for God's sake, tell me what you're talking about."

"Do you remember the night you invited me here for coffee, to meet Tom?"

"Yes." Peyton's eyes are wide with trepidation.

"Remember how I promised you I wouldn't say anything else negative about him? Because I knew you really wanted me to like him, and—"

"I remember. What happened?"

"There's something I should have told you." Rita takes a deep breath. "You asked me to go into the bedroom when he was working on that shelf, to ask him how he took his coffee. Remember?"

Peyton shrugs noncommittally. "Not really, no. What hap—"

"When I went into the bedroom, I found him going through the top drawer on your bureau."

"Oh my God." Peyton clasps a hand over her mouth. "Why didn't you tell me?"

"Because I promised. And because he claimed he was looking for a pencil to make a mark on the wall where the shelf was supposed to go. At the time, I told myself it was a plausible explanation—"

"A pencil? In a dresser? That's plausible?" Peyton's voice rises more shrilly with every word.

"All right, I was reaching. I kept telling myself that I was just looking for reasons to be suspicious of him. But maybe I should have been more suspicious all along."

"Maybe we both should have," Peyton tells her. "Now what do I do? He's coming back here."

"Don't let him in."

"He has the keys." After a pause, she admits, "His own set."

"You need to change the locks again," Rita tells her.

"I know . . . but what am I going to do about him tonight?"

"Tell him to go. You can't stay here alone with him, Peyton."

"He won't want to leave. He knows how upset I am."

"Well, tell him you don't need him. Tell him I'm here to take care of you now."

"He'll want to stay too."

Rita gives her a level look. "Who's in charge here? This is your house. You decide who stays and who goes. Be straight with him."

Peyton doesn't reply immediately.

But as the words sink in, Rita sees a familiar gleam return to her eyes.

"You're right," she says, fists clenched, head held high. "I'm in charge. And he's going."

"How many nights?" asks the night manager behind the desk, obviously bored with the answer before it even arrives; bored with the job, people, life in general.

"I don't know . . . two?"

He looks up at Anne Marie without moving a muscle. "Are you asking me or telling me?"

"I'm telling you two. Maybe three."

"Sunday night, the rate goes up to three hundred forty-nine a night."

"I thought the rates went down after weekends."

"Not out here. We're right next to a corporate park. We get business travelers in during the week. Rate goes up."

"Fine. Rate goes up. *If* I need to stay." Anne Marie fervently hopes that by Sunday, it will all be over.

Dripping ennui, the night clerk hands her the card key and points the way to the elevator.

He doesn't offer a bellhop to help her with her bag. Maybe because there are no bellhops at this suburban hotel; maybe because she only has one bag and it's on wheels; maybe because he doesn't give a damn how she gets up to her room.

She seethes all the way to the elevator, tempted to go back and tell the clerk what she thinks of him.

But she doesn't dare. Displaced rage is dangerous, particularly when one is as tightly wound as she is tonight.

She pulls her bag into the elevator and contents herself with shooting one last dark look in the direction of the desk before the doors slide closed.

You should have just stayed home, or at least in Manhattan, instead of coming all the way out here tonight, she scolds herself. But it's too late now, and anyway, she was anxious to get to her destination. She figured she'll be so nervous by the time tomorrow morning rolls around that driving wouldn't be a good idea.

The room is a guidebook example of three-star mediocrity. Two double beds with ugly quilted turquoise spreads, chair, desk, and television. There's an iron in the closet and a plastic ice bucket on the desk; the shampoo and lotion in the bathroom are in packets, not bottles.

What am I doing here? Anne Marie wonders as she gazes about, suddenly more homesick than she's ever been in her life.

Homesick, oddly enough, not for Bedford and Jarrett and the boys . . .

But homesick, most of all, for her grandmother.

If Grace DeMario had been alive ten years ago, none of this ever would have happened.

She would have been there—always, always there—with her watchful eye and her many rules and her uncanny ability to sense trouble before trouble ever got close enough to strike.

But Grace wasn't there.

The life Anne Marie had somehow managed to build without her help, without anyone's help, was shattered by pure evil.

Despite Rita's advice, Peyton can't bring herself to keep the chain on the door when she hears Tom unlocking it on the other side.

She hurriedly slides the brass knob from its grooved track and as the door swings open, does her best not to look as though she's terrified . . . of him.

Startled to see her waiting in the doorway, he immediately asks, "What happened? Are you okay?"

"Nothing happened, other than . . . that." She points at the purse, still on the coffee table behind her. "I'm just upset."

"This will help." He holds up the white plastic shopping bag in his hand. "I got the milk, and some saltines, too."

"Thank you." She reaches for the bag, knowing he's waiting for her to step aside and let him in.

"You go lie down and I'll bring you the milk." Still holding the bag, he makes a move to come in, awkwardly blocked by her position in the doorway.

"No, actually, I'll just take this"—she grabs the bag from him—"and I'll see you . . . tomorrow."

"Tomorrow?" he echoes, shocked. "You're not staying here alone tonight."

No, she's not. Rita will stay with her. She's in the bedroom even now, waiting silently, listening, just in case something happens.

"I'll be fine," Peyton tells Tom. "I'm just exhausted, and I really . . . I want to be alone tonight. Okay?"

"I don't think that's a good idea."

She studies the concern on his face, wondering if it might somehow be genuine after all, or a practiced mask.

"Really, Tom, I just want to go to sleep."

"I can stay on the couch and stand guard. Just in case—"

"Nothing's going to happen. It was a creepy prank. And I promise I'll call you if I need you. You can be here in two minutes." It's all she can do to keep her voice steady as she echoes the phrase that was once so reassuring to her.

Now it feels ominous.

He just looks at her, as though trying to come up with a convincing argument for his cause.

Then, as though he's realized that nothing he says is going to change her mind, he leans forward and kisses her forehead.

"Okay. If that's what you want. But I'll see you tomorrow."

"Right. Tomorrow."

She twists her clenched jaw into a smile and watches him turn and walk away.

Then she closes the door behind him, locks the bolts, and replaces the chain.

As an afterthought, she turns to the heavy desk, eyeing it as a potential barricade.

"Wait, I'll help you," Rita says, reappearing in the room and instantly reading her mind. "Let me just put this down."

This, Peyton sees, is a meat cleaver her friend must have found in the kitchen drawer.

Noting her startled glance at the would-be weapon, Rita says simply, "I was afraid of him. I didn't know what he might try."

"I didn't either."

"Look, I'm thinking I should probably call J.D. or one of my boys to come stay here tonight with us."

"Oh, Rita, don't do that. I'm sure we'll be fine. He's not going to try anything." There's still a part of her that can't quite accept that Tom, *her* Tom, is capable of hurting her. "Did you tell J.D. what was going on when you called him?"

"Are you kidding? He would have been over here in a heartbeat."

Or in two minutes, Peyton thinks grimly.

"I just told him you were having some light contractions and I didn't think it was a good idea to leave you here alone."

"Was he upset?"

"Trust me, he's used to my being gone all night. It goes with the territory in my business. And sometimes he takes off for a day or two himself."

"He does? Where does he go?" she feels obliged to ask, wondering where Tom is now. Is he still standing outside? Or is he walking home? Did he believe her when she told him she wanted to be alone?

"Oh, we have a cottage out on Long Island," Rita is saying. "We got it before the boys were born. I'll take you out there sometime. You'd love it."

Peyton nods, knowing Rita is trying to distract her from her fear.

As if she realizes it isn't working, she says, "Listen, Peyton, I can call J.D. to come here if that will make you feel safer."

"No, I think we're okay for tonight. I just feel bad making you stay here and lie to J.D."

"Not a big deal. And hey, I'm not complaining. This way, I won't have to listen to him snore."

At last, Peyton manages a smile, grateful for her friend's presence. "You might have to listen to me snore instead. As far as I know I never did before I was pregnant, but Tom said—"

She catches herself.

The expression in Rita's eyes tells her that they're thinking the same thing.

Don't believe anything Tom says.

Aloud, she merely commands, "Step aside, sugar pie, so I can move this desk."

"But . . . it's heavy."

"Good."

Rita gives it a mighty shove, sliding it securely in front of the door.

"There," she says, brushing off her hands. "Safe. For tonight."

"I'll call a locksmith first thing in the morning," is Peyton's glum reply.

Most of the photos laid out on the quilted turquoise bedspread are grainy, snapped from a distance and blown up, with branches and leaves visible around the perimeters of most. They were snapped in a schoolyard, the focal point a big wooden jungle gym with swings, ladders, slides, monkey bars. In the background is a painted sign whose letters are blurred, but that is inconsequential when one knows what they read.

Edgewood Elementary.

The girl with the hauntingly familiar features is in action in all but one of the pictures: climbing, sliding, swinging, her limbs and even her blond pigtails captured as they sail about in midair.

But in one snapshot, she is simply standing, looking straight ahead, almost as though she senses the camera.

"Did she notice that you were taking this?" Anne Marie asked the private investigator the first time she saw it, feeling sick at the possibility that the girl might have realized she was being watched.

"No way. I was in the woods, too far away for anyone to realize I was there."

That's probably true, judging from the few photos that weren't blown up, in which she and the other children are mere specks on the horizon.

Regardless, the magnified photo in which she appears to be staring into the lens makes Anne Marie increasingly uneasy every time she sees it.

She has seen it often these past few months, surreptitiously removing it from its plain manila envelope every waking hour; seeing it even in her sleep, in her dreams, in her nightmares.

She's seen it so often that this child's face has irrevocably morphed with the one she remembers, the one she has carried in her mind's eye all these years.

Now, trying to dissect the features she knows so well, she has no idea where one face ends and the other begins, no way of distinguishing past from present.

Yet it always comes down to the fact that this girl is still alive.

Although sometimes, even now, Anne Marie almost believes the impossible: that her predecessor might be, too.

"You can't do this, Mary," Javier Nueves pleads, pacing the length of the small living room and back again. "You *promised* me that you wouldn't do this. That Father Roberto was the only person you would tell."

"That was before I knew—" She catches herself, unable to say it, even now, a month after the shocking loss. "That was when I thought I would be able to tell him."

"*Ay, por amor de Dios,* Mary! You aren't thinking what can happen."

"Yes, I am." Again, she wipes her streaming eyes with a soggy tissue using one trembling hand, holding her swaddled infant against her breast with the other. "I know exactly what can happen."

Javier stops in front of the sagging couch where she sits, lashing out at her as he never before has done. "You know what can happen? And you're willing to do this anyway? *Usted esta loco!*"

Loco.

An apt description, perhaps, one that has crossed her own mind these past few weeks.

She can't argue with Javier. Perhaps insanity is the only explanation for what they—what *she*—agreed to do.

She went out of her mind with grief every time she lost another baby; was crazed with anguish when the promised adoption fell through. Why else would she have accepted Rose's offer, and the burden of guilt that now goes with it?

The weight of that remorse has grown too heavy to bear, threatening to smother all that now sustains her, including her marriage, even the joy borne of motherhood.

"I have to tell somebody, Javier," she desperately tells her husband, begging his understanding, his forgiveness. "I have to."

"But why? Who will you tell?"

The baby cries out at the sound of her father's harsh demands.

"*Lo siento mucho, mi tesoro.*" Javier bends to kiss his daughter's head, pressing his lips against the pink bow Mary tied around one silken tuft this morning. Pink, to match one of the beautiful dresses Javier brings home by the armload from the thrift store on the corner. Dresses for his little treasure.

How will I live with myself if I tell and destroy him? Mary wonders in anguish.

Yet another, perhaps even more agonizing, question persists. *How will I live with myself—and my sin—if I don't?*

Kneeling before her, resting his clasped hands on her knees as though in prayer, Javier hoarsely repeats, "Who will you tell? Father Roberto is—"

"I know! I know what happened to him. Don't say it, please."

"Well, who will you tell?"

"I don't know," she wails softly. "The police?"

"The police?" Storm clouds obliterate what was left of her husband's attempt at compassion. "You can't tell the police. They'll go to the mother and—"

"You mean the donor."

"I mean the thirteen-year-old *perra,*" he amends crudely, and Mary winces.

This isn't her gentle, loving Javier. This is a man blinded—no, *tainted*—by the delusion she herself once nurtured.

"Javier, please don't—"

"No, *you* please don't," he flings back at her. "If you tell the police what happened, they'll give our daughter back to someone who doesn't deserve her. Is that really what you want?"

"That isn't going to happen. She never wanted the baby, Javier. You know that. The police will know that, too. What makes you think—"

"She has a family, doesn't she? Everybody has a family. What if they want the baby? They'll take her away from us."

"Maybe they won't."

"Maybe they will. We can't take this chance!"

"We have to. *I* have to. Can't you see, Javier? I can't go on like this. I can't live with this sin. I have to leave this in God's hands."

"God doesn't want this innocent child torn from the only parents she knows!" His voice breaks, and he clings to her now, imploring, "Mary, can't you see? You have to open your eyes and see the truth. Dawn was a gift from God."

No, Mary thinks dully, resting her tear-dampened cheek against the baby's black hair, *Dawn wasn't a gift from God.*

She was a gift from a woman who had no right to play God.

CHAPTER FIFTEEN

The sudden ring of the telephone startles Peyton awake.

Reaching for the receiver on the bedside table, she glances blearily at the clock and sees that it's six-thirty. The last time she looked, having watched the minutes tick by for the duration of the night, it was five forty-five.

That was right after she popped the two blue pills Rita handed over with sympathetic reluctance.

"Peyton, it's me. Are you okay?"

"Tom?" Heart pounding, she struggles to shake off a numbing wave of grogginess. She sits up and looks warily around the shadowy room, almost expecting to see the unwelcome caller lurking in a corner.

"I'm going to go pick up bagels and come over."

"No!" Tempering her panic, she manages to say, "I mean, don't come now. Please. I didn't sleep well all night and I need to rest."

"I knew you wouldn't sleep after all that. You'll feel safer if I'm there. I'll just hang around and keep an eye on things while you rest."

"No, really. I just want to be left alone for a while. Please."

He hesitates. "Do you mean left alone so you can sleep this morning? Or left alone for a while . . . period?"

She groans. "Please, Tom, I'm exhausted. I took some Tylenol PM and it's knocking me out. I can barely speak right now."

"You're not supposed to take anything like that when you're pregnant."

Irked by the gentle scolding, she opens her mouth to tell him that she checked with Rita first. That will only require complicated explanations she isn't prepared to give, and he doesn't deserve.

"Look, just let me sleep," she says wearily. "I'll talk to you later."

"Okay. Call me if you need me."

She mumbles an unintelligible reply and hangs up, collapsing against the pillow again.

"I knew he'd call first thing."

She gasps at the sound of the voice and looks up to see Rita standing in the doorway.

"Sorry . . . I didn't mean to scare you, sugar pie."

"I know, I'm just jumpy. Did you sleep?"

"Not much." Rita runs a hand through her disheveled gray hair, her eyes barely visible beneath her unkempt fringe of bangs. "Listen, I'm going to make some coffee. The locksmith will be here in a little while. You just rest."

"Call me when he gets here, okay?"

"I will."

Peyton closes her eyes, already drifting away on a billowing cloud of unconsciousness.

Last night's delightful little stunt was never part of the plan.

Unlike the Bible, the meaningful gift *all* the donors receive, this was an afterthought. Peyton Somerset won't learn anything from it, other than that she isn't in charge of every element of her life.

It's an important lesson, one they could all have stood to learn. But Peyton, more than anyone else. She exudes an inner strength of character that most donors either conceal, or lack entirely. She isn't the least bit leery of the prospect of raising a baby without a loving father to share the blessing.

No, she thinks she can do it all, have it all. She's brazenly claimed as her own the God-given right denied to scores of deserving couples.

For that, she must be punished. This is no longer about the work: the methodical inverted process of take-and-give.

No, and I'll be the first to admit it.

This has become a personal vendetta.

Peyton Somerset is the epitome of the self-indulgent donor,

manipulating the natural order of the universe to suit her own greedy needs.

That's why this time, particularly from here on in, things are going to be different.

Of course there was a momentary lack of organization. First, the unforseen elimination of the Cordells as adoptive parents, then the Khatirs' refusal to accept the proposal. Then there's the cloying recollection of holding a pillow over an innocent man's face until he ceased to breathe.

And a priest, at that.

But you do what has to be done for the greater good. You do whatever it takes to preserve the clandestine nature of the work, do it all without flinching, and then you move on.

As I have.

Everything is under control once again.

Perhaps Peyton Somerset will be the final donor. Perhaps there will be more, but chosen, in the future as in the past, at random once again.

Live and learn.

In any case, the Somerset baby will come into the world to find both a mother and father waiting.

He's going to be so thrilled, and so surprised. I can't wait to tell him . . .

But I will. I'll wait until the time is right.

And in the meantime, there's plenty to do. The bloody gift in Peyton's handbag was the perfect way to knock the infuriating Ms. I've Got It All Under Control off balance.

It was so satisfying that it's tempting to do it again . . . and again . . . if only to banish the impatient boredom that always sets in during the last trimester, when everything is in place, and there's nothing to do but wait.

Mary opens her eyes abruptly to see the sun seeping into the crevices around the perimeter of the drawn aluminum blinds. Slashes of its rays even manage to push through a few of the slats that didn't close all the way, caging the bed beneath the window in strange bars of light.

The angle is all wrong, Mary thinks vaguely, in the moment before it occurs to her to glance at the clock.

No wonder. It's late.

Past ten, already.

A frisson of panic takes hold, and she bolts from the bed, racing for the baby's room.

Dawn has never made it through the night without waking to be fed. Three o'clock, seven o'clock . . .

She should have awakened Mary at least twice by now. Unless Javier got up with her . . .

But he leaves for his Saturday job at the loading dock well before six. Even if he'd given her that first feeding . . .

A frantic, sick feeling washes over Mary as she steps over the threshold into the baby's room, where the blinds are still drawn and the night-light still shines.

How many tragic crib death accounts did she hear about in the bereaved parents' support group she went to for a short time after her first stillbirth? She still recalls the ravaged expressions on the faces of women who described oversleeping, then rushing to check on their babies, only to find them stiff and cold.

Mary remembers thinking, even then, *At least you had them for a little while. At least you got to hold them, feed them, feel like a mother . . .*

I was denied all of that.

Now, as she approaches Dawn's cradle, guilt courses through her. This loss is more terrible, even, than the crippling losses she's already suffered. She's held Dawn, fed her . . .

I'm her mother. And I've lost her.

She closes her eyes as she takes the last few steps, whispering a prayer, asking God for a miracle she doesn't deserve, for strength to face what lies ahead if there can be no miracle.

Then she leans over the cradle, where the white crocheted blanket she tucked securely around her daughter last night lies rumpled at the bottom . . .

And she realizes the cradle is empty.

"I can think of a hundred places I'd rather be," Detective Sam Basir says wistfully.

"I can think of a thousand," Detective Jody Langella replies. Chief among them, down at Breezy Point with her firefighter husband and kids at the annual August beach party.

"Yeah? You're probably wishing you were down at Breezy with Jack and Mandi and Jackie Jr."

Okay, so her longtime partner has the uncanny ability to read her mind. Jody shrugs. "Drunken firemen, burnt hot dogs, jellyfish stings . . . who needs that?"

"You do," Sam tells her. "Maybe you'll get down there in time to have a cold one and see the fireworks."

"I doubt it."

Leaving behind the blazing afternoon sunlight, they walk into the towering Co-op City building.

Jody flashes her badge at the building manager she met last month, and learns that nobody has been picking up mail for the Cordells' apartment.

"What am I supposed to do? Just let it keep piling up?" the manager asks, wringing his hands.

"You could always just open it."

The swarthy little man's eyes shoot toward his receding hairline at Sam's brazen suggestion.

"He's just kidding." Jody shakes her head at her partner, wondering why he insists on riling the innocent.

Moments later, they're being escorted to the fourteenth-floor apartment where Linden Cordell lived with his wife Derry.

After unlocking the door, the manager asks, "Do you need me to stay here this time? Because I have to get back—"

"Go, go." Jody is already in the living room, intent on looking the place over with a fresh perspective.

Nothing has changed in the month since she was here, aside from a staler smell, more cobwebs, a thicker layer of dust. Particles are stirred to dance in the air wherever she walks, glinting like glitter in the sunlight streaming in.

The place is stuffy; Sam swiftly opens every window.

Glancing over a stack of CDs beside the stereo in the living room, he plucks a few off the shelf to examine them. "Check it out, Langella. I haven't even heard of most of these bands since high school. AC-DC? Rush? Hey, I'd love to hear—"

"Come on, we're not here to relive our youth, Sam."

Obviously still convinced they're wasting their time investigating a random murder, he tosses the CDs aside and asks, "So what is it that we're looking for?"

"Whatever we can find."

"I'd like to find something cold to drink." He steps into the kitchen, opens the refrigerator, and makes a face, quickly closing it. "God, that reeks."

"What did you expect? Nobody's cleaned it out in over a

month." Jody shakes her head and leaves him there, heading to the bedroom.

The closet isn't full, despite the fact that there is only one, and it contains both a man's and a woman's wardrobe. Jody is no fashionista despite her thirteen-year-old daughter's efforts, but even she can tell by the labels and fabric quality that the Cordells' clothing budget was limited.

There are a number of empty hangers on the woman's side. Plastic hangers, unlike the wire ones that hold all but two of the remaining garments: inexpensive summer blouses that still have tags on them. One is blue with ruffles, the other peach with a wide collar. Both are from Strawberries, marked down with final clearance prices, probably from the end of last season. Thanks to Mandi's obsession with clothes, Jody recognizes the style as having been popular last summer.

"What'd you find?" Sam asks from the doorway.

"She must have packed a lot of her stuff." Jody stares at the blouses. "But not everything. Wouldn't you think a woman who was leaving her husband—a woman who had very little clothing in the first place—would take everything? Or at least, almost everything?"

"Not necessarily. Maybe she wanted to travel light."

"But she left behind stuff that's new. Why would she do that? Wouldn't she want to bring the new stuff with her, at least?"

"Maybe she had other new stuff."

Jody shakes her head, lost in thought.

Something definitely isn't adding up.

"I still can't believe you forgot to tell me about Wanda last night," Peyton can't help chiding Rita as they step out of an air-conditioned cab into a blast of humid midday heat.

"Yeah, well, we were both a little preoccupied, remember?" Rita struggles to balance a large bouquet in one arm as the driver hands her the gift-wrapped boxes from the trunk.

"Here, give me the roses." Peyton reaches for them.

"No, the vase is heavy. I've got it."

"I'm not an invalid, Rita. I can help. At least give me a couple of boxes. They're not heavy, and it was my idea to buy all those little pink outfits, so it isn't fair that you have to lug them all."

"Yeah, yeah, yeah, I've got them." Rita shakes her head good-naturedly. "I should have known better than to take a pregnant woman to the layette department at Lord and Taylor."

"You're just lucky I didn't buy stuff for my own layette."

"Oh, I think that saleswoman figured you'll be back."

Peyton can't help smiling.

Rita was right earlier when she said shopping for baby gifts would be therapeutic. It was just what Peyton needed this afternoon to sweep away the bitter aftertaste of last night's trauma. She knows it'll come rushing back later, when at last she's forced to go home again, but for now, she has other things to think about.

As they make their way across Amsterdam Avenue to the entrance of Saint Luke's Hospital, she finds herself looking forward to seeing Wanda and her newborn baby girl, though certainly not the controlling philanderer who put them both in danger.

She still can't get over the shock of learning that Wanda delivered her baby girl without letting anyone know she was in labor. Anyone other than Eric, that is.

Peyton isn't hurt, exactly, that she didn't get a phone call. She's just surprised. Wanda promised to call her.

As for Rita—well, she's definitely hurt over the slight. Troubled, too. She wasn't thrilled with Peyton's suggestion that they bring the baby gifts they'd bought right over to the hospital this afternoon.

"I don't know if she wants to see anyone," was Rita's uncertain response. "Eric is probably there."

"Well, then we'll just have to meet the bastard, won't we?"

"I'm not up for that. You go."

"Come with me, Rita. Come on. We owe it to Wanda. She probably needs to know we care."

Peyton's little speech might have swayed Rita, but she privately has to admit to herself that her motives aren't entirely noble. She figures holding an infant in her arms will remind her of her own priorities, and help take her mind off everything—not to mention, keep her away from home . . . and Tom.

At least he can no longer get into her apartment. The locksmith arrived right on schedule this morning and had the new locks in place before Peyton even emerged from a welcome, much-needed slumber. By the time she woke up, Rita had paid him and sent him on his way, not to mention having made a large, healthy breakfast and cleaned the apartment.

"What would I do without you?" Peyton asks her again now, as they walk through the doors into the hospital.

"You'd be fine. You must have reminded me a dozen times last night and this morning that you can take care of yourself . . . remember?"

"I *can* take care of myself. Absolutely. It doesn't mean I don't appreciate a good friend."

"Unlike certain other people we know." Rita follows up with a tight-lipped shake of her head as they stop to look at the building directory.

"Come on, don't be mad at Wanda."

"I'm not as much mad as I am disappointed. How could she put herself and the innocent baby in jeopardy out of convenience for a man like that? I gave her more credit than that."

"She's insecure." Peyton shrugs. "She's not as strong as you are. Or as strong as I am. She thinks she needs him."

"Well, I need J.D., but I'm not going to compromise myself to keep him happy."

Peyton says nothing, just leads the way to the visitor registration desk, thinking about Tom.

As Rita gives the security officer Wanda's name, Peyton wonders whether Tom has been trying to call her all afternoon. Or maybe he came over, tried to use his key, and found out the locks have been changed.

"I'm sorry, what was the name?" the guard asks, after tapping a few keys and scrolling down the computer screen.

"Jones," Rita repeats. "Wanda Jones."

He checks the screen again. "I'm sorry, I don't have any patients by that name."

"She's a maternity patient. She was admitted yesterday through the emergency room. She delivered by C-section so she could be in surgical recovery."

"She'd show up on here no matter how she was admitted."

"Was she already released?" Peyton asks, puzzled. Surely they wouldn't let somebody go home less than twenty-four hours after major surgery.

"Figures," Rita mutters, rolling her eyes. "Big Daddy probably got tired of sitting around a hospital room."

"Can you check and see when she was released?" Peyton asks the guard. To Rita, she says, "We can always just take a cab down to her apartment and—"

"I don't have to check," the guard interrupts. "I have all the information I need right here. According to our records, your Wanda Jones was never a patient here at all."

* * *

Jody hangs up the telephone and looks at Sam. "Richie said Linden's wife definitely didn't have a laptop. She had a big old white desktop computer with a clunky tower and bulky monitor."

"Meaning . . . ?"

"Meaning she brought the computer with her when she left," Jody says, crossing over to the desk, where the computer must have stood. A surge protector power strip still occupies the outlet underneath.

"I wonder if she sent her husband the e-mail saying she was leaving him before or after she actually left. Is there any way to tell where it was sent from, and exactly when?"

"Not unless somebody saved it, and even then . . ." Sam shrugs.

"Richie doesn't know what Linden's password is—I already asked him," Jody tells him. "But he did see the e-mail when Linden opened it. He said he remembers it word-for-word."

"I don't know what you're getting at with all this stuff."

Jody isn't quite sure, either. But she knows there's something here, something she might be missing.

Thinking aloud, she says, "She took a big old P.C. with a clunky monitor, and she left the surge protector behind. Wouldn't she need it where she was going?"

"Maybe she forgot to grab it."

"She also left behind two relatively new blouses with tags on."

"Ah yes. The scintillating fashion angle."

Jody ignores his sarcasm, musing, "She didn't have a car. Did she get into a cab with all that stuff? She couldn't have lugged it on the subway or a bus—"

"Unless she had help."

"Even then . . . do you know how bulky those old computers are? And she'd have had luggage with her, too."

"You don't know that for sure."

"Sam, there isn't a single piece of luggage in this apartment. Not a suitcase, not a duffel bag."

"Maybe they don't travel."

"Everybody has some kind of luggage. Which means either one or both of the Cordells packed and took all whatever they had."

"Well, if that's the case, and it was her, with bags and a computer out on the street, she would have been pretty noticeable. We can start canvassing neighbors, bus drivers, regulars on the subway . . . but I still don't get it. Why? Why not just go with the random murder theory? That makes more sense to me than anything here."

"Because something just isn't adding up. And because I have a gut feeling about this, Sam," Jody says simply.

Before he can make the anticipated comment about her "woman's intuition," a voice calls from the hall.

"Hello?"

They turn to see an elderly woman standing in the doorway of the apartment, a purse in one gnarled hand and a shopping bag in the other. Clad in baggy stockings, terry cloth scuffs, and a nondescript housedress, she has white curly hair, glasses, and a hearing aid Jody can hear whistling from even across the room.

"Hi, can we help you?" Sam asks.

"I'm Myrtle Steiner. I live next door. What's happened now?"

Jody and Sam look at each other.

When Sam doesn't speak up, Jody reluctantly begins, "I'm afraid Mr. Cordell—"

"What's that?" the woman asks, motioning at her hearing aid and coming into the room.

"I said, Mr. Cordell had an accident a few weeks ago—"

"He was run over by a train. I heard about that."

"Did you know the Cordells then?" Jody's voice is still raised, but the woman talks over her as if she doesn't hear.

"I felt so bad about that poor man. What a terrible way to go. And what about her, poor thing? I haven't seen her around at all. Maybe she went to stay with family. I would, if I were widowed with a baby on the way."

Jody's heart skips a beat and she has to hold back a gasp.

She shoots a look at Sam, who barely raises an eyebrow as he calls out, "I'm sorry, what did you say, Mrs. Steiner? I must have heard you wrong."

"And they all tell me I'm the one who's deaf," she mutters good-naturedly, then shouts, "I said, poor thing was widowed with a baby on the way."

"Derry Cordell was pregnant?"

"You didn't know? She was pretty far along, I think. She was really showing."

"I just don't get it," Peyton is saying as she follows Rita across the broad sidewalk toward the towering brick and glass apartment building. "Why would she lie about where she delivered the baby?"

"I don't get it, either. And I don't like it."

Walking from the bright afternoon sunshine into the dimly lit lobby, it takes a moment for Rita to adjust her eyesight.

When she does, she's disappointed to see that the uniformed doorman is a stranger. If Jamil were here, he'd recognize her.

"We're here to see Wanda Jones in 28J," Peyton tells him.

"Your names?"

Rita looks at Peyton. "Think we should make something up so she'll let us in?" she asks under her breath, only half facetiously.

Peyton shakes her head disapprovingly. To the doorman she says, "Just tell her it's Peyton and Rita."

"Peyton and Rita?"

"She'll know us."

"Hang on a second."

She'll know us . . . but will she want to see us?

Rita has a feeling this is futile. She should never have agreed to come down here. Wanda obviously doesn't want to see either of them. Why else would she lie about where she delivered the baby?

The doorman has the desk phone up to his ear, head cocked, obviously listening.

Rita clenches and unclenches her hands, her short fingernails digging painfully into her palms.

The doorman hangs up the phone.

Rita knows before he speaks what he's going to say, yet a disappointed sigh escapes her when he informs them, "Nobody home up there. Sorry."

"Are you sure? Maybe she just couldn't answer the call," Peyton suggests. "She just had a baby. She's probably got her hands full."

"Can we just go on up?" Rita asks, knowing what the answer will be.

"Sorry, no."

"If we go up," Peyton persists, "we can knock and she'll let us in if she's up to it."

He shrugs, shaking his head. "I can't help you, ladies. I can't let you up without the tenant's permission."

"Thanks anyway." Peyton turns away. Looking at Rita, she says simply, "She has to be here."

"Obviously, she doesn't."

"She has a newborn. Where else would she possibly be?"

"I don't know . . . the boyfriend's house?"

"With his wife and kids? I doubt it."

"She told me they're out East this weekend," Rita points out.

"She told you a lot of things. Who knows if any of it is true?"

There's nothing for them to do but walk toward the door, their shoes making hollow tapping noises on the polished marble floor.

The door might as well be a mile away. Rita's legs suddenly feel like shoelaces, the sleepless night catching up with her at last. She covers her mouth to stifle an enormous yawn, wishing she were home, curled up in bed . . . which, as Peyton pointed out, is precisely where one would expect to find somebody who just had a baby.

Something occurs to Rita, then, a thought so outlandish, so chilling, that she stops in her tracks.

Peyton, two steps behind, almost walks into her. "Rita! What's wrong?"

"Nothing. I . . . I'm sorry."

Not daring to even mention to Peyton the preposterous idea that's forming in her mind, she resumes walking, her mouth set grimly.

Peyton is silent as she follows her out the door, but her earlier question echoes ominously through Rita's mind.

Why would she lie about where she had the baby?

What if, Rita can't help wondering, Wanda didn't just lie about where she had the baby?

What if she lied about having had the baby at all?

CHAPTER SIXTEEN

Somebody's home, Anne Marie realizes, as she walks up the creaking, slightly listing front porch steps of the house she's visited before, but only undercover of darkness.

Now, the peeling paint, missing spindles, and broken shutters are boldly visible, yet the house lacks the forlorn, run-down air of others on the block. Bright, dappled sunshine filters through a leafy canopy of old trees onto a dandelion-spotted lawn and overgrown blooming shrubs. Rather than seeming unkempt, there is a somehow a wild, natural beauty to the surroundings.

Fittingly, a lone butterfly flits close to the vibrant Rose of Sharon hedge that borders the porch rail.

Seeing it, Anne Marie is reminded of the day at the Bronx Zoo, the day when she glimpsed the face that triggered a year's worth of renewed agony . . . and led her to this very spot.

There are no coincidences in life, Grace DeMario used to say, and Anne Marie knows now that she was right about that.

She was meant to be in the butterfly garden that day, meant to make the earth-shattering discovery, meant to see this through to the end.

Music floats through the screen door and open windows, the kind of music that once drove Anne Marie crazy. Back when it infiltrated her own home day in and day out, she called it bubblegum pop.

She wonders what they're calling it these days.

It certainly sounds the same. Lyrics that contain lots of *baby, babys* and *yeah, yeahs,* a strong base beat, a synthesized background version of the vocalist echoing herself in falsetto.

There was a time when Anne Marie was certain she would scream if she heard any of those redundant songs again.

Then, as though her wish had been granted by a sadistic genie, the music, and the girl who used to sing along, were silenced forever.

She arrives on the no-frills, black rubber mat emblazoned with the word *Welcome.*

Welcome.

Yeah, I doubt that, she thinks with the closest thing to irony that remains of her long lost sense of humor.

She won't be welcome. But she's here anyway. And she's not leaving until she gets some answers.

Anne Marie takes a deep breath and rings the doorbell.

"If Derry was pregnant, I would have known about it," Linden Cordell's friend Richie insists, leaning back on a sofa that's seen better days, hands folded across his Harley Davidson T-shirt.

"Maybe they wanted to wait awhile before they told people," Jody suggests. She herself kept the news of both pregnancies secret until she was safely past her first trimester.

"I ain't 'people.'" Richie's furrowed brows descend beneath the swoop of his bandanna do-rag. "Linden and me were like brothers. He woulda told me right away if she was pregnant. I knew all about how hard they were trying for a kid for all those years. . . ."

"So they had difficulty conceiving?"

"She couldn't get pregnant. That what you mean?"

"That's what we mean," Sam says dryly. "So if Linden was like a brother to you, is Derry like a sister?"

"Nah. She don't like me that much."

Jody wants to ask him to elaborate, but Sam has already moved on to, "When was the last time you saw her?"

"Oh God, who knows? I guess March? April, maybe?"

So it's possible Derry was pregnant but not showing at the time, Jody concludes.

But why didn't Linden tell his closest confidant? Or his elderly mother?

Jody spoke to the elder Mrs. Cordell herself, when she broke the news about her son's death. After the initial shock and extended silences Jody perceived as emotionally reflective, she asked about her daughter-in-law.

But she never mentioned a baby on the way. Nor did she seem particularly distressed when she found out Derry had left Linden.

"I never expected that to last," is what she said offhandedly, with a detachment that didn't sound like any mother—or even mother-in-law—Jody has ever encountered.

"Do you think Linden didn't tell you because the baby wasn't his?" Sam asks Richie, echoing Jody's next thought exactly.

"Nah. If she was pregnant by another guy, trust me, he woulda said something. I asked him if she left because of someone else, and he said no way. She didn't cheat. He was positive about that. Look, the guy was desperate to find her. By the end, he was going crazy trying to figure out where she was. He musta talked to every single person she ever knew in her life."

"But he didn't file a missing-person's report."

"Nah. Why would he? She wasn't kidnapped or anything. She wasn't some runaway kid. She was a wife who took off and left her husband. She even told him she was going, remember?"

"But he never heard from her again, after that one e-mail?"

"Nope. Not a word. She didn't want to be found, just like she said in the e-mail."

"What did she say again?" Jody asks.

"She said, 'I'm leaving New York. I need space to get my life together. Don't look for me. I'll come back if I'm good and ready.' "

"She said that? 'If I'm good and ready'? Not 'when'?"

"Somethin' like that," he concedes. "Let's put it this way: she didn't have a round-trip ticket to wherever she was headed."

"So you're saying Linden was pretty sure she left. That she wasn't abducted."

"Right. He said they were fighting a lot lately. He spent a lot of time at my place."

"And you're saying," Jody muses, "that she couldn't have been pregnant, because if she was, it would have been Linden's baby, and if it was, you would have known about it? Is that right?"

"That's right."

"But she *was* pregnant," Sam reminds her a few minutes later, as they walk down East 222nd Street, away from Richie's building. "The deaf old lady wasn't the only one who knew that. All the neighbors we asked said the same thing."

"I know. But . . . why wasn't there anything even remotely related to pregnancy or babies in that apartment?"

"Maybe she took it all with her."

"That would explain the empty hangers, and why she hadn't worn the new blouses. If she was showing, she was in maternity clothes. She must have packed them all."

"Why wouldn't the husband tell the best friend she was pregnant?"

"And why wouldn't he at least check in with the police after she left? I still find it hard to believe there's nothing in our files, not a single report involving this. If he was so worried he was asking everyone she ever knew if they'd heard from her, wouldn't he have at least checked to make sure she didn't, I don't know, get run over by a bus?"

"Or a subway train. What, you're thinking it runs in the family, huh?" Sam smiles at his own gallows humor.

"I'm thinking Linden Cordell didn't want the police involved."

Sam's smile fades. "Yeah, I'm starting to think the same thing. You think he offed the wife, then put up a big concerned-husband front, pretending he was looking all over for her? Maybe he even sent himself that e-mail, huh?"

"Maybe. But that still doesn't explain the pregnancy."

"Maybe these people are wrong. Maybe she wasn't pregnant. Maybe she just gained a lot of weight."

Jody rolls her eyes. "She told all the neighbors she was pregnant, Sam. She said she was due in October. She wasn't trying to hide anything. You heard what that old man, Abe, said. He said she was thrilled about it."

"Maybe her husband wasn't."

"Right. If he didn't tell his friend about the baby, the friend he confided in about absolutely everything else, it's because he wanted to keep it a secret. Why? The rest of the world already knew. Everybody who saw her knew."

They reach the light, and Sam looks at his watch. "So what's next? How about cold beers at the beach?"

"How about track down Derry Cordell's obstetrician and talk to him?"

"How about you're no fun at all?" He sighs. "Let me guess, we have to haul ourselves back to Co-Op City and try to figure out who her ob-gyn is, then wait for a search warrant?"

"Nope." Jody reaches into her pocket and pulls out the appointment card she found on the dusty floor beside a wastebasket in the Cordells' master bedroom earlier. It must have missed the trash and fallen, unnoticed, just out of sight beneath the hem of the dust ruffle.

Sam looks over her shoulder, reading the card. "Dr. William J. Lombardo. Are you sure he's the one?"

"According to this card, Derry Cordell had an appointment with him back in February. He must know something. Let's go."

"What about the search warrant?"

"We'll just question him. We aren't going to search medical records or anything. Yet," she adds as an afterthought, already striding toward the downtown subway.

"Did you say the patient's name is Derry Cordell?" echoes Dr. Lombardo's nurse, a pleasant-faced middle-aged woman named Nancy who was summoned to the small conference room by the receptionist.

The doctor himself is reportedly assisting with a delivery and may not be back to the office today.

"Derry Cordell, right." Jody notes the unmistakable recognition—as well as piqued interest—in the woman's eyes. If they tread carefully enough, they might be able to get valuable information out of her. "Is she a patient here?"

"She *was* a patient here. The last time we saw her was in February, although . . ."

When Nancy trails off, Sam prods, "Although . . . ?"

"Although her husband did come in here a few months back, wanting to know if we'd seen her. He said she was missing and he was trying to track her down."

"Why would he think you might know where she was?"

"Who knows?" Nancy shrugs. "He said he was desperate to find her and he was talking to everybody his wife ever knew, trying to figure out if she told anyone where she was going. I guess he figured she might have confided in Doctor Lombardo. A lot of our patients do."

"Did Derry Cordell?"

"Not as far as I know. We haven't heard from her since she was here last winter. But even if we had . . ." The woman shakes her head. "I'm not supposed to be discussing any of this. Patient confidentiality is—"

"I totally respect that, but we're conducting a homicide investigation here," Jody cuts in.

The nurse's eyes widen. "Did something happen to Mrs. Cordell?"

"We're not sure. But something definitely happened to her husband."

"What happened?"

"He was murdered."

Nancy gasps, pressing a row of polished pink fingernails over her mouth. "Murdered? But when? How?"

Jody is uninterested in providing the gory details, particularly to somebody who looks as intrigued as she does horrified. She's familiar with people like Nancy; can see the wheels turning even as she assumes a not-quite authentic sorrowful expression.

She's probably exhilarated to be privy to a juicy murder investigation, already imagining what she'll tell her coworkers and acquaintances.

"We'll have a warrant to seize access to her medical files," Jody tells her, "but in the meantime you might be able to help us."

"Why? Did she have something to do with it?"

"She's missing, and we need to find her," Sam says simply.

"Like I said, we haven't heard from her in months. I can't believe somebody killed him. Do you think she could have done it?"

Jody and Sam exchange a glance.

"Let's put it this way," Sam says. "Do *you* think she could have done it?"

"No."

"Why not? Because they were expecting a baby, or . . ." Jody trails off, hoping Nancy will take the bait.

"No, she wasn't pregnant."

"How do you know?"

"Because that would be impossible."

"Impossible is a strong word, Nancy."

"Trust me, impossible is the right word to use here. I was there when Dr. Lombardo told Mrs. Cordell that she was physically incapable of conceiving and carrying a child."

The woman on the other side of the screen door looks nothing like the child whose pictures are in the manila envelope back in Anne Marie's hotel room. Olive-complected with short black hair and elfin features, she's barefoot and wearing rolled-up denim overalls and a sleeveless T-shirt.

"Can I help you?" she asks, head tilted as if she's trying to remember if she was expecting a visitor.

"Mrs. Clements?"

"Yes . . . ?"

Countless times in the last few days, in the last few minutes, Anne Marie rehearsed what she was going to say in this moment. The settled-upon speech was concise and unemotional, and she managed to get through it time and again without tearing up or losing track of where she was going.

But that was when she was talking to herself in the mirror.

Now that it's real, now that she's facing the woman who has what is rightfully hers, she finds herself faltering.

She finds herself focusing on a small tear in the screen as she mumbles, "I was wondering if I can speak to you about . . ."

About your so-called daughter.

Say it, she commands herself. *Speak up and say it.*

But the moment has passed, and she can hear footsteps pounding down the stairs. Coltish, running footsteps that belong not to an adult, but to an impetuous child.

"Mommy?"

That word . . . in that voice . . .

And there she is, a golden girl with a long waist and bare bronzed limbs, sun-streaked hair, an innocent smile; there she is, as though she stepped out of the past, out of a grave, alive once more.

Oh my God. Oh my God.

Anne Marie's hand flies out to keep her steady, resting on the door frame so abruptly that the woman beyond the screen takes a startled step backward. Her hand is raised in front of the girl, an age-old, instinctive maternal shield from danger.

She thinks I'm the danger, Anne Marie realizes incredulously. *This woman, who stole the most precious thing in the world from me, is looking at me like she thinks I'm here to destroy her.*

Ask her where the child came from. Ask her for proof that she belongs to her.

Trembling, Anne Marie turns her attention from wary adult to curious child, and finds herself gazing into a pair of unusually shaded blue-green eyes.

That's when reality hits her.

It isn't her.

The girl looks like her, sounds like her, moves like her . . .

But the eyes are different, in shade and in shape.

And the lips. The lips are wider, and . . .

And she has braces.

Heather never wore braces. She needed them, the dentist concluded after a series of X-rays, but they were well beyond financial reach.

So Heather was forced to live with a gap in her smile, and the X-rays were dumped into a file folder, not to be seen again until they would be used to identify sparse, dismembered remains found in a landfill.

But Anne Marie never knew until that morning in June, when her cell phone rang with the Brahms lullaby tone she'd assigned to Mason Hertz. He was the private detective she'd hired with Jarrett's money.

That morning, while her children played in the next room and the sun streamed in the windows of her beautiful Bedford mansion, he broke the news that should have been broken to her years ago.

The authorities must have tried to locate her way back then with their somber news, Mason Hertz informed her. But by then, Anne Marie DeMario had disappeared from Staten Island, where she had lived her whole life. She had fled north, to the Hudson Valley, without leaving a trace. The person she once was had ceased to exist, replaced by a shell of a human being who lived every day wishing she were dead.

Then Jarrett came along and gave her the opportunity to reinvent herself as Anne Marie Egerton. Neither he, nor anybody she met after she left the city, ever knew she had been a teenaged single mother.

A mother who was too overwhelmed by the sheer financial responsibility of providing for her child to realize that somebody might steal her away.

Heather. Oh, Heather.

Heather's eyes were brown, not aquamarine, with a wide-set, distinctive roundness, like her great-grandmother's.

"She has my chestnut eyes," Grace DeMario would say proudly. "And a mind of her own, that one, just like me."

A mind of her own, yes, and it led her down a rocky path and well beyond Anne Marie's grasp.

I did everything I could to keep her out of trouble, and safe with me, she tells herself adamantly, jabbing the base of her palm into eyes that are suddenly tear-blinded.

"Mommy, what's wrong with that lady?"

That lady.

That's all I am to her. All at once, Anne Marie isn't here to accuse, to condemn, to reclaim. Not yet. Maybe not ever.

Maybe all she needs now is to know how the path wound its

way here, to this comfortably lived-in house in suburban Long Island.

She clears her throat, looks up at the woman, begins to speak.

But she's cut off by an abrupt "You're her, aren't you? You called me that day, asking crazy questions . . ."

She trails off and glances at the girl, who is hanging on every word.

"Kelly, go get Daddy. Hurry," she commands urgently, her eyes boring into Anne Marie.

Kelly. Not Heather.

The girl takes off running toward the back of the house, calling, "Daddy! Daddy, come quick!"

"Please," Anne Marie manages to say. "Please just tell me how you got her. I know she isn't yours."

"What are you talking about?"

"Look, I saw her birth certificate, but it isn't real. How did you get it? How did you get *her?*"

The woman takes a step back, shaking her head in angry denial, but she's frightened.

Anne Marie can smell her fear, can feel it breaking out like beads of sweat on a condemned inmate's brow.

Yet she summons her self-control with a blatant inhale-exhale to steady herself, and she glares at Anne Marie. "Listen, I don't know who you are, or why you're here, but—"

"I'll tell you who I am," Anne Marie says, in the instant before she hears a masculine voice calling, approaching from somewhere inside. "And I'll tell you who your daughter is."

"What are you talking ab—"

"She's my dead daughter's baby—she's my grandchild!" Anne Marie flings at her before turning and fleeing for the car at the curb.

"Gil? It's me, Peyton," she calls in response to the voice on the intercom. "Can I come up?"

There's no verbal reply, merely an abrupt buzz and a sharp click as the lock on the security door is released.

He only lives on the third floor but she waits for the elevator, balancing a hand on top of her belly.

Too much stress today, she tells herself, cringing as she feels yet another sharp twinge down low in her pelvis, well beneath the spot where she's grown used to the baby's kicks and squirms.

She promised Rita she would go straight home and lie down

when they said good-bye outside Wanda's apartment building. It was the only reason Rita agreed to let her go on her own; otherwise, she said, she was going to insist on staying at Peyton's again tonight.

"Go, Rita," Peyton insisted. "You miss J.D., snoring and all. Go home to him. I'll be fine."

And she really believed she would be.

But when she found herself in a cab, heading downtown to face God only knows what, she decided to make a pit stop at Gil's.

Not because she's anxious to rehash her perceived slight, or his failing marriage, or his being fired.

More because she dreads going home.

What if Tom shows up at her door?

What if he breaks in?

Do you actually think Tom is going to hurt you?

She steps into the small elevator and presses the button marked 3.

Maybe she does.

Maybe she doesn't.

Maybe she isn't sure what she's supposed to be thinking, feeling, doing.

The only thing she knows without a doubt is that with the new alarm system and dead bolts, and the bars on the windows, she should feel safe.

The elevator arrives on the third floor with a jarring bump that is echoed by another strange twinge in Peyton's pelvic region.

If she were further along in the pregnancy, she might think it could be labor. But of course, she still has ten weeks to go. It's too early for labor.

From here, she can see that the door to Gil's apartment is ajar. She walks toward it, wishing she had just gone home after all. What she needs, despite the solid six hours of sleep she got thanks to the Tylenol PM, is more rest.

For all she knows, the disgusting, bloody mess in her bag was some kind of sophomoric prank played by somebody at work who wants to get her riled up.

But what about the Bible?

Maybe that's unrelated.

Yeah, right. And maybe this thirty pounds Peyton has gained is unrelated to the fact that she's pregnant.

But she's weary of riding this dizzying carousel of possibilities. She's no longer as frightened as she is fed up.

She'll say a quick hello to Gil, mend the fences if she can, and be on her way.

"Gil?" she calls, pushing the door open.

He's sitting on the couch, surrounded by newspapers, magazines, empty snack bags, plastic laundry baskets containing heaps of clothes that are either clean and need to be folded or dirty and need to be washed.

Dirty, most likely. Nothing in this place looks or smells clean.

"Hi," he says, blinking up at her like somebody who's just been awakened—except that, judging by the smoldering cigarette in his hand, he wasn't sleeping.

At least, she hopes he wasn't.

"I didn't know you smoked." She closes the door behind her reluctantly, making a face at the toxic air.

"Yeah."

"Do you mind if I open a window?"

The old Gil would have opened it for her, putting out the cigarette and apologizing along the way, calling her Runt in that affectionate tone he uses with her.

This one merely says, "Go ahead."

Peyton crosses the room, sidestepping domestic debris along the way.

"I'm surprised to see you," Gil comments, after she tugs the window open and resists the urge to remove the screen and stick her whole head out into the fresh air.

She can't help retorting, "Yeah, well, I'm surprised to see you *this way.*"

He shrugs.

"What's going on with you, Gil?"

"You really want to know?"

"No, actually, I already know. Unless some new personal crisis has struck in the last few weeks?"

He stares at her for a long moment. Then he says, "You never used to be cruel."

"I'm sorry." She shakes her head, filled with remorse. "I didn't mean to be cruel. I'm just frustrated, seeing you this way."

And frustrated, seeing myself this way. I hate being afraid, and exhausted, and uncertain.

"So why did you come over?"

"Because I was worried about you, and you never called me back."

"I thought you were the one who never called back."

She clenches her jaw—then doubles over at an unexpected cramp.

Gil is on his feet and beside her in an instant. "What happened?"

"Ow . . ." The tightening sensation has passed.

"Come on, Runt, sit down." He's the old Gil again, hurriedly stubbing out the noxious cigarette, helping her to the couch, patting her shoulder, again asking what happened.

"I don't know. I think I'm okay now," she tells him, but alarm bells are sounding loud and clear in her mind.

"Do you need some water or something?" he asks, hovering.

"No," she says slowly, her thoughts careening once again. "But I think I need the telephone."

Hours have gone by with no sign of Javier or the baby.

Hours in which Mary has gone from frantic tears to silent anguish to stoic resolution.

Now she sits beside the empty cradle silently bargaining with God to give her back her family . . . including the child who isn't rightfully hers.

I know I have no right, Father. I know Javier and I can't give her everything she'll ever want.

But we can give her everything she'll ever need: a family, a roof over her head, our unconditional love. Things she might never have had if she hadn't come to us.

Mary rocks back and forth, hugging her empty arms against her barren breast.

She can't stand another minute of solitary silence. She needs to speak to someone, *anyone.*

But who is there to call? Javier has no family in this country; Mary had no one other than her mother. They have friends, of course, but contacting any of them would be inviting trouble. Questions would be asked, suspicions formed.

You can call the police, she reminds herself. *File a missing-person's report.*

No. That, at last, is out of the question. She won't have her husband branded a kidnapper, his photo and Dawn's plastered on Missing Children notices.

Wherever they are, Dawn is safe, and . . .

Javier was justified in taking her.

If he hadn't, Mary would have gone to the police, and the baby would have been wrenched from their lives.

What on earth was she thinking?

She wasn't thinking. She was merely feeling; feeling guilt, and remorse, and a selfish need to unburden herself at her daughter's—and her husband's—expense.

Well, Mary is no longer interested in exposing the deception that led to Dawn's arrival. Nothing could be worse than this soul-numbing grief. Nothing. Not even a lifetime of carrying the shameful secret.

It's time she called the one person who might be able to help her now.

Rose Calabrone.

The shrill ring of the cell phone in her pocket wakes Rita from a sound slumber. She opens her eyes to find that the living room has grown dark while she was sleeping; the occupants of the six o'clock news desk have been replaced by the ten o'clock weekend anchors.

"Rita. Did I wake you up?"

Doing her best to sound alert, she replies, "No, I was just . . ."

"Sleeping?" Peyton asks with a faint semblance of her usual wry wit.

"Yes," she admits. "What's wrong? Is everything okay at home?"

"I wouldn't know."

"What do you mean?"

"I'm in the hospital. I had some cramping, so I called Dr. Lombardo's office, and—"

"What?" Rita sits up straight in her chair, her heart sinking. "What is it?"

"Preterm labor."

"Oh, Peyton, no." Swept by emotion, Rita swallows hard, trying to find the right words. "You've been through so much, sugar pie. What did Bill say?"

Peyton pauses for a split second. Then, as though she just realized that Bill is Dr. Lombardo, she tells Rita, "He wasn't at the hospital with me. He was busy with a delivery so the on-call doctor came in. He said the baby's okay, but they want to keep me here until the morning, just to be sure. Then I have to go home and stay on bed rest until the baby is viable."

After a quick calculation, Rita asks, "About six weeks?"

"About that. I'm still in shock. What am I going to do about work?"

"They'll have to get along without you," she says, peeved that it's even an issue. "This is life and death, Peyton. You've got to take care of yourself and that baby."

"I know. And I will." She yawns deeply. "Listen, I need you to do something for me. They won't release me tomorrow unless I have somebody here to bring me home."

"I'll do it," Rita offers quickly.

"I knew you would. Thank you."

Peyton describes what happened, then, and apologizes profusely for going back on her word to just go home.

"Where's Gil now?"

"He stayed here with me until he was sure I was okay. Then he went to my apartment to meet the alarm installer."

"The alarm installer?" Rita echoes.

"I can't spend the next two months in that apartment without a security alarm. I can't even spend a night there without one. So Gil called a place from the hospital, and they said they could do it tonight."

"You gave him your keys?"

There's a moment of silence. "Rita, it's Gil. I've known him forever."

Rita shakes her head in disbelief. "And that's a reason to trust him? I thought you realized that you can't trust anyone."

"Not even Gil? I was thinking I might ask him to be my labor coach."

"Not even *anyone.* You never know, Peyton. The person you think is your closest friend might be an enemy."

There's a moment of silence.

Then Peyton asks, "Have you heard from Wanda again?"

"Not a word. I tried calling her when I got back home. No answer."

"Did you leave a message?"

"No. If I'd have said what I felt like saying to her, I doubt we'd ever see her again." Rita sighs. "Look, don't worry about Wanda right now. Worry about you."

"I can't help it. First Allison disappeared, and now—"

"Wanda hasn't disappeared. I spoke to her just yesterday, remember?"

"I know. But she wasn't in the hospital where she claimed to be, and she wasn't home. I just keep feeling like maybe she's in trouble."

Not about to disclose to Peyton her disturbing theories about Wanda Jones, Rita purses her lips, then says, "I'm sure she's fine. Just take care of yourself now, Peyton, for the baby's sake."

"But what am I going to do alone in my apartment for weeks on end? How will I survive?"

"I'll help you," Rita says simply, knowing she'll do whatever it takes to get Peyton through the rest of this pregnancy. There is nobody else the woman can turn to, nobody else she can dare trust with her baby's life. "I won't let anything happen to this baby, sugar pie. Everything is going to be just fine. I promise."

"Thanks, Rita." Peyton sniffles. Peyton, whom Rita has never seen cry. "Because the baby is all I care about now. Nothing else matters. Not work, not Tom, not anything else. You're a mother. You understand."

Rita nods. "Exactly. I'm a mother. I understand. Now get some sleep, okay?"

"Absolutely. And thanks, Rita." Speaking around an enormous yawn, Peyton says, "Nancy was right. She told me I'd be able to count on you."

Rita frowns. "Nancy?"

"She answered the phone when I called the office, and she met me over at the hospital. She stayed after Gil left, to help me get settled in and keep me company. She even offered to go take care of the alarm, but Gil insisted on doing it. Nancy's great, though, you know?"

"Yes, she is great," Rita agrees, biting back a warning there's really no reason to give.

For the next two months, Peyton will be cocooned in her apartment, protected from the rest of the world by alarms, locks . . .

And me, Rita reminds herself with fierce resolve. *As long as I'm there at her bedside, standing guard, nobody's going to get to her, no matter what.*

Mary is about to press the last digit on the telephone dial when she hears a sound so faint she wonders if she imagined it.

A baby's whimper.

Her heart stops.

Dawn?

Mary throws the telephone aside and hurries toward the sound, calling her daughter's name.

By the time she reaches the front door, it's already opening.

Javier stands there, the baby in his arms.

"Where were you?" Mary sobs.

He doesn't reply.

She hurtles herself forward, reaching for the fussy infant, holding her close. "How could you put me through that?"

But the words aren't accusatory, nor is her gaze when at last she lifts her head in his direction.

He says only, "I thought you needed to see more clearly."

Unable to speak, she can only nod, hoping he can see in her eyes all that she needs him to know.

In those terrible hours, she lost the only things that will ever truly matter.

Now that she has them back, she'll fight to keep them at any cost.

"You won't tell?" Javier asks, his dark eyes boring into hers, and she shakes her head.

"Do you promise you'll never bring it up again?"

She swallows hard, whispers, "I promise."

Satisfied, he nods, and turns his attention to Dawn, now settled contentedly into Mary's arms.

"She cried a lot," Javier informs his wife. "I think she missed her mother."

For a split second, Mary thinks of the teenaged girl. Then, with newfound resolve, she shoves her firmly from her mind.

Gazing down at the cherished baby in her arms, she croons, "*Es bien, mi tesoro. Su madre esta aqui.*"

Yes.

Your mother is here.

Alone in the hotel room, Anne Marie stares down at the red Bible in her lap.

She showed it to the police when Heather disappeared, but nobody ever considered it evidence that she had met with foul play—even when Anne Marie pointed out that she had never seen the Bible until she found it hidden in her daughter's room.

Convinced Heather was another pregnant teenaged runaway, the detectives were unfazed by the odd, highlighted passages in the Book of Wisdom.

. . . the numerous progeny of the wicked shall be of no avail; their spurious offshoots shall not strike deep root nor take firm hold . . .

. . . for children born of lawless unions give evidence of the wickedness of their parents . . .

"Your daughter must have been doing some soul-searching," Anne Marie was told by an older cop with judgmental eyes.

Ryan, to whom Heather was closer than anybody else, repeatedly assured Anne Marie that wasn't the case. Not that she had any doubts. In her last days, Heather seemed serenely accepting of the next phase in her life.

According to Ryan, Heather found the Bible in her backpack a few weeks before she vanished, and thought one of the kids at school had put it there as a joke. She never worried much about it, and neither did he. It wasn't the first time one of their peers saw fit to condemn her condition, just a more anonymous and creative alternative to whispering behind her back.

Anne Marie knows now that it wasn't a mean-spirited teenager who highlighted those Bible passages. It was somebody whose intention was far more malevolent.

Whoever left the Bible was responsible for her daughter's disappearance and death.

But the baby survived.

Nobody could have guessed that. Heather's remains had been dismembered and scattered, making it impossible for forensics to speculate that the fetus had been removed.

Who took the baby?

Who killed Heather?

She needs answers.

She needs closure, now more than ever.

That's why she hired the private investigator to reexamine her daughter's disappearance, unable to shake the vision she had glimpsed at the Bronx Zoo last summer. On several occasions this past spring, she snuck away to confer with Mason Hertz at his office in Upper Manhattan, telling Jarrett she was at the theater, or shopping, or meeting friends for lunch.

There were times when she knew he believed her grief had conjured the girl in the crowd at the zoo, times when she believed that herself. After all, it was preposterous to believe she had actually seen that hauntingly familiar face in a vast metropolitan area inhabited by tens of millions of faces . . . wasn't it?

But then, she had spent a decade scanning every face in every crowd, everywhere she went, for her daughter, looking for her lost child in every little girl who passed.

In her heart, she knew Heather was long dead; she just needed proof in order to move on, to start living again.

But Mason Hertz didn't just find proof of Heather's demise.

He found Edgewood Elementary School, and he found Kelly Clements.

He also found a legal birth certificate that confirmed she had been born to the couple who are raising her.

"I don't give a damn what that piece of paper says," Anne Marie had told him that day in his office, flinging it back at him. "She's Heather's. And she's mine."

Ten years, wasted. Ten years when she might have been able to watch Heather's baby grow, might have been able to raise her as she raised her own daughter and is raising her boys now. Just as Grace DeMario raised her.

There are no coincidences, Anne Marie.

No, there aren't.

Yet there's no use dwelling on what might have been.

She can only accept what is . . . and decide where to go from here.

She thinks of Ryan, all grown up now, working for a bank and planning a Christmas wedding to a woman he now lives with in Brooklyn. It wasn't hard for Mason Hertz to track him down.

When Anne Marie called him that day from the pay phone to tell him that his daughter might be alive, she expected an incredulous gasp, joyful tears; a barrage of questions at the very least.

But her bombshell was met with silence, followed eventually by a weary "You have to let go, Ms. DeMario. Just like I have."

"But . . . don't you want to find your daughter?"

"No, I'm sorry . . . I don't believe she's really alive. How can she be?"

Ann Marie opened her mouth to convince him, but he went on, "And even if she is, I just . . . I can't. I have a whole life now, I'm getting married, and I can't go back to all that . . . pain. Please try to understand."

But she couldn't understand. And she didn't try.

She hung up, knowing that she alone is responsible for uncovering the truth. She alone carries on in memory of the lovely young woman who is all but forgotten by the rest of the world, her child ripped from the womb and her body nothing more than a discarded incubator left to rot with rat-infested garbage.

Swallowing hard at the memory of the two calls she made on that day in the commuter parking lot, she picks up the telephone on the bedside table and dials.

She won't call Ryan again.

Nor will she call the Clementses.

A groggy voice answers after several rings.

She looks at the clock, belatedly recognizing the late hour as she says softly, "Jarrett? I'm coming home."

The water is boiling now, bubbling furiously in the small stainless steel kettle used solely for this sacred purpose.

A pair of tongs are propped against the rim, the pincers resting on the bottom beside the submerged knife, its extended blade camouflaged in the silvery depths.

Five minutes. That's the length of time necessary for sterilization. Less than a minute to go.

If only the remainder of Peyton Somerset's pregnancy could tick away as rapidly as the seconds on the stove timer.

But you don't have to wait until her actual due date. The baby will be able to breathe on its own well before that. All you have to do is get through another few weeks . . .

All the while, resisting the temptation to stoke her paranoia.

The situation has become too precarious. One false move, and it could all come crashing down.

Better to lie low than risk being discovered now, when the plan is teetering on the verge of fruition.

Yes. Far, far better to be invisible, to watch, to wait until the time is right, and then—

The timer emits a low-pitched buzz.

It's ready.

The knife is removed from its steaming bath with the tongs, and carefully dried on some sterile pads.

Then, in front of the bathroom mirror, the ritual begins.

There is no longer pain on the site of the scar when the blade slices carefully along the crimson line. Not physical pain, anyway.

With practiced expertise, the skin high on the forehead is split open just below the hairline, the blade dragged down a fraction of an inch to gouge the shallow flesh beneath.

Ah, there's the blood. A scarlet trickle forms a droplet that clings for a tantilizing second before falling onto a ledge of pink tongue that savors the salty warmth.

When the ritual is finished, the knife is washed clean in hot, soapy water.

Then it's set aside in a drawer, where it will remain until the wound begins to heal once again.

Month Eight
September

CHAPTER SEVENTEEN

The telephone rings just as Peyton is straining past her enormous stomach to turn over her final card in yet another futile game of solitaire.

"Rita? Are you going to grab that?" she calls, before remembering that her friend ran to Duane Reade to pick up more Tums for Peyton's worsening heartburn.

The phone is just out of reach on the bedside table. She debates whether to bother answering. It rarely rings these days, and when it does, she's never the one who picks it up.

Rita fielded the few calls from her office that came early on in her bed-rest sentence, as well as occasional inquiries from concerned family and friends. Aside from her mother's nightly long-distance check-ins, Peyton's contact with the outside world seems to have tapered off.

Gil initially popped in a few times, as did Nancy, and Kate, and Julie. But Rita discouraged prolonged visits, telling everyone Peyton needs her rest.

And she does. It feels good to hide away from the world, not having to deal with anything or anyone. It's as though she's been indefinitely cast adrift on a sea of tranquility, the weighty problems of the past having been cast away like anchors whose chains have been severed.

Legally unable to interfere with Peyton's medical leave, Tara has all but ceased to exist. Candace stopped by last week to drop off the pretty handmade quilt now draped over the side of the crib beside the bed. She mentioned that Alain's position remains open.

"I bet it'll be yours if you want it, whenever you come back," she confided.

If you want it.

Peyton, who has always known exactly what she wants, and how she's going to get it, is no longer certain of anything.

Funny how now that she has all this time to lie here and think, her thoughts are more muddled than ever.

She might be inclined to throw herself headlong into her career as soon as the baby is born.

Or she might be tempted to give up on Kaplan and Kline, on corporate America altogether.

The same uncharacteristic indecision hasn't just infiltrated her views on her professional life. She still isn't sure who, if anyone, to ask to be her labor coach. Rita keeps telling her there's time, that she can get through it without a coach if she chooses. Peyton doesn't know what to think about it.

Then there's Allison.

Is she still alive? Was she a victim, or an instigator of her own disappearance?

In the dead of night, when Peyton has trouble sleeping, she believes Allison is dead, and that something sinister is lurking nearby, ready to strike her as well. She's sure that the Bible and the bloody placenta are harbingers of catastrophes soon to come.

Then the sun comes up, Rita arrives to bustle around the apartment, and Peyton invariably decides Allison ran away, and that she herself merely fell victim to relatively benign pranks that may—or may not—have been played by a man she foolishly allowed herself to fall for.

The phone is still ringing. No caller ID on the bedroom receiver, either.

I should answer it. It might be Rita.

What if it's Tom?

When she first came home from the hospital last month, he repeatedly tried to see her, tried to convince her to at least talk to him.

Finally, in a single, terse telephone conversation, Peyton apologized for the sudden breakup, but informed him that she was no longer equipped to focus on anything but the baby. When he persisted, she dutifully handed the phone over to Rita, who was loyally standing by.

The midwife told him under no uncertain terms that the slightest mental anguish could be dangerous for both Peyton and the baby.

"You need to leave her alone, Tom," she said firmly. "And if you don't, I'll get the police involved."

That was the last time he called.

Rita has since reported that she's seen him from the window, lurking outside the building on occasion. But he's never attempted to come in.

Not that he can. The place is a fortress. Peyton has learned to feel safe here even when Rita goes home at night, thanks to the dead bolts, the bars, the alarm—and the six-inch carving knife she secretly keeps under her pillow.

Now, as she reaches for the phone, Peyton prays she isn't walking into an unwelcome confrontation with Tom—or another hangup. Rita told her there have been a few this week, most likely coming from pay telephones whose numbers don't appear on caller ID.

"Peyton, turn on the news," a female voice exclaims in response to her tentative "hello." "Channel seven. Now!"

"Who is this?"

"It's Julie. Hurry!"

It takes her a moment to locate the remote control amidst the stacks of cards on the rumpled bed.

"Do you see this?" Julie's voice rises in panic. "Oh God . . ."

"What is it, Julie?" Peyton aims the remote at the television, presses Power, and changes the channel.

Then, yes, she sees it.

And she realizes, in one sickening flash of recognition, that her life is in grave danger.

After a vigorous morning at preschool, the droopy-eyed triplets have been lulled into placidity by a *Blue's Clues* video, peanut butter and jelly triangles, and milk-filled sippy cups.

With any luck, Anne Marie thinks, they'll stretch out on the couches after they eat and fall asleep for a while. That will give her a chance to read this morning's newspaper, still untouched on the kitchen table, and to return several phone calls from mothers of overtly social preschoolers requesting play dates with one or another of the vivacious Egerton boys.

It's hard to remember now that there was ever a time when the trio lay in adjoining isolettes in the neonatal intensive care ward, their monitors bleating whenever one of them drifted too close to oblivion.

The nightmarish vigil lasted for weeks, with Anne Marie and Jarrett seeing each other only in passing, taking turns keeping watch over their delicate children who had been born too soon.

That was the turning point in their marriage, she realizes, looking back.

They had made it unscathed through courtship and commitment, then through the trials of infertility when she attempted to conceive as her age closed in on forty.

She didn't dare tell Jarrett that she knew she could carry a child, that she had already been pregnant and given birth, already been a parent.

Her gynecologist knew about her past pregnancy, of course, but he believed the lie she told him—that she had been pregnant as a teenager and given up the baby for adoption. She asked him not to tell her husband and he was legally bound to oblige.

He gave her a list of esteemed fertility specialists.

Among them she spotted a chillingly familiar name: Dr. William Lombardo. He had evolved from the straightforward obstetrician-gynecologist he'd been just a few years earlier, when he was Heather's doctor at the Staten Island branch of his practice.

He'd never had a chance to deliver Anne Marie's grandchild; now he would not have a chance to treat Anne Marie herself. She chose a stranger, a specialist in Connecticut who eventually assisted her in conceiving the triplets and becoming a mother again.

God bless him, she thinks as she removes a mug of this morning's reheated coffee from the microwave and sinks into a kitchen chair.

She wonders wearily, as she does every afternoon around this time, where the first half of the day went.

She thought she'd have more time to herself now that the boys are in school. But by the time she drops them off at nine and runs a few errands, it's already eleven and time to head back for a pre-pickup parking spot.

It's been a hectic few weeks, settling into the new fall routine. Too hectic to have done much soul-searching.

Not that Kelly Clements isn't in the back of her mind every moment of every day.

She just isn't sure where to put her yet.

While supportive, and forgiving of the lies his wife told him, Jarrett is reluctant to go to the police.

Anne Marie knows he must be worried about appearances, as always.

Of course he claims he merely wants to protect the boys from the upheaval of a long-term, potentially high-profile investigation.

"My daughter was abducted and murdered," Anne Marie has been forced to remind him more than once, as loath to say the terrible words aloud as she is to let the resolution languish indefinitely. "My granddaughter is living with strangers who are passing themselves off as her parents."

"They *are* her parents, legally," Jarrett has reminded her, more than once.

Yes. The birth certificate. So far, nobody in Jarrett's furtive team of attorneys and investigators has found any reason to question it. They've reportedly even found a witness who will attest that Mrs. Clements was visibly pregnant and delivered Kelly herself.

"It's all a con," Anne Marie screamed at Jarrett when he told her that.

"Maybe it is," he agreed with maddening calm.

At least he didn't reiterate, yet again, that there isn't a shred of evidence other than Anne Marie's fierce, purely instinctive conviction that Kelly Clements is Heather's baby.

She's determined to prove it through DNA testing.

But until they reach that milestone, Anne Marie is forced to inhabit this oddly bustling limbo as if nothing has changed.

She swallows some coffee and reaches for the newspaper, deciding to relax for a few more minutes before getting out the calendar to schedule play dates.

She leafs through the front section with its grim global headlines, then takes the last few sips of her coffee while skimming the local section for anything that might capture her interest before she tosses the paper into the recycling bin.

The name jumps out at her in bold black and white for the second time in her life, as though summoned to the page by her thoughts of mere minutes before.

Dr. William Lombardo.

If Rita hadn't stopped impulsively at the newsstand to pick up a couple of magazines for Peyton, she might not have found out for hours.

By then it could have been too late.

But she happens to glance down at the *Daily News* as she's paying for *People* and *Glamour,* and there it is, utterly unexpected, a pair of familiar faces staring out from beneath a sensational tabloid headline.

Oh no. Oh God.

She doesn't even wait for the man to give her the change for the twenty she's just handed him, but takes off running down the avenue, through the pouring rain, magazines in one hand and plastic drugstore bag in the other.

Is she being followed?

She checks over her shoulder at every intersection she must wait to cross, half expecting to see somebody dogging her zigzag pattern toward Peyton's apartment.

But she makes it safely to the door.

She's hurriedly pushing her key into the lock when she hears pounding footsteps splashing down the street.

She looks up to see Tom Reilly racing through the downpour in her direction, waving his arms at her.

In a panic, she manages to get the door unlocked, slips through, and slams it behind her just as he reaches the steps.

"Rita, wait, no!" he shouts.

Ignoring him, she rushes down the stairs with a fervent prayer that she'll find her patient intact. She can hear Tom pounding on the door upstairs, to no avail. He must know the building, inhabited by professionals, is deserted at this time of a weekday morning, same as always.

"Peyton?" Rita calls, bursting into the apartment. "We have to get you out of here, sugar pie."

She finds her in the bedroom, staring at the television, tears streaming down her face.

She already knows.

"You hear about this crazy shit?" Sam Basir throws a morning tabloid paper onto Jody's desk.

She doesn't bother to glance at it. "What, the hostage beheading in Iraq? Yeah, it's—"

"No, that was the front page of the *Post.* This is the *Daily News.* Take a look."

The attractive face that stares back from the cover is unfamiliar, as is the name in the caption.

It's the headline that gets her.

In the month since they obtained a search warrant and ascertained that Derry Cordell was not indeed capable of being pregnant, Jody has managed to push the subway pushing homicide to the back burner.

Yes, she's still convinced the missing wife murdered Linden Cordell. No, she doesn't understand why she was pretending to be pregnant. Perhaps she even fooled her husband into believing it, or maybe he knew the truth. Maybe that was why he didn't share the news with anyone.

In the end, Jody came away with the realization that the enigmatic Derry Cordell managed to disappear, perhaps never to be found, not even if Langella had the means and the time and the leads to try.

But she didn't. She left her card with the doctor, the receptionist, and Nancy, the nurse, asking them to get in touch if anyone thought of anything that might help.

She didn't expect to hear from them.

And that was that.

Until now.

She flips through the paper to the cover story, skims it, and looks up at Sam. "Think it's related to Derry Cordell's disappearance?"

"What do you think?"

"I think we'd better move on it," she says, already on her feet and heading toward the door.

"We have to call the police, Rita," Peyton says urgently, still holding the phone from the call she hastily ended from Julie.

Her heart is pounding as the midwife tugs a pair of sneakers over her bare feet, her stomach roiling with the baby's squirms and twitches, as though it's been stirred into action by a sudden injection of fear-induced adrenaline. Peyton rests a hand on what she believes is the baby's elbow protruding beside her navel, as if she can somehow calm her child despite her own teeming apprehension.

"We will call the police, from my cell after we get out of here." Rita ties one lace and then the other, hands flying, voice quaking. "Any second now, Tom is going to find a way into this building."

Tom.

This feels like her worst nightmare come to life, but it's real. Peyton can hear his frantic pounding and angry shouts from the street even from here.

"We'll go out the back of the building to the garden and through to the next block where I parked my car."

"Car? I thought you took the subway."

"I do, most days. " Rita is pulling Peyton to her feet even as she says, "J.D. usually drives to work but today I have the car, thank God. Let's go."

Thank God, Peyton echoes silently, feeling dizzy as she allows herself to be led through the door, down the shadowy basement corridor, to the back exit opening onto the courtyard.

She hasn't taken more than a few steps at a time in a month. Now, heaven help her, she might have to run for her life.

"Rita," she says, stopping to grab on to the cool, painted concrete wall for balance. "I don't know if I can do this."

"You have to, sugar pie," the midwife says grimly, giving her hand a squeeze. "Come on, I'll be with you every step of the way."

"But . . ." She doubles over as a pelvic cramp slices through her.

"Contraction?" Rita's voice is laced with concern.

"I think so."

Overhead, Peyton vaguely realizes, the pounding and shouting have given way to momentary, ominous silence.

"I'm going to give you something to hold it off as soon as we get to the car," Rita promises, wielding the medical bag she wisely remembered to grab on their way out. "And I'd better take you straight to the hospital."

Mary rarely watches television during the day.

Now that the dog days of August have given way to golden September, she spends most afternoons wheeling Dawn through the nearby park in the secondhand baby carriage Javier bought.

But she awakened this morning to the rumble of thunder and an overcast sky that soon spilled sheets of rain.

It's just as well. She spent the morning catching up on all there is to do around the house. Her daughter looked on, gurgling happily from her high chair in the kitchen and her swing in the living room.

Now Dawn is dozing in her cradle, the house is back in order, and the sky appears to be clearing. Wondering about the forecast, Mary turns on the noon news and settles on the couch with a bowl of canned soup to watch it. If the weather is supposed to be nice later, she might put the baby into her carriage and walk down to the park.

Channel seven's meteorologist has appeared twice already in

teaser segments before the broadcast breaks away to commercials. Every time the newsroom and anchors reappear, Mary expects the weather report, but they keep turning to other stories.

Grim accounts of carjackings and rapes, robberies at gunpoint, and now a violent suicide.

Mary shakes her head as the victim's picture appears: a lovely African-American woman, a young mother with a new baby. The mother hurtled herself from the balcony of her high-rise apartment on Manhattan's Upper West Side, leaving her newborn daughter safely asleep in her cradle, and no sign of a note.

"Police are investigating Wanda Jones's death and have not confirmed sources who say that there may be a link between this woman and the disappearance of a close friend back in May. That woman, Allison Garcia, was almost nine months pregnant when she vanished from her home on Mother's Day."

Mother's Day?

Mary's breath catches in her throat. Frowning, she sets the soup bowl on the coffee table and picks up the remote, raising the volume.

"While Jones's death is officially being called a suicide, and there is no evidence of foul play, police have learned that both she and Garcia were members of a local support group for unwed mothers. Anyone with any information regarding Allison Garcia's disappearance is asked to call this number."

The anchorwoman's face is replaced by a graphic screen: an eight hundred number printed below a photograph.

The moment she sees the ebullient-looking young woman with a halo of black ringlets, Mary knows.

She *knows.*

The facts slam into her like a series of metal gates, clanking one after another into place with numbing finality.

Dawn was born on Mother's Day.

Dawn's face is a miniature version of the missing Allison Garcia's.

And Rose Calabrone lied.

"Hey, Langella," a desk sergeant calls as Jody and Sam head for the door. "I got an urgent call for you."

"Who is it?" Not that it matters, she realizes, not even slowing her pace. "I can't take it now, Jimmy. Not unless it's life-and-death."

He shrugs. "It's somebody from a Dr. Lombardo's office. You decide."

Life-and-death?

Her decision made in an instant, Jody does an about-face and hurries toward the phone, trailed by Sam.

Lying in a fetal position on the backseat of Rita's car, Peyton fights off another painful contraction. She hugs her stomach, fearful for her child, and asks, "How long until that pill starts to work, Rita?"

"Any second now," the woman promises, careening around another corner.

"Are we almost to the hospital?"

"Almost," Rita replies . . . and then curses.

"What is it?"

"I think we're being followed by somebody in a cab. Hold on, Peyton. I'm going to try to lose him."

"Tom?" she asks dully, her body taut with pain and her head suddenly swimming.

"I think so."

The car jerks and jolts. The brakes slam on, followed by the gas pedal.

"I'm sorry, sugar pie," Rita calls as they bump and sway around another corner.

Too woozy to reply, Peyton closes her eyes and prays.

"Who was it?" Basir asks anxiously, as Langella hangs up the phone.

"Lombardo's nurse. Nancy. Remember her?"

"The gossip. Yeah. Why's she calling now?"

"She said she might have more information about the Cordell case." Jody is already retracing her steps toward the door, with Sam right behind her. "She wants us to meet her."

"Yeah? Where? At the office?"

"No, she said the place is a zoo. Reporters are camped out all over the place."

"So where are we meeting her?"

"Calvary Cemetary in Queens."

"What?"

"You heard me. Let's go."

"How do you know she isn't some loony tune pulling one over on us?"

"I don't," Jody tells him grimly. "But we're going anyway."

Once again, it all comes down to carelessness.

Killing Wanda was a stupid, impulsive move, albeit a necessary one, because she had somehow figured it out.

She was never supposed to figure it out, and she was never supposed to die.

Only the donors were supposed to die.

Wanda wasn't a suitable donor. She wasn't married, but her baby was going to have a father. She didn't engineer her pregnancy with anonymous sperm and a test tube. The father has his faults, but he's raised two other children, and he's clearly going to be there for this one.

Wanda didn't have to die.

But she got suspicious, and she got scared. She instinctively went into hiding when she found herself in labor, as though she'd sensed the danger lurking nearby. She must have delivered at some suburban hospital, where she felt safe . . . not that it matters now.

She never even knew for certain whether her suspicions were founded. Not until that final confrontation in her twenty-eighth-floor apartment with its lovely terrace.

Until yesterday she probably thought she was well protected, hidden away in her elegant tower like a princess, behind triple dead bolts with an obedient doorman to protect her.

Just as Peyton Somerset finally believed she was safe in *her* elegant fortress with loyal Rita to protect her.

But, in a misguided attempt to warn Peyton of her suspicions, Wanda crossed the wrong path. All those fancy precautions of hers meant nothing in the end. It was laughably easy to slip past the doorman and up to the twenty-eighth floor. It wasn't even all that difficult to cajole Wanda into unlocking the door.

What a shame she only lived a few minutes longer to regret that fatal move.

What a pity tiny Erica, dozing peacefully in her Ethan Allen crib as Wanda fell to her bloody death, won't have a mother.

You could have taken the baby. . . .

No. You couldn't have.

You've already got a baby of your own on the way, a baby who's going to come into this world, one way or another, before this day is over.

CHAPTER EIGHTEEN

"This is crazy," Jody mutters to her partner as they stride through the misty autumn rain falling over a sea of gray slabs, green grass, and a scattering of early fallen yellow leaves.

"You're telling *me* this is crazy, Langella? I'm the one who said we should just forget it."

"We can't just 'forget it,'" Jody retorts. "Three women who saw Dr. Lombardo are either dead or missing. Derry Cordell might have been a victim, not a killer. This nurse might really have a break in the case, Sam."

"Or she might be a nut job leading us on a wild-goose chase."

"Nut job?" She smirks. "I thought you said she was a loony tune."

"Nut job, loony tune . . . same—"

"Wait." Jody stops walking and consults the scribbled note in her hand. "We were supposed to turn back there to get to the plot where we're supposed to meet her."

Sam grumbles as they backtrack, and grumbles again when they reach the designated grave site to find it occupied solely by the dead.

"So where is she?" he asks with a scowl, looking around.

"I don't know." Jody gazes down at the twin granite markers of the plot Nancy cited.

These stones are much smaller than the surrounding ones. Each is etched with the words *Beloved Son* and the image of an angel with an infant in its arms.

"What does this have to do with anything?" Sam asks after briefly scanning the rectangular slabs.

Jody doesn't reply, absorbed in reading the carved dates that depict the tragic deaths of two young brothers, Gianni and Paolo Zaterino.

They were born a little over a year apart, more than ten years ago.

And both died the same day they were born.

Jolted into awareness by an intense wave of pain, Peyton opens her eyes with a gasp.

For a moment, all she can think about is the agonizing contraction that has clenched her stomach, so intense she's afraid she's going to die.

When she can no longer stand it, the tide of pain begins to ebb.

That's when she realizes she's not in her bed.

She's not in her apartment.

Wanda.

A wave of emotion washes over her to replace the physical pain with grief, uncertainty . . . fear. She closes her eyes again, dragging her hand toward her belly.

Protect the baby.

Snippets of truth have begun to emerge through the haze of dread and confusion.

Wanda is dead.

Tom was after me.

Rita was trying to save me.

Rita!

She opens her mouth to call her friend's name, but her voice is a feeble croak, her mouth oddly dry.

She tries to swallow, but doesn't have the strength. She's too weak to move again, barely able to lift her eyelids. And when she accomplishes that, she can't turn her head to see what's around her.

After a moment, she realizes that she can, however, shift her pupils to the left and then the right, looking for Rita, looking for clues.

Where am I?

White.

Everything is white.

Walls, ceiling, blinds on the windows.

White.

Peyton manages to snatch a vivid detail from the elusive fragments whirling in her mental maelstrom.

Hospital.

Rita was taking her to the hospital.

Hospital.

Good.

I'm safe now, she tells herself lethargically, closing her eyes again. *The doctors and nurses will take care of me and the baby, just like before.*

Rita will take care of us, too.

Before she can drift back to blissful oblivion, another fierce ache takes hold within . . . along with the sudden memory that somebody was in a cab, following Rita's car. . . .

"Where did you leave the boys?" Jarrett remembers to ask, after they're settled into a cab heading uptown to the police precinct near Dr. Lombardo's office.

Her thoughts preoccupied, it takes a moment for Anne Marie to process the question, and another few to remember the answer.

"They're with Karen," she tells her husband, who nods. She doubts he knows exactly who Karen is. But he trusts her judgment. And he believes her.

That means more than anything else now.

When she called him and told him what she'd read in the paper, and that she was certain Heather's disappearance was somehow connected to Dr. Lombardo, he didn't ask questions. He told her to get on the next train to Grand Central, and he'd meet her on the platform.

She spotted him before he saw her. The moment she caught sight of him, intently searching the crowd of disembarking passengers, something stirred to life within her.

Jarrett isn't perfect, but she loves him. And he doesn't always show it, but she knows he loves her.

When this is all over, Anne Marie promises herself, she'll remember to tell him both of those things.

Maybe she'll be able to start living again, after all these years.

"All right, Mrs. Nueves," the detective says, reading over the last of his notes. "Is there anything else you can tell me about this

Rose Calabrone? Anything you can remember that might help us to locate her?"

Mary shakes her head, utterly spent. She looks at Javier, seated beside her on the couch.

His eyes are downcast, his slumped posture signifying utter defeat.

But he didn't protest when she called him to tell him what she'd seen on the news. He just listened, then told her he'd be right home.

He made it to the door moments before the police arrived.

"Mr. Nueves?" the detective asks from his seat adjacent to the couch. "Is there anything you can add?"

Javier looks up at him, simultaneously laying a hand on Dawn, asleep on Mary's shoulder.

"Are you taking our daughter away?" he asks.

Mary opens her mouth to protest that she isn't their daughter, but the detective says it first, firmly.

"I'm sorry, Mr. Nueves. She'll be placed in temporary foster care until we can confirm that she belongs to Allison Garcia. I'm sure the family will want custody in that event."

It's Mary who falls apart first, and Javier who does the comforting.

"*Lo siento, Javier . . . lo siento,*" she says over and over. "Please forgive me."

"You did nothing wrong," he manages to tell her, before he, too, loses his grip on his emotions.

And they cling to each other on the sofa long after Dawn has been taken away.

The window is small.

Small, with blinds.

Peyton closes her eyes to rest for a moment, then opens them again, struggling to focus.

Blinds.

They're drawn.

Plain beige curtains hang on either side, suspended from a metal rod above.

She closes her eyes again, trying to remember.

Were there blinds in the hospital? Curtains? Were the windows this small?

This just . . .

It doesn't feel right.

There are no nurses here. There's no equipment.

And no sounds.

No beeping monitors.

Or doctors being paged.

Clattering carts rolling down the tiled corridor.

Is there even a corridor?

At last, Peyton summons the strength to turn her head.

She sees only more white wall.

With supreme effort, she turns a little farther, and is rewarded with the edge of a door.

The invisible, pitiless fist begins to tighten its grip on her insides once again.

"No . . ." she whispers, petrified of the hurt.

Focus on something else.

Focus on the door.

A plain, white door.

It's closed.

Ouch. Oh God. Make it stop. Take me away from here.

The door.

Think about the door.

Something about the door.

She can't bear the pain. She's beginning to slip away . . .

Oh!

It isn't the kind of door that you'd find in a hospital.

It's the kind of door you'd find in a house.

She's fading fast.

Is she in a house?

The door is opening.

Wait, she commands herself, as unconsciousness swoops in to save her from another wave of pain.

Don't sleep yet . . .

See who's on the other side of the . . .

Anne Marie thanks the young police officer and sips lukewarm water from a small paper cup.

"Better?" Jarrett asks, seated beside her at the table in the claustrophobic interrogation room.

She nods, still feeling overwhelmed by emotion. Just coming into the station brought it all back: the shock when her daughter failed to come home, the anguish of the futile search, the frustration with authorities who wanted to write Heather off as a runaway.

But that was then. This is now. This is different.

The young officer, summoned by Detectives Jacobs and Antares when Anne Marie began to feel faint, hastily takes his leave, closing the door behind him.

"All right, Mrs. Egerton." Antares, the less patient of the pair, leans forward again. He rests his elbows on the table, poised to listen to whatever else she has to say. "Let's go back to the day your daughter disappeared. Where were you?"

"I was at work—my day job, at Macy's in the mall," she says reluctantly, waiting for the inevitable look of disapproval.

Single mother holding down two jobs; latchkey kid left to her own devices.

No wonder the kid got herself into trouble, the detectives are thinking. "Trouble" in this case meaning not just pregnant, but murdered.

They're assuming that if Anne Marie had been around more to keep an eye on her daughter, she'd be alive today.

I don't blame them. I've always believed the same thing.

She sips more of the tepid water, wrinkling her nose at the unpleasant, silky taste, and puts the cup on the table.

"You were working at the same mall your daughter visited that day," Jacobs prods.

"Yes. She stopped in to show me the little outfit she had bought for the baby at Gymboree." Choked up, she can't speak for a moment. How well she remembers the little yellow outfit with its matching cap.

"Look, Mom," Heather said, grinning. "*Can't* you just see the baby wearing this?"

Yes. Yes, she could.

Jarrett squeezes her arm gently. "You okay?"

She nods.

The detectives are waiting silently for her to go on.

After exhaling shakily, she does. "Heather asked if I wanted her to wait around and drive me home when my shift was over, but I told her to go ahead and I would take the bus because I was working later than I expected."

"Why?"

"Because I always took the bus, and I didn't want her out on the road. It was icy."

"No," Antares says, "I meant, why were you working late that night?"

"Because somebody called in sick and they asked me to stay. It was my night off at the restaurant so I said yes. I was taking every extra shift I could, saving up money for . . ."

Again, emotion gets the best of her.

"For what, Mrs. Egerton?" Jacob asks.

"For a christening outfit for the baby. I wanted to buy a special one." She's crying now, burying her face in her hands, thinking of Kelly Clements, wondering if she was ever christened, thinking of all the milestones Heather missed in her daughter's life.

There's a brisk knock on the door.

"Yeah?" one of the detectives calls gruffly, and Anne Marie hears it open.

She looks up to see the young police officer standing there again.

"I'm sorry to interrupt, but I have a man out here who says he has urgent information about a woman who might have been abducted today. She was also a patient at that Lombardo's practice."

The detectives are already on their feet.

"Who's the man?" Antares asks.

Anne Marie hears the reply just before the door closes. "Says he's a friend of the woman's, and his name is Gil Blaney."

If only he'd hurry and call back.

He must have gotten the messages by now.

If he hurries, he might be able to get here before their child is born.

That would be good. Then he'll be able to help me get rid of her.

It would be nice, for a change, not to have to be the one to lug the body, still bloated with all that pregnancy fluid, onto the wheelbarrow. The ground is muddy today, making it harder to push the thing down to the edge of the pond, where the stack of concrete cinder blocks is waiting.

He doesn't know the ritual, but it's not all that complicated.

Haul her into the little rowboat, take her out to the middle, weigh her down, and drop her in so she can sink into the depths with the others.

Except the first, Heather.

And Derry Cordell.

Although, she wasn't a donor.

Neither was Wanda Jones.

Fitting, then, that their remains will rest elsewhere. The pond is strictly reserved for donors.

Funny.

That's actually kind of funny.

Maybe I should make a little memorial stone for it someday.

Here lie the wicked, whose progeny have been rescued.

But then some trespasser might stumble across it and get suspicious.

Not that it will matter.

We'll be long gone by then, the three of us. We'll be a family at last, living far away from here. Maybe we'll go to California. Or Europe. I've always wanted to go to Europe.

A fitful whimper escapes the next room.

Oh well. Time to put the knife aside and get back to the patient.

At the sound of footsteps moving through wet grass, Jody looks over her shoulder.

Dr. Lombardo's nurse, Nancy, is making her way toward the detectives.

Jody sees Sam's hand rest briefly on the holster concealed beneath his jacket as he calls, "Why are we here, Nancy? What's this about?"

"I needed you to see it for yourselves, so you'll believe me."

"What are we supposed to see for ourselves, Nancy?" Jody asks as the woman comes to a stop a few feet away with a shudder.

"The graves." She pauses, then reaches into her pocket.

Jody instantly goes for her gun, as does Sam.

But Nancy has merely pulled out a packet of tissues, using one to dab at her teary eyes. "I'm sorry," she says, her voice quavering. "I haven't been in a cemetery since . . ." She pauses, takes a deep breath, goes on. "Since my mother died suddenly, the week before Mother's Day. She and I were really close. We lived together, my whole life. It was a heart attack, and I found her—" Her voice breaks.

Jody looks at Sam, who shrugs, nonplussed. He opens his mouth as if he's about to prod the nurse along, but Jody cautions him to wait.

"I don't have a husband or children, and Mommy . . . she was all I had. It's hard for me to talk about her, even now."

Having lost her own mother last year, Jody is struck by the poignant sorrow in her voice.

But Sam is getting impatient, gruffly asking, "What about the graves, Nancy? What did you want us to see?"

"All these years, she's been talking about her sons, John and Paul. The surgeon and the pediatrician."

"Who, Nancy?" Jody asks, trying to follow

Caught up in her meandering tale, the woman has knelt on the soggy ground to touch the small granite stones, running her fingers over the letters.

"She lost them the day they were born, both of them. Maybe that's what put her over the edge. Maybe that's why she lied about everything—being a mother, being married. She doesn't have anyone at all. She lives alone. Her neighbor told me her husband left her years ago for another woman. He's remarried, has a family of his own. I guess that's why he left her. Because she couldn't give him children."

"Who are we talking about, Nancy?" Jody repeats, her heart pounding.

"Rita. Rita Calabrone."

"It's okay, sugar pie," a familiar voice croons, and Peyton opens her eyes again to see Rita standing over her bed.

"Thank God," she murmurs. "What's wrong with me? I feel—"

"Shhh, I know." Rita pats her arm. "You're in labor."

Labor.

"It's too soon," Peyton grunts, trying to gather her thoughts as a strong contraction wracks her body.

"No, it's early, but the baby can survive just fine if you deliver now. Here, sit up and drink this . . . it'll help ease the contractions."

"Wait," Peyton moans, writhing. "No."

"Try to breathe."

"Make it . . . stop!"

"Don't fight it," Rita says abruptly in an oddly harsh tone. "If you fight it, you're going to hurt worse. Just let it happen."

"Ow . . . owww," Peyton howls, trying to focus, but unable to think of anything but the searing pain.

"Come on, don't waste your energy on crying. You're not a baby, you're having one. Just breathe, and get through it."

She breathes.

And she gets through it.

When the contraction subsides, she sips from the steaming cup Rita holds up to her lips. The liquid is bitter.

"What is it?" She makes a face.

"Special herbal tea."

She shakes her head, pushes it away when the cup is raised again.

"Drink it, Peyton," Rita orders. "Unless you don't mind the contractions?"

Another twinge of agony has already begun to take hold, as if cued by Rita's words.

Peyton seizes the cup from her hand and gulps the hot liquid, not caring that it burns her throat all the way down.

No pain, she tells herself, oblivious of her last, rapidly dwindling moments of naïveté, can compare to the torment of labor.

"Good," Rita tells her, taking back the empty cup with a smile. "That should kick in any second now."

In the midst of a full-blown contraction now, Peyton cries out, reaching desperately for something, anything to grab on to.

Her flailing arm encounters a wooden bedpost.

She clings to it.

Somewhere in the back of her mind, it occurs to her that hospital beds have metal rails, not wooden bedposts.

Frightened, she turns toward her friend for reassurance . . . and spots the odd trickle of blood that has emerged beneath the fringe of Rita's overgrown bangs.

At last Detectives Antares and Jacobs have returned to the interrogation room, accompanied by a shaken-looking man they introduce as Gil Blaney. His female friend, on the verge of giving birth and becoming a single mother, is missing from her apartment.

"Mrs. Egerton," Jacobs asks, "do you know a woman named Rita Calabrone?"

"Rita Calabrone?" She frowns, shaking her head.

"She may also use the aliases Rose Calabrone, and . . ." He consults his notes before adding, "Rose Cascia. Although she may not have used that one in years."

"Rita . . . *Cascia?*"

"You know her?"

"She's a saint."

"She's no saint, Mrs. Egerton," the detective says grimly. "She's a suspect in—"

"No, I mean Rita of Cascia is an actual Catholic saint."

"That's right, she is!" Gil Blaney exclaims, as Anne Marie's thoughts pivot back to parochial school, to the time she had to write a report about the origin of her name.

That was when she found out Grace had named her after Anne, the patron saint of pregnant women. But Margarita Taylor claimed that *she* was named after the patron saint of pregnant women. Anne Marie argued with her until the teacher, Sister Mary, stepped in.

She explained that both girls were right. Saint Anne was the patron saint of pregnant women. Saint Rita of Cascia, whose real name was Margarita, was the patron saint of pregnant *and* infertile women.

Anne Marie remembers being jealous, thinking her own boring essay paled compared to mean old Rita Taylor's interesting report about the enigmatic saint, who became a nun after tragically losing her sons and husband.

"What do you know about this Saint Rita?" the detective asks now, obviously intrigued.

He glances from Anne Marie to Gil, who shrugs and admits, "I don't remember much. Just the name. What about you?"

Anne Marie frowns, trying to remember, pulse racing and skin crawling at the possibility that a stranger boldly invoking a saint's name might have something to do with her daughter's death.

"Tell them what you know." Jarrett touches her trembling hand. "It's okay."

"She, um, lived in the fifteenth century and . . . there were supernatural legends associated with her. . . ."

"Like . . . ?" somebody asks when she trails off, lost in her memories.

She settles on the starkest image, the one that frightened her as a child and stayed with her all these years.

"She was a recipient of stigmata."

Realizing nobody but Gil comprehends that, Anne Marie quickly manages to explain, "That's a word for inexplicable bleeding on the site of Christ's wounds."

Blaney concurs. "It's been documented by the church to have happened for centuries to especially pious people."

The detectives exchange a dubious glance.

"Saint Rita always had a mysterious, bleeding gash in her forehead that corresponded with the crown of thorns," Anne Marie tells them. "Oh, and the bees! There were—"

She breaks off, realizing something else, to ask, "You said she was going by Rita *Calabrone?*"

"And Rose Calabrone."

Rose.

Yet another shock jolts through Anne Marie. "Neither of those can possibly be her legitimate name."

"How do you know that?"

She explains as quickly as she can the two most relevant miracles associated with Saint Rita.

The first miracle: when she was born, a strange swarm of snow-white bees appeared above her cradle and buzzed around the infant, inexplicably without harming her. The bees, which are unable to sting, reputedly continue to appear every year on the Feast Day of Saint Rita in the convent where she died.

The second miracle: as she was dying on a harsh January day, Rita asked a visitor for a blooming rose from her family's estate. There was no hope of finding one, but the visitor was compelled to look. On a seemingly dead bush, against a stark winter landscape, one perfect rose was found in bloom.

"So you think that's why this woman is using the name Rose?" the detective asks Ann Marie, and she nods.

"What about the bees?" Jarrett asks. "What does that have to do with anything?"

Anne Marie, whose grandmother Grace frequently lapsed into her native tongue, informs them all, "The word *calabrone* means 'bumblebee' in Italian."

"So you think this woman is some kind of deluded religious fanatic?" the detective asks.

Anne Marie reaches into her bag, pulls out the red leather Bible, and slides it across the table with an icy hand. "I know she is."

"Your head," Peyton manages to tell Rita, her mouth clenched in pain. "It's . . . bleeding."

Rita reaches up to touch the trickle of red above her brow. An unsettling look comes over her face, yet she says nothing.

Another monstrous contraction attacks without warning.

"It . . . still hurts," Peyton moans, thrashing in the bed.

Her friend nods, merely watching, an oddly detached expression in her eyes.

There's something different about her, Peyton realizes, through the haze of pain.

When at last the intense cramping has briefly subsided, she manages to ask, "Where are we?"

"My house. Out on Long Island."

Bewildered, Peyton reaches for Rita's hand, mere inches from the bed but just beyond her grasp. Rita looks down but makes no move to touch her.

"Why?" Peyton asks, dread washing over her like a bone-chilling wave that comes out of nowhere. "Why are we here?"

No reply.

"What about—" She winces. Oh God. Here it comes again.

"What about the hospital?" she asks in a rush, while she can still speak.

"We couldn't go to the hospital." Rita is looking down into her eyes, watching her suffering, doing nothing to stop it.

A long, excruciating minute passes before Peyton can ask, "Why not . . . the hospital?"

"It wasn't safe."

Peyton is distracted by an ominous tightening in her stomach. Too soon. They're coming so close together.

What about the tea? Why isn't it helping?

As soon as there's another fleeting window between contractions, she begs Rita to give her something to ease the hurt.

"I can't do that."

"More tea . . . please . . . not working . . ."

"Oh, the tea." Rita laughs. The sound is eerily humorless. "It's working, all right. It's doing what it's supposed to do. And so did the nice little pills I gave you in the car."

I must have heard her wrong, Peyton thinks wildly, *because that doesn't make sense. If anything, the pain is getting worse.*

Rita is looking down at her, and her features seem contorted, her face a grotesque, leering mask that bears little resemblance to her trusted friend.

Spinning away from the woman in the bed, Rita paces across the room again.

If only the phone would ring.

Funny how you can go from loathing that sound to longing for it.

It hasn't even been twenty-four hours since Wanda Jones called Peyton's apartment for the very last time.

When Rita saw that the number was blocked on caller ID, she realized that it must be the same caller who kept hanging up whenever she answered.

Well, this time she wouldn't answer.

Peyton was sound asleep in the bedroom with the television blasting, and the volume on the answering machine was low enough that she'd never hear.

Rita screened the call, and Wanda, foolish Wanda, left a detailed message.

She told Peyton that she thought Rita might not be what she seemed. That she had snooped into her background and found out her real name, and her addresses—both of them. She left the information on the answering machine for Peyton and asked her to accompany Wanda to the police with it. She said Eric had forbidden her to get the authorities involved because he was afraid their affair would be exposed.

Rita wonders how he feels today, with his dead girlfriend's picture and rumors about her married lover splashed all over the tabloids.

You're not feeling so terrific about that yourself, Rita can't help thinking. You should have realized the media would put two and two together even if the police didn't think to link Wanda to Allison.

Which, eventually, they would.

But she wasn't thinking clearly when she shoved Wanda to her death. She only knew that she had to get her out of the way quickly, before she got to Peyton.

She stopped to cuddle Wanda's infant daughter before she left, and she imagined what it would be like to hold her own baby.

That was when she realized she couldn't afford to wait for Peyton to go into labor on her own.

It was time to stop preventing it and start inducing it.

Peyton never even noticed that her breakfast coffee was laced with a little extra kick this morning.

* * *

"And how did you find out Rita Calabrone wasn't who she claimed to be?" Jody asks Nancy as she and Sam hurriedly escort her back to the parking lot, intent on turning her over to the precinct handling the Lombardo investigation.

"I went to her apartment this morning when I found out about Wanda. I'd never gone there before, because it was out here in Queens, and I live in Jersey."

"And never the twain shall meet," Sam says dryly. "Right?"

"Exactly. You know how it is."

"Absolutely. I live in the Bronx and I can't tell you the last time I visited Langella here in Brooklyn."

Jody rolls her eyes. "So getting back to your situation, Nancy . . . you never had any occasion to visit Rita's apartment even though you were good friends?"

"No, we always just got together at the office or somewhere in Manhattan. And, frankly, Rita never invited me."

"Obviously she had reason not to," Sam points out and asks, as if he finds the whole scenario hard to believe, "You were never suspicious of her?"

"Why would I be? I've known her for years. She was wonderful at her job. The patients raved about her bedside manner."

A chill slithers down Jody's spine at that. She wonders how many laboring women entrusted themselves and their babies into the care of a woman who might very well be a serial killer.

"And anyway, some people like to keep to themselves," Nancy goes on. "I just figured she was one of them. And it wasn't like she didn't say anything about her personal life. She talked a lot about her sons, and her husband, and their charming little house in Queens, and their farmhouse way out on Long Island." She snorts, shaking her head. "She doesn't even live in a house. It's an apartment building and it's seen better days. At first I thought I had the wrong address when I saw it. I was thinking maybe I should have called her first."

"Why didn't you?" Jody asks.

"Because I was scared. Of Dr. Lombardo," Nancy says reluctantly. "I didn't know where he was, and I just wanted to get out of my apartment, just in case . . ."

"He was brought in for questioning this morning," Sam informs her, referring to the information they received right before they left the precinct.

"Did they arrest him?"

"I doubt it," Jody tells her. "Why did you think he had something to do with this?"

"I don't know . . . maybe I didn't, really. But he was the only person I could imagine . . . I mean, I never thought Rita could be involved. Never in a million years."

I'm hallucinating, Peyton realizes. *That has to be it.*

That woman across the room isn't Rita. She's probably some nurse and I'm thinking she's Rita because Rita makes me feel safe and I need her.

The pain is bearing down on her again, roaring at her like a freight train. Helpless to get out of its path, she has no choice but to let it crush her.

Somehow, she survives it.

I'm not in a house, I'm in the hospital, she reassures herself when the train has roared past and she can think clearly again. *It just looks like a house because I want it to be a house because I want this to be over.*

Here it comes again.

Dear God, please, have mercy.

"Please, just tell me . . . how much longer?" she begs the stranger who isn't Rita, as she returns to stand over the bed.

"Oh, it could be hours. Trust me, though. You don't want to wish it away."

Again, the chilling cackle fills Peyton with dread as potent as the relentless siege on her body.

Trust me, though . . .

Trust me . . .

What was it Rita said to her the night she called from the hospital and told her about Gil?

She can't think straight for the blinding ache that contorts her once more.

Only when it's begun to ebb does she remember Rita's words . . . and finds herself gripped by a terror as acute as the next contraction already sweeping in to claim her.

You never know, Peyton. The person you think is your closest friend might be an enemy.

"So you absolutely trusted your friend Rita," Jody says, just to be sure she has Nancy's story straight.

"Yes. Absolutely. And when I heard the news about Wanda this morning, I needed to see her. I just had to get out of the city, and find a safe place to hide. So I looked up her address and I went out to Queens."

"You had her address, then?"

"Yes, both her addresses, here and on Long Island, are in the files at the office. But I bet the farmhouse is a fake, too. Or it's probably really run-down like the apartment building was. I should have known. I mean, the neighborhood didn't look anything like she described it."

"How did she describe it?"

"Oh, you know . . . trees and parks and families. It was more like gangs and drugs and garbage. I was looking around, trying to figure out where her cute little house was, when this woman came out of the building. She asked if she could help me and I told her I was looking for Rita. She said she knew everyone in the building and she had no idea who I was talking about until I showed her a picture."

"You had a picture of Rita with you?" Jody asks incredulously. She doesn't even carry pictures of her own children.

Nancy looks embarrassed. "It was from a few years ago. One of those photo booth places. I . . . I guess I don't have many friends, and I thought she was one."

Once again, Jody can't help feeling sorry for the woman. She comes across almost as an overly eager, insecure adolescent, trying too hard to fit in and make friends.

Typically unmoved, Sam nudges, "So what happened when you showed the picture?"

"The neighbor said, 'Oh, that's Helen Zaterino.' And that's when I found out Rita isn't Rita after all. And that she lives alone, and she's been here forever. Her husband left her because he wanted children and she couldn't carry them to term."

Sam emits a low whistle, shaking his head and muttering, "Harsh."

Jody asks, "So Gianni and Paolo were their sons?"

"Yes. I guess losing them destroyed the marriage. It had to have destroyed Rita—I mean, Helen—too." Nancy shakes her head. "It's sad, in a way. Poor thing. Do you think she really believed they were alive?"

"Who knows what she's thinking?" Jody shrugs, thinking of all the criminally insane killers she's encountered through the years. "It's hard to tell."

They've reached the detectives' car, and Sam climbs in, saying he's going to radio the latest to the precinct.

Left alone with Nancy, Jody tells her somberly, "I'm glad you called us. You did the right thing."

The woman offers a tremulous nod. "I was afraid you might think I was crazy unless I showed you the graves. If you'd heard the way she talked about her sons . . . how proud she was of them . . ." She shudders.

"Do you have any idea where her husband is?"

"No, but I bet that neighbor might know. She's been living there forever, she said. I bet it was a decent neighborhood years ago."

"We'll need to talk to her. Did you get her name?"

"Alice something. Detective Langella, do you think . . . Rita did something to Mrs. Cordell?"

"I don't want to speculate, Nancy. Let's just take this one step at a time."

Sam pokes his head out of the car. "Nancy, do you know a patient named Peyton Somerset?"

The color drains from the woman's face. "Oh God. Rita was taking care of her. Is she . . . ?"

"She's missing," Sam says, "Come on, get in."

Everything will be okay as soon as J.D. calls, Helen promises herself.

Or maybe he won't call.

He hasn't called in . . .

When was the last time?

It's been a while.

She probably doesn't let him call. That's why he hasn't returned Helen's messages in so long. Of course he wants to. Of course. But he can't.

Well, maybe he'll just show up, to surprise her. He used to do that years ago. Pop up where she least expected it. Sometimes he'd bring her flowers, or a little gift . . .

Or a big gift, she thinks, looking down at her diamond engagement ring.

Unlike her, J.D. came from money. Not big money, but enough to afford the apartment in what was, just a decade ago, a nice part of Queens, as well as a weekend house on Long Island.

When he left, she got to keep the ring, the apartment, and the house. Not that she cared. She just wanted him.

And now I'll have him back, she thinks with a smile. *I'll finally be able to give him the one gift he always wanted from me, the one his money couldn't buy.*

She can just imagine the look on his face when he sees her holding a baby.

Their baby.

A live, pink, happy, hungry baby.

She pushes aside the memory of the stiff little boys she clung to on the darkest days of her life, willing them to come alive again, to come back to her.

Sometimes, when she's telling nosy Nancy about them, she can almost convince herself that her prayers were answered, that she has two strong, grown boys of her own.

Gianni and Paolo.

John and Paul.

Her babies.

The woman behind her in the bed lets lose an agonizing shriek.

Helen flinches at the grating sound, wishing she would just shut up.

She looks out the window again, checking to see if J.D.'s truck is turning down the lane yet. Wouldn't that be a sight for sore eyes.

She hasn't seen that old red truck in years. Who knows if he even has it these days?

Maybe *she* doesn't let him drive a truck. Maybe it doesn't fit into their lifestyle in that upscale town in Nassau County, on the island's north shore—a stone's throw and a world away from both the Queens apartment and the farmhouse where J.D. and Helen were supposed to live happily ever after.

Jealousy bubbles within her like a cauldron, spilling over into venomous hatred.

What she probably should have done, years ago, was get rid of the woman who stole J.D. away from her, the woman who could give him what she couldn't.

But then, that would have been murder, plain and simple.

Helen isn't a cold-blooded killer.

Yes, she's disposed of a handful of donors, as well as a few unfortunates who got in the way. But that's all part of the work. God will forgive her for that. Of course he will. Look at all the good she's done, punishing the wicked, unselfishly saving the worthy from her own barren fate.

Unselfishly, Helen?

All right, maybe she always secretly believed that if she blessed enough infertile couples with children, she would be rewarded.

She closes her eyes, and her mother's face appears before her. Mama, alive again, dressed in her solemn Sunday black, all fired up from the latest sermon.

Mama drilled into her little girl's head that it was every God-fearing person's duty to see that sinners were punished. She said that was why God had taken Daddy away from them, that horrible day he was electrocuted in the bathtub—because he had been adulterous, and adultery was a sin, one of the worst imaginable.

Only later, when she overheard Mama praying for forgiveness, did Helen realize that Mama must have punished Daddy on God's behalf. Hadn't she always said that a God-fearing person was obliged to do just that, wherever she saw fit?

Mama said that even children were sinners. Throughout all those years of enduring whatever punishment Mama handed out for Helen's sins, real and imagined, the little girl prayed for redemption. She read her Bible and she dutifully prayed to the saints, just as Mama taught her to do. She prayed frequently to Matilda of Saxony, patron saint of the falsely accused, and to Perigrinus, patron saint of open sores, to heal the angry red welts and burns her mother was forced to inflict.

As a teenager, after the tables turned and she was at last obliged to punish her mother for her sins, Helen prayed to Mark the Evangelist, patron saint of impenitence, and Frances Xavier Cabrini, patron saint of orphans.

When God sent J.D. into her path, she knew she had been rewarded for her piety; knew in her heart that they would be blessed with the children they longed for.

She prayed to Rita of Cascia, the patron saint of infertility, all those years that she was trying to have a child.

She told J.D. they had to be patient, that it would happen for them. And it did. Twice, God and Saint Rita blessed her with pregnancy.

When their sons died, she begged her husband not to give up on their family, on her.

He left anyway.

She always knew in her heart that if she kept praying, if she kept up her God-fearing obligations, then he would bless her with a family. That J.D. would come back to her, and they'd have another chance at the happiness that slipped so tragically from their grasp. . . .

"Rita," the woman in the bed calls plaintively. "Please, Rita . . ."

Helen pointedly ignores her, anger flaring once again to obliterate her sorrow.

She was the mistake. Peyton Somerset. The biggest mistake of all.

I should have stuck with strangers, she tells herself again. *That was always the plan. After what happened with the first one, that girl Heather whose mother went crazy looking for her, I knew I shouldn't mess with Lombardo's patients.*

For ten years, she kept the business discreet, far removed from her daily life, tempting as it was to choosing donors and recipients from among those she knew through her work.

The humble recipients were relatively easy to locate, thanks to her scattered volunteer work with several gynecological free clinics in the metropolitan area. She found a few of the donors that way as well: women who weren't likely to be the subject of a high-profile search, if they were missed at all. Hookers, homeless women, throwaway street kids who'd been raped.

Then Nancy, damn her, came up with the brilliant idea of a Pregnant and Single support group, with Rita as reluctant moderator.

What else was she supposed to do? She couldn't say no. Nor could she resist the donors who were all but rolled to her doorstep on a doomed gurney.

Allison was the first, so damned ripe to be taken down a few notches. She actually laughed about having used a sperm donor; actually dared to mock her mother, who tried to warn her that she was a sinner.

Helen initially did her best to overlook Allison's brazen attitude, but she just couldn't seem to get past it. Allison deserved to be her next donor and that humble Nueves couple from New Jersey would be the perfect recipients of her baby.

And so it began . . . the beginning of the end.

Once she gave in to that first bold impulse, she could have been tempted to choose all the women in that group as donors. But of course, she knew better. She didn't want anybody to grow suspicious. She figured one was plenty . . .

Until she saw Peyton Somerset strutting confidently around the office like she was entitled to whatever she wanted.

Look at her now.

Sweating, squirming, screaming like a sick, wounded animal.

I even tried to warn her. I told her not to trust anybody.

But she trusted me. She was so obedient, climbing into the car. She lapped up those pills so willingly, never asking me what they were for.

Surprisingly, it's almost a shame now to see the confidence beaten right out of her.

Helen quite honestly expected her to put up more of a fight.

But then, the sedative was powerful. So powerful she slept throughout the journey to Long Island and the wheelchair ride into the house.

As much as she hated to use medication that will cross the placenta prior to delivery, she had no choice. And in the end it was a much appreciated blessing. There was no need to carry on the charade, pretending to be outrunning a predator in a yellow cab. All she had to do was drive, and plan.

"Oh . . ." Peyton moans, eyes closed, perhaps both in severe discomfort and exhaustion.

The sedative probably still hasn't worn off entirely; nor have the effects of the drug Helen used to induce labor, hurrying along what Mother Nature herself already triggered.

In the grips of perhaps the most intense labor experience Helen has ever generated, Peyton Somerset is truly suffering.

Well, in the end, everybody gets what they deserve, Helen thinks smugly. *She's finally going to get what's coming to her . . .*

And so will I.

"Getting . . . worse," Peyton pants in desperation, as another brutal contraction takes hold almost before the last has faded.

Rita, staring through a lifted slat in the blinds, merely nods. She's been going back and forth to the window for what seems like hours now, as if she's waiting for somebody.

Perhaps it has been hours.

The light that filters in through the gap seems grayer than before. This grueling day might be drawing to an end at last.

But what about the night? Peyton wonders in despair. How many more hours can she endure this torment?

"Help . . . me," she begs Rita again. "Please."

Finally, the woman turns away from the window. With a

gleam in her eye, she reaches for the latex gloves she tossed aside earlier.

"No!" Peyton cries out, realizing what she's about to do. "Please, no. Not again."

Rita marches to the foot of the bed. "I need to see how far you've progressed, sugar pie. Come on, open up."

"Noooo . . . God, no . . ." Peyton screams as the savage fingers probe into her like knives.

"Ten centimeters," Rita announces triumphantly when she can bear it no more. "Time to start pushing and have this baby."

The baby.

The word is like a healing balm that cuts through the anguish.

Yes. The baby.

I'm having my baby.

That's why I'm here.

Outside, in the distance, gravel crunches with the sudden approach of a car.

Rita goes absolutely still.

Then she breaks into a grotesque grin and triumphantly yells, "He's here! I knew he'd come."

He's here.

Relief courses through Peyton despite the overwhelming urge to bear down and push.

Clenching her teeth, fighting off the incredible pressure, she grunts, "Is it Dr. Lombardo?"

"Dr. Lombardo?" Rita furrows her eyebrows in amusement, revealing a smudge of dried blood on her forehead.

The blood.

The blood is so strange . . .

Rita makes a move to return to the window, but Peyton grabs on to her arm with sudden, superhuman strength, pulling her back to the bed.

"Let go of me."

"Tell me who it is!" Peyton gasps, trembling uncontrollably. "Who's here? Dr. Lombardo?"

"Of course not. Why would he come all the way out here?"

"To . . . deliver . . . my baby." She's breathing hard, straining against the flames of tension in her lower back and pelvis.

"I guess I'd better break it to you, Peyton. It isn't your baby."

She's crazy, Peyton realizes. She's talking nonsense.

Somewhere beyond the room, there's a knocking sound, then the creak and slam of a door being opened and shut.

"Of course . . . it's . . . my . . . baby," she manages to say despite the explosive ache that's threatening to tear her apart.

"I'm afraid not, Peyton. I'm going to be the mommy. And here's the daddy now," Rita exclaims happily as footsteps approach and a voice calls her name.

"Rita!"

The voice is familiar, Peyton realizes in the midst of her own frantic hysteria.

A voice that reaches through the fog of pain like a lethal hand she can no longer escape.

Tom Reilly's voice.

CHAPTER NINETEEN

Sitting anxiously in the passenger seat, watching the scattered trees and tiny yards of eastern Queens give way to an increasingly urban landscape, Jody can't help feeling as if she and her partner are driving in the wrong direction.

They should be going to Peyton Somerset, the woman she's never met in her life, the woman for whom she suddenly feels responsible.

She's missing, and her life is in grave danger. Jody can feel it.

But their supervisory officer ordered them back to the precinct, assuring them that the address of the farmhouse, obtained from Nancy's files, has been forwarded to the Long Island police with urgent orders for a search and rescue.

Jody wonders if they're going to make it there on time, wonders if the isolated farmhouse is really where Rita took Peyton. It's certainly a possibility. Her Queens apartment and Peyton's Manhattan one are being searched even now. If anything relevant has turned up, somebody surely would have called Langella and Basir in the car.

"I still don't get it," Sam mutters, swerving out of the slow-moving center lane into the left as they approach the Triborough Bridge ramp. "How the hell did Rita, or Helen, or whatever her name is, get away with this? Didn't she think she'd eventually get caught?"

"She's sick," Jody reminds him. As if that offers any insight at all into the character of a murderess who had everybody fooled all these years.

Through snatches of information she and Sam have gleaned in

the last hour via phone calls and radioed updates, Jody has been piecing together the bizarre details of this case. The big picture has revealed implications of a scheme more chillingly elaborate than Jody could ever have imagined.

It was pure gut instinct that told her to look further into Linden Cordell's death.

And it's gut instinct that tells her time might be running out, right this moment, for Peyton Somerset.

"I know the woman's sick," Sam is saying, "but what the hell is her motive? What does she get out of any of this?"

Jody shrugs.

As Nancy put it before Langella and Basir turned her over into protective custody, Helen Zaterino must see herself as a noble Robin Hood figure of sorts. She steals the babies of women she considers undeserving, and hands them over to poor, infertile couples despondent enough to go along with a peculiar nine-month charade.

"You know, desperation does strange things to people," Sam comments, and Jody knows his thoughts are meandering down the same path as hers.

Jody thinks of her children; tries and fails to imagine life without them.

She can almost understand how a couple might be driven to such an extreme.

Almost.

After all, in exchange for their covert efforts, the otherwise helpless couples are presented with healthy infants and nobody, supposedly, will ever be the wiser.

It's an airtight, diabolically clever plan, really. The babies are ostensibly born at home with only a spouse and a registered midwife in attendance. Women give birth in that scenario every day all over the metropolitan area. Nobody bats an eye when the midwife fills out the paperwork for the birth certificate that will be perfectly legitimate. Nobody would dream of questioning whether an apparently pregnant woman has actually given birth.

The radio crackles suddenly and Jody picks up the receiver, speaking briefly with the supervisor.

"Did they find her?" Sam asks the moment she hangs up.

"Not yet," she tells him, knowing he's talking about Peyton Somerset. "But they do think Allison Garcia's daughter may have turned up. She was living with a couple in New Jersey who said they got her from a Rose Calabrone from an adoption agency that of course doesn't really exist. On Mother's Day."

"Unbelievable. The family must be thrilled."

"I imagine they see it as a mixed blessing," Jody points out, realizing that the baby's appearance doesn't bode well for the mother's safe return.

Please let the police get to Peyton on time, she thinks, feeling helpless. There was nothing she and Sam could do from where they were when they found out the address. The house is a good two hours away from Queens, almost at the tip of eastern Long Island.

"Do you think the Cordells were supposed to get this baby?" Sam asks after a moment, gazing intently out the windshield at the crawling bridge traffic.

"Probably. I wonder what happened to Derry."

"Nothing good, that's for sure."

Jody nods, wondering if a replacement stepped in to fill her maternity clothes. She looks out over the cityscape across the water, speculating.

Is there a childless couple waiting out there, even now, for the blessed event to come to fruition?

Anxious to get to the station for another update, she glances at the clock at the dashboard, then asks Sam, "Can you drive any faster?"

"Not if you want to go home to your kids tonight."

Jody swallows hard.

Yes. Yes, she wants more than anything to go home to her kids tonight.

Of course he came. Well, what did you expect?

You knew he'd be here. He wouldn't miss this for the world.

"J.D.! We're in here," she calls, as Peyton heaves her upper body forward, still gripping her arm, using the leverage to lift her massive weight from the mattress.

J.D.'s footsteps have stopped and the door behind her opens.

Helen is about to shake Peyton off and hurtle herself into his arms . . .

Then she realizes that her patient's bare legs are spread, knees bent . . . and the baby is crowning.

"Hurry, J.D.!" she calls without turning around, her giddiness transformed into bold purpose as instinct and experience take over.

The most important thing now is to see that their child arrives safely into the world . . . and immediately see Peyton Somerset out of it.

Then we can be together at last, she promises herself. *All three of us. Forever.*

She looks down at the baby's dark, blood-slicked scalp preparing for the miracle she's witnessed time and time again.

But this is the most miraculous birth of all.

Any moment now, the slippery body of a newborn will slide into its mother's waiting hands.

My hands.

Yes, Helen thinks, barely able to contain her joy, turning at last to look at her beloved husband, *any moment now . . .*

"What made you realize your friend might be in trouble?" Jarrett is asking Gil Blaney, as Anne Marie forces down acrid coffee from a police station percolator that looks like it hasn't been washed in a month.

"I guess I just finally woke up," the man says, his head bent as if in shame. "I've been caught up in my own problems the last few months. Maybe if I hadn't been so self-involved, I might have realized something was wrong with Peyton's situation."

"What situation do you mean?" Anne Marie asks.

"Rita was always there. Whenever I called, whenever I tried to visit. It was like she was standing guard so that nobody could get to Peyton. I just figured she was trying to help since Peyton had to stay in bed. I thought she just wanted her to rest."

"You can't blame yourself," Jarrett tells the man, who shakes his head, looking pale.

"If anything happens to her, I'll never forgive myself. Thank God I saw the news this morning and recognized the name of her doctor and the friends she'd told me about. I went straight over there and let myself in when nobody answered the door, but the place was empty. So I called the police."

Anne Marie swallows hard over a lump in her throat, wishing somebody had been there for Heather. If only somebody had been able to find her, before it was too late. . . .

"Mrs. Egerton?" Detective Jacobs appears in the doorway of the tiny room where Anne Marie has spent the better part of this harrowing day. "I just wanted to let you know . . . the police out on Long Island have brought the Clements couple in for questioning. We'll have to do the DNA testing to confirm it, but I wanted you to know that Kelly Clements is most likely your granddaughter."

Unable to speak, Anne Marie lifts her eyes to heaven and offers a silent prayer of thanks, to God and to the woman who long ago taught her something she never forgot.

There are things a mother just knows, if she listens to her heart.

She's reached her limit, the end of her rope.

This is it.

She can't bear another minute, another second, of the pain.

Her eyes squeezed shut, her body on fire, Peyton fervently wants only to die.

Or maybe that's what this is, this bloody torture. Maybe she's already dying.

Maybe Rita is killing her, or Tom is killing her. . . .

I trusted them both.

I was a fool.

"No! Stop it!"

Rita's angry shout travels across a great distance to pierce the rushing in Peyton's ears.

Who is she talking to?

Her husband . . .

Peyton's body jerks violently against the terrible pressure, the searing sensation in her loins.

No, don't give in to it.

Think. Try to think.

Don't give up.

Who . . . ?

J.D.!

That's Rita's husband, she realizes triumphantly.

He must be here, too. She said he was here . . .

But Peyton heard only Tom's voice.

Dear God, why does this hurt so damned much? Shouldn't the pain be left behind now? Isn't death an escape?

Peyton groans, pants loudly, clutches, screams in agony. Nothing makes it stop. Nothing makes it all go away.

Then her own keening wail mingles with a piercing shriek.

Rita.

Peyton hears a grunt, a crashing thud somewhere beyond the bed.

She strains to hear what sounds like, "Peyton, hang on. You can do it!"

Tom. Tom is calling to her.

Why?

Tom wants to hurt her. He wants to kill her.

She should be afraid. . . .

Fight.

You have to fight.

The voice comes from within, from a well of strength that once belonged to her.

"No," she moans. "No."

She can't fight, hasn't the stamina to fight.

Longing now only for reprieve, for death, Peyton struggles to ignore the voice in her head, the one that's growing more potent with every word, telling her to hang on.

It's her own voice, speaking up at last.

Don't let them do this to you.

You have too much to live for.

You're a mother.

Yes.

Oh God, yes.

The baby.

That's what it's all about now.

So much to live for.

Somewhere deep within a soul that's stirring to life again, the light comes on again. A mere glimmer of the fortitude that's gotten Peyton Somerset every place she ever wanted to be.

"No!" she bellows, pulling herself forward, clinging to the bedpost, clinging to her very life itself. Driven by fury, by need, she bears down with all her might as a tremendous rushing sensation sweeps through her . . .

And then it's over.

The ruthless tension dissolves.

The deafening roar is silenced, as are the voices.

They're gone, all of them: Rita, Tom, J.D.

Spent, Peyton is immersed in utter darkness, attempting to grasp the enormity of what's happened to her.

This is death.

Then she hears it.

And it isn't death.

It's life.

Precious life, punctuated by the unmistakable high, thin wail of a newborn child.

Her skull is gripped in a vise of pain that obliterates everything—sight, sound, smell . . .

There is nothing but the pain, and the shocking knowledge that he caused it.

J.D.

Slugged her with his mighty fist, when all she wanted was to show him their baby . . .

The baby!

Helen struggles to open her eyes, and when she succeeds is met by blinding pain and light that shines far, far above her.

I'm on the floor, she realizes in shock. *He knocked me to the floor.*

It was a mistake.

Of course.

He didn't realize.

He thought I was somebody else.

"J.D., help me. Please . . ."

A shadow looms above her.

"Don't move. If you move, so help me, I'll kill you."

"But . . . I love you," she whimpers, knowing he'll say it in return. He has to say it in return.

But maybe he didn't hear her, or maybe he's gone.

Maybe she's simply closed her eyes.

Her head hurts so badly . . .

The baby!

She hears it.

Her baby is crying.

Her baby needs her.

Helen reaches out, reaches for the baby, finds nothing but emptiness.

"Where's my baby?"

Arms frantically clawing the air, she tries desperately to reach her child as the wails grow louder.

"Hush, little one, hush. Mama's here," she croons, and begins to hum a lullaby, never realizing that she isn't hearing the wail of a baby at all, but the howl of approaching sirens.

* * *

Peyton cradles her daughter against her breast as the medics wheel her out into the night air. They wanted to take the infant out separately, but she refused to let go.

She'll never let go.

Tom, walking beside her, reaches out to tuck in the loose flap of her blanket. "Is there anybody you want me to call?"

So many people will want to know she's arrived, Peyton realizes, serenely gazing down at her daughter's tiny face. She's no longer wide-eyed as she was shortly after her birth, when she gazed unblinkingly into her mother's eyes as if in curious recognition. Now her delicate eyelashes are fluttering like the wings of a butterfly, ready to carry her off to sleep, where there will be no lingering effects of the trauma mother and daughter survived.

"You don't have to call anyone yet," Peyton tells Tom, as the medics roll her down a short path beneath a canopy of old trees, toward the open back of a waiting ambulance.

There will be plenty of time for spreading the happy news.

Plenty of time for everything.

"I'll meet you at the hospital," he promises. "Okay? As soon as I'm done here."

She nods, following his gaze to the cluster of police cars and uniformed officers who swarmed the house in the moments after the baby was born.

What if they had been too late?

If Tom hadn't shown up when he did, there's no telling what Rita would have done to her.

The stranger Peyton once called her friend was hallucinating, babbling incoherently as they took her away in handcuffs, calling for a husband and sons who reportedly don't exist.

Peyton shudders to think that she trusted the woman who wanted to kill her, that she actually believed all Rita's terrible, manipulative lies about the man who saved her life.

None of what Rita told her about Tom was true . . . other than the fact that he was outside the brownstone this morning, trying to break in.

Not to kill her . . . to save her.

"I'll see you at the hospital," Tom says, leaning to kiss her head and lay a gentle, brief hand on the baby's blanket.

"Wait, Tom. How on earth did you find me here?" Peyton asks, holding on to his arm.

A shadow crosses over his face. "Wanda."

"But—" She shakes her head, certain she didn't dream the terrible news this morning. "Wanda is—"

"I know. I'm so sorry."

So it's true.

The momentary glimmer of hope is replaced by somber grief again.

"Wanda had been trying to reach you, Peyton, to warn you. But Rita kept answering the phone at your place. And Wanda got scared. She must have remembered my last name, and where I work, and she tracked down my voice mail there last night."

"She remembered," Peyton says with a nod, hearing Wanda's voice echoing in her head once again.

"I was just making sure he's good enough for you."

"I didn't get her message until I got to the lab this morning," Tom tells her. "She said she had just tried to call you but you weren't home. She had a bad feeling about Rita, and wanted me to check her out if I could. She was worried about her spending so much time with you."

"Oh my God. Wanda . . ." Peyton's voice breaks. "If it weren't for her—"

"I know. She left me Rita's real name and her addresses. That's how I tracked you down."

"Sir? We need to get her out of here now," one of the medics interrupts, as the gurney is pushed to the open door of the ambulance.

"I'll see you at the hospital," Tom promises again. "Both of you."

Both . . . ?

Oh! Yes. How could she have forgotten already?

Gazing contentedly at the child in her arms, she tells Tom with a smile, "We'll both be waiting."

Month Nine
October

EPILOGUE

Wheeling the navy blue buggy into Madison Square Park, Peyton admires the patchwork of vibrant foliage against the slate-colored cityscape and overcast sky. She pauses for a toddler who scampers into her path, chased by a harried nanny.

Glancing down at the buggy's occupant, in the midst of her usual midmorning nap, Peyton thinks, *Next year at this time, Allie, you'll be toddling off on wobbly little legs to explore the world.*

And hopefully, Peyton will be lucky enough to be the one chasing after her most of the time.

One good thing came out of the glaring local publicity that followed her abduction and rescue: she was contacted by the publisher of a parenting magazine and invited to interview for a part-time advertising sales position. She discovered that there's more money—and a far less hectic schedule—in the sales end of the industry. Better yet, there's no Tara.

The job is hers if Peyton wants it . . . and she's decided that she does.

Just yesterday, she called Kaplan and Kline to tell her boss she won't be returning after her maternity leave. Candace promised she'll have Tara return the call as soon as she gets back from Prague.

"How's little Allie?" the secretary asked. "When are you bringing her in to see us?"

"Soon," Peyton promised.

And she will . . . any day now. Soon she'll be ready to share with her concerned former coworkers the baby whose name, Allison Wanda, honors Peyton's lost friends.

For now, she's still feeling too protective to venture far beyond familiar territory. And no wonder, given what she's been through.

Unlike her mother, who is still plagued by occasional nightmares, little Allie sleeps peacefully, eats regularly, and smiles often.

But things are gradually getting easier for Peyton. The therapist Nancy recommended, whom she's been seeing twice weekly, ensured her that the frightening memories will fade a little more every day. In time, she'll be able to stop looking over her shoulder, stop searching for hints of masked insanity in even the most trusted faces around her.

With luck, she'll never again have to face the woman who tried to kill her. It's unlikely that the woman who called herself Rita Calabrone will be found mentally fit to stand trial for more than a dozen murders that have now been linked to her. Allison Garcia's body was found with the others when the pond behind the farmhouse was dredged.

Heather's mother, Anne Marie, sent Peyton flowers in the hospital, and her wealthy husband set up a private school and college scholarship trust for Allie.

"So you won't ever have to struggle as a single mother, the way I did, wondering how I was going to pay for my daughter's education," Anne Marie told Peyton in one of their many telephone conversations.

The woman has become a friend and a source of comfort these last few weeks, as have Gil, and Nancy, and even Dr. Lombardo, who has already broken his no-house-calls rule for Peyton. In her postnatal checkup last week, he pronounced her remarkably well recovered, at least physically, from the ordeal of her daughter's birth.

Emotionally, it's going to take some time.

For all of us, Peyton thinks, recalling the tears she's shed with Nancy, and with Wanda's and Allison's families.

And with Anne Marie, tears of both sorrow and joy. Thanks to DNA evidence, she now has the chance to get to know her granddaughter. The Clements have agreed to let their daughter Kelly get to know the Egertons, and Anne Marie has agreed, in exchange, not to press charges that would disrupt the child's life and possibly rip her from the only parents she's ever known.

"How can I do that to her, and even to them?" she asked Peyton. "They believed everything that lunatic told them. They thought they were rescuing an unwanted baby."

Mary and Javier Nueves thought the same thing. They, too, are expected to be exonerated of any charges. And when they are, Allison's parents are considering returning their granddaughter to the couple's custody. As her mother explained to Peyton, they already have their hands full raising their teenaged grandchildren. And the Nueves will be good parents. They love little Dawn with all their hearts.

Just as I love you, Peyton silently tells her sleeping daughter, as a brisk October breeze rustles the branches overhead and she reaches down to tuck the blanket more securely around her.

Maybe someday, she'll be less vigilant, more relaxed. Maybe the time will come when her last nightly waking thought isn't a fervent prayer for her child's safety.

Then again, maybe not.

As Gil said, "You're a parent now. It goes with the territory. You'll never stop watching, or worrying. Your life will always be centered on this life you created."

That's why he's leaving New York in a few days, to move out to the West Coast where his ex-wife has gone with his children. Peyton is going to miss her old friend, but of course she understands.

Just as she understands why Eric, Wanda's married boyfriend, was forced to choose his newborn daughter over his wife. In time, perhaps, his wife will get past his betrayal and accept little Erica into their home. But for now, Eric is living in Wanda's apartment, taking care of the child who was unfairly left motherless by a madwoman.

Peyton will never understand what led Helen to commit the heinous crimes that robbed countless parents of their children, countless babies of their mothers. Her ex-husband, interviewed in one of the tabloids, said simply, "Helen went crazy with grief when our babies died. She just never recovered."

Peyton shuddered when she read that, cradling her own child closer to a heart that manages, even now, to ache in empathy for another mother's unbearable loss.

But that doesn't mean she's been able to forgive, or forget.

Maybe someday, according to the therapist. And maybe not.

Either way, she'll survive.

She's reached the designated bench in the center of the park, between the reflecting pool and the playground. Keeping a protective hand on the handle of the carriage, she sits and watches the children romping in the faint rays of golden light that are now beginning to poke through the clouds.

"Mommy, Daddy, look," a little girl shouts from high up on a ladder, to a couple on a nearby bench. "The sun is coming out. I'm climbing up to touch it!"

Someday, Peyton thinks with a smile, *I'll be sitting here watching Allie climb up to the sun.*

And maybe, just maybe, she won't be alone. Maybe Allie will be shouting, "Mommy, Daddy, look!"

Footsteps scuffle through the fallen leaves.

Peyton looks up to see the man she's been waiting for.

Tom kisses her cheek, gently touches the bundle in the carriage, and says, "Sorry I'm late. Should we go get breakfast?"

"Let's just sit awhile," Peyton suggests with a smile, patting the bench beside her. "I have a feeling it's going to be a beautiful day after all."